"Can I do anything to help you?"

Ava touched his arm again, this time lightly, brushing her fingertips across the slick material of his jacket.

The human contact and the emotion behind it made him shiver. Max clenched his teeth. "You can't do anything to help. You've done enough."

She grabbed the door handle and swung open the door before the car even stopped.

"Hold on. I'll walk you up."

"I thought you were anxious to get rid of me."

He didn't want to leave Ava, but he had to—for her own safety. "I was anxious to get you away from the lab and back home. The police can pick it up from here."

He followed her to the front door. She dragged her keys from her purse and slid one into the dead bolt. It clicked and she opened the door.

Apprehension slithered down his spine and he held out a hand. "Wait."

But it was too late. Ava had stepped across the threshold and now faced two men training weapons on her.

A̶ ̶ ̶ ̶ ̶ ̶ ̶ ̶ ̶ ̶ ̶glass.

UNDER FIRE

BY
CAROL ERICSON

Published in Great Britain 2015
by Mills & Boon, an imprint of Harlequin (UK) Limited,
Eton House, 18-24 Paradise Road, Richmond, Surrey, TW9 1SR

© 2015 Carol Ericson

ISBN: 978-0-263-25311-5

46-0715

Harlequin (UK) Limited's policy is to use papers that are natural, renewable and recyclable products and made from wood grown in sustainable forests. The logging and manufacturing processes conform to the legal environmental regulations of the country of origin.

Printed and bound in Spain
by CPI, Barcelona

Carol Ericson lives with her husband and two sons in Southern California, home of state-of-the-art cosmetic surgery, wild freeway chases and a million amazing stories. These stories, along with hordes of virile men and feisty women, clamor for release from Carol's head. It makes for some interesting headaches until she sets them free to fulfill their destinies and her readers' fantasies. To learn more about Carol, please visit her website, www.carolericson.com, "Where romance flirts with danger."

Chapter One

The shell casings from the bullets pinged off the metal file cabinets. One landed inches from her nose and rolled one way and then the other, its gold plating winking at her under the fluorescent lights. The acrid smell of gunpowder tickled her nostrils. She smashed her nose against the linoleum to halt the sneeze threatening to explode and give away her position.

Someone grunted. Someone screamed. Again.

Ava held her breath as the rubber sole of a black shoe squeaked past her face. She followed its path until her gaze collided with Dr. Arnoff's.

From beneath the desk across from her, he put his finger to his lips. His thick glasses, one lens crushed, lay just out of his reach between the two desks. With his other finger, he pointed past her toward the lab.

Afraid to move even a centimeter, Ava blinked her eyes to indicate her understanding. If they could make their way to the lab behind the bulletproof glass and industrial-strength locks they might have a chance to survive this lunacy.

The shooter moved past the desks, firing another round from his automatic weapon. Glass shattered—not the bulletproof kind. A loud bump, followed by a crack and the door to the clinic, her domain, crashed open.

Greg bellowed, "No, no, no!"

Another round of fire and Greg's life ended in a thump and a gurgle.

Ava squeezed her eyes closed, and her lips mumbled silent words. *Keep going. Keep going.*

If the shooter kept walking through the clinic, he'd wind up on the other side in the waiting room. At this time of night, nobody was in the waiting room, which led to a door and a set of stairs to the outside.

Keep going.

He returned. His boots crunched through the glass. Then he howled like a wounded animal, and the hair on the back of Ava's neck stood at attention and quivered.

The footsteps stopped on the other side of the desk— her pathetic hiding place. In the sudden silence of the room, her heartbeat thundered. Surely he could hear it, too.

He kicked at a shard of glass, which skittered between the two desks.

Ava turned widened eyes on Dr. Arnoff and swallowed. She harbored no hopes that the doctor could take down the shooter. Although a big man, his fighting days were behind him. Their best hope was to make it to the lab and wait for help.

The black-booted foot stepped between the desks, smashing the other lens of Dr. Arnoff's glasses. A second later the shooter lifted the desk by one edge and hurled it against the wall as if it were a piece of furniture in a dollhouse.

Exposed, Dr. Arnoff scrambled for cover, his army crawl no match for the lethal weapon pointed at him. The bullets hit his body, making it jump and twitch.

Ava dug a fist against her mouth, and her teeth cut into her lips. The metallic taste of her blood mimicked the smell permeating the air.

Then her own cover disappeared, snatched away by some towering hulk. She didn't scream. She didn't beg. The gunman existed in a haze behind the weapon that he now had aimed at her head.

His gloved finger on the trigger of the assault rifle mesmerized her. She mumbled a prayer with parched lips. *Click.* She sucked in a breath. *Click.* She gritted her teeth.

Click. He'd run out of ammo.

He reached into the pocket of his fatigues, and adrenaline surged through her body. She clambered over the discarded desk and launched herself at the lab door. With shaking hands she scrabbled for the badge around her neck and pressed it to the reader. The red light mocked her.

Her badge didn't allow her access to this lab. Her exclusion from the lab had been a source of irritation to her for almost two years. How could she forget that now?

She dropped to her knees and crawled to Dr. Arnoff's dead body. Her fingers trembled as she unclipped the badge from the pocket of his white coat.

Amid the clicking and clacking behind her, the gunman muttered to himself.

Expecting another round of shots at any second, Ava swiped Dr. Arnoff's badge across the reader. The green lights blinked in a row as if she'd just won a jackpot. She had.

She yanked open the heavy door and shoved it closed just as the shooter looked up from his task. Five seconds later, a volley of bullets thwacked the glass.

Knowing the gunman could lift a badge from any of the dead bodies around him just as she had, Ava slid three dead bolts across the door and took two steps back.

This windowless room, clicking and buzzing with machinery, computers and refrigeration, offered no escape, but it did contain a landline telephone. Maybe someone had been able to make a call to the police when the mayhem started, but no cavalry had arrived to the rescue yet.

After his first round, the crazed man outside her sanctuary had stopped shooting. He seemed to be searching the bodies of her fallen coworkers—looking for a badge, no doubt. He wouldn't find Dr. Arnoff's.

Ava pounced on the receiver of the telephone on the wall beside the door. Her heart skipped a beat. No dial tone. She tapped the phone over and over, but it remained dead.

Even if she had her cell phone, which remained in the pocket of her lab coat hanging on a hook in the clinic, it wouldn't do any good. Nobody could get reception in this underground building in the middle of the desert.

The lock clicked and she spun around. The shooter was leaning against the door, pressing a badge up to the reader. The lock on the handle responded, but the dead bolts held the door securely in place.

She'd resented being locked out of this lab, but now she couldn't be happier about those extra reinforcements.

He grabbed the handle and shook it while releasing another roar.

Ava covered her galloping heart with one hand as she studied the glittering eyes visible from the slits in the ski mask. What did he want? Drugs? Why murder all these people for drugs? Why come all the way out here to a high-level security facility to steal meds?

He gave up on the door and shook his head once. Then he reached up and yanked the ski mask from his head.

Ava gasped and stumbled back. She knew him. Simon.

He was one of her patients, one of the covert agents the lab treated and monitored.

Guess they hadn't monitored him closely enough.

"Simon?" She flattened her palm against the glass of the window. "Simon, put down your weapon. The police are on their way."

She had no idea if the police were on their way or not. The lab used its own security force, so she and her co-workers never had a reason to call in the police from the small town ten miles away in this New Mexico desert. Since the lab's security guards had made no attempt to stop Simon, she had a sick feeling Simon had already dealt with them.

"You need help, Simon. I can help you." She licked her lips. "Whatever you need me to say to the authorities, I'll say it. We can tell them it was your job, the stress."

His mouth twisted and he lunged at the window, jabbing the butt of his gun against the glass, which shivered under the assault.

Ava blinked and jerked back. She made a half turn and scanned the lab. If he somehow made it through the door and she got close enough to him, she could stick him with a needle full of tranquilizer that would drop him in his tracks. She could throw boiling water or a chemical mixture in his face.

He'd never let her get that close. He'd come through shooting, and she wouldn't have a chance against those bullets. None of the others had. She gulped back a sob.

The bullets started again. Simon had stepped away from the door and continued spraying bullets at the glass. That window hadn't been designed to withstand this kind of relentless barrage. She knew. She'd asked when she started working here, curious about the extra security of this room.

He knew it, too. Sweat beaded on Simon's ruddy face as he took a breather. He didn't even need to reload. He rolled his shoulders as if preparing for the long haul.

Then he resumed firing at the window.

Again, Ava searched the room, tilting her head back to examine the ceiling. Unfortunately, the ceiling was solid, except for one vent. She eyed the rectangular cover. Could she squeeze through there?

Simon took another break to examine the battered window, placing his weapon on the floor beside him.

She tried to catch his gaze, tried to make some human contact, but this person was just a shell of the Simon she had known. The sarcastic redhead who did killer impressions had disappeared, replaced by this creature with dead eyes.

Ava's breath hitched in her throat. Beyond Simon, a figure decked out in black riot gear loomed in the doorway of the clinic. Was it someone from security? The police?

Not wanting to alert Simon, she inched farther away from the window and kept her gaze glued to Simon's face.

The man at the door yelled, "Simon!"

How did he know who the shooter was? Had someone from the lab seen Simon before the rampage started and reported him?

Simon turned slowly.

"Give it up, Simon." The man raised his weapon. "We can get help, together."

Simon growled and swayed from side to side.

Would he go for his gun on the floor?

Taking a single step into the room, the man tried again. "Step away from your weapon, Simon. We'll figure this out."

Simon shouted, "They have to pay!"

Ava hugged herself as a chill snaked up her spine.

His animalistic sounds had frightened her, but his words struck cold fear into her heart. Pay for what? He'd gone insane, and they'd been responsible for him, for his well-being.

"Not Dr. Whitman. It's not her fault."

Ava threw out a hand and grasped the edge of a counter to steady herself. Her rescuer knew her name? His voice, bellowing from across the room, muffled by the mask on his face, still held a note of familiarity to her. He must be one of the security guards.

"It is." Simon stopped swaying. "It *is* her fault."

He dropped to the floor and jumped up, clutching his weapon. He raised it to his shoulder but it didn't get that far.

The man from across the room fired. Simon spun around and fell against the window, which finally cracked.

Ava clapped a hand over her mouth as she met Simon's blue stare. The film over his eyes cleared. They widened for a second and he gasped. Blood gurgled from his gaping mouth. He slid to the floor, out of her sight.

Every muscle in her body seized up and she couldn't move.

The security guard kept his weapon at his shoulder as he stalked across the room. When he reached the window of the lab, he pointed his gun at the floor, presumably at Simon.

Ava covered her ears, but the gunfire had finally ceased.

Slinging his weapon over his shoulder, the man gestured to the door. "Open up. It's okay now."

Would it ever be okay? She'd just watched a crazed gunman, one of her patients, mow down her coworkers and had barely escaped death herself.

She stumbled toward the door and reached for the first lock with stiff hands. It took her several tries before she could slide all the dead bolts. Then she pressed down on the handle to open the door.

The man, smelling of gunpowder and leather and power, stepped into the lab. "Are you okay, Dr. Whitman?"

She knew that voice but couldn't place it. Tilting her head, she cleared her throat. "I—I'm not physically hurt."

"Good." His head swiveled back and forth, taking in the small lab. "Are there any blue pills in this room?"

She took a step back from his overpowering presence. "Blue pills? What are you talking about?"

"The blue pills." He stepped around her and yanked open a drawer. "I need as many blue pills as you have in here—all of them."

"I don't know what you mean." She blinked and edged toward the door. Had she just gone from one kind of crazy to another? Maybe this man was Simon's accomplice and they were both after drugs.

He continued his search through the lab, repeating his request for blue pills, pulling out drawers and banging cupboard doors open.

A crash from another area of the building made them both jump, and he swore.

Taking her arm in his gloved hand, he said, "We need to get out of here unless you can tell me where to find some blue pills."

"I told you, I don't know about any blue pills, and there's no serum on hand either." Maybe he was after the vitamin boost the agents received quarterly.

He grunted. "Then let's go."

"Wait a minute." She shook him off. "H-he's dead, right? Simon's dead?"

The man nodded once.

"Then why do we have to leave? Maybe that noise was

the police breaking in here." Cold fear flooded her veins and she hugged her body. "Are there more? Is there another gunman?"

"He's the only one."

"Then I'd rather stay here and wait for the rest of your—" she waved a hand at him "—security force or the cops or whoever is on the way. That could be them."

He adjusted his bulletproof vest and took her arm again. "We don't want to wait for anyone."

Confusion clashed with anger at his peremptory tone and the way he kept grabbing her. She jerked her arm away from him and dug her heels into the floor. "Hold on. My entire department has just been murdered. I was almost killed. I'm not going anywhere. I don't even know who the hell you are."

"Sure you do." He reached up with one hand and yanked the ski mask from his head.

Her eyebrows shot up. Max Duvall. Another one of her patients, another agent—just like Simon.

"Y-you, you're..."

"That's right, and you're coming with me. Now." He scooped her up with one arm and threw her over his shoulder. "Whether you want to or not."

Chapter Two

"Let me go!" She struggled and kicked her legs, but Dr. Ava Whitman was a tiny thing.

He could get her to go with him willingly if he sat down and explained the whole situation, but they didn't have time for that. That could be Tempest at the door right now. He couldn't even risk doing a more thorough search for the blue pills. He'd have to just take her at her word that there were none at the lab.

Maybe Dr. Whitman already knew the whole situation. Knew why Simon had gone postal. He couldn't trust anyone...not even pretty Dr. Whitman.

Clamping her thighs against his shoulder, he stepped over the dead bodies littering the floor. When he navigated around the final murder victim in his path at the door of the clinic, Dr. Whitman stopped struggling and slumped against his back. If she'd had her eyes open the whole way, she probably just got her fill of blood and guts.

He crossed through the waiting room and kicked open the door to the stairwell. He slid Dr. Whitman down his body so that she was facing him, his arm cinched around her waist.

"Will you come with me now? I need you to walk up

these stairs and out the side door. I have a car waiting there."

Through his vest, he could feel the wild beat of her heart as it banged against her chest. "Where are we going? Why can't we wait here for the police?"

"It's not safe." He grabbed her shoulders and squeezed. "Do you believe me?"

Her green eyes grew round, taking up half her face. She glanced past him at the clinic door and nodded. Then she grabbed the straps on his bulletproof vest. "My purse, my phone."

"Are they in the clinic?"

"Yes."

He shoved back through the door and pulled her along with him. He didn't quite trust that she wouldn't go running all over the lab searching for the security guards. Wouldn't do her any good anyway—Simon had killed them all.

She broke away from him and yanked her purse from a rack two feet from the body of a coworker. She dipped her hand in the pocket of her lab coat hanging on the rack and pulled out a phone.

Another crash erupted from somewhere in the building, and Dr. Whitman dropped her phone. It skittered and twirled across the floor, coming to a stop at the edge of a puddle of blood.

She gasped and hugged her purse to her chest.

The noise, closer than the previous one, sent a new wave of adrenaline coursing through his veins. "Let's go!"

Her feet seemed rooted to the floor, so he crossed the room in two steps and curled his fingers around her wrist, tugging her forward. "We need to leave."

Still holding on to Dr. Whitman, Max plucked her phone from the floor and headed toward the stairwell again. He half prodded, half carried Dr. Whitman upstairs, and when they reached the door to the outside, he inched it open, pressing his eye to the crack.

The car he'd stolen waited in the darkness. He pushed open the door of the building and a blast of air peppered with sand needled his face. He ducked and put an arm around Dr. Whitman as he hustled her to the vehicle.

She hesitated when he opened the passenger door. The wind whipped her hair across her face, hiding her expression.

It was probably one of shock. Or was it fear? "Get in, Dr. Whitman. They're here."

This time she didn't even ask for clarification. His words had her scrambling into the passenger seat.

He blew out a breath and lifted the bulletproof vest over his head. Would Simon have turned the gun on him after everything they'd gone through together? Sure he would've. That man in there who'd just committed mass murder bore no resemblance to the Simon he knew.

He threw the vest in the backseat and cranked on the engine. He floored the accelerator and went out the way he came in—through a downed chain-link fence.

He hit the desert highway and ten minutes later blew past the small town that served the needs of the lab. The lab didn't have any needs now.

After several minutes of silence, Dr. Whitman cleared her throat. "Are we going to the police now? Calling the CIA?"

"Neither."

Her fingers curled around the edge of the seat. "Where are we going?"

"I'm taking you home."

"Home?" She blinked her long lashes. "Whose home?"

Without turning his head, he raised one eyebrow. "Your

home. You have one, don't you? I know you don't live at the lab—at least not full-time."

"Albuquerque. I live in Albuquerque."

"I figured that. Once I drop you off, you're free to call whomever you like."

"But not now?"

"Not as long as I'm with you."

She bolted upright and wedged her hands against the dashboard. "Why? Don't you want to meet with the CIA? Your own agency? Tell them what happened back there?"

"What do *you* think happened back there?" He squinted into the blackness and hit his high beams.

"Simon Skinner lost it. He went on a murderous rampage and killed my coworkers, my friends." She stifled a sob with the back of her hand.

She showed real grief, but was the shock feigned? Extending his arms, he gripped the steering wheel. "How much do you know about the work you do at the lab?"

"That's a crazy question. It's my workplace. I've been there for almost two years."

"Your job is to treat and monitor a special set of patients, correct?"

"Since you're one of those patients, you should know." She dragged her fingers through her wavy, dark hair and clasped it at the nape of her neck.

One soft strand curled against her pale cheek. Whenever he'd seen her for appointments, her hair had been confined to a bun or ponytail. Now loosened and wild, it was as pretty as he'd imagined it would be.

"And the injections you gave us, the vitamin boost? Did you work on that formula?"

She jerked her head toward him and the rest of her curls tumbled across her shoulder. "No. Dr. Arnoff developed that before I arrived."

"Did he tell you what was in it?"

"Of course he did. I wouldn't inject my patients with some mystery substance."

"Were you allowed to test it yourself? Did you work in that lab?"

"N-no." She clasped her hands between her bouncing knees. "I wasn't allowed in the lab."

"Why not? You're a doctor, aren't you?"

"I…I'm… The lab requires top secret clearance. I have secret clearance only, but Dr. Arnoff showed me the formula, showed me the tests."

He slid a glance at her stiff frame and pale face. Was she still in shock over the events at the lab or was she lying?

"Now it's your turn."

His eyes locked onto hers in the darkness of the car. "What do you mean?"

"It's your turn to answer my questions. What were you doing at the lab? You weren't scheduled for another month or so. Why can't we call the police or the CIA, or Prospero, the agency you work for?"

"Prospero?"

She flicked her fingers in the air. "You don't have to pretend with me. Nobody ever told me the name of the covert ops agency we were supporting, but I heard whispers."

"What other whispers did you hear?" A muscle twitched in his jaw.

"Wait a minute." She smacked the dashboard with her palms. "I thought it was your turn to answer the questions. What were you doing there? Why can't we call the police?"

"You should be glad I was there or Skinner would've gotten to you, too."

Folding her arms across her stomach, she slumped in her seat, all signs of outrage gone. She made a squeaking noise like a mouse caught in a trap, and something like guilt needled the back of his neck.

He rolled his shoulders, trying to ease out the tension that had become his constant companion. "I was at the lab because I found out Skinner was going to be there. We can't call the police for obvious reasons. I'm deep undercover. I don't want to stand around and explain my presence to the cops."

"And your own agency? Prospero?"

"Yeah, Prospero." If Dr. Whitman wanted to believe he worked for Prospero, why disappoint her? The less she knew the better, and it sounded as if she didn't know much—or she was a really good liar. "I'll call them on my own. I wanted to get you out of there in case there was more danger on the way."

"You seemed convinced there was."

"We were in the middle of the desert, in the middle of the night at a top secret location with a bunch of dead bodies. I didn't think it was wise for either of us to stick around."

She leaned her head against the window. "What should I do when I get home?"

He drummed his thumbs against the steering wheel. If Tempest and Dr. Arnoff had kept Dr. Whitman in the dark, she should be safe. Tempest would do the cleanup and probably resume operations elsewhere—with or without Dr. Ava Whitman.

"Once I drop you off and hit the road, you can call the police." He frowned and squinted at the road. "Or do you have a different protocol to follow?"

She turned a pair of wide eyes on him. "For this situation? We had no protocol in place for an active shooter like that."

Maybe the whole bunch of them out there, including Dr. Arnoff, were clueless. No, not Arnoff. He had to have known what was going on, even if he didn't know the why.

"Then I guess it's the cops." Even though the local cops would never get to the whole truth. He pointed to the lights glowing up ahead. "We're heading into the city. Can you give me directions to your place? Is there someone at home?"

She hadn't touched her cell phone once since they escaped from the lab. Wouldn't she want to notify her husband? Boyfriend? Family?

"I live alone."

He supposed she'd want to be with someone, have someone comfort her. God knew, he wasn't capable. "Do you have any family nearby? Any friends to stay with?"

"I don't have any family…here. I'm kind of new to the area and I spend a lot of time at the lab, so I haven't had much time to cultivate friends."

Hadn't she told him she'd been working at the lab for two years? Two years wasn't enough time to make friends? Maybe she'd been taking some of her own medicine.

"When the police come, they may want to take you back to the scene. You'll probably have to lead them to the facility."

She gasped and grabbed his arm. "What do I tell them about you?"

He stiffened and glanced down at her hand gripping the material of his jacket. She dropped it.

Was she offering to cover for him? He figured she'd waste no time at all blabbing to the cops about the man who'd shot Skinner and then whisked her out of the lab. "Tell them the truth."

No law enforcement agency would ever be able to track him down anyway. Tempest had made sure of that.

"I can always tell them you were a stranger to me, that you wouldn't tell me your name." Her fingers twisted in her lap as she hunched forward in her seat.

She *was* offering to cover for him. Why would she do that, unless she knew more than she'd pretended to know?

"You'd lie for me?"

She jerked back and whipped her head around. "Lie? You're an agent with a government covert ops team. If I learned anything at the lab, it was how to keep secrets. I never revealed any of my patients' names to anyone, and I'm not about to start now."

"I appreciate the…concern." He lifted a shoulder. "Tell the cops whatever you like. I'll be long gone either way."

She tilted her chin toward the highway sign. "That's my exit in five miles."

"Then I'll deliver you safe and sound to your home, Dr. Whitman."

"You can call me Ava."

After riding in silence for a while, Ava dragged her purse from the floor of the car into her lap and hugged it to her chest. "What happened to Simon? He looked… dead inside."

"He snapped." His belly coiled into knots. If Simon could snap like that, he could snap, too.

"Did you know about his condition somehow?"

"I had an idea, and when I discovered he was heading out to New Mexico I put two and two together."

"Was it the stress of the assignments? I saw most of you four times a year, but of course you weren't allowed to discuss anything with me. You all seemed well-adjusted though."

Max snorted. "Yeah, I guess some would call that well-adjusted."

"You weren't? You're not? Can I do anything to help you?"

She touched his arm again, this time lightly, brushing her fingertips across the slick material of his jacket.

The human contact and the emotion behind it made him shiver. He clenched his teeth. "You can't do anything to help...Ava. You've done enough."

She snatched her hand back again and studied her fingernails. "This is the exit."

He steered the car toward the off-ramp and eased his foot off the accelerator. She continued giving him directions until they left the desert behind them and rolled into civilization.

He pulled in front of a small house with a light glowing somewhere inside.

She grabbed the door handle and swung open the door before the car even stopped.

"Hold on. I'll walk you up."

"I thought you were anxious to get rid of me."

He scratched the stubble on his chin. That hour-long drive had been the closest he'd come to normalcy in a long time. He didn't want to leave Ava, but he had to—for her own safety.

"I was anxious to get you away from the lab and back home. The police can pick it up from here."

If there was anything left of the lab when they got there. Tempest had to know by now that one of its agents had gone off the rails. The crashes and noises at the lab could've been Tempest.

"Well, here I am." She spread her arms.

He jingled the keys in his palm and felt for his hand-gun and other gear on his belt as he followed her to the front door.

She dragged her own keys from her purse and slid one into the dead bolt. It clicked and she opened the door.

Apprehension slithered down his spine, and he held out a hand. "Wait."

But it was too late.

Ava had stepped across the threshold and now faced two men training weapons on her.

And this time she wasn't behind bulletproof glass.

Chapter Three

Simon was back—in stereo. Ava caught a glimpse of two men with guns pointed at her for a split second before Max snatched her from behind, lifting her off her feet and jerking her to the side.

At the same instant, she heard a pop and squeezed her eyes closed. If the men had shot Max, she was finished.

An acrid smell invaded her nostrils and she opened her lids—and regretted it immediately. The black smoke pouring from her front door stung her eyes and burned her throat.

"Hold your breath. Close your eyes." Max lifted her and tucked her under one arm as if she were a rag doll.

She felt like a rag doll. The jolt of fear that had spiked her body when she saw the gunmen had dissipated into a curious out-of-body sensation. A creeping lethargy had invaded her limbs, which now dangled uselessly, occasionally banging against Max's body.

If she was lethargic, Max was anything but. His body felt like a well-oiled machine as he sprinted for the car, still clutching her under one arm. He loaded her into the front seat and seconds later the car lurched forward with a shrill squeal.

"Get your seat belt on."

Her hand dropped to the side of the seat, but her fingers wouldn't obey the commands of her fuzzy brain. At the next sharp turn, she fell to the side, her head bumping against the window.

A vise cinched her wrist. "Snap out of it, Ava! I need you."

How had Max known that those three little words amounted to a rallying cry for the former Dr. Ava Whitman?

She rubbed her stinging eyes. She sniffled and dragged a hand beneath her nose. She coughed. She grabbed her seat belt and snapped it into place.

Without taking his eyes from the road, Max asked, "You okay?"

She ran her hands down her arms as if wondering for the first time if she'd been shot. "I'm fine. Did they shoot at us? How did they miss…unless…?"

"I'm okay. They didn't get a shot off."

"I thought— What was all that smoke? The noise?"

"I was able to toss an exploding device at them before they could react. I don't think they were expecting you to have company."

"Let me get this straight." She covered her still-sensitive eyes with one hand. "Two men had guns pointed at us when we walked through the door and you were able to pull me out of harm's way and throw some smoke bomb into the house at the same time?"

"I had the advantage of surprise."

Her hand dropped to her throat. "Did you know someone would be there waiting? Because I was sure surprised to see them standing there."

"Let's just say I had a premonition."

She shook her head. "Superhuman."

Max jerked the steering wheel and the car veered to the right. "Why'd you say that?"

She tilted her head. Why the defensiveness?

"When I saw those guns, I thought we were both dead. Somehow you got us out of there alive. Did I ever thank you? Did I ever thank you for what you did at the lab?"

"Not necessary." He flexed his fingers.

"Are you going to tell me what those men were doing at my house? Are they with Simon? Did they come to finish the job he started?"

She held her breath. If she had a bunch of covert ops agents after her, what was her percentage of survival? Especially once Max Duvall left her side, and he would leave her side—they always did.

"I'm not sure, Ava."

The name sounded tentative on his lips for a man so sure of himself. Agent Max Duvall had always been her favorite patient and it had nothing to do with his dark good looks or his killer body—they all had those killer bodies.

Most of the agents were hard, unfriendly. Some wouldn't even reveal their names. Max always had a smile for her. Always asked about her welfare, made small talk. She looked forward to the quarterly visits by Max—and Simon.

Smashing a fist against her lips, she swallowed a sob. Simon had been friendly, too. He'd even admitted to her that he was engaged, although such personal communications from the agents were verboten. Where was Simon's fiancée now?

Did Max have a wife or a girlfriend sitting at home worried about him, too?

"Are you sure you're okay?"

She blinked and met Max's gaze. They were back on the desolate highway through the desert, and Max's eyes gleamed in the darkness. A trickle of fear dripped down her back. Maybe those men back at her house were there to save her from Max. Maybe Max and Simon were in league together.

"Are you afraid of me?" His low, soft voice floated toward her in the cramped space of the car.

"N-no." She pinned her aching shoulders back against the seat. "No, I'm not. You saved my life—twice. I'm just confused. I have crazy thoughts running through my head. Do you blame me?"

"Not at all."

"If you could tell me what's going on, I'd feel better— as much as I can after tonight's events. I deserve to know. Someone, something is out to extinguish my life. I need to know who or what so I can protect myself."

"I'll protect you."

"From what? For how long?" Her fingers dug into the hard muscle of his thigh. "You have to give me more, Max. You can't keep me in the dark and expect me to trust you. I can't trust like that—not anymore."

Tears blurred her vision, and she covered her face with her hands. Hadn't he just told her to snap out of it? If she wanted to prove that she deserved the hard truth, she'd have to buck up and quit with the waterworks.

"You're right, Ava, but I have a problem with trust, too. I don't have any."

"You don't think you can trust me?" Her voice squeaked on the last syllable.

"You worked in that lab."

"The lab that you visited four times a year. The lab that kept you safe. The lab that treated your injuries—both physical and mental. The lab that made sure you were at your peak performance levels so you could do your job, a job vital to the security of our country."

"Stop!" He slammed his palms against the steering wheel, and she shrank against her side of the car.

"That lab, that bastion of goodwill and patriotic fervor, turned me into a mindless, soulless machine." He jabbed a finger in her face. "You did that to me, and now you have as much to fear from me as you did from Simon. I'm a killer."

Chapter Four

Icy fingers gripped the back of Ava's neck and she hunched her shoulders, making herself small against the car door. She shot a side glance at Max. The glow from the car's display highlighted the sharp planes of his face, lending credence to his declaration that he was a machine. But a killer? He'd saved her—twice. Unless he'd saved her for some other nefarious purpose.

Her fingers curled around the door handle, and she tensed her muscles.

Her movement broke his trancelike stare out the windshield. Blinking, he peeled one hand from the steering wheel and ran it through his dark hair.

"I—I won't hurt you, Dr. Whitman."

She whispered, "Ava."

He cranked his head to the side, and the stark lines on his face softened. "Where can I take you…Ava?"

She jerked forward in her seat. She couldn't go home, as if she'd ever called that small bungalow teetering at the edge of the desert home.

But if Max thought he could launch a bombshell at her like that and then blithely drop her off somewhere, he needed to reprogram himself.

Had he really just blamed her for Simon's breakdown?

"Before you take me anywhere—" she pressed her palms against her bouncing knees "—you're going to explain yourself. How is any of this my fault?"

He squeezed his eyes closed briefly and pinched the bridge of his nose. "I shouldn't have yelled, but I don't know if I can trust you."

"Me?" She jabbed an index finger at her chest. "You don't know if you can trust me? You're the one who whisked me away from the lab, led me into an ambush and then threatened to kill me."

He sucked in a sharp breath. "That wasn't a threat. I don't make threats."

His words hung in the space between them, their meaning clear. This man would strike without warning and without mercy. The fact that she still sat beside him, living and breathing, attested to the fact that despite his misgivings he must trust her at least a little bit.

"You warned me that you were a killer, like Simon."

"What exactly do you think the agents of...Prospero do if not kill?"

"You kill when it's necessary. You kill to protect the country. You kill in self-defense."

"Is that what you think Simon was doing?"

She stuffed her hands beneath her thighs. "No, but that's what you were doing when you took him out."

He nodded once and his jaw hardened again. "I won't hurt you, Ava."

She swallowed. His repetition of the phrase sent a spiral of fear down her spine. Was he trying to convince her or convince himself?

"Tell me where I can drop you off, and you'll be fine. Friends? Family?"

"I told you, I don't have any friends or family in this area." She pushed the hair from her face in a sharp gesture, suddenly angry at him for forcing her to admit that pathetic truth.

"I can take you to an airport and get you on a plane to anywhere."

"No." She shook her head and her hair whipped across her face again. "Before I get on a plane to anywhere, I want you to explain yourself. What happened to Simon? Why did you blame me? Why did Simon attack the lab?"

"If you don't know, it's not safe for me to tell you."

"Bull." She jerked her thumb over her shoulder. "Those two men were waiting for me at my house. I wasn't safe back there, and I'm not safe now. What you tell is not going to make it any worse than it already is. And you know that."

Lights twinkled ahead, and she realized they'd circled back into the city after a detour on a desert highway so that he could make sure they hadn't been followed.

He pointed to a sign with an airplane on it. "I can take you straight to the airport and buy you a ticket back home to your family. You can contact the CIA and tell them what happened. The agency will help you."

"But the agency is not going to tell me what's going on. I want to know. I deserve to know after you accused me of being complicit in Simon's breakdown."

"You were."

She smacked her hands on the dashboard. "Stop saying that. This is what I mean. You can't throw around accusations like that without backing them up."

He aimed the car for the next exit and left the highway. "It's going to be morning soon. Let's get off the road, get some rest. I'll tell you everything, and then you're getting on that plane."

She sat quietly as Max followed the signs to the airport. He turned onto a boulevard lined with airport hotels and rolled into the parking lot of a midrange highrise, anonymous and nondescript.

He dragged a bag from the trunk of the car and left the keys with the valet parking attendant.

She hadn't realized how exhausted she was until they walked through the empty lobby of the hotel.

A front desk clerk jumped up from behind the counter. "Do you need a room?"

"Yeah." Max reached for the back pocket of his camouflage pants. Without the bulletproof vest, the black jacket and the ski mask, he looked almost normal. Could the hotel clerk feel the waves of tension vibrating off Max's body? Did he notice the tight set of Max's jaw? The way his dark eyes seemed to take in everything around him with a single glance? *Normal* was not a word she'd use to describe Max Duvall.

"Credit card?"

"We don't use one. Filed for bankruptcy not too long ago." Max offered up a tight smile along with a stack of bills. "We'll pay cash for one night."

The clerk's brow furrowed. "The problem is if you use anything from the minibar or watch a movie in the room, we have no way to charge you."

Max thumbed through the money and shoved it across the counter. "Add an extra hundred for incidentals."

The clerk's frown never left his face, but he seemed compelled to acquiesce to Max. She didn't blame him. Max was the type of man others obeyed.

Five minutes later, Max pushed open the door of their hotel room, holding it open for her.

She eyed the two double beds in the room and placed her purse on the floor next to one of them. If the clerk downstairs had found the request for two beds odd, he'd put on his best poker face. Maybe he'd figured their *bankruptcy* had put a strain on the marriage.

She perched on the edge of the bed, knees and feet primly together, watching Max pace the room like a jungle cat.

He stopped at the window and shifted to the side, leaning one shoulder against the glass.

"Do you want something from the minibar? Water, soft drink, something harder?"

She narrowed her eyes. She hadn't expected him to play host. Despite rescuing her from mortal danger, he hadn't seemed too concerned with her well-being. He'd gone through the motions and had acknowledged her shock and fear, but he'd done next to nothing to comfort her. Because he still didn't trust her.

"I'll have some water." She pushed up from the bed and hovered over the fridge on the console. "Do you want something?"

"Soda, something with caffeine."

The man didn't need caffeine. He needed a stiff drink, something to take off the hard edges.

She swung open the door of the pint-size fridge and plucked a bottle of water from the shelf. She pinched the neck of a wine bottle and held it up. "You sure you don't want some wine?"

"Just the soda, but I don't mind if you want to imbibe. You could probably use something to relax you."

"That's funny." She placed the wine on the credenza and grabbed a can of cola from the inside door of the fridge. "I was just thinking you needed something to relax *you.*"

"Relax?"

He blinked his eyes and looked momentarily lost, as if the idea of relaxation had never occurred to him.

"Never mind." She crossed the room and held out the can to him.

When he took it, his fingers brushed hers and she almost dropped the drink. That was the first time he'd touched her without grabbing, gripping and yanking. Although she'd touched him before, plenty of times.

Like all of the agents, his body was in prime condition—his muscles hard, his belly flat, barely concealed power humming beneath the smooth skin. As a medical professional, she'd always maintained her distance but she couldn't deny she'd looked forward to Max Duvall's appointment times.

But that was then.

She planted her feet on the carpet, widening her stance in front of him. "Are you going to tell me what this is all about now? Why did Simon go on a murderous rampage, why is someone out to get me, and why did you blame it all on me?"

He snapped the tab on his can and took a long pull from it, eyeing her above the rim. "Let's sit down. You must be exhausted."

"I am, but not too exhausted to hear the truth." She walked backward away from him and swiveled toward the bed, dropping onto the mattress. She had to hold herself upright because out of Max's tension-filled sphere, she did feel exhausted. She felt like collapsing on the bed and pulling the covers over her head.

He dragged a chair out from the desk by the window and sat down, stretching his long legs in front of him. It was the closest he'd come to a relaxed pose since he'd stormed into the lab in full riot gear.

"What do you know about the work at the lab?"

"Didn't we go through this already? We support a covert ops agency, Prospero, by monitoring and treating its agents. Part of the lab is responsible for developing vitamin formulas that enhance strength, alertness and even intelligence."

"But you're not part of that lab."

"N-no. I'm the people doctor, not the research doctor."

He slumped in his chair and took another gulp of his drink. "How do you know you support Prospero? Isn't that supposed to be classified information? After all, the general public knows nothing of Prospero...or other covert ops agencies under the umbrella of the CIA."

"We're not supposed to know, but like I said, people talk." She waved her hand in the air. "I've heard things around the lab."

"You heard wrong."

She choked on the sip of water she'd just swallowed. "I beg your pardon?"

"The rumor mill had the wrong info or it purposely spread the wrong info. You don't support Prospero. You support another covert ops team—Tempest."

"Oh." Clearing her throat, she shrugged. "One agency or the other. It doesn't make any difference to me. They must be related groups, since both of their names come from the Shakespeare play."

He nodded slowly and traced the edge of the can with his fingertip. "They are related, in a way."

"So what difference does it make whether we supported Prospero or Tempest?"

"I said the agencies were related, not the same. One is a force for good, and the other..." His hand wrapped around the can and his knuckles grew white as he squeezed it.

The knots in her stomach twisted with the aluminum. "Tempest is a force for evil? Is that what you mean?"

"Yes."

She jerked the hand holding the bottle and the water

sloshed against the plastic. "That's ridiculous. I wouldn't work for an agency like that. Would you? You're a Tempest agent. Are you telling me you all signed up for service knowing Tempest had bad intentions?"

"Not knowingly. Did you? How *did* you come to work at the lab?"

Unease churned in her gut and a flash of heat claimed her flesh from head to toe.

"What is it?" Max hunched forward, bracing his forearms against his thighs.

"Dr. Arnoff recruited me." She pressed her fingers to her warm cheeks. "He gave me the job because I had nowhere else to go."

"Why not, Ava?" His dark eyes burned into her very soul.

"I—I had lost my license to practice medicine. I was finished as a physician before I had even started. Dr. Arnoff gave me a chance. He gave me a chance to be a doctor again." Her voice broke and she took a gulp of water to wash down the tears.

"Why? What happened? You're a good doctor, Ava."

His gentle tone and kind words had the tears pricking the backs of her eyes.

She sniffed. "I'm not a doctor. I made a mistake. Someone betrayed me, but it was my own fault. I was too trusting, too stupid."

He opened his mouth and then snapped it shut. Running a hand through his thick, dark hair until it stood up, he heaved a sigh. "So, Arnoff took advantage of your situation, your desperation to get you to work for Tempest."

"And you? Simon? The others? How did Tempest recruit you?"

He dropped his lashes and held himself so still, she thought he'd fallen asleep for a few seconds. When he opened his eyes, he seemed very far away. "You're not the only one who has made mistakes, Ava."

"So, what is Tempest? What do they do? Wh-what have you done for them?"

A muscle twitched in his jaw, and he ran his knuckles across the dark stubble there. "Tempest is responsible for assassinations, kidnappings, tampering with elections around the world."

"I'm not naive, Max. A lot of covert ops groups are responsible for the same types of missions."

"Tempest is different. An agency like Prospero may commit acts of espionage and violence, but those acts promote a greater good—a safer world."

She crossed her arms and hunched her shoulders. "And what does Tempest promote?"

Max's dark eyes burned as he gazed past her, his nostrils flaring. He seemed to come to some decision as his gaze shifted back to her face, his eyes locking onto hers.

"Terror, chaos, destruction."

"No!" A sharp pain drilled the back of her skull and she bounded from the bed. "I don't believe you. That turns everything we did in that lab, all our efforts, into a big lie. My coworkers were good people. We were doing good work there. We were protecting agents who were protecting our country."

He lunged from his chair, slicing his hand through the air, and she stumbled backward as he loomed over her, his lean frame taut and menacing.

"Tempest agents do not protect this country. Tempest is loyal to no one country or group of nations. Tempest is loyal to itself and the shadowy figure that runs it."

Her knees shook so much she had to grip the edge of the credenza. Despite Max's sudden burst of fury, she didn't fear him. The man had saved her twice. But she did fear his words.

Maybe he was delusional. Maybe this was how Simon had started. Maybe she *should* fear Max Duvall.

"I don't understand." The words came out as a whisper even though that hadn't been her intent. She had no more control over her voice than she did the terror galloping throughout her body.

He ran both hands through his hair, digging his fingers into his scalp. "I don't see how I can be any plainer. Tempest is a deep undercover agency, so rogue the CIA is completely in the dark about its operations and methods. Tempest carries out assassinations and nation building all on its own, and these interests do not serve the US or world peace."

"Then what is their purpose?"

As if realizing his close proximity to her for the first time, Max shuffled back, retreating to the window, wedging a shoulder against the glass.

"I don't know. Tempest's overall goal is a mystery to me."

"If Tempest is so evil, why are you one of its agents? You said you were recruited, but why'd you stay? There's no way the agency could keep you in the dark, not...not like me."

She held her breath, bracing for another outburst. Instead, Max relaxed his rigid stance. His broad shoulders slumped and he massaged the back of his neck.

"You really have no idea, do you? You haven't figured it out yet."

A muscle beneath her eye jumped, and she smoothed her hands across her face. She sipped in a few short breaths, pushing back against the creeping dread invading her lungs.

"Why should I know? You haven't explained that part to me. You've made some crazy, wild accusations, throwing puzzle pieces at me, expecting me to fit them together when I haven't even processed the mass murder I just witnessed."

Her knees finally buckled and she grabbed for the credenza as she sank to the carpet.

Max's long stride ate up the distance between them, and he placed a steadying hand on her shoulder. "Are you okay? We should've saved this conversation for morning, after some sleep and some food."

When she didn't respond, he nudged her. "Can you stand up?"

She nodded, but the muscles in her legs refused to obey the commands from her brain.

He crouched beside her, slipping one arm across her back and one behind her thighs. She leaned into him and he lifted her from the floor and stood up in one motion.

He was careful to hold her body away from his as he carried her to the bed, but for her part she could've nestled in his arms forever. She wanted him to hold her and tell her this was all a joke.

He placed her on the bed with surprising gentleness. "Why don't you get some sleep, and we'll talk about this over breakfast?"

She grabbed a pillow and hugged it to her chest. "I wouldn't be able to sleep anyway. Tell me the truth. Tell me the whole ugly truth about what we were doing in that lab and why you stayed with Tempest."

He backed up and eased onto the edge of the bed across from hers. He blew out a long breath. "I stayed with Tempest even after I discovered their agenda because they wanted me to. Tempest controlled my mind and my body. They still do."

"No." Ava squeezed the pillow against her body, her fingers curling into soft foam.

"It's a form of brainwashing, Ava, but it goes beyond the brain. It's my body, too." He pushed up from the bed and plucked up a lamp with a metal rod from the base to the lightbulb. He unplugged it and removed the shade. Gripping it on either side with his hands, he bent it to a forty-five-degree angle. Then he held up the lamp by the lightbulb, which had to still be hot, and didn't even flinch.

Her eyes widened and her jaw dropped. "Dr. Arnoff's vitamin formula—stronger, faster, impervious to pain."

He released the bulb and the distorted lamp fell to the floor. He examined his hand. "So, he did tell you."

"That's what he was working on, but he told me it was years from completion."

He held up his reddened palm. "He completed it."

"What you're telling me—" she swung her legs over the side of the bed "—is crazy. You're saying that Dr. Arnoff's formula created some kind of superagent and that Tempest sent these agents out into the world to do its bidding?"

"Yes, but I told you it's more than physical." He tapped the side of his head. "Tempest messed with our minds, too."

She bunched the bedspread in her hands. "How? That didn't happen in our lab."

"No. That occurred in the debriefing unit in Germany where we went after every assignment."

She pinned her hands between her knees as her eyes darted to the hotel door. Max Duvall could be crazy. This could all be some elaborate hallucination, one that he'd shared with Simon Skinner. Then her gaze tracked to the metal rod of the lamp, which he'd folded as if it were a straw. So, he was crazy *and* strong—a bad combination.

"How did they do it? The brainwashing?"

He squeezed his eyes closed and massaged his temple with two fingers. "Mind control—it was mind control and they did it through a combination of drugs, hypnosis and sleep therapy."

"What is sleep therapy?"

"That's my name for it. The doctors would hook us up to machines, brain scans, and then sedate us. They said it was for deep relaxation and stress reduction, but…" He shook his head.

"But what?" She wiped her palms on the bedspread. The air in the room almost crackled with electricity.

"It didn't do that. It didn't relax us, at least not me and Simon. After those sessions, a jumble of memories and scenes assaulted my brain. I couldn't tell real from fake. The memories—they implanted them in my brain."

She gasped as a bolt of fear shot through her chest. "They wanted you to forget the assignments."

"But I couldn't." He shoved off the window and stalked across the room, pressing his palms against either side of his head. "Simon and I, we remembered. I don't know how many others did."

He really believed all of this, and he blamed her for administering the serum. Maybe the men at her house had been there to protect her from Max. The pressures of the job had driven them both off the deep end. Simon had snapped, and Max was nearing the same precipice.

"I-is that what drove Simon to commit violence? The implanted memories?"

"No." He pivoted and paced back to the window, a light sheen of sweat breaking out on his forehead. "The implanted memories were fine. It was the flashes of reality that tortured us."

If she kept pretending that she believed him, maybe

he'd drop her off at the airport without incident. She could make up family somewhere, a family that cared about her and worried about her well-being. A fake family.

"The reality of what he'd done for Tempest pushed Simon past the breaking point?"

"It's the serum." He turned again and swayed to the side. He thrust out an unsteady hand to regain his balance. "Simon tried to break the cycle, but you can't go cold turkey. I told him not to go cold turkey."

A spasm of pain distorted his handsome features, and Ava tensed her muscles to make a run at the door if necessary. "I'm not sure I understand, Max."

"The pills." He wiped a hand across his mouth and staggered. "I need the pills. I'll end up like Simon without them."

She braced her hands on her knees, ready to spring into action. The pills, again. He'd been going on about blue pills at the lab when he rescued her, too.

Max was talking gibberish now, his strong hands clenching and then unclenching, his gait unsteady, sweat dripping from his jaw.

"What pills?" She licked her lips. Her gaze flicked to the door. If she rolled off the other side of the bed, she could avoid Max, pitching and reeling in the middle of the room. Then she'd call 911. He needed help, but she didn't have the strength or the tools to subdue him if he decided to attack her.

"Pocket. The blue." Then he pitched forward and landed face-first on the floor.

Chapter Five

"Max!" She launched off the bed and crouched beside him. If he decided to grab her now, she wouldn't have a chance against his power.

His body twitched and he moaned. He *had* no power to grab her now. She could make a run for it and call hotel security. The hotel would call 911, and he could get help at the hospital from a doctor—a real doctor.

Max's dry lips parted, and he reached for her hand.

And if any part of his story was true? She knew the secrecy of that lab better than anyone. Those two men with the automatic weapons had been waiting at her house, for her. Max had saved her.

She curled her fingers around his and squeezed. "I'll be right back."

She ran to the bathroom and grabbed a hand towel. She held it under a stream of cool water and grabbed a bottle of the stuff on her way back to Max. She swept a pillow from the bed and sat on the floor beside his prone form.

He'd rolled to his back, so at least he wasn't unconscious.

Pressing two fingers against his neck, she checked his pulse—rapid but strong. She dabbed his face with the wet towel and eased a pillow beneath his head.

"Can you drink some water? Are you in any pain?" She held up the bottle.

"The pills." His voice rasped from his throat.

They were back to the pills? "What pills, Max?"

His hand dropped to his side, and she remembered what he'd said before he collapsed. His pocket.

She skimmed her hand across the rough material of one pocket and then the other, her fingers tracing the edges of a hard, square object. She dug her fingers into the pocket and pulled out a small tin of breath mints, but when she opened the lid no minty freshness greeted her.

Five round blue pills nestled together in the corner of the tin. She held up the container to his face. "These pills?"

His chin dipped to his chest, and she shook the pills into her palm.

He held up his index finger.

"Just one?"

He hissed, a sound that probably meant yes.

She picked up one pill between two fingers and placed it into his mouth. Then she held the water bottle up to his lips, while curling an arm around the back of his head to prop him up.

He swallowed the water and the pill disappeared. His spiky, dark lashes closed over his eyes and he melted against her arm. Her fingers burrowed into his thick, black hair as she dabbed his face with the towel.

His chest rose and fell, his breathing deeper and more regular. His face changed from a sickly pallor to his usual olive skin tone, and the trembling that had been racking his body ceased.

Whatever magic ingredient the little blue pill contained seemed to work. She peered at the remaining pills in the tin and sniffed them. Maybe he was a drug addict. Hallucinogens could bring on the paranoid thoughts.

His eyes flew open and he struggled to sit up.

"Whoa." Her arms slipped around his shoulders. "You just had a very scary incident. You need to lie back and relax."

"It passes quickly. I'm fine." He shrugged off her arm and sat up, leaning his back against the credenza. He chugged the rest of the water.

"Are you okay? I almost called 911."

"Don't—" he cinched her wrist with his thumb and middle finger "—ever call the police."

Her heart skipped a beat. She should've run when she had the chance.

His deep brown eyes widened and grew even darker. He dropped her wrist. "I'm sorry. I scared you."

She scooted away and rested her back against the bed, facing him. "And I'm sorry you're going through all this, but there's nothing I can do to help you. You need to see a doctor, and I—I'll go to my family and contact the CIA about what happened at the lab."

"You *are* a doctor." His eyes glittered through slits.

"Not exactly, and you know what I mean. You need to go to a doctor's office, get checked out."

"You mean a psychiatrist, don't you?"

"I mean…"

"You don't believe me. You're afraid of me. You think I'm crazy." He laughed, a harsh, stark sound with no humor in it.

"It's a crazy story, Max. My lab was just shot up and two men tried to kill me—or you."

"Both of us."

"Okay, maybe both of us, but I don't belong in the middle of all this."

"You're right." He rose from the floor, looking as strong and capable as ever. "Try to get some sleep. I'll take you to the airport tomorrow."

"And you?"

"I'll keep doing what I've been doing."

"Which is?"

"You don't belong in the middle of this, remember?" He tossed the pillow she'd tucked beneath him onto the bed and took a deep breath, the air in his lungs expanding his broad chest, his black T-shirt stretching across his muscles. "Would you like to take a shower? I need to take one, but you can go first."

"I would, but I can wait."

Still sitting on the floor, she'd stretched her legs in front of her.

Max stepped over her outstretched legs on the way to the bathroom and shut the door behind him.

Blowing out a long breath, Ava got to her feet and grabbed her purse. She could get a taxi to the airport before he even got out of the shower.

MAX BRACED HIS hands against the tile of the shower and dipped his head, as the warm water beat between his shoulder blades.

She'd be gone by the time he came out of the shower. And why shouldn't she be? She thought he was crazy. She didn't trust him. And she was right not to.

If she stayed, if she believed him, she could probably help him. She didn't seem to know about the pills, but she'd worked with Arnoff. She might know something about those blue pills that stood between him and a complete meltdown like Simon.

He'd warned Simon to keep taking the pills, but his

buddy was stubborn. He'd wanted nothing more to do with Tempest and its control over their lives.

Max faced the spray and sluiced the water through his hair. Maybe he'd made a mistake showing his hand to Tempest. As soon as he'd refused his last assignment, Foster had suspected he'd figured everything out—not everything. He and Simon hadn't realized quitting the serum would have such a profound effect on their bodies and minds.

He cranked off the water and grabbed a towel. At least he'd been able to save Dr. Whitman—Ava—from Simon. Stupid, stubborn bastard. Who was going to tell Simon's fiancée, Nina?

He dried off and wrapped the towel around his waist. A few hours' sleep would do him good, and then he'd reassess. He could contact Prospero, but he didn't know whom he could trust at this point. He didn't blame Ava one bit for hightailing it out of here.

He pushed open the bathroom door and stopped short.

Ava looked up from examining something in the palm of her hand. Her gaze scanned his body, and he made a grab for the towel slipping down his hips.

"You're still here."

"Did you expect me to take off?"

He pointedly stared at the purse hanging over her shoulder. "Yeah."

She held out her hand, his precious pills cupped in her palm. "What are these? They have a distinctive odor."

"They should." He adjusted the towel again and glanced over his shoulder at his clothes scattered across the bathroom floor. He couldn't risk leaving her alone with those pills another minute. She might just get it in her head to run with them. She probably thought he was a junkie.

Her body stiffened and she closed her hand around the blue beauties. "Why would you say that?"

"They're a milder form of the serum you inject in us four times a year." He cocked his head. "You really don't know that?"

The color drained from her face, emphasizing her large eyes, which widened. "Why would you be taking additional doses of the serum?"

"Weaker doses. To keep up. To be better, faster, stronger, smarter. Isn't that what the serum is all about?"

"Did you know what they were when you started taking them?"

"By the time the pills were introduced into our regimen, we didn't care what they were for. We needed them."

"They're addictive?" She swept the breath-mint tin from the credenza and funneled the pills into it from her cupped hand.

Max released the breath he'd been holding. "More than you could possibly know."

"Then tell me, Max. I deserve to know everything. I stayed." She shrugged the purse from her shoulder and tossed it onto the bed. "One little part of me believed your story. There was enough subterfuge in that lab to make me believe your wild accusations."

"Can I put my pants on first?" He hooked his fingers around the edge of the towel circling his hips.

Her eyes dropped to his hands, and the color came rushing back into her pale cheeks. "Of course. I'm not going anywhere."

He retreated to the bathroom and dropped the towel. Leaning close to the mirror, he plowed a hand through his damp hair. It needed a trim and he needed a shave, not that he'd given a damn about his appearance before Ava came onto the scene.

He pulled on his camos and returned to the bedroom.

Ava had moved to the chair and sat with her legs curled beneath her, a look of expectancy highlighting her face.

He'd memorized that face from his quarterly visits with her. Dr. Ava Whitman had been the one bright spot in the dark tunnel of Tempest. He believed with certainty that she had no idea what she'd been dosing them with. At first, he'd been incredulous that a doctor wouldn't know what was in a formula she was giving her patients, but her story made sense. Tempest sought out the most vulnerable. The agency used blackmail and coercion, and in Ava's case, hope, to recruit people.

Dr. Arnoff had kept her in the dark, had probably shut down her questions by reminding her that she wouldn't be working as a doctor if it weren't for the agency and then using the illegality of that work to keep her in line.

And she'd been good at her job. He had a hard time remembering the two missions he'd been on last year, but he could clearly recall Ava's soft touch and cheery tone as she checked his vitals and injected him with the serum that would destroy his life.

Ava cleared her throat. "If the blue pills are a weaker dose of the T-101 serum, why are you still taking them?"

"I have to."

"Because you're addicted? Why not just ride out the withdrawal?" She laced her fingers in her lap. "I can help you. I—I have some experience with that."

He raised his eyebrows. She had to be referring to a patient. "It's more than the addiction. I could ride that out. You saw Simon."

She drew in a quick breath and hunched forward. "Simon went over the edge. He lost it. The stress, the tension, maybe even the brainwashing—they all did him in."

"It's the...T-101, Ava. Is that what you called it? Without the serum, we self-destruct. Another agent, before Simon, before me, he committed suicide. Tempest put it down to post-traumatic stress disorder because this agent had killed a child by mistake on a raid. Now I wonder if that was even a mistake or his true assignment."

"Adam Belchik." She drew her knees to her chest, wrapping her arms around them.

"That's right. I thought he was before your time."

"He was, but I heard about him."

"He was the first to go off the meds, and he paid the price. He had a family, so he killed himself before he could harm them."

"Is that why you were jabbering about cold turkey? You can't quit cold turkey like Simon did, like Adam did. You have to keep lowering your dosage by continuing with the blue pills."

"That's it." He pointed to the tin on the credenza, the fine line keeping him from insanity and rage. "I find if I take one a day, I can maintain. I tried a half, and it didn't work."

"You have only five left." Her gaze darted to the credenza and back to his face.

"Four now. Four pills. Four days."

She uncurled her legs and almost fell out of the chair as she bolted from it. "That's crazy. What happens at the end of the four days?"

He lifted his shoulders. "I'll be subject to incidents like the one you just witnessed until they kill me or I snap… or Tempest gets to me first."

"And if they do?"

"They'll either kill me or I'll be their drone for the rest of my life."

She folded her arms across her stomach, clutching the material of her blouse at her sides. "There has to be another way. If we get more of the pills and you take smaller and smaller doses, maybe eventually you can break free. You tried taking a half, but it was too soon."

"Where would I get more pills? You said yourself you never saw them at the lab. They weren't administered at the lab. My quick search there revealed nothing."

She snapped her fingers. "Max, there has to be an antidote somewhere."

"Why would you think that? Tempest had no intention of ever reversing the damage they'd done to us."

"Maybe not to you, but Dr. Arnoff tested the T-101 on himself."

His heart slammed against his chest. "Are you sure?"

"I'm positive, or at least I'm positive that he told me he'd tried it on himself. He said he felt like a superhero—strong, invincible, sexually potent."

She reddened to the edge of her hairline and waved a hand in the air. "You know, that's what he said."

Sexual potency? It had been a long time since he'd been close enough to a woman in a normal situation to even think about sex.

He cleared his throat. "If he acted as his own guinea pig, he'd want something to counteract the effects in case things didn't go the way he planned."

"Exactly—an antidote."

"We could be jumping to conclusions." He dragged in a breath and let it out slowly in an attempt to temper his excitement. He'd learned to be cautious about good news. "Maybe Arnoff didn't develop an antidote. He could've dialed back by taking the blue pills—fewer and fewer of them until the cravings stopped and the physical effects dissipated."

"That could be, but it also means there must be more of those blue pills floating around." She dropped onto the bed. "What about the other agents? Can you all pool your resources and wean yourselves off of the serum?"

He cracked a smile and shook his head.

"What's so funny? That's the first real smile I've seen from you all night, and I wasn't even making a joke."

"I just got a visual of a bunch of Tempest agents sitting around a campfire sharing little pieces of their blue pills."

A smile hovered at her lips. "Not possible?"

"I don't even know who more than half of the agents are."

"I do."

His gaze locked onto hers. "You don't know all their names. You don't know where they live, and most of them are probably on assignment anyway."

She shook her finger at him. "You'd be surprised how many of them opened up to me."

"Not surprised at all." She'd obviously been a ray of sunshine for the other agents, too. "But we can't go knocking on their doors asking them to give up their meds. Unless they've already suspected something or had incidents like Simon and I did, they're not going to see the problem."

"I meant to ask you that." She fell back against the mattress and rolled to her side to face him, propping up her head with one hand. "What made you and Simon realize what was going on?"

"There were gaps, glitches in our response to the treatment. For me it was the memories. I recalled too much about my operations. The memories they tried to implant in my brain didn't jibe with my reality. On one assignment, Simon and I started comparing notes and then experimenting with the pills."

"Simon didn't show up for his last appointment with me. He never got his injection."

"He decided to make a clean break. He shrugged off the seizures even though I tried to warn him." He dropped his head in his hands, digging his fingers into his scalp. What would they tell Simon's fiancée?

The bed sank beside him, and he turned his head as Ava touched his back.

"You had to shoot Simon. He would've killed you. He would've killed me." The pressure of her hand between his shoulder blades increased. "Now, since you saved my life—twice—I'm going to save yours."

He wanted to believe her. He wanted to stretch out on the bed next to Ava and feel her soft touch on his forehead again.

"And how to you propose to do that, Dr. Whitman?"

Her hand dropped from his back. "Don't call me that. I told you, I never finished. I don't deserve the title."

"Ava."

"We're going to find that antidote or a million blue pills to get you through this." She yawned and covered her mouth with the back of her hand. "But first I'm going to sleep away the rest of what's left of this evening."

"And your family? I thought I was taking you to the airport tomorrow so you could fly out to be with your family."

"My family." She launched from his bed to hers, peeled back the covers and slipped beneath them. "I have no family."

Chapter Six

Ava buried her head beneath a pillow and ran her tongue along her teeth. She needed a toothbrush and a meal.

"Are you awake?"

Lifting one corner of the pillow, she peered out at Max sitting in front of a tablet computer at the table by the window. "What time is it?"

He flicked back the heavy drapes and a spear of sunlight sliced through the room. "It's around ten o'clock. You must be hungry. When was the last time you ate?"

"I had my dinner at the lab before…before everything went down."

"That was a long time ago."

"An eternity. A lifetime." She retreated beneath the pillow. How was she supposed to do this with Max? Why did her life always manage to get upended?

She heard his footsteps across the room and the crackle of plastic.

"I went down to the little store in the hotel and bought you a few things."

"A new life?"

The silence yawned from across the room and engulfed her. She tossed the pillow away from her and sat up.

Max stood in the center of the room, a plastic bag dangling at his side. "You don't need to do this, Ava. In fact, I'm going to take you to the airport right now. I'll pay for a ticket anywhere you want to go. Then you can call the CIA or whatever number the lab gave you in case of an emergency and you can forget about all of this."

She sighed. "I was trying to make a joke. I want to help you. I feel responsible for your predicament. If I hadn't been so anxious for a job, any job, I wouldn't have been injecting you and Simon and countless others with poison."

"Not your fault. They would've found someone else." He chucked the bag onto the foot of the bed. "Toothbrush, comb, deodorant, some other stuff. Take a shower. I have some stuff to get out of the car, and then I'll meet you in the restaurant downstairs for breakfast. You can let me know then what you want to do."

The door closed behind him and she stared at it for several seconds. A ticket to anywhere. A new start—again. How many new starts did one woman need?

She threw off the covers and grabbed the bag of toiletries. She didn't need a new start. She needed a finish. She needed to help Max Duvall.

Forty minutes later, freshly showered but wearing the same clothes from yesterday, Ava made her way down to the lobby. She spotted Max immediately. Did everyone else notice the aura of power and menace around him or did she just have that special switch that flicked on when danger sent out its Siren's call?

He glanced up from his newspaper and watched her approach with an unwavering gaze, as if willing her to his side. He didn't have to throw out any lures. She was all in.

He rose to his feet when she reached the table and pulled out her chair. "Do you feel better after your shower?"

Sitting down, she flicked the collar of her blouse. "I'd feel even better if I had some clean clothes to step into."

"I wouldn't recommend going back to your house for a while."

"Ever?" She turned her coffee cup over and nodded at the waitress bearing a coffeepot.

"When this all blows over."

"When will that be?" After the waitress came by with the coffee, Ava poured a steady stream of cream into her cup, watching the milky swirls fan out in the dark liquid.

"When the CIA or Prospero gets a handle on Tempest and puts a stop to its clandestine operations."

The spoon hovered over her cup. "In other words, I'd better get used to these clothes."

"Buy new ones."

"Is that what you do?" She took in the dark blue T-shirt, very similar to the black T-shirt he'd been wearing last night. He'd swapped the camouflage pants for a pair of faded jeans.

"I've been carrying my clothes—and everything else—with me for the past month. I have one bag for my clothes and a second one for my...tools."

She slurped a sip of coffee, wondering how best to ask him about his tools, when the waitress came back and saved her from doing something stupid.

They both asked for omelets, but Max added a bowl of oatmeal and some fresh fruit to his order.

She folded her hands on the table and tilted her head. "When was the last time you ate?"

"It's been a while." He brought the coffee cup to his lips and stared at her over the rim. "Airport?"

She gripped her hands together and sucked in a breath. She let it out on one word. "No."

"Are you sure?"

"I have some ideas, Max."

The waitress placed Max's oatmeal between them, and

he dumped some brown sugar and raisins into the bowl. "I'm listening."

The maple smell of the brown sugar rose on the steam, creating a homey feel completely at odds with their conversation.

"I know where Dr. Arnoff lives—lived." She pushed her cup out of the way and tapped a spot on the table. "The lab is here and Albuquerque is this way. He lives in a suburb, a high-end suburb. We can start with his house and see if he has anything there, any of those blue pills. I know he keeps a work laptop at home."

"Is he married? Does he have a family?"

"He is married, but his children are adults. One lives overseas and the other one is in Boston."

"You think his wife, his widow, is going to invite us into her home so we can snoop around in her dead husband's personal effects?" He plunged his spoon into the oatmeal.

"You're a spy, aren't you? We either break in or gain entrance through some kind of subterfuge."

He raised an eyebrow. "I repeat. You do not have to do any of this. You can hop on a plane and put this behind you."

"No, I can't." Whatever happened, she'd never forget Max Duvall. She'd always wonder if he made it or not, and if he didn't make it she'd always blame herself.

He left his spoon in the bowl and pushed it to the corner of the table. "You mentioned you had no family. Do you have friends you can stay with?"

"Out of the blue like this?" She spread her hands. "No."

"If anything happened to you…"

She pressed her fingers against his forearm, and his corded muscle twitched beneath her touch. "I'll be with you. For better or worse, you still have T-101 pulsing through your system. You're practically indestructible."

"I may be, but you're not." He covered her hand with his own, his touch rough, awkward but sincere. "You can give me directions to Arnoff's and I'll go there on my own."

"What am I supposed to do? Where am I supposed to go?"

They broke apart when the waitress delivered their food. "You had the Denver and you had the spinach? Ketchup? Salsa?"

"Both, please." Ava flicked the napkin into her lap.

When the waitress returned with their condiments, Max spooned some salsa onto his plate and took up the conversation without missing a beat. "You can stay here."

"Stay here?"

"I'd come back after going to Arnoff's in case nothing panned out there. You could help me find a few other agents and be on your way." He sawed off an edge of his omelet with his fork. "Once you decide where you want to go."

"I'd need to call the CIA or rather the emergency number I have."

"You have an emergency number?"

"I thought I told you that." She stabbed a potato and dragged it through the puddle of ketchup on her plate. Then she remembered the blood all over the lab and placed the tines of her fork on the edge of her plate.

"You told me you planned to call the CIA."

"Yeah, the emergency number."

"You know for a fact that the emergency number goes to the CIA?"

"I just assumed it did." She wrapped her hands around her cup, still warm from the coffee the waitress had topped off. "D-do you think it's the number for someone at Tempest?"

"Could be." The blood-red ketchup didn't seem to bother him as he squirted another circle of it on the side of his plate.

Her hands tightened around the mug. "I can't call that number. Those men at my house could've been from Tempest."

"They *were* from Tempest." He tapped her plate with his knife. "Eat your breakfast."

She spooned the ketchup from her plate into a napkin. "So, who am I supposed to call? The number for the CIA isn't exactly in the phone book."

"You should call Prospero—once I'm out of the picture."

"You don't trust Prospero but you expect me to?"

"You're not an agent formerly working with Tempest. Prospero has no reason not to trust you."

"Really? Because you trusted me immediately?"

"I can't trust anyone, Ava."

"Maybe I can't either."

"You can trust me."

"As long as you keep taking the reduced dosage of T-101 in those pills."

He glanced up from his plate, his dark eyes narrowing to slits. "I'm glad you recognize that. Don't forget it."

His tone made her a little breathless. What would she do if Max turned into Simon? She'd have to be long gone before that ever happened. He'd make himself long gone before that ever happened.

She finished her omelet and put her hand over her cup when the waitress swung by to offer refills.

Max pushed his plate away and crumpled up a napkin next to it. "Do you have Arnoff's address?"

"Yes. When are you going out there?"

"I think it's best if I wait until night."

"In case Mrs. Arnoff isn't cooperative?"

His hand jerked and the water in the glass he'd been holding sloshed and the ice tinkled. "I wouldn't hurt Dr. Arnoff's wife."

Her cheeks burned. "I didn't mean that at all. I just… I mean in case you have to break in or something."

His shallow breath deepened and he seemed to unclench his jaw. "I won't hurt her. I won't do that."

She didn't want to probe too deeply into whether or not he'd hurt civilians for Tempest. Whatever he'd done for the agency, it disturbed him profoundly.

"She must know by now her husband's dead. Maybe she's not even home." She patted the newspaper on the chair between them. "I suppose there's nothing in the paper about the mayhem at the lab."

"No journalists even know about the lab, do they? Do the police in that area make a habit of patrolling around the lab?"

"No. We had our own security force. No police."

"They knew it was there?"

"They knew it was a top secret government entity. The lab's security force had given the local cops instructions to keep their distance."

"Then maybe nothing's been discovered yet. Did family members ever drop by?"

"I…"

"Other employees' family members."

She pursed her lips. She hadn't been about to tell him she had no family again. Guess she'd already beaten that particular dead horse. "I was going to say, I never saw any family members there. A lot of the lab employees didn't even reside in New Mexico. They lived elsewhere and had come out here for the assignment. I got the impression most left their families behind."

"Except Dr. Arnoff."

"He was the head of the lab, so he was a permanent fixture."

"Did he tend to work long hours? Sleep at the lab?"

"He did."

"Then his wife may not even know he's dead."

"Perhaps not. You're not going to tell her, are you?"

He held up his hands. "Not me, and I doubt if she'd take kindly to a stranger snooping around and asking questions."

She sat forward in her chair, hunching over the table. "That's why I need to go with you. I'm sure she remembers me. We met a few times. I can get us into the house by telling her Dr. Arnoff sent me to collect something. Once we're in the house, you can do your spy thing."

"As you delicately pointed out before, I can get into the house and she'll never know I was there."

"But my way might be easier."

"I think you'd be safer here at the hotel."

Folding her arms, she sat back in her chair while Max left some money on the check tray. He didn't plan to leave until dark, so she still had some time to work on him. "What are your plans in the meantime?"

"Shopping."

"A little retail therapy? I never would've guessed you were the sort."

He waved his finger up and down to take in her wrinkled blouse. "I was thinking of you. Do you want to pick up a few clothes here?"

"That would be great, but you don't have to come along."

"Humor me."

FOR THE NEXT few hours, she humored him. She picked up some jeans and T-shirts, a comfortable pair of ankle boots and some sneakers. She added some underwear and a few more toiletries. Max picked out a small carry-on suitcase for the plane trip he was convinced she'd be taking. She let him believe that.

He paid cash for everything from a seemingly endless supply of money even when she offered to use her credit card, which he refused and told her to put away.

She wasn't going to allow him to pay for everything, so when he ducked into a sandwich shop to get some drinks she headed toward an ATM.

Placing the edge of her card at the slot, her hand wavered. It had to be okay to use her card just once. The machine piled up the bills for her to snatch. She tucked them into her purse and returned to the front of the sandwich shop.

Max approached her, carrying two drinks in front of him. "Are you going to get that other pair of shoes?"

"No, I decided against it. I don't want to spend any more of your money." She held out her own cash to him. "And I really want to pay you back."

Max reached out and squeezed her shoulder. "Don't worry about it. I appreciate the gesture, but you keep the cash just in case." He handed her a soda and picked up her shopping bags. "I don't know about you, but I need a nap after last night's activities."

She could use a nap, too, but sleeping in the same room as Max was awkward—at least for her. He seemed all business now, definitely not as friendly as when he was her patient. But he hadn't known the extent of his enslavement to Tempest at that point and that she'd been injecting him with poison. He had no reason to be friendly to her.

He'd parked his car in the parking structure below

the mall, and they took the elevator into the bowels of the garage.

As they approached the blue sedan, she turned to him suddenly. "Where'd you get this car? Why do you have all that cash?"

He clicked the remote and put a finger to his lips. "I still have some secrets."

She eyed the car as he opened the trunk and swung her bags inside. It didn't look like a spy's car unless it had special, hidden gadgets.

"Does this thing have an ejection seat or turn into a hovercraft?"

He opened the passenger door for her and cocked his head. "I don't think it can even do eighty miles an hour."

The car went sixty on the highway on the way back to the hotel. Max rolled into the hotel's parking garage, and they returned to the room.

He pulled the drapes closed on the gray day and stretched out on the bed with his tablet propped up on his knees.

She pointed at the computer. "I thought you were going to sleep."

"I am. I'm actually reading a book. Even though it's a good one, I should be drifting off any minute—and you should, too."

She sat on the edge of the bed and toed off her shoes. Then she fell backward, her knees bent and her feet still planted on the floor, and stared at the ceiling.

She should've never taken the job offer from Dr. Arnoff. It had seemed too good to be true—a chance to practice medicine without the medical license. Now she was paying for her lies. She always did.

"Do you generally sleep with your legs hanging off the bed?"

"I'm almost too tired to move."

"Shopping does that to me, too."

"I don't think it was the shopping." She hoisted herself up on her elbows. "I think it's more the threats on my life and the fact that my job was a sham."

"Sorry."

She studied his face. Was he being sarcastic?

He stared back at her, his dark eyes serious, not a hint of sarcasm. Had he lost that ability, too?

No, he meant it. His life was in the toilet and he still had empathy for her. Guess the T-101 hadn't worked that great on him if it had been designed to erase human emotions. Max kept a tight rein on his feelings, but he definitely had them.

"Thanks. I'm sorry, too. Sorry that you're going through this. Sorry that I was a party to it."

He dropped his gaze to his book. "Let's try to get some sleep."

Folding her legs on the bed, she rolled to her side and closed her eyes. If Max thought he was leaving her here when he went to Dr. Arnoff's, he had another think coming.

This agent, this damaged man, was her only hope of returning to a life with any semblance of normalcy—not that she'd ever had that before.

This time she woke up first. She scooted to the edge of the mattress and peered through the gloom at Max fast asleep on the other bed, the tablet rising and falling on his chest with every deep breath.

Even in repose, sleeping on his back, he looked primed and ready. Could he ever really relax?

She rolled to the other side of the bed and slipped off

the edge. Tiptoeing around the room, she gathered a few of her new purchases and retreated to the bathroom.

She peeled off the clothes she'd dressed in yesterday morning, never dreaming she was heading into a nightmare, one worse than the previous nightmare she'd already lived through.

Did the nightmares ever end?

She brushed her teeth and washed her face. She dabbed on some moisturizer and added a little makeup. She didn't want to scare Mrs. Arnoff before she could talk her way into the house.

She padded on bare feet back into the room, her dirty clothes tucked under one arm, her shoes hanging from her fingertips.

"I was getting used to those slacks and blouse."

She jumped and dropped a shoe.

In the darkness of the room, Max was watching her from the bed, a pillow wedged beneath his neck.

She swept the shoe from the floor and stacked the armful of clothes on top of the suitcase Max had bought, still believing she would hop on a plane to somewhere.

"If I never see these slacks again, it will be too soon. I could toss them down the trash chute and be perfectly happy." She scraped at a spot on the navy blue pant leg. "Th-there are spots of blood on them that I never noticed before."

"You can send them to the dry cleaner while you wait for me." He swung his legs from the bed, raising his arms above his head in a long stretch.

"Yeah, about that." She busied her hands folding the clothes. "I'm going with you."

"No." He dropped his arms and shoved off the bed. "I have no idea what I'm going to find at Arnoff's house."

"You're probably going to find Mrs. Arnoff." She wedged

her hands on her hips. "She knows me. She'll let me in the house. She'll let me go through her husband's things if I tell her he sent me. She'll give me his computer."

"Unless she knows he's dead somehow."

"I don't think she will. You said yourself that news of the lab won't leak out until everything's cleaned up. And if she does—" she shrugged "—I'll make up another story to get us inside based on what she thinks she knows."

"Why are you so hell-bent on coming along? You don't owe me anything. I believe you that you knew nothing about the T-101 and Tempest's true mission."

"I'm not volunteering out of a sense of guilt." Clearly, she needed to use a new justification. "I don't want you to leave me here alone. You're the only person who can help me now, the only one I can turn to."

His nostrils flared. "Are you really afraid to stay here by yourself?"

"I'd feel better if I came along with you." She waved a hand at the window. "I don't know what's out there. I don't know who's out there, and I'm certainly not prepared to meet them if they come after me."

He crossed to the window and pressed his forehead against the glass as if assessing the danger below. "I think you'd be fine here, but if you're not comfortable, you can come with me."

Ava released a measured breath, not quite a sigh. "I would feel more comfortable, and I think I can get us into the house."

He held up his hand. "We'll see when we get there. I'm going to brush my teeth and get some gear together."

It was exactly that gear she was counting on to keep her safe. She'd played on Max's natural protective instincts to get him to agree to let her come along, but it hadn't been a total ruse. What would she do here alone? What would she do if someone came after her?

For now she'd stick to Max and his gear.

While he got ready, she turned on the TV, not that she expected to see any news about the lab. Tempest or the CIA would clamp down on that story. When she and Max parted ways, could she trust the CIA? Tempest had presumably been operating, unchecked, right under the nose of the agency.

Max slung a bag across his chest, gripping the strap with one hand. "Are you ready?"

She'd think about whom to trust when she and Max parted once they reached that point. She hadn't been lying to him. Right now, he was all she had.

She tossed the remote control on the bed. "Ready."

They took the elevator to the second floor and then jogged down the stairwell, their shoes slapping against the metal steps.

Max pushed through the fire door and she followed him across a short hallway to a side exit that led to the parking structure.

The parking lot had cleared out some since they'd returned to the hotel from shopping, and it looked as if they'd missed the dinner crowd leaving for their restaurants.

Max unlocked the car and hoisted his bag into the backseat.

She scrambled into the passenger side of the car before he could change his mind.

They snapped their seat belts in unison and Max slipped the key into the ignition. It clicked.

"What the…?" His fingers hovered over the dangling keys.

Ava's nostrils flared. "What's that smell?"

"Ava, get out!" He yanked off his seat belt as she stared at him with her mouth agape.

He popped the release for her and then nudged her shoulder. "Get out of the car now and run for the exit!"

He reached into the backseat and a surge of adrenaline pulsed through her veins. She snagged her bag from the floor of the car and shoved at the door. It fell open and she stumbled out of the car.

"Get to the stairwell." Max sprinted behind the car, the black bag banging against his hip.

She didn't know why the hell they were running, but when Max Duvall yelled "run" in that tone of voice, she obeyed.

He crowded behind her, urging her to move faster.

Just when she smacked her palms against the cold metal of the stairwell door, an explosion rocked her off her feet, driving her against the door.

As Max smashed against her back, she jerked her head over her shoulder—just in time to see their ride go up in flames.

Chapter Seven

Max cranked his head around, squinting through the black, acrid smoke billowing from his stolen car. No collateral damage. *Please, God, no civilians.*

He peeled himself away from Ava, flattened against the stairwell door. "Are you okay?"

She nodded, covering her ears with her hands.

The noise from the explosion hadn't affected him. He still had enough T-101 coursing through his bloodstream to make him immune to such things.

"Did you see anyone else up here when we went to the car?"

"What?"

He put his lips close to her ear, which had to be ringing. "Any other people. Was anyone else on this level?"

"I didn't see anyone."

"Let's get out of here." He reached around her and pressed the door handle down. The door swung open, and he had to catch Ava around the waist as she tripped.

They'd been discovered. How?

Footsteps echoed in the stairwell, and Max pulled the gun from its shoulder holster and held it against his chest, beneath his jacket.

A man and two women, faces white, eyes wide, met

them on the next landing. The man gripped the handrail. "What happened?"

"A car on level four is on fire."

"Fire?" One of the women grabbed the man's arm. "That sounded like an explosion."

Max shrugged. "I don't know. Maybe the flames reached the gas tank. We called 911."

As if on cue sirens called in the distance.

Ava put her hand out. "I wouldn't go up there. It's dangerous. Let the firemen handle it."

The man asked, "Nobody's up there? Nobody in the car?"

"No." Max grabbed Ava's hand and tugged her downstairs. He whispered in her ear. "When we get to the hotel room, throw your things in that suitcase. We're out of here."

Back in the room, Ava moved like a robot, but at least she moved like a fast robot. She swept the items she'd bought that afternoon into the new bag without one question on her lips. Despite the quick movements, she had a dazed expression on her face. That would change to fear soon enough when the shock wore off.

By the time they returned to the garage, the fire department had cordoned off every level except the first. In the confusion, people had abandoned their cars in the circular driveway. Max scanned the cars lined up, waiting for the valet.

"This one." He propelled Ava toward an older SUV with its hatchback open. He threw his bags in the back and pried her suitcase from her fingers and tossed it in after his.

With his hand against the small of her back he maneuvered her to the passenger side of the car. She stalled and for a minute he thought he was going to have to pick her up and drop her on the seat.

Then she placed one foot on the running board and he helped her inside.

Glancing around him at the chaos, he strode to the other side of the car, turned the keys dangling from the ignition and rolled away from the curb.

He paused to let another fire engine careen into the garage, and then he floored the accelerator and whipped around the corner.

Ava kept her eyes glued to the street in front of them as he dodged between cars, glancing at his rearview and side mirrors at every turn.

Tempest had tracked them down. He'd figured someone had been monitoring the cameras at the lab, and chances were his car had been made. He should've ditched it at the first possible opportunity instead of shopping with Ava.

He'd let his guard down.

As he zigzagged around the city making sure to lose any possible tail, Ava maintained a stony silence on her side of the car. His eyes darted to the side once or twice to make sure she was still breathing.

At the end of his circuitous route, he took one more look at his mirrors and headed for the freeway on-ramp. They still had a date with Dr. Arnoff's widow.

Ten minutes later, Ava shifted in her seat and expelled a long breath.

"Are you okay?"

"It's my fault."

He swiped a hand in the air between them. "Don't be ridiculous. It was my idea to go shopping. We probably should've just stayed in the room and left the car in the parking lot."

"No." She hiccuped and then covered her mouth with her fingers. "I led them to us by using my ATM card."

His gut rolled. "You used your ATM card?"

She nodded, covering her face with her hands. "I'm sorry. I didn't think. I didn't realize."

"When? At the mall when I was getting drinks?" He opened and closed his hands on the steering wheel. He shouldn't have left her alone for a second.

"Yes. I—I just wanted to pay you back. I guess it never occurred to me that they could track me that way." She dragged her fingers through her long, chestnut-brown hair and sighed. "That's not true. I had a moment right when I stuck the card in the slot, a moment of panic."

"Why didn't you tell me?"

"I convinced myself it meant nothing. It was too scary to contemplate that someone would be tracking me."

A muscle ticked in his jaw. He couldn't expect Ava to have the same instincts that he did. He should've warned her against using her cards. Obviously, she didn't understand the significance of the large amounts of cash he carried with him. Or she understood the importance for him but not herself. It probably was a form of denial.

Hunching his shoulders, he braced his hands against the steering wheel and extended his arms. "Don't worry about it now. It's a done deal."

"Your car…"

"Not mine."

"Stolen like this one?"

"Yes."

She blew out a ragged breath. "How did they find the car? How did they know what you were driving?"

"They probably have it on video from the cameras at the lab. I tried to take out as many cameras as I saw on my way into the lab, but I'm sure there were others hidden from view. Once you used your card at the mall, they knew where to look. They could've trained a satellite on the area."

"They're relentless, aren't they?"

"That's one word for it."

"And they have the advantage because they know who we are, and they're just some nameless, faceless assassins to us."

"Maybe, maybe not." He slowed the stolen SUV until the car behind them passed on the left and sped out of sight.

"Do you think you might know the man or men after us?"

"I might and you might if Tempest is sending its agents to take care of us."

She pinned her hands between her bouncing knees. "I can't imagine even one of my patients trying to kill me."

"Have you forgotten Simon already? Your patients, as you call them, are programmed to do just that. Tempest will tell lies to get them to do the job. Keep your eyes open for a familiar face."

"Ugh." She wrapped her arms around herself. "Where are we going now?"

"Dr. Arnoff's house, as planned."

She whipped her head around to face him. "Won't Tempest figure we'll be heading there?"

He squinted into the rearview mirror at a pair of headlights behind them and then let out a breath when the car turned off. "Tempest doesn't know what I know. They don't know if I've gone off the rails like Simon or if I've put any of the puzzle pieces together yet. That car bomb was meant to kill me or warn me."

"Uh, it blew up that car. I think the message was pretty clear."

He held up a finger. "Ah, but it didn't ignite right away. It's not like Tempest to make a mistake like that. As soon as I turned on the ignition, I sensed the danger. They had to know I'd figure it out."

"And if you hadn't?"

He shrugged. "We'd both be dead."

Her body stiffened and he silently cursed his insensitivity. She wasn't like him—cold, unfeeling.

"Sorry." His hand shot out and covered hers, clutching her thigh. His fingertips brushed her soft skin, and he felt her tremble. He slid his hand from hers and rested it on the console between them.

"Anyway, Tempest might not realize I need to search Arnoff's house. They know I know he's dead—end of story."

"And if they *are* at his house?"

"We'll take every precaution. Going to Arnoff's is worth the risk."

"If you say so. They'd probably figure us for a couple of lunatics going to Arnoff's after that car bomb, so we just might be safe."

"I can drop you off on the way, Ava." He wiped one palm on his jeans. "I can still take you to the airport."

"Then what? I go underground? Go into the witness protection program for spies?"

"I told you. Prospero can help you. You get on a plane to anywhere and call Prospero once you reach your destination. I can give you a contact number."

"You implied earlier that you couldn't trust Prospero."

"I can't trust anyone, but once you separate from me, you should be okay. You can tell them whatever you want. Just don't tell them you believed me. Tell them I'm insane. Tell them I held you against your will."

"What about you?"

"I'll figure it out."

"You'll figure it out a lot faster with me by your side. I may not be a real doctor, but I'm familiar with formulas, especially this one. If there's an antidote out there, I'm going to recognize it faster than you will."

"I appreciate the offer, but..."

She pounded the dashboard. "You keep getting this crazy idea that I'm doing this for your benefit. Don't you get it? I don't have anywhere else to go. You're it. You're my protector whether you want to be or not."

He wanted to be. The thought came out of nowhere and slammed against his chest. Just as quickly, he stuffed it away.

Skimming his palms along the steering wheel, he said, "It's going to be dangerous. I can't guarantee your safety."

"You've done a pretty good job of it so far." She jabbed a finger at the windshield. "Two more exits."

"Do me a favor when we get there."

She crossed her arms and gave him a wary look. "What?"

"Follow my lead."

"I've been doing that ever since you dragged me out of the lab."

"Any complaints?"

"I'm alive, aren't I?"

So far they both were and he intended to keep it that way.

Following her directions, he maneuvered the car through a well-heeled neighborhood. Looked like being employed as a mad scientist had its rewards.

Ava pulled a slip of paper from the pocket of her hoodie and peered at it. "Have we hit Hopi Drive yet?"

"Nope."

"It should be coming up."

"I'm not driving up and parking in front of the house. I'll drive by first and tuck the car away somewhere."

"Good idea, considering it's stolen."

"Any complaints?"

"Considering our car had been…disabled, none at all."

She directed him to Dr. Arnoff's house, and he slowed the car down to a crawl as he passed in front of it. Lights burned somewhere in the house and a late-model Mercedes crouched in the driveway.

"Do you know if that's Arnoff's car?"

"It's his wife's. He drives a Caddy and as far as I know it's still at the lab."

He wheeled around the corner, made a U-turn and parked at the curb. "I'm going to leave the doors unlocked and the key in the ignition. If anything happens in there, make a run for it. Take the car and don't look back."

Her tongue darted from her mouth and swept across her lower lip. "I'd wait for you."

"That might not be an option."

He cracked the door and she put a hand on his arm. "Are you really expecting trouble?"

"I always expect trouble."

She slid from the car and dropped to the ground on silent sneakers and then pushed the door closed. *Good.* He didn't have to tell her to be quiet. She was a fast learner.

"I hope nobody steals the car."

A dog barked in the distance and another howled an answer. Max put a finger to his lips.

He held out his hand behind him and she took it. Then he hunched over and crossed the street, pulling Ava close in his wake. Might as well not make it easy for someone watching to distinguish two figures in the night, even though they planned to knock on the front door.

When they reached the other side of the street, Max

followed the hedges bordering the sidewalk, the shoulder of his jacket brushing the stiff leaves.

He tucked Ava behind him as he edged around the corner, glancing up and down the block. Lights dotted the houses along the quiet residential neighborhood, but everyone must've turned in early for the night.

He kept to the available shadows and Ava stuck close to him, the flowery perfume she'd gotten at the department store tickling his nostrils.

They made their way up the driveway, skirting the luxury car. The porch light created a yellow crescent, encompassing the porch and a flower bed under the window. The fragrance from the colorful blooms matched the scent wafting from Ava.

Funny how smells could distinguish a place and time. Whatever happened, the particular smell of those flowers would always remind him of this night with Ava. No drug could take that away from him.

She whispered, "Are we going to knock? Unless she's already heard about the lab, she won't be surprised to see me."

"Go ahead."

Max turned and faced the street as she rang the doorbell. A footfall from inside the house had Ava standing up straight and plastering a smile on her face.

A muffled voice reached them through the heavy door. "Who is it?"

"Mrs. Arnoff, it's Ava Whitman—from the lab?"

A chain scraped and the door eased open. Mrs. Arnoff, a robe wrapped around her body, peered at them. "I thought that was you. Is everything okay at the lab?"

Mrs. Arnoff didn't know.

Ava widened her smile until her cheeks hurt. "Everything's fine. Dr. Arnoff is hard at work and sent me over to pick up a few things for him."

The door swung open. "I've been trying to call him for two days. He didn't mention that he was spending the night at the lab this time."

"You know how it gets there sometimes—crazy and our cell phone reception is nonexistent."

"He usually does get out to call me though." Her gaze shifted to Max. "Come on in."

Ava waved her hand at Max. "This is…Mike, my friend."

"Hello, Mike." Mrs. Arnoff offered her hand to Max. "I'm glad to see Ava has made some friends."

Ava winced. So, Dr. Arnoff had told his wife about her pathetic social existence.

"Ava and I have been friends for a while." Max draped his arm across her shoulder.

For a man with no emotions, he sure seemed to be getting into this role.

Mrs. Arnoff gestured to a half-full wineglass on the coffee table in front of the muted TV. "Would you like some wine? Something else?"

Ava folded her hands in front of her, trying not to twist her fingers. "No, thank you, Mrs. Arnoff."

"Lillian—please call me Lillian. I feel like I know you even though we've met just a few times. Charles talks about you a lot."

"Really?" Ava coughed. "Dr. Arnoff is brilliant. I'm so lucky to be working with him."

"Well, the feelings are mutual." Mrs. Arnoff shook her finger and Ava realized Lillian was slightly drunk.

That could make things easier.

"What did my husband want? It's just like him to send a woman to fetch for him."

Max stepped close to Ava and nudged the side of her hip. "His laptop. Isn't that what you told me, Ava? And samples, some kind of samples."

Ava nodded, the stupid smile still on her face, a breath trapped in her lungs. Max had just decided to go for it.

Lillian's brow furrowed and she tucked strands from her gray bob behind her ear. "His laptop's in his office, but I'm not sure what samples you mean. He doesn't keep any of his lab work at home."

"Let me grab the laptop first." Ava pivoted toward the hallway. "His office?"

"I'll show you."

Max cleared his throat. "Do you mind if I use your restroom?"

Ava shot him a glance beneath her lashes. Did he think he'd find the T-101 pills in the medicine cabinet?

"Right across from the office, Mike." She patted Ava's hand. "Follow us."

Lillian weaved toward the hallway and Ava got the crazy idea that if they shared a bottle of wine with her, she might just pass out.

When they reached the first two rooms in the hallway, Lillian pushed at the door on the right. "Bathroom in here."

Then she reached into the room across from the bathroom and flicked on a light. "He usually leaves his laptop on the corner of his desk. Did his computer go down at the lab or something?"

"He didn't tell me, Lillian. I just obey orders. He asks me to pick up his laptop—" she snapped her fingers "—I pick up his laptop."

"And samples?"

Ava scooped up the laptop from the desk and hugged

it to her chest. "He meant the blue pills. You know, the blue pills?"

Lillian tilted her head. "He doesn't tell me much about his work. Can you email him or something and ask him where they are?"

"I-it was an afterthought. Maybe they're not very important."

Lillian led her out of the office and winked before she turned off the light. "Maybe if we forget about it, Charles will come home to get them himself."

They stepped into the hallway, and Max came from the opposite end.

"Hope you don't mind. There was no hand soap in this bathroom, so I found another."

"That's fine."

As Lillian headed back to the living room, Ava squeezed Max's hand and he shook his head. No blue pills in the medicine cabinets, but at least they got the laptop.

"Are you sure you don't want some wine?" She grabbed her glass and gulped down the remainder of the burgundy liquid. "God knows, my husband's never home anymore to join me."

"Ava, why don't you have a glass with her? If you don't mind, Lillian, I'll just take a quick look in the garage since Ava mentioned he sometimes works out there."

Mrs. Arnoff blinked her eyes. "He does?"

"Yes, yes, he did say something about storing some work in the garage." Ava swept past Lillian and grabbed a glass from the wet bar in the corner. "I'd love to join you."

The boozy smile erased the confusion from Lillian's face. "Wonderful. It's an outstanding year for this particular cab."

She almost knocked the bottle over and Ava grabbed it. "Allow me."

Max had disappeared through the door to the attached garage, and Ava poured a generous amount of wine into Lillian's glass and a splash in her own.

She clinked her glass with Lillian's. "Here's to Dr. Arnoff."

"Wherever he is." Lillian took a long pull from her glass.

The knock on the front door startled them both.

Lillian put her glass down and brushed her fingers together. "Looks like we're going to have a party tonight without Charles."

She took a halting step toward the front door as Ava glanced at the garage. If that was the police reporting Dr. Arnoff's death, she'd better do some quick thinking and she could use Max's help.

Mrs. Arnoff was halfway to the front door when Max came barreling into the room. "Don't answer that."

"What?" Lillian stumbled to a stop.

"You shouldn't answer your door when you're home alone at night."

"But I'm not alone." Lillian spread her arms to take in the two of them and proceeded to the door.

"Wait." Max held up his hand.

A man yelled from the porch. "Mrs. Arnoff? It's the cable company. Several people in your area have been reporting outages."

Ava's heart thumped and she stepped back, glancing at the TV, still flickering with images. Lillian must have a great cable provider if they came out at this time of night.

Mrs. Arnoff reached the door and placed her hand on the knob while leaning toward the peephole. She called out, "I think my TV's fine." She glanced over her shoulder at Ava. "Don't you think so?"

Max charged forward and grabbed the laptop. Then he

took Ava's arm and whispered in her ear. "We need to get out of here. She just announced our presence."

"We still need to check, ma'am," the voice on the porch insisted.

Lillian took the chain off the door and Max yanked Ava toward the sliding door in the back.

As soon as Max slid open the back door, a crackling sound rang behind them and Lillian fell back into the room—missing half her head.

Chapter Eight

Ava didn't have time to react. Didn't have time to let loose with the scream gathering in her lungs.

Max yanked her out the back door and sped across the patio toward the fence on the side. She moved mechanically, still in shock. His voice grated in a harsh whisper. "I don't know if they saw us or not, but they'll know someone was there. Even if they didn't hear Lillian speaking to you, they'll notice the second wineglass."

They reached the fence and Max bent over and cupped his hands to hoist her up.

She wedged one sneakered foot in his hands and grabbed the top of the stuccoed fence. She pulled herself up and over, landing in some dirt on the other side. "Slip the laptop over."

She stepped onto a sprinkler cover and reached up with trembling hands. The hard edge of the laptop met her grasping fingers and she eased it over the wall and hugged it to her chest. "Got it."

Two seconds later, Max vaulted over the fence, landing beside her. "Any vicious beasts in residence?"

She gulped. "Not yet."

She followed his lead across the backyard, hunching forward and keeping to the shadows, her knees trembling with each step. The next fence presented a bigger problem, as spiky hedges bordered the entire length.

She huffed out a breath, as fear clawed through her chest. "How are we going to get over that fence?"

"Don't worry. We got this. The hedges are stiff enough to use as a ledge."

Before she could respond, he took the laptop from her and his hands encircled her waist. He lifted her off the ground, high into the air. "Find a stable point to get a foothold."

With her legs dangling in the air, she tapped her foot against the dense hedge until she found a stationary spot. "I think I'm good here."

"Is there a place to put your hands?"

She groped along the edge of the bush, ignoring the sharp pain from the nettles, and found the rounded top of the stucco fence that separated the two houses. "Yeah."

"Are they coming?"

Glancing across the yard, she shook her head. "I don't see anything coming this way."

He released her and she put her weight on her hands, her feet lightly dancing over the hedge until she could swing her legs over the fence. She let herself drop to the ground.

Her panting merged with the panting coming from behind her and she spun around and nearly tripped over a furry, four-legged creature.

Before she could warn Max, he dropped down beside her with the laptop tucked beneath one arm. The dog backed up, lifted his nose and let out a howl.

"Shh." Ava dropped to her knees and placed her hands on either side of the mutt's head and rubbed his ears. "You don't need to do that."

The howl ended and the little dog pranced around their feet in excitement.

Max nudged her back with his knee. "Let's get going before he changes his mind."

Rising to her feet, Ava chucked the pup under the chin, reluctant to leave the one spot of normalcy in the entire evening. "You're a good boy."

They dashed across the yard with the dog at their heels, but at least he'd decided they were friends instead of foes.

The fence on the other side, leading to the street where Max had parked the car, posed less of an obstacle than the other fence, and they both hopped over easily, landing on the sidewalk across from the stolen SUV.

Ava took a step toward the curb, but Max had other ideas. He grabbed her wrist and pulled her back.

"Hold on." He nudged her behind his back as he ventured into the street, looking both ways. "Stay with me."

She practically stepped on his heels as she jogged across the street in his wake.

When they reached the car, he cupped his hands at the window to peer inside. He nodded and carefully opened the door.

She did the same on her side and let out a long breath when she collapsed on the passenger seat. She twisted around and placed the laptop on the floor of the backseat.

Max started the car and then manually turned off the headlights that came on automatically. He put the car in Reverse and backed up, avoiding Dr. Arnoff's street.

It didn't do any good.

JUST WHEN HE reached the next cross street, a car, its headlights blinding them, came roaring around the corner.

Max didn't miss a beat. The Tempest agents must've gone out to the street, listening to every sound in the night—the howl of the dog and the engine of the car. He continued his reverse turn around the block, and when the other car turned down the same block, Max punched the accelerator and sped past the car in the other direction.

His eyes darted to the side mirror. The driver of the other car hadn't bothered turning around. He'd taken off after them in Reverse. That gave him and Ava an advantage.

Max clenched the steering wheel. Now if he only had a high-performance car instead of this clunky SUV. They were fast approaching the end of the block, and he'd have to make a hard right turn or end up in someone's living room.

He glanced at Ava's white face. "Hang on."

The other car was almost abreast of them. Max eased off the accelerator and jerked the steering wheel to the right. The tires squealed but stayed on the road—for the most part.

Cranking her head around, Ava peered between the two front seats and out the back window. "They made the turn. Now they're facing the right direction."

"That's good. Now they can go even faster."

"How is that good? They're going to catch up to us."

"I noticed something on that first road we turned on just off the freeway. I was cursing this SUV a few seconds ago, but I think its wide body is just what we need."

"If you say so. Are they going to start shooting into this car?"

"If they get the chance." With the other car roaring closely behind them, Max kept floating to the left to keep them from drawing up next to them. But he had plans to take them to a wider stretch, as long as they didn't start taking potshots at the back of the SUV.

He careened around the next corner toward the freeway, keeping the SUV in the middle of the road so the other driver couldn't see what was on the horizon.

When Max neared the dip in the road that he'd noticed before, he slowed the SUV until the other car was almost at their bumper. Then he pulled to the right and slammed on the brakes.

The black sedan screamed past them and hit the dip going almost seventy. The front end of the car flew into the air, its spinning wheels leaving the asphalt. It seemed to float for a second and then crashed to earth with the shrill sound of twisting metal. Max saw a single wheel go airborne before he headed down another street for the freeway.

A siren wailed in the distance and Ava pressed her hands to her heart. "Someone had already called the police."

"Too bad there are no witnesses to the crash since we'll be long gone. I wonder if the cops are going to discover Mrs. Arnoff's body?"

Ava pinned her hands between her knees. "I'm slowing you down, aren't I? They wouldn't have tracked us down if I hadn't used my ATM card like an idiot."

"Don't keep beating yourself up about that. You're a civilian. Your mind doesn't work like mine. I should've known Tempest would pay a visit to Mrs. Arnoff—just didn't realize they'd show up so soon and kill her."

"You did know they'd pay her a visit, but in the end it was worth the risk, wasn't it?" She jerked her thumb at the backseat. "We got Arnoff's laptop."

"That's another thing. I never would've known about that laptop, Ava."

She sighed and tilted her head back. "What now?"

"We need to take a look at Arnoff's computer, see if he has any information about an antidote or the location of more blue pills."

"Even looking at his notes on the serum will help us, help me. I just might be able to figure out a way to neutralize the drug's effects."

"And I need to warn the other Tempest agents."

He could feel her gaze searching his face.

"Why do you need to do that?"

"Tempest is planning something big. All of my assignments have been leading to something big. If Simon hadn't gone off the rails like he did, I'd still be working for Tempest, still be on the inside."

"You still wouldn't have gotten all the names of the other agents. Tempest kept you apart, right?"

"That's right, unless we worked an assignment together like Simon and I did. My guess is Tempest won't be putting any agents together anymore. Anyway, I'm hoping to get the other agents' names from Arnoff's laptop, unless you have their names."

"I just knew a few names, usually first names only. Most of my patients didn't want to get personal."

He slid a quick glance her way. He'd wanted to get personal with her even though she'd known them by their numbers. "They may have given you phony names anyway."

"Did you and Simon discuss your memory lapses and suspicions when you had that assignment together?"

"Not then, but we became aware of each other. Later he found me in Brussels. I don't know how he found me and I don't know how he knew I was having the same experiences he was having, unless it was something he noticed during that joint assignment."

"Did you ever ask him?"

"Of course I did. He wouldn't tell me. I don't know if it was for his safety or mine."

"Or someone else's."

He raised an eyebrow. "You think he had someone on the inside?"

She shrugged. "Where are we going?"

"We're going to drive for a while and find a place to spend the night. Then we're going to delve into the private world of Dr. Charles Arnoff."

He bypassed the lights of Albuquerque and headed toward a small town on its outskirts. He'd need to swap this car for another. He had the cash to buy a used car and avoid the danger of getting pulled over for auto theft.

Ava tapped on the window. "How about that place? Not too small, not too big."

"Why don't we want a small motel?"

"Too few people checking in, so we'd be more memorable."

"And why not too big?"

"Too crowded, so we wouldn't be able to keep track of the other guests coming and going." She tilted her head. "Was that a test?"

"If you're going to help me out for a little while longer, I need to prepare you better."

"But you did tell me not to use my cards. I wasn't listening to the subtext of your words."

"You shouldn't have to listen for subtext—this is life and death. I'm going to spell it out for you from now on."

From now on? He took the next turn a little too fast. Ava could help him figure out what was on Arnoff's computer, and then she needed to get out of here—away from him.

He swiped the back of his hand across the beads of sweat on his upper lip.

"The pills?" She hunched forward in her seat, her brow furrowed.

"Yeah, I could use another, but I'm going to try to hold out."

"You're not going to hold out as long as you did yesterday. That's just dangerous."

"It'll be dangerous when I run out of the meds, too."

"That's not going to happen."

He swung into the parking lot of the midsize motel. The night clerk was talking to another guest when they walked into the lobby.

Max sized up the other man with a glance—tourist looking to escape his room filled with the wife and kids.

Although he had some cards with an alternate ID, Max repeated his bankruptcy story and the clerk was only too happy to take cash.

"The luck's with you tonight. We have two rooms left and both have a king-size bed."

"Great." He'd be spending the night on the floor.

Max handed over the cash and the clerk slid two key cards across the counter. "Enjoy your stay."

Ava tapped her card against her chin. "Free Wi-Fi?"

"Yes, ma'am."

They left the clerk and the guest to their conversation and headed for the side door that led to their room. Steam rose from the outdoor pool and Jacuzzi to their right, and heads bobbed above the gurgling water.

Max rolled his shoulders. "That looks inviting about now."

"Tell me about it." Ava rubbed her head.

He stopped and placed his hands on her shoulders. "Are you okay? That was a wild car ride and you must've gotten jostled around. I'm sorry I didn't even ask if you were hurt."

Her lashes fluttered as her chest rose and fell quickly.

The pulse in her throat beat out her scent, and it was as intoxicating as the bougainvillea creeping along the gate surrounding the pool.

"I—I'm fine. I didn't think we were going to get out of there alive."

He gave her shoulders a squeeze before releasing them. "Too bad they heard Mrs. Arnoff talking to us before she opened the door. We could've gotten away and they would've never known we were there."

"Too bad Lillian opened the door at all. She'd still be alive."

"No, she wouldn't be, Ava." He turned back to the lit pathway, and she followed him silently.

He told her he was going to be truthful, and that meant making sure she knew the tenacity of the enemy they faced. Tempest came to do a job and Mrs. Arnoff's death was the goal of that job. Finding him and Ava there had just been a bonus.

They reached their room, and Max opened the door for Ava, pushing it wide. The big bed dominated the space, but Max did his best to ignore it.

He dropped his bag in the corner. "You must be starving. I noticed a pizza place a few doors down. I'm sure they deliver here."

"That sounds fine." She parked the laptop on the credenza next to the TV and placed her suitcase next to his duffel. "Should we start in with the laptop?"

"Let's get some food in first. It might take some work to get around Dr. Arnoff's security." He reached into the front pocket of his jeans and shook the tin back and forth, tumbling the pills inside. "Besides, I've got four pills left. We have plenty of time."

She rolled her eyes at him. "Is that your attempt at humor?"

"Not very funny, huh?" He tossed the tin onto the nightstand.

"Don't give up your day job."

"Now, *that's* funny." He yanked open the single drawer of the nightstand and pulled out a telephone book. "Pizza, pizza. Here it is. We're on Cochise Road, right?"

She perched on the edge of the bed, reached across him and plucked up the notepad next to the phone. "Yep, Cochise Road."

He held the receiver of the phone to his ear. "What do you want? The works?"

"Excluding anchovies and pineapple." She wrinkled her nose, looking adorable, and *adorable* wasn't a word he used often—ever.

He ordered the pizza and then pulled some change from his pocket. He jingled it in his palm. "I saw a vending machine out by the pool. Do you want something to drink?"

"Diet anything."

His gaze swept her lithe frame from head to toe. "Because you look like you need to diet."

"When you're short, you always need to watch what you consume."

"You're the doctor."

"Not really."

Her solemn voice and downturned lips had him taking two steps toward her and brushing her jawline with his fingertips. "You were the best damned doctor I ever had."

"I was injecting you with poison, and I didn't even know it. Some doctor."

"You had a great bedside manner when you were doing it." He tugged on one wavy lock of her dark brown hair, and she flashed him a quick smile from her tremulous lips.

"Lock the door behind me and don't open it for anyone. The pizza's not going to get here that fast."

"Got it."

He stood outside the door of the motel room until he heard the dead bolt and the chain. Then he followed the path back to the gated pool with a whistle on his lips.

He hadn't felt this hopeful in a long time—not since he and Simon had figured out what Tempest was doing to its agents. He finally had someone on his side—someone who offered real help, not a hothead like Simon.

What had Ava done to lose her chance at a medical license? He couldn't imagine her doing something illegal, although she hadn't been squeamish about stealing cars and lying to Lillian Arnoff. In fact, she'd adapted to life on the run more quickly than he would've imagined.

He braced a hand against the soda machine outside the pool gate and studied the selections. A woman's low laugh bubbled from the hot tub, followed by a soft squeal and a sigh.

He closed his eyes. He'd like to try to make Ava sigh like that—a sigh of contentment instead of one of exhaustion or fear.

His lids flew open, and he fed some coins in the slot and punched the button for a diet soda and then repeated the process for a root beer. He'd try to get a good night's sleep tonight and pop one of the precious pills in the morning.

Gripping a cold can in each hand, he glanced over his shoulder at the steam rising from the hot tub, the heads so close together now as to be indistinguishable. Lucky bastard.

When he returned to the room, he tapped on the door with the edge of one can. "It's me."

She slipped the chain from the door and opened it.

"I hope you looked out that peephole before opening the door."

"I did, although that didn't help Mrs. Arnoff, did it?"

"Mrs. Arnoff was a fool—and drunk. A bad combination."

She took her soda from his hand. "She paid a high price for a few glasses of wine."

"She paid a high price for being married to Dr. Arnoff." He slammed the door behind him and threw the chain in place again. "And you're paying a high price for working with the man."

"Maybe Dr. Arnoff didn't realize how Tempest was using its agents. Maybe he truly thought you were a force for good."

"Then why all the secrecy? Why keep you out of the loop?"

"That's easy." She popped the tab on her can and bubbles sprayed from the lid. "What he was doing was completely unethical. T-101 hadn't been properly tested or vetted or reviewed or approved by the FDA. It was a dream situation for Dr. Arnoff. Tempest was funding an illegal lab for him, a lab where he had complete control."

"And unwitting guinea pigs at his disposal."

Ava wandered to the laptop on the credenza. "I powered it up while you were gone. It's password-protected and there's not much life left on the battery."

"We're going to have to crack that password." A pulse pounded in his temple, making his eye twitch.

"And we're going to have to get a new power cord."

"How much juice does it have left?" He rubbed his eye with his fist.

"About an hour, and I just might be able to figure out that password."

"How are you going to do that?" He dropped into the

one chair in the room, stationed by the sliding door that led to a small patio.

A rosy pink blush rushed across her cheeks. "I went through Dr. Arnoff's desk once at the lab."

"Really?" He cocked one eyebrow at her. Definitely not as sweet as she appeared.

She spread out her hands. "It was because of the lab. He was so secretive, I decided to do a little digging of my own."

"You obviously didn't dig very far if you didn't find out the real purpose behind T-101."

"No, I never did get that far, but I did discover a bunch of his passwords. There's a good reason why cyber security people advise against writing down your passwords."

He pointed at the computer. "Have you tried any of them yet? Do you even remember them?"

"I remember some of them. I'd just tried a few when you knocked on the door, but I was afraid of draining the battery."

Another knock sounded on the door, and Max held up one finger. "Hang on."

He squinted through the peephole while grabbing the door handle. "It's pizza time."

Still, he felt for his weapon tucked into his holster before opening the door. Anyone could impersonate a pizza delivery guy, just like anyone could impersonate a cable repairman.

The pizza guy held the box in front of him. "Pizza?"

"That's us. How much do I owe you?"

"That's fifteen ninety-five."

Max traded a twenty for the pizza. "Keep it. Thanks."

"Thank you."

Max locked up again and put the pizza on the credenza next to the laptop. "Do you want to try again?"

"My mind is in a fog right now, and I don't want to waste the battery trying out twenty different passwords. I'd rather wait for that power cord."

He tapped the box. "Sit down and have a slice or two before you faint from hunger." Or was he the only one ravenous?

Ava looked around the room. "Our seating options are limited, aren't they?"

"You can have the chair. I'll take the bed."

"Just don't leave any crumbs in there."

He could've said something about crumbs in the bed and whether or not he'd kick her out for the offense, but he refrained. She obviously hadn't considered the sleeping arrangements yet.

He dropped two pieces of pizza on one of the paper plates provided by the pizzeria and handed it to Ava. "Looks good."

Then he filled up his own plate and reclined on the bed against a couple of pillows. The cool pillow felt soothing against the back of his head, which had started throbbing, along with his temple, in the past ten minutes.

Had to be hunger. He tore into a slice of pizza with his teeth. The flavor of the spicy pepperoni filled his mouth, and he wiped his chin with a napkin.

Ava took a small bite from the tip of the triangle and dabbed her lips. "Mmm, that hit the spot."

He waved his pizza at her. "You *are* going to eat more, right?"

"Of course." Her gaze slid to the computer on the credenza. "I'm dying to find out what's on there."

"It's almost eleven o'clock, Ava. We're not going to find a power cord at this time of night. We can pick up a cord first thing tomorrow."

"You have a point." She leaned forward and closed the lid of the laptop. Then she collapsed back in the chair and took a big bite of her pizza.

"Are you going to tell me how Tempest recruited you?"

He dropped his crust on the plate and brushed his fingers together, trying to buy time.

"The short answer?"

"Do you have any other kind?"

"I was a Green Beret, and I disobeyed orders. Tempest saved me from a court-martial."

"D-did you do something wrong? Something illegal?"

"I saved four men in my unit." His mouth twisted. "But I still disobeyed orders. They were bad orders."

"Tempest must've been on the lookout for guys like you."

"Yep."

"Where's your family? Do they know you're going through this?"

"That's another thing Tempest looks out for—I have no family."

"Parents, siblings?"

"I was an only child and my parents died in an embassy bombing in Africa. My dad was with the State Department."

"I'm sorry."

"That's why I enlisted." He rose from the bed and placed two more pizza slices on his plate. "I didn't tell you my sob story to ruin your appetite. Eat up."

She nibbled at the edges of her second piece of pizza. "Did you go into the service with the intention of saving the world or just avenging the deaths of your parents?"

"Does it matter? It led me to the same place."

"I never knew all this about you when you were my patient."

"It's not something I'm going to blurt out to a medical doctor."

"Stop calling me that." She took a fast gulp of soda and her eyes watered.

"You know it's coming, don't you, Ava?"

She looked up from wiping her eyes with a napkin. "What?"

"How did Dr. Arnoff recruit you? I showed you mine, and now you definitely have to show me yours."

The pink tide rushed into her cheeks once again.

He hadn't meant that as a sexual reference, but if she'd taken it that way then maybe this attraction he felt for her wasn't one-sided.

She tossed the napkin onto her plate and folded her hands in her lap. "While I was still in medical school, a clinical student, my brother thought it was a good idea to use my credentials to steal meds and write prescriptions."

"Addict?"

"Yes, just like our father before him."

"How did his actions impact you? I can see reprimanding you for carelessness or poor judgment, but you didn't steal the stuff."

The knuckles of her laced fingers turned white, and she clamped her lower lip between her teeth.

"Did you?"

"I didn't steal anything…but they thought I did."

"Because you let them believe it." He rolled the can between his palms. "You took the fall for your brother."

"I had to. He was facing his third strike." Her chin jutted forward, and her lips thinned out to a straight line. "He has an illness, and he was not going to be let off with a slap on the wrist and a treatment plan."

"So, you allowed him to ruin your career and everything you'd worked for?"

"It's complicated." She rose from the chair and wedged her shoulder against the sliding glass door. "Our parents were a mess. Mom crashed her car into a tree while driving drunk and Dad dealt with the loss of his drinking partner by ingesting even more drugs before OD'ing. Even before they died, I'd always taken care of Cody. I guess I didn't do a very good job."

"Because raising a child is not the job for another child." He plumped the pillows behind him and massaged his temples. "Where is your brother now?"

She traced a pattern on the window with her fingertip. "He's in Utah, working at one of the ski resorts near Salt Lake as a snowboard instructor. I think he's tending bar until all the lifts are open up there."

"Did he even feel a shred of guilt letting you take the fall? Did he ever make any kind of restitution?"

"Sure he did." A half smile curved her lip. "He hooked me up with Dr. Arnoff."

A shaft of pain flashed behind his eyes, and he squeezed them shut.

"Are you okay?"

"Slight headache." He pinched the bridge of his nose. "Your brother knew Dr. Arnoff?"

"He'd met him on a hike in the Grand Canyon." She turned to face him, leaning her back against the glass of the door. "Cody didn't tell me at the time, but he and Dr. Arnoff had shared some hallucinogens."

His eyes flew open, his brows jumping. "Dr. Arnoff was into psychedelics?"

"Dr. Arnoff was into experimentation. Anyway, when Cody told Dr. Arnoff about me, the doctor said he might have a job for me at his lab. The rest—" she spread her hands "—is history."

"That's gotta be the weirdest job referral ever."

"Yeah, and look where it got me." She pushed off the door and folded her plate in half. "All kinds of alarms were going off in my head after I spoke to Dr. Arnoff, but I ignored every last one of them. I just wanted to see patients, treat people. I allowed that desire to override my common sense."

"I get it, Ava."

"You would." She buzzed around the napkins and packets of cheese, ending her confessional.

He did get it—and her. No wonder Tempest had targeted them both.

He forced his heavy limbs off the bed and helped her clean up. "Do you want the rest of the pizza?"

"We can have it for breakfast."

"My kinda girl."

He just wished he didn't mean that so literally. He'd always looked forward to seeing Ava at the clinic, and spending this time with her under dire conditions had strengthened that attraction even more for some crazy reason.

He coughed. "Do you want to use the bathroom first?"

"Sure."

While Ava was in the bathroom, he dropped a couple of pillows on the floor and found an extra blanket in the closet. He'd set up a serviceable place to sleep by the time she finished brushing her teeth.

She exited the bathroom with a hitch in her step. "What's that?"

"My bed for the night."

Her gaze shifted to the real bed. "You can have the bed. You were just complaining about a headache. You take it. That blanket isn't even going to cover your feet."

"I've slept on a lot worse."

"I'm sure you have, Max, but that's not the point." She

stuffed her clothes in her suitcase and perched on the edge of the bed in the long cotton T-shirt she'd bought for a nightgown. "If you won't trade, then just join me. This bed is big enough for the two of us."

His pulse thudded thickly in his throat. "I don't want to crowd you."

"I don't take up a lot of room, and I wouldn't be able to sleep knowing you were on the hard floor."

"It's not that bad." He tapped his foot on the blanket.

"Max."

"Okay, you don't have to twist my arm. Pick your side and I'll hit the bathroom."

After he brushed his teeth, he braced his hands on the sink and leaned into the mirror. He had no intention of making a move on Ava, but sleeping next to her just might drive him crazier than the lack of T-101. With any luck, she'd be sound asleep by the time he made it back to the bedroom.

He stripped to his boxers and then considered putting his T-shirt back on. He could always sleep on top of the covers with that blanket he'd found in the closet.

He turned off the light and eased open the door to the room. He could barely discern Ava's small frame on the far side of the bed, lying on her side, the covers pulled up to her nose.

The lamp on his side of the bed still burned, and he crept across the carpeted floor and placed his folded clothes on top of his bag. On his way to the bed, he snatched up the blanket and pillows from the floor and settled on top of the covers, wrapping the blanket around his body.

Ava couldn't be sleeping over there with that shallow breathing, but her pretense was probably a good thing.

He closed his eyes and tried to block out the images

that always marched across his mind at night. He had no way of knowing which ones were real or fake anyway.

A sliver of pain lanced his temple. He'd hoped to put off taking a pill until morning, since that would mean progress.

A bead of sweat rolled down his face, and he licked his dry lips. He'd left the tin of pills on the nightstand and tried to raise his arm to reach them, but the familiar numbness invaded his limbs.

The pictures in his head flashed like a slide show across his vision, and his hands curled into fists. The blood. The carnage. The destruction.

A strangled cry rose from his throat. A surge of adrenaline reanimated him. He clawed the blanket from his body.

He had to make them stop. He reached for the form next to him and sank his fingers into the soft skin.

Chapter Nine

Max's hand grabbed the back of her neck. Already on alert, she twisted away from him and shouted his name.

She tumbled from the bed and landed on the floor with a thud.

The thrashing and moaning continued from the bed, so she crawled on the floor around the foot of it. He'd tossed the blue pills on the nightstand.

She reached up from the floor and plucked the tin from the bedside table. She popped it open and pinched one of the pills between her thumb and forefinger.

She turned her attention to Max, his limbs flailing, frightening, guttural sounds emanating from his lips. The same sounds Simon had been making.

She let out a long breath and hopped onto the bed. "Max. Max, listen to me."

His head thrashed to the side, and she straddled his body, clutching the pill.

"Max, it's Ava. I'm going to put this pill beneath your tongue. You'll be fine in a few minutes."

Did his dark eyes gleam with understanding from the pain etched across his face?

She slipped her fingers inside his mouth and tucked the pill beneath his tongue, covering his lips with one hand.

He bucked beneath her, his hands cinching her around the waist. Another minute. "C'mon, Max. You can do it. It's me. It's reality. You're coming back."

His frame lost its rigidity. He pulled in a couple of long breaths. He blinked and swallowed. "Ava."

Despite the raspy edge, it was the sweetest sound she'd ever heard. Leaning forward, she cupped his jaw with her hand. "That's right. It's Ava. I'm here."

The hands around her waist tightened before they dropped.

His spiky, dark lashes shuttered his eyes, and he dragged the back of his hand across his mouth. "Did I...did I hurt you?"

Her heart pounded. "Absolutely not. I wasn't in any danger at all."

He cursed and shifted her off his body. "I could've killed you."

Lying next to him, she didn't move one muscle. "I don't believe that, Max."

He sat up and shook his head, his chest heaving with every breath. "I should've taken another pill when we ate. I had no right to push my luck—not with you here."

"It's a good thing I was here. I was able to do something for you this time."

"I haven't done anything for you except drag you into a mess of epic proportions."

"You've saved me so many times, I'm beginning to lose count, and you didn't drag me into anything. I walked into this mess with my eyes wide open. I posed as a doctor and worked for a man I already knew to be unethical."

He rolled out of bed—away from her—and stumbled toward the credenza. He grabbed a bottle of water and chugged the contents.

"Now, I'm going to spend the rest of the night on the

floor, and if you had an ounce of sense, you'd sneak out of here while I'm asleep."

For the first time in a long time, something made perfect sense to her. She whipped back the covers on the bed and patted the mattress. "You need a good night's sleep now more than ever, and the floor is not going to cut it."

He hesitated halfway to the bed, folding his arms over the sculpted chest she couldn't help noticing.

"I mean it, Duvall. Doctor's orders, even if they're from a fake doctor. Get back to bed and relax. You have a small dosage of T-101 running through your veins. No chance of another seizure now."

He snorted. "Is that what you're calling it?"

But at least he was moving toward the bed—and her.

He crawled in beside her and she let out a pent-up breath. "Feeling better?"

"Anything's better than what I just went through." He held his hands in front of him and flexed his fingers. "I could've hurt you."

"You didn't."

He turned away from her and shifted to his side.

Did he think he could get rid of her that easily?

She rolled to her side facing his back and stroked the hair away from his forehead. "It's going to be okay, Max. You're going to be okay."

And she would be okay as long as she had this damaged man to protect her. Then she would return the favor—she was going to fix Max Duvall.

THE WARM SKIN felt smooth beneath her fingertips. Ava moved in closer and rested her cheek against Max's broad back as she brushed her knuckles across the hard plates of muscle on his chest.

She'd examined his beautiful body, scars and all, at

the clinic before, but never in such an intimate way. She uncurled her hand and ran her palm up to his shoulder.

He sighed and halfway rolled onto his back, flinging his arm to the side where it rested across her hip.

She took his hand in hers and smoothed her fingertips over the rough spots where his fingers met his palm. They had to make this right. He could keep lowering his dosage, but an antidote would counteract the drug's effects in his system. Arnoff had to have one somewhere.

"What time is it?"

His gruff voice startled her, and she dropped his hand. "Sorry."

He shifted completely to his back and stretched his arms over his head. "For what?"

She held up her hands, spreading her fingers. "For mauling you in your sleep."

He hitched up to his elbows. "If that was mauling, I'm all for it."

"How are you feeling?"

"Okay." He ran his tongue over his teeth. "Dry mouth, slight headache, but I still have my sanity—thanks to you."

"All I did was give you a pill." She tugged the hem of her T-shirt over her thighs.

"That's all I needed."

"You need that antidote."

"Yeah, that too."

She sat up and tilted her chin toward Dr. Arnoff's laptop. "And we just might find the clues to that antidote in there."

"I'm claiming the shower first, and then I'll go out and pick up some breakfast. Bagels, coffee?"

"Anything like that." Max had just put an end to her visions of lolling in bed with him while they discussed strategy. Who was she kidding? If he wanted her, he could've had her. She'd had her hands all over him. Wasn't that obvious enough for him?

The slam of the bathroom door put a punctuation mark on her foolish imaginings.

She scooted off the bed and flipped the lid on the laptop. Sleep had recharged her brain if not the battery, and she had recalled several different letter, number and character combinations that Arnoff had written down using his wife's name. She'd give those a try and then wait for the power cord.

She powered on the computer, checking the battery life. Looked as though they had about an hour—an hour to save a life.

She wrote down each password as she tried it and then squealed when she entered the fifth combination.

Max charged out of the bathroom, sluicing his long hair back from his face, his jeans hanging low on his hips. "Are you okay out here?"

"More than okay. I got the password."

"I'm impressed, especially after the night you just had."

The night she'd just had was her best in recent memory. "I recalled that he'd written down his wife's name using different letters, numbers and characters. It just took a few tries, but we're still going to need that power cord."

"We can at least make a start." He rubbed his knuckles across the dark stubble on his chin. "I was thinking in the shower, Ava."

Her gaze flicked to his flat belly and back to his face. "I'm listening."

"If we can't locate any more blue pills or an antidote in the next few days, I want you gone."

She tapped the computer's keyboard. "We're going to find something, Max. Dr. Arnoff may have been unethical, but he was brilliant. He wouldn't have developed a drug like T-101 without an escape plan."

"You find that escape plan while I go round up some breakfast." He pulled a T-shirt over his head, strapped on his shoulder holster and shrugged into a jacket. He turned at the door. "Lock up behind me and don't answer for anyone."

She padded to the door after it closed and put the locks and chain in place. Then she picked up the pad of paper with the hotel logo on it and dragged the chair in front of the computer on the credenza.

She wrote down the names of all the folders on the desktop, arranged them in alphabetical order and double clicked on the first one.

She was into the third folder by the time Max returned with breakfast. She opened the door wide as he walked through with coffee in each hand and a white bag pinned to his side with his elbow.

"Nothing fancy—just a couple of bagels with some cream cheese and coffee. I did throw some sugars and creams in the bag."

She pointed to the coffee cups. "Are these the same?"

"Plain old black coffee."

"Fine with me once I douse it with cream."

She popped the lid on her coffee and dumped in three little containers of cream. "I'm systematically going through the files on the desktop. I haven't even opened the hard drive yet to see what's on there."

"Discover anything so far?" He ripped into the bag and twisted two halves of a bagel apart.

"Nothing, but I'm only on the third of seven folders."

"I'll help you as soon as I devour this bagel. In fact—" he reached out and hooked a finger beneath the sleeve of her nightshirt "—why don't you take a shower and get dressed and let me take over folder duty."

Her cheeks burned as she glanced down at the hem of her T-shirt where it hit her midthigh. "I completely forgot."

"I know. You couldn't wait to delve into that computer." He licked some cream cheese from his thumb. "What am I looking for?"

"Formulas, calculations, numbers, any reference to T-101."

"Agents' names."

"Yeah, that too." She shoved the laptop in his direction. "I'll make myself presentable."

He grunted and started tapping at the keyboard, which was not the response she'd been fishing for.

Max didn't play those games. He dealt in black and white, not subtleties.

She dug through her suitcase for clean clothes and retreated to the bathroom. This morning she washed her hair and scrubbed her body to remove all traces of Max that still clung to her from spending the night in the same bed with him. If someone had told her a month ago that she and Max Duvall would sleep in the same bed and actually sleep, she would've sent them to have their head examined.

She toweled off her hair and scrunched up her waves with some mousse on her hands. She pulled on the same jeans from yesterday, a white camisole and a blue V-neck sweater over it. She stroked on a little makeup and even added a swipe of lipstick. Just because Max didn't actually voice his compliments, it didn't mean he didn't notice.

She stepped from the bathroom and folded her nightshirt on top of her suitcase. "Find anything?"

"I'm not as methodical as you, but I may have located

some of the other agents. I entered the names I knew in the search engine, and they pop up in a few places."

"While I understand your desire to warn the other agents, it's more important right now for you to get an antidote flowing through your veins." She hooked her thumbs in the front pockets of her jeans and sauntered to the credenza.

He lifted one shoulder. "I didn't know what to enter in the search field for a formula or antidote. I entered what I knew."

"Okay, then." She leaned over his shoulder and peered at the screen. "What came up?"

He jabbed his finger at the display. "They come up in a database in some program, but I'm not sure how to launch it. It's not some static file. It updates automatically."

"Let me see if it looks familiar." She wedged her hip on the arm of his chair, hunching forward. "Okay, I think we can open it with this database program."

She clicked on a menu and selected the icon for the program. It launched a map of the world and she opened the file with the agents' names Max had found from inside the program.

Red dots began flashing on the screen. A man's face would appear and then zoom to a different area of the map.

She held her breath as the dots populated the map, and Max swore softly.

"It's some kind of locator for the agents."

When the last dot found its home, Ava expelled a long breath. "Are you on here?"

"I didn't see myself." He poked at the middle of New Mexico. "And there's nothing coming up in our location."

"How is this program tracking agents?"

"I'm not sure. I'm just relieved Tempest didn't inject

some kind of tracker beneath my skin. I'd been worried about that."

"Have you gotten rid of anything issued by Tempest?"

"A few things, most notably my phone. Tempest could've easily put a tracking device in our phones. We're supposed to carry them with us at all times. They have a hotline to Tempest and not much else." He flicked a finger at the map somewhere south of them. "But this is what I'm interested in. This looks like the agent closest to us—somewhere in Central America."

"Wait. Click on the red dot so we can see who it is."

Max clicked on the dot, and a head shot appeared on the screen with a name.

"You know him?"

"That's Malcolm Snyder, or at least that's the name he gave me. He's very quiet, almost shy. Are you going to try to track him down?"

"My goal is to get to all of them, help all of them break free."

She laid her hand over his on the mouse. "You need to break free first, Max. You can't save every Tempest agent unless you save yourself."

"I know that, which is why we'll keep looking through Arnoff's files. We may have to venture onto the next big town so we can buy a power cord for the laptop. I don't think the local hardware store is going to have one."

"Looks like we have another half hour or so." She tugged on his arm. "Let me get on there. If we're not following my system, I might as well start searching for some common formulas."

They switched places, and he pulled another bagel from the bag. "Do you want one?"

"You take it." As the laptop's battery drained, she started typing more furiously. Every action seemed like a race against time—if not the battery, then the blue pills. What would happen to Max when he ran out? To save his life, he might have to throw himself on Tempest's mercy. He wouldn't allow himself to go down the same road as Simon—possibly hurting other people, possibly hurting her.

She glanced over her shoulder at him lounging across the bed, biting into a bagel and watching a football game on TV. Would he take himself out rather than submitting to Tempest again? She shivered and slurped a sip of lukewarm coffee.

She entered another chemical from Dr. Arnoff's original T-101 formula and clicked on Search. Three files popped up and she sucked in a breath.

"I got a hit here."

He muted the TV and joined her at the credenza.

"This chemical is in the original formula." She opened the first file and the formula for T-101 was laid out on the screen. Her pulse rate ticked up. "We're onto something."

"You're onto something. That looks like gobbledygook to me."

"Very important gobbledygook." She minimized the file and opened the next one. Her gaze darted down the screen, and she squealed and grabbed Max's arm. "I think this is it. I think this is the formula for the antidote."

He squinted at the letters and numbers against the white background. "What's that going to do for us?"

"Max—" she bounced in the seat "—this is the antidote. You can take one dose of this and it will counter effect the T-101 in your body—no blue pills, no more shots. You're done."

He scratched the sexy stubble on his chin. "It's just a formula on a computer. How do we actually get the antidote?"

She shoved back from the credenza as a low-battery message flashed across the screen. "We make it."

"You can make—" his finger circled the air in front of the computer screen "—that."

"I know how to mix a formula. I know what these chemicals are. I was allowed to do that work with Dr. Arnoff, and I've done it before in other labs."

"Yeah, but you had an actual lab. Where are you going to cook up that stuff now? In the sink at the Desert Sun Motel?"

She jumped up from the chair and paced the floor. "I know who can find me a lab—and those chemicals."

His voice rose. "Really? Who?"

"My brother."

Chapter Ten

Max folded his arms, his rising excitement extinguished by Ava's words, which acted like a splash of cold water. "Your brother? The guy who completely screwed up your life?"

"My brother the druggie. My brother, who has dabbled in the production of meth and probably knows about every meth lab in the southwestern corner of the United States."

"A meth lab? You're going to cook up a batch of T-101 antidote in a meth lab?"

"Exactly."

"You can't trust your brother, and you can't trust anyone who cooks meth." Hadn't she learned that lesson about trust the hard way? He balled his fists against his sides. Obviously not, since she was still here with him.

"Who said anything about trust?" She waved her fingers in the air as if she was sprinkling fairy dust. "We rent the lab, cook up our own batch of drugs and leave it the way we found it."

"You said your brother's in Utah?"

"That's right. I know he'll help us. Cody owes me."

Max dragged a hand through his hair. "That Tempest agent we located on the computer is in the other direction—south."

She stopped pacing and marched toward him. She grabbed his arms with surprising force. "Unless that other agent has a storehouse of blue pills that he can share, it's pointless to warn him. We need to stabilize you first. I don't care about any Tempest agent right now except Max Duvall."

With her flushed cheeks and bright eyes, Ava looked ready to take on the world—for him. He reached out and brushed his thumb across her smooth cheek. "Why *do* you care, Ava? Am I another homeless dog to save? Another broken family member?"

Her words came out on a whisper, her warm, sweet breath caressing his throat. "You saved me. You're protecting me, and I'm going to do the same for you. Right now, you're all I have, a-and I think I'm all you have."

His thumb traced her bottom lip. "You are."

She met his gaze steadily and something passed between them—a pact, a bond. At that moment, he knew he'd do anything to protect this woman. He'd already killed for her…and he'd die for her. But not yet.

"Can you reach your brother?"

She blinked and nodded. "Yes. Should I call him now or track him down when we get to Utah? I know which resort he's working at."

"You know your brother best. Is he going to bolt if he knows you're on your way?"

"No, but I'm afraid to use my cell phone. Once I used my ATM card and they tracked us down, it got me thinking about other methods they could use to get to us. You said yourself, the program on Dr. Arnoff's laptop is probably tracking the agents through their cell phones."

He kissed her mouth because he couldn't help himself anymore and then chucked her beneath the chin. "I'm going to turn you into a covert ops agent yet. Dump your cell phone, pick up one of those temporary ones or use mine and then call your brother."

Stepping back from him, she said, "I'll get a phone at the same place where we buy a power cord for Arnoff's computer."

"We have at least a ten-hour drive ahead of us, so let's get going."

"What are we going to do about that SUV? Even if nobody saw us careening through Dr. Arnoff's neighborhood last night, the owner has definitely reported the car stolen."

"I have a bottomless pit of cash and a few fake ID's that I haven't even used yet. I'm going to purchase a car at a used-car lot, so we can drive to Utah in relative safety."

"That would be a first." Ava pivoted away from him and started shoving clothes into her bag, her long hair creating a veil over her face.

He eyed her stiff shoulders. He shouldn't have kissed her. No, the kiss was okay, but he shouldn't have made light of it after. If he'd never kissed her in the first place, he wouldn't have had to shrug it off.

Damn it. Being a robot had been a hell of a lot easier than dealing with these human emotions.

He strode across the room toward her, and she made a surprised half turn at his approach. He pulled her into his arms and planted a kiss on her parted lips.

Running his hands through her hair, he tilted her head and deepened the kiss.

One hand still clutching a T-shirt, she wrapped her arms around his waist and pressed her body against his.

The pressure of her soft breasts and intoxicating scent lit a fire in his belly. He hadn't felt this way in a long time, if ever. Tempest had tried to steal those memories from him, as well, and had mostly succeeded. Had he ever loved a woman? Did he even know how?

Was it fair to use Ava as his guinea pig?

He pulled away and dropped a kiss on her forehead, her cheek and her nose, ignoring the stab of guilt that twisted in his gut at her confused expression. "We'd better go trade that SUV for something legal."

"Good idea."

He turned and she grabbed his hand. "Max?"

"Yeah?" Her deep green eyes drew his gaze like a magnet.

"I don't regret that kiss. Do you?"

"No."

With that single word, her face brightened and he left it at that. She didn't need to know about the confusing emotions warring in his brain right now.

Ava was a big girl and had been making her own choices for years. He couldn't help it if they'd all been bad.

AVA LEANED AGAINST the headrest of the compact car as Max drove it off the used-car lot. That had been easier than she expected, but then, Max did have a boatload of cash and a few alternate identities.

He should just use one of those to get out of the country—after she injected him with some T-101 antidote. Maybe he could get an extra ID for her, and they could ride off into the sunset together.

She bit the inside of her cheek, trying hard not to draw blood. What *would* she do once she got Max stabilized? He was a man who flew solo. He'd let her help him, and then he'd let her go. She could tell by the way he kept fighting his attraction to her.

And he *was* attracted to her, just as she was to him. All she could do right now was help. She owed him that.

"Drives like a dream." He tapped the steering wheel.

"A three-thousand-dollar dream with ninety thousand miles on it?" She rolled her eyes. "Let's just hope it can get us up to Salt Lake without incident."

He tapped the GPS that the dealer had thrown in with the deal. "Once we get the name and address of the resort where Cody's working, we can enter it and be on our way. Are you sure you don't want to use my phone to call him?"

"I'll wait until I get one of my own. Cody's not going anywhere. The ski season hasn't officially started yet."

He handed her the GPS. "Do you want to find the next midsize town? Someplace with a decent electronics store for the power cord? You can pick up a throwaway phone anywhere."

"Like I said, I'm in no hurry." She patted her gurgling tummy. "I'm more interested in finding some food."

"You should've had one of those bagels. How about a quick drive-through so we can get on the road?"

"Find me a breakfast burrito and I'll be happy."

"There are usually a few fast-food places around the freeway, so I'll keep going that way."

One block before the freeway on-ramp, Ava tapped the window. "That'll do."

Max pulled into the drive-through, ordered a burrito for her and a couple of coffees, and they were on the freeway five minutes later.

After Ava polished off her breakfast, she reached for the laptop in the backseat. "Do you think the battery's dead?"

"Not sure. What are you going to look for?"

She opened the computer and tried to power it on, but the battery had died. "I just wanted to check out the formula again. We should probably buy a thumb drive so we can copy the formula and print it out somewhere. If something happens to this computer, we'll be lost."

"Who knows? Tempest may even have a kill switch to Arnoff's laptop. If it leaves his possession, they may be able to shut it down remotely."

"They can do that?" Her fingers curled around the sides of the computer, her palms suddenly sweaty.

"Tempest employs top-notch people. You said it yourself—Dr. Arnoff was brilliant."

"He was. Too bad he used that brilliance for a terrible cause."

"He paid for it."

She rubbed the goose bumps on her arms. "As did everyone in the lab, whether they knew about the true purpose of T-101 or not."

"I'm sorry."

Turning her head toward the window, she blinked back tears. Max's sincerity ran deep. Maybe because he was in danger of losing his emotions, he relished them more than the average man.

There was no way she'd let him morph into Simon. She'd mix up a batch of that antidote if she had to hijack a hospital to do it.

A few hours later, they started seeing signs of civilization. Max pulled off the freeway, and they spotted an outdoor mall with several stores.

Max said, "We're in luck. We can get computer accessories in that electronics store on the corner."

"And find a place to work in one of the restaurants on the other side."

They bought a power cord that fit Dr. Arnoff's computer, a thumb drive and two temporary cell phones.

Ava nodded toward a coffeehouse at the edge of the mall. "If you're not too hungry, we can get a snack in there and plug in the laptop. That's probably the only place with an outlet for us to use."

"That's okay with me."

They settled into a corner table next to a woman tapping away at her keyboard, and Max held up the plug. "Can I use the outlet beneath your table?"

The woman glanced up from her computer. "Sure."

Leaning back, Max plugged in Arnoff's laptop.

While Ava powered it, he pointed to the counter. "Sandwich and coffee?"

"Just a latte for me."

The laptop woke up, and Ava dipped into the plastic bag on Max's chair and unwrapped the thumb drive. She inserted it into the USB port and navigated to the file containing the antidote formula. By the time she'd dragged the file to the external drive, Max had returned with her latte.

"They're microwaving my sandwich. Did you copy it over?"

"I did." She leaned back in her chair, wrapping her hands around the large coffee mug, inhaling the milky sweet aroma of her drink. "Now I can relax a little. You really had me on edge with that comment about a kill switch."

"Like I said—Tempest has experts in every field." He tapped the back of the computer's cover. "Are you going to print it out, as well?"

"I think that's a good idea. Did you notice a copy place in this shopping center?"

"I didn't see one, but I'm sure we'll find a printer we can use in this town." He looked at his watch. "Now we just have eight hours until we get to Salt Lake. Are you going to call Cody now?"

"I'll turn on my cell long enough to copy his number from my contacts into this temporary phone and call him from the car when we can get some privacy." She scrolled through her contacts and punched Cody's number into the new phone.

The barista called from behind the counter. "Sir, your sandwich is ready."

As Max carried his sandwich back to the table, Ava pressed the button to turn off her cell phone and asked, "Who *is* behind Tempest, Max? Do you even know?"

"I know." His lips formed a firm line, and she raised her eyebrows.

"Does he have a name?"

"He has a code name—Caliban."

She snapped her fingers. "I get it. Caliban was the monstrous little character in *The Tempest*."

"Yeah, emphasis on *monstrous*." He picked up one-half of his sandwich and paused. "If I'd been more well-read, maybe I would've figured out the allusion. I didn't read that play in school. Then I found out the Caliban character tried to kill Prospero, and the code name suddenly made sense."

"Have you ever met Caliban?"

"No, but I know he's former military—special ops."

"Do you think someone turned him?" She blew on her coffee and took a sip.

"Someone or something, but he must've been off in the first place. You don't flip a switch like that and become a bad guy overnight. He definitely used his time in the military to make contacts. Tempest is a worldwide organization. It has no boundaries or loyalties—only to itself and its agenda."

"How do you know all this and the other agents don't?"

"I told you, Ava. The T-101 never worked right on me, or Simon. I don't know who else. I have to believe there are others. So, we suspected something was not right. I did some investigating while I was still in the fold. That's why I warned Simon to hang tough, but he couldn't do it."

"Does anyone else know anything about this? The CIA? Prospero?"

"God, I hope not." He broke his sandwich in half and prodded the crumbs on his plate with the tip of his finger. "The implications that the CIA or Prospero knows what Tempest is up to is too chilling to contemplate."

She narrowed her eyes. "But you've contemplated it."

"That's why I haven't contacted either agency. I'm not willing to take the risk." He took a bite of his sandwich and wiped his fingers on a napkin. Then he spun the laptop around to face him. "Have you checked the agent tracking program?"

"No. We're not going after anyone, Max. We need to work on this antidote. As it is, Cody is going to have to come up with the chemicals for the formula, even if he can find me a lab."

"We may not have far to go." He turned the laptop sideways on the table and flicked the screen. "It looks like this agent has come up from Mexico to Texas. It'll be easier to reach him now that he's in the States."

"After—" she closed the lid on the laptop "—we shoot you up with antidote."

"The sooner the better." He tapped her phone. "When you make that call to Cody, put him on Speaker."

"You don't trust me?"

"I don't trust him. Do you blame me?"

"Not at all." She popped the last bite of his sandwich in her mouth and dabbed her lips with a napkin. "In that case, I'd better make the call from the car. I don't want the cops coming down on me now as I discuss meth labs with my brother."

Max brought the plate and cups back to the counter and rapped his knuckles on the wood. "Is there someplace nearby where we can print a file from a thumb drive?"

"There's a twenty-four-hour copy shop about a mile down this street."

"Thanks."

When they got back to the car, Ava pulled the phone from her purse. "I'm not sure he's going to pick up a call from an unknown number."

"Leave a message."

She punched the speed-dial number for her bro pressed the speaker button on the side. As she suspected, the phone rang four times and then voice mail picked up.

"Hey, man, I'm probably shredding. Leave me a message."

"Hi, Cody. It's me, Ava. Give me a call ASAP. I need a favor."

Max cocked an eyebrow. "Do you think telling him you need a favor is the best way to get him to call back?"

"*The* best way." She winked. "I told you he feels guilty about what happened before. I never ask him for favors, so he'll jump at the chance."

"Is he going to balk at the request?" He started the car and maneuvered out of the shopping center's parking lot.

"Coming from me? Maybe. Coming from anyone else? Just another day in the life of Cody Whitman."

Max parked in front of the copy shop, and Ava patted the side pocket of her purse where she'd stashed the thumb drive. "Got it."

The clerk behind the counter directed them to a computer in the corner. "You can use that one. It'll scan your media first, and if there's a problem, you won't be able to continue."

Max waved. "I'm sure it's fine, thanks."

Ava inserted the thumb drive and printed out a copy of the file with the formula. When she took it off the printer, she folded it and stuffed it in her purse. "Okay, that's two backups."

On the way back to the car, her phone rang. "Cody?"

"Yep. What's up, Ava?"

"Hang on just a minute."

Max unlocked the car and they both slid inside. Then put the phone on Speaker. "I need your help, Cody."

"I figured that from your message. Anything. You know I'm good for it."

Ava rolled her eyes at Max. "You're at Snow Haven, right? I'm on my way up to Salt Lake, and I need a lab."

"Yeah, yeah. Snow Haven." He coughed. "A lab? Aren't you still working for Dr. Arnoff?"

"It's a long story. I'll tell you later, but right now I need a place to work."

"I'd like to help you out, but how am I supposed to find you a lab?"

"Don't yank my chain, Cody. If you're not using, you know who is."

"Whoa, whoa. We are *not* discussing this over the phone."

"All right. We'll discuss it up there. I should be in town around ten o'clock tonight."

"Should I pick you up at the airport?"

"I'm driving in."

He whistled. "I don't even know what's going on with you right now, but I'm not sure I want to get involved."

"You don't have a choice, little bro." She looked at Max and shrugged. "Why are you so jumpy?"

"I didn't want to tell you, didn't want to worry you, but there's some weird stuff going on up here."

Ava's pulse picked up speed. "What are you talking about?"

"At work the other day, one of the other snowboard instructors told me someone was sniffing around looking for me—didn't sound like anyone I knew and he didn't give her a name."

"Maybe it was someone looking for lessons."

"I don't think so."

"Why are you so sure? You're in a tourist resort. It could be anyone asking about you."

"Two days later, I came home late from a party and someone had broken into my place and trashed it."

"What?"

"Yeah, and the weird thing is I think whoever trashed it was still there…waiting for me."

"What makes you say that?" Her hand gripped the small phone so tightly it almost popped out of her grasp.

"I just felt it, so I didn't go inside. Turned right around and headed for my buddy's place."

"Did you call the police?"

"I don't want to draw attention to myself here. My friend and I just went in and cleaned up later and then I got some new locks."

She blew out a breath. "Be careful, Cody. I'll call you when I get in tonight."

After she ended the call, Ava cupped the phone between two hands and twisted her head to the side to look at Max. "What do you think of all that?"

"I think Tempest tracked him down."

Chapter Eleven

Ava's eyes widened, but her grim mouth told him she'd already suspected the same.

"It makes sense. Tempest wouldn't have any trouble tracking down your brother, especially if he's already in the system." He closed his hand around hers to soften his words.

"I don't know about that, Max. I never put Cody's name on any paperwork. Dr. Arnoff knew about him, of course, but I didn't have him listed with HR. If they did track him down, d-do you think they'll hurt him?"

"They might…ah…try to get him to talk if they think he knows your whereabouts."

Her right eye twitched, and he smoothed his hand across her brow.

He said, "If they're watching him and he goes about his business, maybe they'll leave him alone."

"But not if he goes about his business finding me a lab."

He squeezed her hands. "Tempest is good but not that good, Ava. They still don't know how much we know, what we're after. They only know I've pieced together parts of their scheme and what they've been doing to the agents. They have no idea we're looking for a lab to mix up an antidote. They may not even know about the antidote."

"I'm pretty sure Dr. Arnoff didn't go blabbing to his superiors about testing the T-101 on himself, so maybe he never mentioned the antidote." Her fingers twisted beneath his hold. "I just don't want to drag Cody into this."

He got that. He hadn't wanted to drag Ava into this either, but Tempest had already done its part to make sure she was up to her neck in it. "We can turn around right now, find some other lab, abandon the whole project."

"No." She pinned her shoulders to the back of the seat. "This is your only chance, Max. We have to see it through."

"It's up to you."

"Snow Haven it is."

They crossed through a corner of Colorado, and the temperatures dropped as the elevation rose. Ava offered to drive, and they switched places.

They drove through another fast-food place for dinner, and Max vowed to wine and dine Ava once they got to Snow Haven. It sounded like a perfect place to relax and sink into luxury, but it wouldn't turn out to be much of a haven for them with Ava cooking up potions in a meth lab while they looked over their shoulders.

Maybe they'd both jumped to conclusions. Given Cody's lifestyle, it could've been anyone going through his stuff—maybe even the cops.

"We still have a few hours. You can take a nap if you like." She patted the GPS stuck to the windshield. "I can get there."

"We should've asked your brother for a hotel recommendation."

"Aren't we going straight to his place? I was going to call when we got to town to get his address."

"I don't want to go rushing up to his apartment, especially if it's been compromised. Let's get a feel for the place first."

"Cody's probably tending bar tonight anyway. I didn't even ask him."

He peeled the GPS from the glass and tapped it. "I think this will list hotels and restaurants, too. We can look something up when we get to Snow Haven."

"I wonder if they have any snow yet. Do you ski?"

"Yeah. Do you?"

"That's an expensive sport, and my family didn't exactly have money."

"How did Cody learn to snowboard?"

"Cody's been playing pretty much since he graduated from high school—snowboarding, surfing, mountain climbing. He's done it all."

"How'd he afford that lifestyle?"

"Don't ask." She pursed her lips and stared at the highway.

Max closed his eyes, but he'd never mastered the trick of sleeping in a moving car or plane or bus. He never got tired though. He was wound too tight to relax. Tempest must've thought he was prime material for their spy games.

"Are you okay to drive the rest of the way? I can't sleep anyway."

"I'm good." Her brow furrowed. "You need to get some rest."

"You mean because it's almost time for Mr. Hyde to come out?"

"I'm just wondering if you could hold out for a little longer if you practiced meditation or deep breathing or something like that."

He lifted his shoulders and let them drop. "Never tried it."

"My point exactly."

He slumped in his seat and closed his eyes again. "I'll start working on it right now."

A few seconds later, Ava was poking his arm. "We're here."

He blinked and rubbed the back of his stiff neck. "Where?"

"In Snow Haven, and it's not snowing."

"You're kidding." He pressed his forehead against the cold window, as the outline of stark trees rushed by in the dark. "I actually fell asleep."

She scrunched up her face. "It wasn't a very deep sleep—lots of mumbling and twitching."

"That must've been attractive. Any drooling?"

She giggled. "Not that I noticed."

He wiped his chin with the back of his hand anyway and dug the GPS out of the cup holder. He tapped the display for places of interest and selected hotels.

Several popped up and he scrolled through the list. "How about the Snow Haven Lodge and Resort."

"Sounds expensive."

"Tempest is footing the bill."

Her jaw dropped. "Is that where you got all this cash?"

"They owed me—big-time."

"Let's do it. It's not like you're going to return any left-over funds to Tempest, is it?"

"Not unless they pry them from my cold, dead hands."

Ava sucked in a breath and punched his shoulder. "Don't even joke about that."

Hadn't she figured out yet that he didn't have much of a sense of humor? He rubbed his arm. "Ouch."

"There's more where that came from if you insist on tempting the fates with that kind of talk."

Ava Whitman could be a fierce little thing.

He selected the Snow Haven Lodge and Resort, and the GPS told them to take the exit in two miles.

He yawned and shook his head. "I don't think I could take your brother tonight anyway. I need a good night's sleep, a meal and a shower first."

She tilted her head. "You don't think you could take Cody? I can't imagine you'd have anything to fear from him."

"Fear?" He snorted. "I'd be hard-pressed not to clock him for the way he treated you."

"Really?" Her voice squeaked.

"You've never had anyone look out for your interests?"

"I wouldn't say *never*. One of my professors in med school took me under her wing." She shook her hair back from her face. "Of course, she abandoned me when she discovered what I'd done."

"What Cody did. Didn't you ever tell her the truth?"

"I've never told anyone that truth, except Dr. Arnoff, who'd already heard the story from Cody. And you."

"Like I said, that brother of yours will be lucky if I don't knock his block off."

"Please, don't. We need his connections."

A little smile hovered around her lips as she took the exit, so he knew she kind of liked the idea of someone knocking her brother's block off for what he'd done to her.

A few miles in, Max pointed to an alpine structure set back from the road. "There it is. I'm hoping they have a vacancy since the season hasn't officially kicked off."

She pulled the tired little beat-up car up to the valet station and popped the trunk.

As she took the ticket from the valet, she asked, "Are there rooms available?"

"Yes, ma'am. We won't fill up for another month unless the snow comes early."

The bellhop pulled the duffel from the trunk first, staggering under its weight. Max made a grab for the strap and hoisted it over his shoulder. "I'll get this one. It has some sensitive equipment."

They approached the front desk with the bellhop wheeling the rest of their belongings behind them.

Max booked one of the suites. This way they'd have two different rooms for sleeping without actually asking for two separate beds. He didn't know if he could handle another night lying next to Ava. He couldn't trust himself to keep his hands to himself.

The clerk slid two key cards toward them. "You're going to appreciate this suite. It has a fireplace and a wonderful view of the mountain."

Ava smiled brightly. "Perfect."

The bellhop trailed them to their room, and Max slipped him a tip after he'd unloaded their bags.

Ava wandered to the window and pulled back the drapes. "We could see the skiers from here if there were any."

"Are you hungry?" He shoved his bag in the closet.

"Not after driving all day and that icky fast food. Are you?"

"No, but I could use some water or a can of soda. Should we brave the minibar?"

"It's all courtesy of Tempest, right?"

He flung back the door beneath the flat-screen TV and opened the minibar. "Soda? Juice? Wine?"

"If you don't mind, I'll have some wine."

"Why should I mind?"

"I just figured you didn't drink. That's what you used to tell me during your checkups."

"I don't drink, but I don't mind if you do."

"We never recommended abstinence—from drinking. Did Tempest have some sort of rule against it? Not all of my agent patients were teetotalers."

"Red or white?" He held up two half bottles of wine.

"I'll take the red. It wasn't in the fridge, was it?"

"Next to it." He twisted off the lid and poured the ruby liquid into a glass. "My reasons for not imbibing aren't medical. I just never wanted to feel impaired in any way on the job."

"And you were always on the job, weren't you?" She strolled to him and took the wineglass from his hand.

"Twenty-four seven."

"When's the last time you had a vacation?" She ran her fingertip along the rim of the glass before taking a sip.

"I can't even remember." He snapped the tab on his soda and gulped back the fizzy drink. "That was the point of the Tempest agents on T-101. We didn't need vacations. We're superhuman."

She dropped to the love seat in front of the fireplace and toed off her shoes. "I suppose I should call Cody and let him know we're here."

"Tell him we'll meet him for breakfast."

She put her phone on Speaker again and called her brother.

When he answered, he shouted across the line over raucous background noise. "Ava? What is this number, anyway? Not your usual."

"Never mind. I'm here at the Snow Haven Lodge and Resort. Do you want to come by here for breakfast tomorrow morning? Ten? I know you're not an early riser."

A shrill whistle pierced through the noise. "The Snow

Haven Lodge and Resort? Dr. Arnoff must be paying you well."

"Can you get over here at ten?"

"I'll be there. Enjoy your fancy digs."

She pushed up from the love seat and plugged her phone into the charger. Then she placed her wineglass on the mantel and fiddled with the switch on the side of the fireplace.

"I think that ignites the pilot." He strode to the fireplace and picked up a box of long matches. "Turn it to the right, and I'll light the fire."

A little blue flame flickered beneath the logs and he struck a match and lit the kindling. The blaze raced along the log and then shot up into an orange fire.

"I like that." He grabbed his can and sat on the floor before the fire, leaning against the love seat Ava had just vacated and resting his forearms on his bent knees.

She took a sip of her wine and gazed into the fire. "This feels good—almost normal."

"Have a seat." He patted the cushion behind him.

Cupping the bowl of her glass with one hand, she took a few steps toward the love seat and lowered herself to the edge.

The soft denim of the jeans encasing her legs brushed his arm. She stretched her feet out to the fire and wiggled her polished toes.

"How's the wine?"

"It's good. It's been a while since I've had a drink, too, except those few sips with Lillian Arnoff." She swirled the wine in her glass and took a gulp. "I can feel it sort of meandering through my veins, relaxing each muscle set as it warms it."

He twisted his head around to look at her. "Are you tipsy already?"

A slow smile curved her lips, which looked as red as the wine in her glass. "I don't think so, but I sure feel relaxed."

"Good. You've had a rough few days."

She sat forward suddenly, her hand dropping to his shoulder. "No, you've had a rough few days—a rough few months and maybe even a rough few years."

Tears gleamed in her green eyes. Maybe that wine hadn't been such a good idea after all.

He patted her hand. "I'm okay, Ava."

She slid off the love seat and joined him on the floor, stretching her legs out next to his. "What are you going to do once you get the antidote?"

"*If* I get the antidote, I'm going to try to reach out to the other agents. Tempest will have a tough time carrying out its plans without its mind-controlled agents doing the dirty work."

"Once we have the proof for the CIA or even Prospero, those agencies can take care of Tempest. You don't have to be a one-man show anymore." She yawned, and her head dropped to his shoulder.

"I'm not a one-man show." He snaked his arm around her shoulders. "I have you."

"Mmm." She snuggled against him. "Pill. Don't forget your pill."

Ava's breathing deepened, and Max let out a pent-up breath. Her exhaustion just saved him from battling his attraction to her. The suite, the view, the fireplace had all made him forget for just a minute who and what he was.

He disentangled his arm from Ava's shoulders. She stirred. He swept her up in his arms and carried her into the bedroom. He dipped and stripped back the covers on the bed with one hand. Then he placed her on the cool sheet and tucked the other sheet and the blanket around her chin.

She murmured, "Max?"

"Shh. Go to sleep."

He fished the breath-mint tin from his pocket and plucked out one of the blue pills. He swallowed the pill with the rest of his soda and then stretched out on the couch by the window.

He'd just protected himself and Ava from another one of his spells, but if Ava couldn't cook up that antidote he'd have to take more drastic measures to protect her.

He'd have to leave her.

AVA FLUNG HER arm out to the side, clutching a handful of sheet. Her lids flew open and she squinted against the light filtering through the drapes.

She ran her tongue along her teeth in her dry mouth. Had she gotten drunk and passed out? No wonder Max hadn't spent the night with her.

Max. A spiral of fear curled down her spine. Had he taken his pill last night or did he try to tough it out again?

She scrambled from the bed, still wearing the clothes from yesterday. "Max?"

She shot out of the bedroom and plowed right into his chest.

"Whoa." He grabbed her around the waist to steady her. "Are you okay?"

Brushing the hair from her face, she studied his clear, dark eyes and the smile hovering around his mouth. "I was worried about you."

He cocked his head. "Me? I'm not the one who went comatose after one glass of wine."

"I—I mean, I didn't know…"

"I took a pill before I went to sleep." He dropped his

hands from her waist. "In fact, you reminded me right before you passed out."

She poked his hard stomach. "I didn't pass out. At least, I don't think I did."

"You were wiped out after that drive. Anyone would've fallen asleep after a glass of wine."

"At least it was one glass instead of the ten it took to put my mom under the table." She dropped her lashes. "You didn't have to sleep in the sitting room. I think we proved the other night that a king-size bed is big enough for the two of us."

His eyes flickered. "I didn't want to disturb you."

"No…incidents last night?"

"If you mean did I start gnashing my teeth and breaking out in a cold sweat, the answer is no. The pill worked just like it always does."

"Glad to hear it, but now you have just two left, so I need to get to work. Cody's meeting us at the restaurant at ten."

"No, he's not."

"Oh my God, did he call or something? Is he backing out?"

"I didn't talk to Cody, but I don't want him coming over here on his own. He might be followed. We still don't know who broke into his place and why or if they're still here."

"Should I have him meet us somewhere else?"

"Tell me where he is, and we'll pick him up so I can make sure he's not being tailed, and we can stop for breakfast somewhere else."

She ducked around Max and snatched her phone from the charger. "I'll call him right now."

When her brother answered the phone, he sounded half-asleep.

"Change of plans, Cody. My friend and I are going to pick you up. Is there someplace for breakfast around there?"

"Tons of places in the town of Snow Haven."

"Give me your address and wait outside for us. We'll be there at ten."

Cody rattled off his address and asked, "Who's your friend? Is she hot?"

"He is hot—very hot."

She ended the call and turned to face Max, who had looked up from his tablet. "I think you just disappointed Cody. Is he going to be a no-show now?"

"He'll be more curious than ever."

Forty-five minutes later, they were on the road to Cody's. Ava had shoved Dr. Arnoff's laptop into her bag and had the printed-out formula folded up and stuffed in her pocket. They'd put the thumb drive in the hotel safe, along with stacks of cash from Max's bag.

Max followed the directions from the GPS, and when they pulled onto Cody's street Ava tipped her chin toward her brother, dressed in jeans and a red flannel shirt, his hair scraggly. "That's him."

Max rolled the car to a stop at the curb, and Cody bent over and peered into the car. When he saw her, he broke into a smile, wreathed by a scruffy brown beard.

Max popped the locks on the car and Cody climbed into the backseat. "Hey, Ava, good to see ya."

"Cody, this is Max. Max, my brother, Cody."

Max looked into the rearview mirror and nodded.

"How you doing, man?" Cody settled against the backseat. "There's a breakfast place called Holly's about a half a mile up and to the left. So, what's this all about?"

"I'll tell you when we get to Holly's."

Assured they hadn't been followed from Cody's place,

Max parked the car in a metered lot a half a block from the restaurant.

On the walk, Cody peppered her with questions about her job and Dr. Arnoff, which she avoided and deflected. Since Cody was a master of both, he didn't pressure her for answers.

They snagged a table in the back of the restaurant, near the kitchen. Cody and Max ordered full breakfasts with the works while she stuck with blueberry pancakes.

They traded comments about the weather and the drive and Cody's job until he planted his elbows on either side of his plate. "Are you going to tell me about this favor you want me to do, Ava?"

Max pointed his fork at Cody. "And don't forget, you owe her for destroying her career."

Cody's eyes bugged out. "You told him about all that, Ava? Are you crazy?"

"He had to know. It's all tied to what I need from you now."

"Spit it out."

"Are you still using, Cody?"

He glanced over his shoulder. "If by 'using' you mean addled, dazed and confused—no. I use a little for recreational purposes, mostly weed these days."

She sighed. "With our family background and your own past addictions, I don't understand why you risk it."

"It is what it is, Ava." He shoveled more food into his mouth.

"Do you have a dealer in Snow Haven?"

As he wiped his mouth with his napkin, his murky green eyes narrowed. "Who wants to know?"

She shoved her plate away from her and her fork clattered to the table. "If I wanted to turn you in, I would've done so a long time ago."

Cody leveled a finger at Max. "You're not a cop, are you?"

"Do I look like a cop?" He glared at Cody's finger, and Cody dropped his hand.

"No, but you could be one of those undercover guys."

"I'm not. Look, we don't give a damn about your drug use, or at least I don't. We need a lab, and we need it yesterday."

Cody's brows disappeared under the messy curls across his forehead. "You mentioned a lab before. What is this all about, Ava?"

"I know you've been involved in the production of meth, Cody." She held up her hands. "Don't even bother lying to me."

"And you want me to secure a meth lab for you?"

"Exactly." She slid a piece of paper across the table. "And it needs to be stocked with these chemicals."

He glanced at the list before pocketing it. "Why do you need all this?"

She folded her arms. "You have your secrets, and I have mine. You don't need to know. I need a place to work, and I need those specific chemicals."

"What about Dr. Arnoff? Don't you already have a lab where you work?"

"That lab is no longer feasible." Max took a sip from his coffee cup, watching Cody over the rim.

Cody balled up his napkin and tossed it onto his plate. "Are you in some kind of trouble, Ava? Is this guy taking advantage of you?"

Ava held her breath as her gaze darted to Max's clenched jaw.

"You have some nerve saying that after what you put her through."

Cody flinched. "I know I'm a jerk, but that doesn't

mean I want my sister to get mixed up with anyone else who's going to hurt her."

Max's dark eyes got even darker. "I'm not going to hurt your sister."

Ava waved her hands between them. "Hey, I'm right here at the table. You don't have to talk about me like I'm not."

The waitress broke the tension with her coffeepot. "Refills?"

When the waitress left, Ava turned to Cody. "All you have to know is that Max and I are helping each other. I wouldn't be here right now without him."

"Okay, I believe you. So, I'm supposed to find you a lab, no questions asked."

"Last time I checked, cooking meth was illegal. We're the ones who won't ask any questions." Max wrapped his strong hands around his coffee cup.

Cody swallowed, his Adam's apple bobbing in his throat. "Deal. I have an option in mind, but just so you know, it won't be my lab and it won't come cheap. I don't cook the stuff."

"I don't care, but your sister does. For her sake, you should think about cleaning up your act."

Before Cody irritated Max any more, Ava tapped his water glass. "Tell me about the break-in. Was anything stolen?"

"Not that I could tell, but then, I don't have much stuff. I had my phone with me. I have a roommate and none of his stuff was taken either. The place was tossed. That's why I figured it might be the cops."

"The cops are going to break into your place without a search warrant and go through your stuff?" Max shook his head. "I don't think so."

"You sure you're not a cop?"

"I'm sure, but I don't think the police operate that way."

Cody snorted. "You don't know the cops like I do."

"I'm sure nobody knows the cops like you do, Cody." Ava rolled her eyes. "How soon are you going to know about the lab?"

"Today." Cody scratched his beard. "He'll want to be paid. You good for that?"

"I am, but he'd better not try to gouge me." Max's voice had rolled into a growl.

"He won't, he won't. He's a good guy."

Ava made a noise in the back of her throat and her brother had the grace to turn red.

"I mean, for a guy who cooks meth."

Ava waved her hand in the air for the waitress. "Don't come to our hotel to see us. Give me a call on that number when you have something."

Max added, "And watch your back."

Cody's hand collided with his water glass. "Why do I need to watch my back?"

"Someone broke into your place, right?" Max lifted one shoulder. "I don't think it was the cops."

"Are you telling me that break-in had something to do with this lab business?"

Ava reached across the table and encircled Cody's wrist with her fingers. "Maybe. Just do me a favor and be careful."

"You too, Ava." He grabbed her hand. "You deserve to be happy. And safe—you've never been safe."

She slid a glance to Max tossing some bills on the check tray and whispered, "I'm safe now."

Max handed the money to the waitress. "Cody, can you get back to your place from here?"

"I get it. You don't want us to be seen together." He winked. "Done deal, man. Ava, I'll be in touch."

He leaned across the table and tugged her hair, and then he scooted out of the booth.

Max slumped in his seat. "He's a character. You two are nothing alike, except…"

"Except what?"

"Hard to explain." His hands formed a circle. "A certain naiveté about the world, I guess."

"I'm not naive anymore, Max. I've seen too much."

"Sure you are, and that's part of your charm. You're able to hold on to the good even among waves of bad. It's a gift."

"You don't have to dress it up."

"I'm not." He tapped the table. "Let's get back to the hotel. I was looking at the spa services, and a massage sounds pretty good about now, doesn't it?"

"Sounds like heaven."

He opened the door for her and they stepped onto the sidewalk.

Max stopped in front of a kiosk and grabbed a local paper, perusing the front page while Ava scanned the notices pinned to the bulletin board.

Out of the corner of her eye, she noticed a man pivot suddenly and hunch forward to look in a shop window.

As she studied his profile, beneath the baseball cap pulled low over his forehead, her heart jumped. She grabbed Max's wrist. "I recognize that man to your left in front of the T-shirt shop."

Max didn't move a muscle, but his frame stiffened. "Who is he?"

"He's a Tempest agent."

Chapter Twelve

Max didn't turn around despite the adrenaline pumping through his veins—the adrenaline and the T-101, but that Tempest agent shopping for T-shirts would have even more T-101 pumping through his veins.

He dug into his pocket and pulled out some change and a pen. He shoved the coins in the slot for the paper and put his lips close to Ava's ear. "Take this pen. We're going to split up, so I can draw him away from you. If he comes after you and he gets close, flip off the lid to this pen and jab him. It's not ink… It's poison."

She sucked in a quick breath but she took the pen from him and curled her fingers around it. "What about you?"

He gave a slight nod to his right. "I'm going to lure him into that public restroom by the bus stop. I have my weapon."

"He'll have a weapon, too."

"He will." He nudged her hip. "Head down the street like you're shopping. Go into one of those shops. He may follow you, but he's not going to shoot you down in broad daylight in the middle of a store."

"What if he has a knife or a poison pen of his own?"

"Like I said, Ava, if he gets close, stick him first."

Cupping her cheek with one hand, he kissed her mouth. "Goodbye, Ava."

He looked both ways before crossing the street, taking in the man with the baseball cap. He never would've known the guy was from Tempest.

When he reached the other side of the street, he glanced over to make sure Ava was on her way.

He window-shopped along the way to the bathroom, releasing a long sigh when the Tempest agent crossed the street to follow him. At least Ava was safe—for now. If he didn't come out of this encounter alive, she'd have the good sense to contact the CIA, or maybe she'd have the good sense to leave the country. Would Caliban want to leave any loose ends? He didn't think so.

The man was shortening the distance between them, but he wouldn't shoot him on the street, even with a silencer. The streets weren't crowded, but there were enough people to deter him.

He tensed his muscles and headed into the bathroom. The door had been taken off its hinges, but a divider wall separated the entrance from the urinals and stalls.

He slid his gun from his shoulder holster beneath his jacket and approached a urinal, turning to face the entrance.

The thought had crossed his mind that this agent might be someone like him and Simon. Even if he had the opportunity, could he just start shooting as soon as the guy walked in?

He didn't have to worry about that.

The agent emerged from behind the divider, his gun drawn.

Max immediately raised his own weapon. He recognized him now—the agent that was positioned in Central America on Arnoff's locator. So, he couldn't have been the same person who broke into Cody's apartment. He couldn't have made it here that quickly.

Snyder stretched his lips in what passed as a smile for a Tempest agent. "I should've known you'd be ready for me, Duvall. I'd considered tossing an explosive device in here, but that would've caused a scene. You know how much Caliban detests scenes."

"Yeah, he's a real low-key guy." He trained his aim right between Snyder's eyes. "Looks like we have a stand-off here."

"Not really. I don't care if I die for Tempest. You do. That gives me the upper hand. I start shooting, you start shooting, we both end up dead. And without you to protect her, Dr. Whitman will be next."

A quick, hot rage thumped through his system. He'd never allow that to happen. "Dr. Whitman already knows too much, and she'll know what to do once I'm gone."

"I don't think so."

"You're a drone, Snyder. Don't you care? You're a dispensable pawn to Tempest and your hero Caliban. You're drugged. You're a machine. I can help you."

"I don't want help. I've committed great acts of heroism for Tempest. We will rule the world one day."

"Is that what Caliban is after? He wants to rule the world?" Max tightened his finger on the trigger. Snyder had an automatic and would cut him down as he was getting his own shot off. But he *would* get the shot off.

"Caliban is a madman, like many before him. He'll never rule the world. He'll just succeed in murdering a lot of people and causing strife among countries."

"And that, Duvall, is the first step."

Snyder had lied. If he didn't care about dying, he would've pulled the trigger already.

"Come back to the fold, Duvall. You're too valuable

an agent for Tempest to lose. Get back on the program. I know you have to be hurting right now. We can shoot you up with the juice and make it all better."

So that was Snyder's motive, to get him back to Tempest. If he pretended that was what he wanted, he could buy more time.

Max rubbed his temple. "It's hell coming down off the stuff."

Snyder's voice turned silky smooth. "You don't have to. The lab where Dr. Whitman worked, where we used to get our shots, has been destroyed. She destroyed it. She's our enemy now."

Was that the lie Tempest was spreading among its agents? It was designed to make Ava enemy number one, which would be laughable if it weren't life-and-death.

Max cleared his throat. "Where are we getting our shots now?"

Snyder hesitated, his eyes flickering. Tempest agents didn't do well when they had to make decisions like this on their own.

Straightening his spine, Snyder said, "Germany. We're going to Germany now, where the other testing takes place."

The other brainwashing, but Max was supposed to be a good little agent and not state the obvious.

"I don't know, man. It's hard."

"Come back, Duvall. We need you. The cause needs you."

Maybe if he went with Snyder, Tempest would forget about Ava, or he could convince them she knew nothing, was no threat.

"You'd take me to Germany now?"

"Yes. If I had orders to kill you, I would've done it before I walked into this bathroom."

He believed that. "And Dr. Whitman? We just leave

Dr. Whitman? She really doesn't know anything. Hell, *I* don't know anything."

"Yes. We leave her here." Snyder shifted his gaze to the wall and back.

He was lying.

Max's muscles coiled. He'd take the shot and then die for it. Die for Ava. It would be the most human action he'd taken in a long time. He'd go out a man, not a machine.

His gaze focused on a point right between Snyder's eyebrows.

Max sensed a whisper behind the divider and then Ava emerged from behind it. In a flash, she lunged at Snyder and plunged the pen into the side of his neck. He dropped like a brick, his automatic weapon slipping from his hands.

It all happened so fast, Max still had his weapon pointing at thin air.

Ava grabbed a paper towel, wiped off the pen and tossed it in the trash. "Let's get out of here before the lunchtime bus service starts and someone actually comes into this bathroom."

"We can't leave him here with this weapon. The drug you just injected him with mimics a heart attack."

"Do your thing. I'll watch out for witnesses."

While Ava hovered near the door, he crouched beside Snyder's body and started breaking down his weapon. He threw some pieces into the trash can. The rest he'd toss into the Dumpster around the corner.

When he had the two longest pieces of Snyder's gun in his hands and his own weapon tucked back into its holster, he joined Ava at the door.

"Let's slip around the back. Do you see any cameras around here? I checked when I headed inside, but I didn't have much time."

They scanned the outside of the small dilapidated build-

ing and Max didn't detect anything. He grabbed Ava's
hand and pulled her to the back of the bathroom. Then
he leaned into the Dumpster and buried the two pieces of
metal beneath a mountain of trash.

He wiped his hands on the thighs of his jeans. "Let's
do a little window-shopping on our way back to the car."
He took her hand again and they strolled down the sidewalk like a couple of tourists, except Ava's skin had an
unnatural pallor and her hand was shaking in his.

When they got to the car, she folded her frame in half
and covered her face with her hands. Her shoulders shook
and heaving sobs racked her body.

Although he wanted to take her in his arms, he wanted
to get out of the area more, so he let her cry alone until he
pulled the car into a turnout for a view point.

When he threw the car into Park and turned off the engine, he reached for her, running his hand along her back.
"I'm sorry, Ava. I'm sorry you had to kill a man. You
shouldn't have followed me, but you saved my life."

She rolled her head to the side, looking at him through
wet lashes. "I don't care about killing him, Max. He was
evil. I was just so afraid I wouldn't get there in time. And
when I heard the last part of your conversation, when I
heard him lie about letting me go, I knew you were going
to shoot him. I knew you were going to die."

"Ava." He pulled her upper body across the console
and she rested her head against his chest as he stroked
her hair back from her moist face.

"I never expected you to come to my aid like that. The
pen was for your own protection. You shouldn't have put
yourself in danger. Snyder would've been only too happy
to shoot you dead if he'd seen you before you pulled that
ninja move."

"I know, but I had to take the chance. You've taken so many chances for me."

He kissed the top of her head. "I appreciate it more than I can express. I'm just sorry it came to that. I never wanted to put you in a position like that."

She wiped her nose on his shirt. "Desperate times, desperate measures. Speaking of desperate, I need to check on Cody. He left the restaurant ahead of us. What if Snyder harmed him?"

"Call him."

She placed the call, holding the phone against her ear. "Yeah, yeah, I don't expect you to have anything yet. I'm just calling to see if you're okay."

She paused and nodded to Max. "Just checking. Everything's fine and we still need that lab and the chemicals."

She ended the call and dropped her phone in the cup holder. "He's okay. I didn't want to tell him what happened. He doesn't need to know any more than he already does."

"Do you think he'll suspect anything when he finds out a man died of a heart attack in the bus station bathroom minutes after we met for breakfast?"

"Cody pays very little attention to anything that doesn't involve Cody."

"Are you sure you're okay?" He threaded his fingers through hers.

"I'm fine. I'll be fine."

"Let's get back to the hotel, monitor the news and relax." He started the engine and pulled back into the stream of traffic.

"Maybe we can schedule those massages at the same time." Grabbing the back of her neck, she tilted her head from side to side as if to get the process started.

"I mentioned the massage for you, not me."

She jerked her head toward him. "Why not? You're the one Snyder was holding at gunpoint. You need it more than I do."

"I can't." He hunched his shoulders. "I don't really like massages."

Was there any good way to tell Ava that he didn't like to be touched? Except by her.

"I understand." She placed her hand on his thigh and he didn't even flinch under the gentle pressure.

He didn't need to explain. She got it. She got him.

He pulled in front of the hotel and left the car for the valet. As they walked into the lobby, he whispered in her ear. "I'm taking it as a good sign that there are no police here to greet us."

"Nobody saw what went down. That bus stop was deserted. I think it's mainly used during ski season as a shuttle stop and at lunchtime."

They got into the elevator with another couple, and Ava stopped talking. As soon as the couple got off, she turned to him as if she'd never stopped. "There weren't any cameras there either. What are the police going to find when they check his ID?"

"A man who has a convenient next of kin only too happy to take care of all the details."

When the elevator reached their floor, she straddled the doors holding them open. "Do *you* have convenient next of kin?"

"Absolutely."

"What about Simon Skinner? He had a fiancée—Nina. He talked about her all the time."

He corrected her. "He *had* a fiancée. They'd split up. She left him."

"So, Tempest won't even notify her?"

"No, but I wanted to notify her. It doesn't seem right. She'll never know what happened to Simon."

"It doesn't, but don't you think Tempest is going to be monitoring her now? They might suspect that you'll contact her."

He unlocked the door to their suite and pushed it open. "You're probably right."

"Like I said before, you need to worry about yourself right now. Look at Snyder. You were all ready to rush off to warn him and he was on his way to capture or kill you." She swayed on her feet and he caught her around the waist.

"You're not fine, Ava. You just killed a man."

"I-it was self-defense." A tremble rolled through her slight frame.

"And totally justified. I know that, but it doesn't make it any easier. Even if you took him out while he was pointing a gun right at your head, you'd still feel traumatized. Anyone with any human emotions would feel the same way. That's why Tempest had Dr. Arnoff create T-101—to develop agents without those human emotions. Killing machines."

She looked into his eyes. "That's not you. They couldn't do it to you."

"I've done my share…"

"Shh." She placed two fingers against his lips. "That wasn't you, and then you fought it. You're still fighting it…and you're going to win."

He kissed her fingertips. "Only with your help."

"It's the least I can do after you saved me from Simon and then those two assassins at my house, even after I'd been responsible for your predicament."

"I thought we were over the blame game. You didn't know what you were doing."

"And neither did you when you were working for Tempest."

"Then we're both guilt-free and can move on." He stuck out his hand. "Agreed?"

"Agreed." She shook his hand, and he rubbed his thumb across her smooth skin.

"I meant it about that massage. You look all wound up."

"And what are you going to do while I'm getting pampered?"

"Work." He walked to Dr. Arnoff's laptop on the desk by the window and turned it on. "I'm curious if that agent-locator program shows Snyder here in Snow Haven."

"That would be one way to make sure it's accurate. You're off that grid, so we can't check the accuracy that way."

Max drew his eyebrows over his nose. "So, how did Snyder find me? How'd he know to head to Snow Haven, Utah?"

Ava stopped digging through her suitcase and looked up. "I thought we determined that they'd tracked us down through Cody."

"Maybe someone on Tempest's orders initiated the break-in at Cody's place, but that was no Tempest agent or he would've shown up on the locator."

"Tempest found Cody and sent an agent here to follow up. He didn't show up on the locator because he wasn't here yet."

"The agent knew we were here one day after we arrived. How'd they get that info from Cody's apartment? They couldn't have."

"You said you got rid of your cell phone. That's how they'd been tracking you before. They must've just gotten lucky this time."

"Yeah, lucky." He navigated to the agent-locator program and pulled up the map. "Son of a... Ava, look at this."

She stood rooted to the floor, clutching a T-shirt to her chest. "I'm almost afraid to see."

"You're the kind of woman who wants to know what you're up against, right?" He didn't want to heap any more bad news onto her already fragile psyche, but they were partners in this thing and he needed her up to speed.

She squared her shoulders and joined him at the desk. "What are we looking at?"

"The locator map." He jabbed his finger at the display. "It shows Snyder here in Utah."

"Okay, so we know it works. That's a good thing, right?"

"Look at the other dots." He trailed his finger across the map from east to west. "You notice anything about the location of these agents?"

"One's on the West Coast and one's on the East Coast. So what?"

"Yesterday, this one was in Southeast Asia and this one was in France. They're converging on us, Ava."

Chapter Thirteen

His words sucked the air from her lungs and she grabbed for the desk with one hand. "Snyder must've told them we were here."

"Impossible." He exited the program. "These agents were already on their way before Snyder even made contact with us. Tempest always knew we were headed to Snow Haven."

She licked her lips. "How? How could they be so sure just because Cody was here? Tempest can't possibly know what we have planned and how Cody can help us. Caliban may not even be aware of the antidote."

Max shoved the laptop and then landed his fist on the desk beside it. "It's the laptop. It's reciprocal. While the program tracks the agents, Tempest can track Dr. Arnoff. They found us at Arnoff's house. They knew Arnoff was dead, and they killed his wife. Once the laptop went on the move, they had to know it was us."

She stepped back from the desk on wobbly legs. "We thought it was such a great find at the time, and it ended up betraying us."

"It's not human, Ava, and it *was* a great find. You discovered the formula for the T-101 antidote. Now you have the antidote printed out and on a thumb drive. It's time to get rid of the laptop."

"If we just destroy it, they'll have no reason to believe we left Utah."

"Exactly, which is why we have to do something other than destroy it."

"Which is?"

"Send it on a trip."

"How are we going to do that?" She clutched her hands in front of her. Everything was moving too fast.

"Think about it." He tapped his temple. "We're in a tourist area, in an upscale resort. People are flying in and out of Snow Haven all the time."

"Are you crazy?" She took a turn around the room, scooping a hand through her hair. "Nobody is going to take a laptop from us. TSA agents even warn people against it at the airports."

"Did I say we were going to ask?" He spread his hands. "I'm going to get into the hotel luggage area and slip it into someone's bag, after deleting everything on it except the locator program, which won't make sense to anyone else anyway."

"How are we going to do that?"

"There's no *we* this time. You go off and get your massage, and I'll get rid of the laptop." He strode toward her, cupped the side of her head in his large hand and smoothed a thumb between her eyebrows. "Don't worry about it. This sort of thing is a piece of cake for me. This laptop will be on its way to Boston or Atlanta or San Diego in no time, and those agents will have to adjust their travel plans."

To forget about everything for an hour or two and leave this in Max's capable hands sounded too good to pass up. Besides, those Tempest agents were still thousands of miles away, weren't they?

She took a deep breath and blew it out, ruffling the edges of his long hair. "Okay, but what if you get caught?"

He folded his arms and raised one eyebrow. "Really?"

"Okay, okay, piece of cake."

"Get on the phone and see if you can get an appointment right now. I'll start deleting stuff from the laptop."

The spa had an available appointment for a full body massage in twenty minutes and she took it.

She peered over Max's shoulder as he dragged files into the trash can and then emptied the trash. "It's a ninety-minute massage. Will the deed be done by then?"

"Yep. You just relax and enjoy, knowing we're sending those Tempest agents on a wild-goose chase."

"Not sure I'll be able to relax."

"Sure you will. I've got this, Ava."

She believed him. She trusted him. He'd been ready to take a bullet for her in that bathroom or even return to Tempest. She'd had to prove that he hadn't misplaced his trust even though sticking that man—Malcolm Snyder—in the neck with the pen had been just about the most frightening action she'd ever taken. She'd had to stuff down every memory of Snyder, every feeling she'd ever had about him, and go on autopilot.

That was how the T-101 worked. It put those agents on autopilot to allow them to do their jobs without question.

She shivered and pulled on a clean T-shirt. She didn't blame Max one bit for wanting off the stuff.

"I'm going to head down to the spa now. Should I just meet you back up here?"

"Hang on." He clicked the mouse without looking up. "I'm going to walk you there."

She wrinkled her nose. "I thought you said we were safe for now, no Tempest agents in the immediate vicinity."

He dragged one more file to the trash can and looked

up with a half smile on his face. "I just want to walk you down."

"I thought you wanted to let me in on the whole truth and nothing but the truth?"

He shoved a card key in his back pocket and placed his hand on her lower back. "I think we're safe right now, but nothing is one hundred percent."

"Okay, I can accept that."

They took the elevator down to the basement floor, one level below the lobby, and Max walked her to the door of the spa. He touched his lips to hers. "Enjoy yourself."

Ava checked in, relaxed in the waiting room with a cup of tea and some aromatherapy and then followed her masseuse to one of the back rooms. When the masseuse left her, she undressed and slipped beneath the sheet on the table.

She closed her eyes, the hushed atmosphere of the spa already working its magic and the gentle New Age music soothing her nerves. What if she told the masseuse that she'd just killed a man in a bus station bathroom? The Hippocratic oath she'd taken never seemed further out of reach.

The masseuse returned to the room, and they exchanged very few words as she started working on her back.

The masseuse cooed. "You have a lot of tension in your shoulders and neck. I'm going to work on those knots."

Lady, you have no idea.

Ava responded with an unintelligible murmur as the masseuse dug her thumbs into her flesh.

Ninety minutes later, kneaded, pinched and pounded, Ava rose from the table a new woman. She paid with Tempest's cash and left a generous tip.

Back in the real world, she hoped Max had gotten rid of that laptop without getting detained by hotel security.

She hoped someone had discovered Snyder in the bathroom and had already ruled his death a heart attack. And she hoped her brother had come through with a usable lab and the chemicals she'd need to mix up a batch of T-101 antidote. Was that asking too much?

She could feel the tension creeping back into her shoulders already. Maybe the spa could give her a daily appointment—she'd need it.

Stepping from the spa, she spotted Max lounging against the wall down the hallway past the gym. The stress that had been clawing its way back into her muscles melted away.

Maybe she just needed a daily appointment with Max.

When she approached, he pushed off the wall. "I don't even have to ask how it was. You look…relaxed."

"I'll be more relaxed once you tell me how things went on your end." Despite herself, she scooped in a breath and held it.

"Arnoff's laptop is safely on its way to Florida."

"Where it will get plenty of fun in the sun." She touched his arm. "Do you think it'll work?"

"It bought us a little time, although we don't know who's here checking up on your brother."

"Maybe that was a simple break-in. God knows, Cody attracts his share of trouble without even trying."

"I doubt it, but at least we know the person here working for Tempest is not one of the T-101 agents. They're all being tracked with that program. I might have some trouble handling another T-101 robot, but not anyone else."

"That massage made me incredibly hungry. Did you eat lunch yet?"

They continued past the gym and he pointed at the weight machines behind the glass. "I could use some lunch, and then I'm going to work out. If I can't take advantage of the spa here, I'm going to at least use the gym."

"Sandwiches in the lobby restaurant?"

He took her arm and propelled her down the hallway. "If you don't think you'll float away."

She covered a yawn with her hand. "Do I look like I'm floating?"

"Yep, and I'm glad to see it. I told you I'd take care of the computer."

She pressed the elevator button. "What about Snyder?"

"It just so happens that I overheard a couple of the bellhops talking about a man found in the men's room at the bus stop—an apparent heart attack victim."

She held up her crossed fingers. "Let's hope the coroner concurs with the initial finding."

"Believe me, Snyder's next of kin will make sure that they relate a history of heart disease. Tempest protects and conceals the deaths of its agents. You haven't heard anything about what happened in New Mexico, have you?"

"Not a word."

They sat down at the restaurant and she ordered a salad while Max stuck with a French dip sandwich. Just as she was about to dig into her salad, her cell phone buzzed in her pocket.

She pulled it out and smiled. "It's Cody. He says he's working on it."

"That's vague, but I'll take it."

"That's a lot from Cody. He's really trying to communicate."

"Let's hope he can nail this down for us."

She crunched through her vegetables to avoid the question on her lips. What would happen if Cody couldn't find them a lab? The formula and instructions for the antidote wouldn't do her any good without the chemicals to cook it and a lab to cook it in.

Since Max had taken a huge bite of his sandwich, she had to assume he didn't want to discuss it either.

He had two blue pills left, and he had to take one tonight. That didn't leave them a lot of time until…

She grabbed her soda and slurped through the straw. "If you don't mind, I'm going to let you hit the gym on your own. I'm going to take a nap. That massage made me feel like a limp noodle."

"That's okay. I'm not a very social gym rat. I'd rather listen to music than talk."

She traced a bead of moisture on the outside of her glass. "I suppose talking's a girl thing, huh?"

He crossed one finger over the other and held them in front of his face. "My mother taught me never to stereotype girls."

"Smart woman, your mom."

"Yeah. Smart and a little bit reckless." He clinked his glass with hers. "Like someone else I know."

"I'm not reckless. I just always end up in the wrong place at the wrong time."

"Like in the men's room at the bus stop with a poison pen clutched in your hand."

"Okay, maybe a little reckless."

Max paid the bill and Ava took a soda to go. When they returned to the room, Max retreated to the bathroom and changed into some basketball shorts and a tank.

"Just to be on the safe side, when I'm gone lock the dead bolt and don't answer the door. I'm not going to send you room service or a special note or anything else. If it's the housekeeping staff, it can wait. Okay?"

"Okay, but your words keep belying your assertion that we're safe."

"Ava." He sat next to her on the bed. "We're not going to be safe until this is over. You know that, right?"

She dipped her chin to her chest. "I do, but sometimes I just need to hang on to the illusion. Do you know what I mean?"

He curled a lock of her hair around his finger. "I know exactly what you mean. We can pretend everything's normal once in a while."

She parted her lips because she really, really wanted him to kiss her—and not one of those soft, gentle kisses he'd been bestowing on her as if she'd crack beneath any pressure from his lips. She wanted a real kiss—a hot, full-bodied, gasping-for-air kind of kiss.

He released her hair and stood up, reaching for his tablet on the bedside table. "You're welcome to go through my library and read something if that'll help you fall asleep."

"I'm not sure I'll need help. I'm pretty exhausted."

"You have reason to be." He peeled his card key from the credenza and pointed it at her. "Lock the dead bolt behind me."

She bounded from the bed when he closed the door, knowing he'd be waiting to hear the dead bolt. After she flicked it into place, she smiled as she heard his footsteps retreat down the hallway.

So, no hot kiss. Maybe she wouldn't get one until this was all over. He'd get so carried away when she shot him up with the antidote, he'd crush her into his strong arms and kiss her silly.

She snorted. She'd better hang on to that daydream because that was all it was. And did she really want a gratitude kiss?

She grabbed his tablet and fluffed a pillow behind her.

Actually, she'd take anything he had to offer, motivated by anything.

She clicked the tablet, and his current book popped up. She scanned the text—one of Homer's epic poems. Didn't he say he wasn't well-read? Maybe after missing the Caliban reference, he decided to get well-read—or he was using this as a sleep aid.

She clicked back to the book list and noted some history, some true crime and a fantasy series. Max Duvall would probably never cease to surprise her.

She started in on the fantasy because she needed a little escape from this world. After reading about ten pages, she realized the fantasy world was no better than the real world—at least her real world.

She clicked the remote for the TV and crossed her legs at the ankles, tapping her feet together. She stopped the channel surfing at a reality dating show. Now, *this* was a fantasy she could get into.

By the time the show ended, Max was at the door. She peeked through the peephole and flipped back the dead bolt. "Wow, did you lift every weight in there?"

He pushed a damp lock of hair from his eyes, and his biceps bulged. "Yeah, sorry. I need a shower. Any news from Cody?"

"Nothing yet, but I think that woman should choose the dog trainer for the next date."

His brows shot up. "What?"

She flicked her fingers at the TV. "I got very engrossed in that show. Now I'm going to have to follow it and see who she picks."

"I thought you were supposed to take a nap."

She muted the TV. "I didn't feel that tired, but honestly vegging in front of the TV is pretty relaxing."

"Don't do much of that?"

"Not usually." She ran her gaze up and down his body, trying not to get hung up on a particular part of it. "How was the gym?"

"Good. I've lost some strength."

"That's good?" She covered her mouth. "Oh, the T-101 is having less of an effect on your body."

"Seems like it." He jerked his thumb over his shoulder. "I'm going to take a shower. You can indulge in more reality TV if you like."

"Funny thing about reality TV."

He cranked his head over his shoulder when he got to the door of the bathroom. "What's that?"

"It's so much more fake than real life, I don't know why they call it reality TV."

"Probably to make it seem like your own life is incredibly boring."

"Those reality TV people don't know my life."

"Right." He shut the door behind him.

She skimmed through the rest of the channels and left the TV on the local news. Maybe there would be some more information about Snyder. She hoped by the time his so-called next of kin came to Snow Haven to pick up the body, Tempest would be tracking them to Florida.

Max emerged from the bathroom with a towel around his waist. "I forgot to bring some clean clothes in with me."

She'd seen it all before, but the first time she'd seen him half-naked she still thought he was a crazy person. Now he was everything to her.

She clamped her hands over her waist, stilling the butterflies. She didn't want to feel that way. Red flags and danger signs were waving and flashing in front of her eyes.

He stopped on his way to his bag and turned. "Are you okay, Ava?"

"Yeah, I'm fine."

He crossed the room and put the back of his hand against her forehead. "You looked pale. The whole incident in the bathroom rattled you more than you probably even realize. You could even experience some post-traumatic stress."

She'd been more upset about her unrequited feelings for Max than about killing a man. What did that say about her? She'd never admit that to Max.

"I'm just anxious."

He stroked her hair. "Understandable."

Her phone rang and she jumped to grab it from the nightstand. When she saw Cody's name on the display, she punched the speaker button.

"What do you have for us, Cody?"

"Nothing. I got nothing for you, Ava. There is no lab."

Chapter Fourteen

Her legs turned to rubber and she sank to the bed. "What are you talking about? You know people. There has to be someone in the area cooking meth."

"I'm not getting any hits, Ava. I'm sorry." He cleared his throat. "On the plus side, I got the other stuff you needed."

"What am I supposed to do, Cody, cook it up in the hotel bathroom?"

"I don't know what to tell you. The only possibility I have is out of town. He'll be back next week. I can probably set you up then."

She gripped the phone with two hands. "We don't have until next week. We don't have two days."

"I'll keep working on it, Ava. Maybe something will come through. These guys are cagey."

"Obviously. That's why we gave you all that money." Tears had filled her eyes and she dashed them away. "You owe me, Cody. You ruined my life, my career. I protected you, and now you owe me."

"I know that. I'll keep looking, Ava."

When she ended the call, she chucked the phone across the room and fell back on the bed, the tears running into her ears.

Max had stood silent and still like a statue during her conversation with Cody. Now the mattress dipped as he sat down beside her.

He wiped away her tears with the back of his hand. "It's okay, Ava. Don't cry."

She hoisted herself up on her elbows. "How can you say that? You know what it means, Max. You have two pills left—one for tonight and one for tomorrow. After that, you're cut off."

"Maybe I'll find more. That's where I was when I met up with you. I had no hope for an antidote then. I'm back to my original position."

"No, you're not." She tossed her hair back from her face. "You had five pills when you rescued me from Simon."

"If I had never gone to that lab to chase after Simon, I'd still have two pills today—and you'd be dead." He lay down next to her and captured her hand. "I'd say I'm in a lot better position now."

She sniffled. "What will you do, Max? How can I help you?"

One corner of his mouth lifted and he kissed her fingers. "You've already helped me, Ava. Nothing more is necessary. Nothing more is required. We have a new goal now—get you to a secure location."

"Max." She twined her arms around his neck and pulled his head close to hers, pressing her forehead against his. "I don't want to lose you. Stay with me. I'll help you ride it out."

He wrapped one arm around her waist, and his other hand skimmed up her spine and cupped the back of her head.

Slanting his mouth across hers, he whispered her name against her lips.

The towel had come loose from his waist, and she trailed her hand down the warm, smooth skin of his back. Her fingers dug into the hard muscle of his buttocks, and she moved in closer to him, drawing him closer to her.

He deepened the kiss, thrusting his tongue inside her mouth, lighting a fire in her belly, curling her toes. Here it was at last—the hot kiss she'd longed for, but now it meant goodbye.

He yanked off his towel and tossed it over his shoulder onto the floor.

Her eyes still closed, she let her hands create the visual as they roamed over his naked body, skimming the hard muscle and the flat planes, caressing the smooth skin.

He ended the kiss, leaving her panting and disoriented. Her lashes fluttered and her gaze met his dark eyes, alight with passion and desire. The look from those eyes melted her core.

Then she drank in what her hands had been exploring, and the beauty of his form took her breath away. Pure muscle cut through his lean frame. The nicks and scars on his body relieved it of perfection but added a layer of sexiness and danger that fueled her attraction.

On impulse, she ducked her head and planted her lips against the chiseled slabs of muscle on his chest. Her tongue toyed with one brown nipple, and she felt his erection plow into her belly.

With one hand, she reached down between his thighs and encircled his hard, tight flesh with her fingers.

A groan escaped his lips as he thrust into her hand. His fingers curled around the hem of her T-shirt. "Why are you still dressed?"

Before she could form a coherent answer, he had tugged the shirt from her body and over her head. It joined the towel on the floor. He slipped one hand into the cup of her bra, kneading her breast, swollen and aching with want.

His thumb trailed across her nipple, and she sucked her lower lip between her teeth to keep from screaming. He unclasped her bra and cupped both of her breasts in his hands. Dipping his head, he encircled one nipple with his tongue and then sucked it into his mouth.

"Oh." She dragged her fingers through his thick hair, her nails digging into his scalp. She hitched her leg over his hip to get even closer to him, and the head of his erection skimmed her bare belly.

She needed more of that.

She struggled with the buttons of her jeans with trembling fingers until Max drew back from her.

"Need some help with that?"

"If it means you have to stop doing what you were doing to my left breast, I think I got this."

He chuckled and unbuttoned her fly with deft fingers. "I have plenty of time to return to that luscious left breast."

At the mention of time, her heart jumped and she yanked off her jeans and her panties in one stroke. They had precious little of that and she intended to make every second count.

She kicked her pants to the floor and rolled onto her side again where Max awaited her. Wrapping his arms around her, he pulled her body against his. They met along every line, bare skin touching bare skin, fusing together in heat and passion.

With their arms entwined around each other, Max bent his head and captured her lips again. She invited him inside, their tongues dueling and exploring.

His heart beat against her chest, strong and steady while hers galloped and skipped. She stroked him from his broad shoulders to the curve of his buttocks, reveling in the raw power tingling beneath her fingers.

He cupped her derriere with one hand, the calluses on his palm tickling her tender skin. He caressed her flesh and fit her pelvis to his as his erection prodded her impatiently.

When he broke away from her, he planted a path of kisses from her chin, down her throat and between her breasts. Then he cinched her around the waist and rolled her onto her back.

Missing the contact already, she reached for him, dragging her nails lightly across his six-pack.

He shivered, and then rising to his knees, he positioned himself between her legs, his body proud and masculine on display before her. If just the sight of him turned her to jelly, how would she be able to hold herself together once he entered her?

She'd have to wait to find out, since Max had other ideas.

Slipping his hands beneath her bottom, he lifted her hips. He leaned forward, kissed each breast, flicked his tongue down her belly and nibbled the soft flesh of her inner thighs.

She thrashed her head from side to side. "You're going to drive me crazy."

He rested his head against her leg, his hair tickling her. "Do you know how long I've waited to drive you crazy like this?"

She rolled her eyes toward the ceiling. "Ever since I saved your life in the bathroom?"

"Nope, before that." His tongue darted from his mouth, flicking against the sensitive skin between her legs.

She sucked in a sharp breath. "Ever since I saved your life at the Desert Sun Motel?"

"Before that." He teased her again with his tongue.

She squirmed, her hips bouncing from the bed. "Ever since I saved your life that first night in Albuquerque?"

He raised his brows. "Do you think this is gratitude I feel for you right now?"

"Mmm, this feels a lot better than gratitude."

"I'm glad you recognize that." He trailed his tongue up the inside of her thigh and brushed it across her throbbing outer lips.

She closed her eyes and let out a long sigh, even though her muscles had coiled in anticipation of a sweet release. "So, how long have you been waiting to drive me crazy?"

"Ever since you first had me strip to my skivvies in your examination room."

Her lids flew open. "Really?"

"Oh, yeah. You couldn't tell by my—" he coughed "—reaction to you?"

She giggled, the heat rising to her cheeks. "I thought your heart rate was a little elevated."

He snorted. "It wasn't my heart rate that was elevated, sweetheart. Now it's payback."

He ran his thumb along the outside of her moist flesh and then used his tongue and lips to drive her crazy.

All at once, everything came unraveled and she cried out as her orgasm jolted through her body. This was no smooth wave of pleasure. Instead her ecstasy clawed at her over and over, driving her to new heights. Max rode it out with her, shoving his fingers inside her, prolonging her release as she tightened around him.

When she lay spent, her breathing ragged and her chest heaving, he straddled her. Was the T-101 responsible for that erection? If so, she gave a silent, guilty thanks to Dr. Arnoff.

And then the guilt and the fear and the desperation all

dissipated like feathers in a strong gust of wind as Max thrust into her. She closed around his thick girth as if he was a part of her.

He was a part of her. Whatever happened to him, to them, he'd always exist deep in her pores.

Each time he pulled out, even though it was for a nano-second, she ached for his return. He plowed into her, over and over, as if he couldn't get enough, couldn't get close enough.

Her sensitive flesh, still tingling from her orgasm, responded to the close contact of Max's body, the tension building in her muscles again. She clawed at his buttocks, wanting more of him, needing more of him.

When he paused to capture her lips with his own, she shattered beneath him, her orgasm sending rivers of tingles throughout her body. She thrust her hips forward to engulf him and the motion acted like a trigger.

His frame stiffened as he plunged deep into her core. Then he howled like a wild, untamed beast and she trembled beneath him.

His release racked his body until sweat dripped from the ends of his hair, and his legs, still straddling her, trembled. He held himself above her, wedging his arms on either side of her shoulders. Then he lowered himself and kissed her mouth.

He growled. "I could do that all over again."

She dabbed her tongue against his salty shoulder. "Is that the T-101 talking?"

Grinning, he pulled out and rolled to her side. "Is that why you instructed your brother to fail on the lab?"

"Max." She drew her brows over her nose, and he tweaked it.

"I'm just kidding. You have to excuse my sense of humor. It's been AWOL for a few years." He smoothed the back of his hand across her cheek. "Let's just enjoy the time we have left."

Blinking back the sudden tears that flooded her eyes, she shifted to her side and smoothed her hand along the hard line of his hip. "I can do that."

"Glad to hear it." He rolled onto his back and pulled her close, molding her against his side. "You think we can find that reality dating show again?"

She twisted around and felt for the remote control on the bedside table. "Not sure about that show, but I'm sure we can find something that has more drama than our lives."

She aimed the remote at the TV and clicked the power button.

The hotel phone on the nightstand jangled and the hand Max had been circling on her belly froze.

They both stared at the phone as it rang again.

Ava swallowed. "I-it could just be housekeeping."

"Don't answer it."

They watched the phone ring three more times, Ava holding her breath until it stopped.

Max's entire demeanor had shifted from the passionate, considerate lover to the wound-up spy on the run, his jaw tight and his fists curled. She wanted to smash the phone with her own fist.

"Maybe we should call the front desk and see if it was housekeeping."

Max leveled a finger at the phone. "Whoever it was left a message."

She jerked her head to the side and eyed the blinking red light on the phone with trepidation. "That's good. Maybe they just want to drop off towels."

Max sat up and reached across her. He pulled the phone

onto the bed. He punched the message and the speaker buttons in succession.

The automated voice droned. "You have one new message. To listen, press two."

He punched the two button. A rasping breath burst over the line, followed by a man's harsh voice. "Max, it's Adrian Bessler. I'm a Tempest agent and I need help."

Chapter Fifteen

Max put his finger to his lips as Ava started talking, her voice rising with each word.

The agent—Bessler—coughed and cleared his throat. "This isn't a trap, I swear. I know what happened to Skinner. I know what's happening to you. It's happening to me, too. We can help each other. I'll tell you more, but you have to meet me. I'm afraid to talk on this phone. I'll keep it for a while longer to wait for your call, and then I'm throwing it away. Hurry." He recited his phone number and then the message ended.

Max stared at the phone in his hands. "It's too convenient."

"I know Adrian Bessler, Max, and he didn't show up on the agent-locator program. I never thought to count those red dots on the map to verify if all the agents were accounted for, but I know Bessler's name wasn't among them."

"That doesn't mean anything." He slammed the phone in its cradle and Ava jumped. He closed his eyes. "I'm sorry."

"It's okay." She rubbed the back of his hand with her fingers. "I realize it all could be a ruse, but he wasn't on that map."

"That could all be by design. Maybe Tempest figured since you were with me and had treated all the agents that you would've noticed Bessler's absence on the map, making this call more believable."

"But what if it's the truth?" She curled her fingers around his hand and squeezed. "You said yourself that you wanted to track down the other agents and warn them. Now you don't have to. One has come to you."

He pinched the bridge of his nose, squeezing his eyes closed. "I'd have to be very careful meeting him."

"Of course, and I'll be there, too."

"Forget it."

She squeezed his hand tighter. "I thought we were partners. I, at least, will know what Adrian Bessler looks like. That'll give us an advantage. You'll be walking in blind. He could be anyone—and that's dangerous."

"You could describe him to me. I'll tell him to wear something specific for the meeting."

She opened her eyes wide. "Didn't I ever tell you I'm really bad at describing other people? Besides, he could tell you he'll be wearing a red baseball cap and then blindside you. With me, there will be no blindsiding."

He shoved the phone to the foot of the bed and took Ava into his arms again. Her silky, soft skin soothed him. "I don't want you in harm's way, my love."

She sipped in a small, quick breath and he mentally gave himself a good swift kick. He hadn't meant to mention anything about love, but after the incredible connection they'd just shared, the words had come to his lips naturally.

"If you don't want me in harm's way, then don't leave me—ever." She nuzzled his neck and pressed her lips against the pulse beating in his throat. "Call him back.

Let's meet him and see what he has to say. We can use all the allies we can possibly get on our side."

With her soft breasts pressed against his chest and her wavy hair tickling his chin, he couldn't refuse her anything.

He sat up and reached for the phone. He put it back on Speaker and punched in the number Bessler had left.

The agent picked up on the first ring. "Yeah?"

"Bessler, I got your message."

"Duvall?" Bessler released a long, ragged sigh.

"Start talking."

"I'm in the same boat as you, man. The juice stopped working on me or something. I started remembering things, terrible things I'd done."

Max flinched and Ava ran her hand down his back.

"How did you find me? Why are you off the grid?"

"I knew you were with Dr. Whitman. I knew Dr. Whitman had a brother in Snow Haven. She told me herself that he was headed there to be a snowboard instructor. And I'm off the grid because I chucked my phone, just like you."

Max glanced at Ava and she pressed three fingers to her lips and nodded.

"I tracked her brother down, broke into his place to see if I could find out anything about Dr. Whitman. But I didn't know I'd be running straight into a Tempest trap."

"What does that mean?"

"You took him out, didn't you? The agent in the bathroom. I knew it was you as soon as I heard the circumstances. If he had seen me here, I'd be dead. I may still be dead. I can't talk any more, Duvall."

"We meet in broad daylight, tomorrow."

"In public."

"Exactly. There's an ice-skating rink in the center of town. Be there at noon in a green scarf and cap."

"And how will I know you?"

"I'll be in a green scarf and cap, too." Max drummed his fingers on the receiver. "And I have one more question for you."

"Yeah?"

"How many blue pills do you have left?"

"Not nearly enough, man, not nearly enough."

When the call ended, Ava took the phone and placed it back on the nightstand. "He sounds legitimate, doesn't he?"

"He said all the right things."

"His story makes sense, Max. I did tell him about Cody because Adrian is a snowboarder, too. He must've heard about the massacre at the lab and somehow knew I escaped. He ditched his phone to go off the grid and then figured he might find us here. It all adds up."

"I repeat—too convenient."

She stretched out on the bed, raising her arms above her head and grasping the headboard. "I believe him."

He dusted his hands together. "If you believe Agent Adrian Bessler, so do I."

"Really? That was easy."

"We'll find out if he's legit one way or the other tomorrow, and I'm not gonna lie, I care more about getting back to you than I do about Bessler because you look totally irresistible like this." He ran the flat of one hand down from her neck to her belly, and she shimmied beneath his touch.

The worry lines around her mouth and eyes dissolved, and the knots in his own gut loosened just a little. He had no idea if Bessler would try to kill him or if he'd have to take out Bessler.

It didn't matter right now. Regardless of what Bessler had to offer, he had limited time with Ava and he wasn't going to waste another minute of it discussing Tempest.

Or how he'd have to leave her in two days to protect her from the inevitable rage that would take over his mind and body.

She wiggled her toes. "We still need to eat dinner, but I'm all for room service in bed."

"With reality TV?" He flipped open the room service menu.

"What else?"

They ordered cheeseburgers and French fries and chocolate cake and spent the evening in bed eating and talking and laughing. And he'd never felt so alive.

Then he popped a blue pill, leaving one in the tin, and made love to Ava again as if it was his last night on earth.

MAX STOOD IN front of a mirror in the hotel's ski shop and wrapped the scarf around his neck. "Why did I pick green?"

"Probably because it stands out in the crowd." She adjusted the ends of his scarf and patted his chest.

"It stands out in the crowd because nobody wears it." The matching hat Ava held in her hands brought out the emerald color of her eyes, and he knew why he'd chosen the color—he'd been thinking about her eyes.

He took the hat from her and pulled it onto his head. "Bessler will definitely be able to pick me out."

"And you him, but wait for the signal from me first. If I see him at the skating rink and he's not wearing green, that's a sure sign he's planning to ambush you."

"He could just be the lure with someone else waiting there to ambush me. That's why you stay out of sight and keep your distance from me."

"Got it."

He swept the cap from his head and yanked the scarf from his neck. "I guess these will do."

He paid for the hat and scarf and took Ava's hand as they walked out of the store. "Are you hungry? You hardly touched your breakfast."

"I'm too nervous to eat. I hope…" She lifted her shoulders and then dropped them.

"You hope what?" He brought her hand to his lips and kissed each knuckle, one by one.

"I don't know. I just hope Adrian has a plan, that he's discovered something we haven't." Her green eyes sparkled with tears. "You have one pill left, Max."

"I know that, Ava."

She rounded on him and dug her fingers into his shoulder. "What do you plan to do when it's gone?"

"I'm not going to subject you to another Simon. I'm not going to subject anyone to that."

She bit her lip and one tear trembled on the edge of her long lashes. "We can get you help."

"A padded cell?" He shook his head. "T-101 is not exactly an FDA-approved drug. No doctor is going to know what to do with me, and they won't have a chance to even experiment. Tempest wouldn't allow that."

"What about the CIA? Prospero?"

"I told you, Ava." He caught the tear on the end of his thumb. "I don't know who I can trust, except you. I trust you."

She stared past him bleakly, her eyes dead. "I love you, Max."

The words rushed over him in a warm wave, and he closed his eyes to savor every sensation those words inspired. With Ava's faith in him, he'd achieved a monumental goal. Caring for her, loving her had made him human—more human than any antidote.

He kissed her right there in the hallway outside the ski

shop. "I love you, too, Dr. Whitman. Now let's get some coffee or hot chocolate and get ready to skate."

In the coffee shop, Max planted his elbows on the little table between them, hunching forward. "What do you remember about Bessler?"

"He's husky, blond, usually has a buzz cut." She skimmed her finger through the mountain of whipped cream floating on her cocoa and sucked it into her mouth.

He dragged his gaze away from her lips. He had to stay focused on this meeting with Bessler. "I don't mean his physical appearance. What was he like? Seems like he was one of the talkers if he told you he was a snowboarder and you mentioned your brother to him."

"He was nice, young." She snapped her fingers. "He was like you and Simon—friendly, talkative. A lot of the guys were reticent, didn't have much to say for themselves."

"So, you think Bessler could be on the up-and-up because he was friendly?"

"It kind of makes sense, or at least it's a positive sign. You three were not affected by the T-101 as much as the others." She sipped her hot chocolate and ended up with a fluff of whipped cream on her nose.

He reached over and dabbed it off. "Would you stop doing all that with the whipped cream?"

"Doing what?" She rubbed the back of her hand across the tip of her nose, her eyes widening.

"I'm supposed to be running through my plan for meeting Bessler and you're flicking whipped cream all over your body."

Her lips twitched into a smile. "You need to get your mind out of the gutter."

"It's not the gutter I'm imagining." He drew a line with his fingertip from her slender throat down to the V of her sweater. "It's a big bed with tousled covers and tousled hair and lots of whipped cream."

She swallowed and whispered, "Maybe if everything goes well with Bessler, we'll have time to live out that fantasy."

It always came back to that. She had to stop dreaming. He had one blue pill left, one pill between him and sure madness. And he planned to be as far away from Ava as possible when that madness descended.

"Hmm, don't know about that." He rolled his eyes to the ceiling.

"Wh-what? I have faith."

"I don't know if I want whipped cream or warm fudge and strawberries—maybe both, maybe all three."

Blinking her eyes, she smiled through her sniffles. "Once we get out of this mess, you can have me any way you want me."

He smacked the table. "You just pumped up my motivation tenfold."

She tapped her phone. "It's time. It's eleven forty-five."

"So it is."

They left their cups on a tray and made their way to the front of the hotel for the lunchtime shuttle into town. A few other guests from the hotel joined them, and then the driver hopped in.

He looked in his rearview mirror and called out, "This shuttle is going into town, makes one stop and then turns around."

The driver cranked the doors shut, and the bus lurched forward.

Max closed his eyes, trying to visualize his meeting with Bessler, but instead of a green scarf, all he saw was a pair of sparkling green eyes, and the thought kept pounding his brain that this could be his last day with Ava.

Even if Bessler hadn't called to lure him out and kill him, the other agent probably didn't have much to offer and he hadn't had Ava to help him. Bessler had called out for help—not much chance he could solve the problem.

The shuttle turned the corner and threw Ava against his shoulder. She stayed put, and Max draped his arm across the back of her seat and drummed his fingers on her collarbone.

She'd put on a good face today, but she'd been tense and had seemed on the verge of tears a couple of times. He'd take the coward's way out and slip away in the middle of the night. Ironic for a man who'd been searching for human emotion for the past two years only to escape from it in the end.

She pointed past his shoulder at the yellow tape tied to a post near the restrooms and waving in the breeze. "The bathroom isn't cordoned off, so it's obviously not a crime scene."

"Obviously. I heard a man dropped dead of a heart attack in there."

"This time it will be different." She laced her fingers through his and kissed the back of his hand.

He put his lips close to her ear. "Remember, we part company when we get off the shuttle. Head to the skating rink via the main drag, and I'll slip through the backstreets."

She nodded.

"If you don't see Bessler at all or you see him and he's not wearing green, just send me the text we agreed upon."

"No green."

"I'm gonna make a spy out of you yet." He pinched her soft earlobe. "We give him fifteen minutes to show. Then you return to the restaurant where we had lunch with Cody."

"Holly's. If he's there and wearing green, I'll text you *green.*"

"And the most important part of the plan?"

"I stay out of Bessler's sight, keep out of the open and stick with other people."

"You got it." The bus rumbled to a stop and the doors, front and back, creaked open.

"Have a great day, folks. The shuttles are still running on a reduced schedule, so we'll just have five more runs with the last one at two o'clock, and then we start up again for dinner at five."

Ava stood up first. She leaned over and kissed him on the lips. "Good luck."

She was the only luck he needed.

He brushed a knuckle across her cheek. "Be careful."

He watched her hop off the bus and tag along behind a couple on their way to the main street.

"Sir, are you getting off or going back to the hotel?"

"Just looking for my hat." He plucked it from his lap and pulled it over his head. "Found it."

He jumped onto the sidewalk, still wet from the rain the night before, but not icy. He slipped around the corner of the bathroom, wondering if the Tempest cleanup crew had ever found Snyder's weapon.

With his muscles tense and all his senses on high alert, he navigated the backstreets of Snow Haven, which was neither snowy nor a haven for anything but traps. Total fail on that name.

He reached an alley between two buildings that led to the town square at the end of the main street. On one end of that square was the ice-skating rink, which abutted the end of a ski run. That town run hadn't yet opened for the season, and brown patches and clumps of trees dotted the side of the hill.

Reaching the end of the alley, he poked his head out and looked down the sidewalk both ways. The crowds of people that would usually clog the streets during the full ski season were thinned out, but enough people milled around the shops and restaurants to give him some cover.

He let out a breath and leaned against the wall, pulling his phone from his jacket pocket where he cupped it in his palm. A chill seeped through his veins as his adrenaline merged with the T-101 still pumping through his system.

He recognized the feeling. He welcomed it.

The phone buzzed in his hand and he glanced at the display. He read the one word aloud as if to connect him with Ava. "'Green.'"

Game time.

Squaring his shoulders, he pushed off the wall and stepped onto the sidewalk, his gaze sweeping the town square. He joined a clutch of people heading for the skating rink as he hunched his shoulders and pulled his scarf around his face.

He spotted Bessler immediately hanging over the side of the rink, watching the skaters, his green scarf tucked into a black jacket. What else did he have tucked in there?

Max waited in line at the booth and then paid to rent a pair of ice skates and for an afternoon of ice-skating. He picked out a pair of skates and slung them over his shoulder.

Bessler had raised his head and was staring across the rink. He'd been made, but did Bessler have to be so obvious? Ava was right. The other agent was young and green—another good reason for the chosen color.

Max stalked toward the skating rink, waiting for Bessler to make his move. The agent clumped toward the opening of the circular rink and glided onto the ice. At least the guy could ice-skate.

Max edged around to a less populated rim and gripped the wooden railing that circled the ice. He smiled and waved to a little girl, hanging on to her mother's hand and wobbling across the ice. Maybe her mother would have him arrested before he could even talk to Bessler.

Bessler skimmed around the ice, even doing a few turns and jumps. Then he started making wide circles around the perimeter of the rink, stopping every few laps to watch the rest of the action.

He neared Max and then bent over to adjust his laces. He came to a stop a few feet away from Max.

Max leaned forward and waved again. "How'd you know where we were staying?"

Bessler replied to the ice, his head still bent. "I bugged Dr. Whitman's brother's place. I heard him on the phone. Tempest doesn't know about Cody Whitman. They tracked you here some other way. Do you still have your Tempest phone?"

"Of course not." Max didn't want to reveal too much to Bessler just yet, so he didn't need to know about Arnoff's computer. "What do you know?"

"I know they're pumping us full of juice to brainwash us, to create some superagent, but it's not working on me, at least not completely. I heard Skinner went nuts and shot up the lab but Dr. Whitman escaped. I know she's with you."

"She's not with me anymore." Max laughed and waved at his imaginary daughter. "You're doing great, sweetheart."

"Cut it out, Duvall." Bessler untied his laces again. "I heard a lot more from Cody Whitman than where you two were staying. He's trying to find a lab for you. Why?"

Max whistled between his teeth. He had to admit the guy had skills. "How do I know this isn't a setup?"

"If it were, you'd be dead by now."

"Or you would. Don't flatter yourself, kid." A woman barreled into the side of the rink, almost tripping over Bessler.

Catching her arm, Max said, "Be careful."

"I don't think this is my thing." She laughed and then skated off.

Max leaned back and looked over his shoulder. "Besides, I don't think Tempest wants to kill me. Snyder already had his chance."

"Snyder?" Bessler finished tying his skate and brushed ice chips from his snow pants.

"The guy in the bathroom."

"Why does Dr. Whitman need the lab, Duvall? Can she create more of the juice? A weaker strain like the blue pills? Because that's one thing I do know. We can't quit cold turkey or we'll wind up like Skinner—and I have no intention of winding up like Skinner."

Bessler rose from his crouch and then his blue eyes widened as he clapped the side of his neck.

Max dropped to the ground and hugged the ice rink's barrier. He didn't need to see it—he'd heard it.

Bessler crashed to the ice.

Chapter Sixteen

Adrian Bessler fell to the ice and Ava stifled a scream when Max disappeared behind the ice rink's barrier. They'd both been hit.

She dropped the cup of hot chocolate she'd been drinking on the ground and rushed toward the ice rink, her heart pounding, her mouth dry.

A few people had stopped next to Bessler, but nobody had panicked yet. Did they think he'd just fallen? Wasn't there any blood? And why had nobody gone to Max's aid on the other side of the barrier?

She ran onto the ice, her booted feet slipping beneath her. Five feet away from Bessler, she fell, her hands hitting the cold, solid surface. Sobbing, she crawled toward the fallen agent on her hands and knees.

He looked as though he was sleeping. There was no blood on the ice, no gaping wound in his head.

"Is he your husband? I think he might've fallen and hit his head. He's out."

Ava gazed past the woman's blurry face to the place where Max had just been standing. Had nobody on the other side of the wall seen him go down?

As she dragged herself toward Bessler's inert form,

attracting more and more attention, Max's head popped up on the other side of the barrier.

"What the hell are you doing?"

She nearly collapsed to the ice in relief. "I—I thought…"

"Doesn't matter what you thought. Stand up and do it quickly. I'm going to yank you over this wall."

The eyes of the woman attending to Bessler bulged from their sockets as they ping-ponged between her and Max.

An attendant in a blue parka started skating toward them.

"Wait!" Ava grabbed the lapels of Bessler's jacket. "His pills."

The Good Samaritan sat back on her heels. "Oh, does he have a heart condition?"

"Yes, yes."

Max growled. "Let's go."

Ignoring his command, Ava unzipped Bessler's jacket and patted his pocket, her hands tracing over his weapon. In a tiny inner zippered pocket, she felt the outlines of a pill bottle. With trembling fingers, she unzipped the pocket and snatched the pill bottle.

"You need to get off that ice—now."

The attendant skated up. "What happened? Does he need an ambulance?"

"He might have had a heart attack." The woman pointed to Ava, now crawling across the ice toward Max behind the wall. "His wife was looking for his pills."

"Ma'am?"

Ava twisted her head over her shoulder. "I'm not his wife. I've never seen this man before in my life."

When she reached the barrier, Max leaned over and pulled her over the wall. She landed on top of him.

"Stupid, stupid thing to do." He pinned her against the

wall, clamping his hands on her shoulders. "Stay down and keep to the wall."

Bending forward, they edged along the wooden barrier, as the buzz on the ice grew. Was Bessler dead? Why had he gone down? "Max…"

"Shh. We're going out the front way. I think they hit him from behind the rink, from the mountainside."

He whipped off his hat and shed his scarf. "Take off that jacket in case they saw you."

She shrugged off her jacket, shoving the pill bottle in the front pocket of her jeans.

Max grabbed her hand and pulled her behind the rental booth. "We can't sit around and wait for the shuttle. I saw some taxis by the ski rental shop back toward the bus stop."

They weaved up and down a few streets, sidling along the walls of buildings, joining groups of pedestrians on the sidewalk. They meandered through the ski shop and exited on the other side.

Max hailed the first taxi he saw. He bundled Ava into the backseat and said, "Snow Haven Lodge and Resort."

Bessler's bottle was radiating heat in her pocket and it took all her self-control not to dig it out and discover its contents.

When the taxi reached the hotel, they marched through the lobby without speaking one word. Finally, when Max slammed the door of their suite behind him, she pulled out the bottle.

He took a turn around the room, raking a hand through his hair. "What were you thinking? You were supposed to stay out of sight—no matter what."

"I thought you'd been hit. I saw Bessler go down and almost at the same time you went down, too."

"Doesn't matter."

"It does matter. Nothing else matters." She flipped off the lid of the bottle and peered inside. Her heart did a somersault in her chest. "Look, Max."

He stopped pacing and pivoted. "What?"

She dumped the blue pills into her palm and held out her hand. "Two of them. We have two more days together."

Her smile faded as she studied his face, his jaw hardening, the lines deepening. "I-it's two more days, Max."

His harsh laugh frightened her.

"Is that how I'm supposed to measure out my days left on earth? By counting little blue pills?"

She closed her hand around the pills and dropped her lashes. "These represent two days we didn't have before."

"It doesn't make any difference, Ava. Are we going to lure other Tempest agents here, get them killed and steal their stash?"

Anger flashed across her chest. "That's not how it happened. I'm sorry for Adrian, but he found us. I just took advantage of a terrible situation. Does that make me selfish? Then, yes, call me selfish for wanting to spend another two days with the man I love, the man I can't live without."

He reached her in two long steps and crushed her against his body. He buried his face in her hair. "You have to, Ava. You have to go on without me."

She clung to him, tears stinging her eyes. "I have the formula for the antidote, Max. I can save you."

"And what lab, what hospital is going to allow you to mix it up?" He drew back from her, cupping her face in his large hands, strands of her hair still clinging to his beard.

"A lab at the CIA or Prospero. They're the good guys. They'll help you."

"They've also put their trust in Tempest. Don't you think Tempest has already put out the word? Rogue agents, armed and dangerous. If the CIA doesn't kill me first, they'll send me back to Tempest to deprogram. I'm an intelligence asset. They can't allow me to walk the streets spouting crazy conspiracy theories."

"And Prospero?"

Furrows creased his brow. "I don't know. They're a wild card. Why did Tempest's leader choose that name and moniker of Caliban for himself?"

"You said it yourself. Tempest is the dark side of Prospero. Where Prospero is a force for good, Tempest is a force for evil."

"That's just it. Is Tempest the flip side of Prospero? Two sides of the same coin? I can't take that chance. I'm not going to end up in Tempest's clutches again."

"Caliban doesn't want to kill you, does he?"

He released her and fell across the bed, toeing off his shoes. "Do you know what happened to Bessler?"

"No." She sat on the foot of the bed. "He wasn't shot. There was no blood."

"Someone shot him in the neck with a tranquilizer dart."

"Do you think he's dead?"

"I don't know, but the same type of attack was planned for me and I know my dose wouldn't have been lethal. I would've wound up in the hospital, and my helpful brother or doctor or even wife would've come to collect me, bearing all the necessary ID and paperwork to airlift me to a facility of their choosing."

"They're diabolical."

"To say the least." He punched a pillow. "Tempest wants me back, but I'm not playing along. Before I'd go back to my so-called life at Tempest, I'd rather…"

Her nose tingled and she gulped back a sob. He'd rather kill himself. And what could she do to stop him? He didn't want to be around her once the withdrawal from the T-101 turned him into a raging machine.

She shivered as she recalled Simon Skinner's dead eyes through the glass at the lab. She never wanted to look into Max's deep, dark eyes and see that look. Better to remember the warmth kindling there as he made love to her.

She'd have that memory forever, and she'd never let it go.

Opening her hand, she stretched it out toward him. "We still have three more days. Let me have those three last days with you."

He pinched the two pills between his thumb and forefinger, took the tin from his pocket and dropped them inside to join the other. "We'll make these three days feel like an eternity."

She scooted between his legs and rested against his chest, feeling at home against the steady beat of his heart. "Let's start now."

He stroked her hair. "God, I was so terrified when I saw you on the ice, I didn't even ask if you were okay. *Are* you okay?"

"I'll probably have a couple of bruises on my knees. I'm sorry that I tore out there like an idiot, but you disappeared right after I saw Adrian collapse. I thought they'd gotten to you, too."

"I have no doubt they planned to nail both of us, but I think they wanted to get me first. Bessler stood up suddenly and that's when he was hit. I knew immediately what had happened, so I dropped."

She ran a hand along his belly. "I'm glad I did go out there. I remembered he'd said something about not having enough blue pills, so I figured he must've had a couple. And he did."

"Poor kid. I kind of have to believe now that he was on the up-and-up, unless Caliban plans to kill him to tie up a loose end."

"What else did he say before he was hit?"

"I'd forgotten all about what he said, but it was interesting." He toyed with her fingers. "He's the one who broke into your brother's place, and he bugged it. That's how he knew we were staying here, and he knew your brother was trying to secure a lab for us."

"That's two pieces of good news." She balanced her chin on his chest. "Maybe Tempest doesn't know about Cody. They tracked us here through Dr. Arnoff's computer, and so far they don't know we're holed up here."

"And the second thing?"

"That my brother was actually trying to find a lab for us."

"You doubted that?"

"He's my brother. I know him too well." She shifted to Max's side and twined her leg through his. "Did you tell Bessler why we needed the lab?"

"No. I didn't trust him until the moment he got shot with the dart. I still don't trust him, but he figured you might be mixing up a batch of weak T-101 to get us through the withdrawals."

"Adrian was sharp. He removed himself from Tempest's tracking system and managed to find us faster than Tempest did." She sighed. "What a waste."

"At this rate, Tempest isn't going to have any agents left to do its dirty work."

"He'll recruit more, won't he? Caliban. This whole thing—" she fashioned a big circle in the air with her hands "—is bigger than you and me. It's not just about developing an antidote to T-101. It's about stopping Caliban."

"We have to find out who he is before anyone can stop him."

"Do you really believe the CIA and Prospero are in league with him? It seems to me they're the two agencies that *can* stop him."

He ruffled her hair. "That's for you to find out, Ava. You're going to see this thing through. I have faith in you."

She clenched her teeth and pushed the dark feelings aside. When she and Max were lying here together, so close both physically and mentally, she could forget that they had just three more days together before he left her. And she'd never see him again.

He must've sensed her funk because he curled his toes against her feet and nuzzled her neck. "We picked at breakfast and skipped lunch completely. Are you down with another feast in bed?"

"I could go for that." She twisted her fingers together. "What's going to happen to Bessler?"

"If he's still alive, Tempest probably has him. If he's dead, the cleanup crew will take care of all the details."

"I'd like to think he's alive. Tempest can have him for now, but when I produce that antidote we'll get him back." She sat up, her heart galloping. "That's it, Max."

"Hmm?" He looked up from the room service menu and she snatched it from his hands.

"Tempest can have you back, too. Eventually, I'll have that formula ready to go and we'll save all of the Tempest agents, including you."

One side of his mouth quirked up in a half smile. "How will you ever find me again?"

She blinked. "I'll find you, Max. Wherever you are in the world, whatever you're doing, I'll find you."

"I almost believe you when you talk like that." He rubbed his hand up her arm, and she shook him off impatiently.

"Tell me you'll think about it. We may even get the antidote to you before Tempest can send you out in the field again."

"I'll think about it." He shook open the menu again and ran his finger down a row of items. "Cheeseburgers were good, but I could go for some pasta."

She stared at him over the edge of the menu and held her breath. It wouldn't do any good to shout at this immovable piece of granite. She'd work on him gradually. Hell, she wasn't above using her body to convince him. She'd give him such a mind-blowing experience in bed tonight, he'd agree to anything.

"You're smiling." He tapped her with the corner of the menu. "I see you like the idea of pasta."

"Let me see that thing." She held out her hand for the menu. "Do they have any whipped cream, hot fudge and strawberries?"

He raised an eyebrow at her. "I don't know what the strawberries would be like this time of year, but I'm sure they can scrape up some hot fudge and whipped cream."

"Purrrfect." She arched her back and tousled her hair.

He grabbed her around the waist and pulled her into his arms. "You're damned sexy, Dr. Whitman."

She wouldn't even correct him this time. He could call her Dr. Whitman until his dying day, as long as he delayed his dying day by turning himself over to Tempest.

Closing her eyes, she lifted her face for his kiss. When it didn't come, she opened one eye to find Max searching her face.

She thrust out her bottom lip. "What happened to that kiss?"

"You are so beautiful." His fingers dabbled lightly over her nose and mouth. "I'm imprinting you on my memory."

"You're already imprinted here in my heart." She tapped her chest, tight with emotion.

He tossed the menu over his shoulder. "It's a little early for dinner anyway. I think I want my dessert first—forget the whipped cream."

Just when they got comfortable under the covers, her phone rang. As always these days, the sound caused a shaft of fear to plow through her heart.

She rolled to the side and swept it from the nightstand. She met Max's eyes over the glowing display and peeled her tongue from the roof of her mouth. "It's Cody."

"Answer it."

"What's up, Cody? Are you okay?"

"Besides a string of crazy things happening in Snow Haven ever since you and that cyborg showed up, I'm fine. And you're gonna be fine, too."

"Why? What happened?"

"I got you a lab."

Chapter Seventeen

"Where? How? What?" She bounced on the bed. "I love you. You're the best brother in the world."

"Wow, before I was the scourge of mankind for mixing you up in my illegal activities. Now I'm freakin' hero material."

"Cut to the chase, Cody." Max threw off the covers and swung his legs over the side of the bed.

"You could've told me I was on Speaker, Ava." Cody coughed. "Hey, man, I totally meant that cyborg comment as a compliment."

Max grunted. "Whatever. Spill."

"That one guy I knew who was out of town got back to me when he heard about the money involved. He knows I'm no snitch."

"Which is coming in very handy right now." Ava's voice squeaked. She could barely contain her excitement. "Go on."

"Anyway, he has a place that he abandoned because the DEA was onto him."

Max interrupted. "Does the DEA know about this place?"

"No. My friend abandoned the place when the DEA started tailing him. Nobody knows about the lab except him and his partner, and now us."

Max asked, "Where's his partner?"

"Uh, dude's in jail."

"Great." Ava nibbled the side of her thumb. "Where is this place, Cody? Is it ready to go?"

"I already have the key and the code and someone's delivering all the chemicals you need as we speak. I gave the guy your money already, including the dude who got the chemicals, and I kept my cut. You said I could keep a percentage, right?"

"We did." Max walked to the window and peered through the blinds. "How are we going to get the key from you? I don't want you near the hotel right now."

"I don't think I'm being followed. Haven't noticed anything since the break-in."

"Humor the cyborg."

Cody choked. "A friend of mine works at the Haven Brewery in town. Her name's Dina. I'll leave it with her— no questions asked."

"Got it." Max grabbed the hotel pad of paper by the phone. "Now, where is this lab?"

Cody gave them detailed directions to a place south of Salt Lake City, along with the code for the door. "You have to follow these directions exactly because you'll never find the place using your GPS or a map. As far as I can tell, it's in the middle of nowhere."

"That's exactly what we're looking for." Ava took a twirl around the room. "Cody?"

"Yeah?"

"Have I ever told you you're the best brother in the world?"

"Yeah, like five minutes ago. Look, I don't know what you two are up to, but be careful. And, cyborg?"

"Are you talking to me?" Max rolled his eyes at Ava.

"Don't let anything bad happen to my sister. She's all I got."

"I won't." Max joined her at the foot of the bed and curled his arm around her shoulders, pulling her close. "She's all I got, too."

When Cody hung up, Ava jumped into Max's arms, wrapping her legs around his waist. "He came through. I can't believe it. He came through."

"Are you sure you want to do this?" He smoothed her hair back from her face. "It's going to be dangerous."

She wrinkled her nose. "How? I've been working in labs for the past ten years of my life. I know my way around a lab."

"Adrian Bessler had your brother bugged. How do we know Tempest hasn't done the same?"

"You said yourself, Tempest tracked us here from Arnoff's computer. Tempest doesn't know about Cody. He's off their radar."

"He was, but nothing remains a secret from Tempest for long."

"Then we'd better get moving." She wriggled out of his arms. "I've got a batch of T-101 antidote to cook up."

"Before we start packing up—" he shook his tin of pills "—I'm going to pop one of these for what I hope is my last time."

A half an hour later, they'd packed their bags and Ava stood at the door looking back into the room.

Max nudged her. "Are you ready?"

"I just want to remember where I spent one of the happiest nights of my life."

He kissed her ear. "I'm going to give you plenty of those, Dr. Whitman."

With the car packed up, they drove into town and

parked in a public lot. Max hesitated before opening the door.

"What's wrong?"

"Every time we come into this town, something bad happens."

Before she opened her door, she blew him a kiss. "Our luck just changed."

The crowds on the streets of Snow Haven were thicker at night than during the day, the restaurants bustling with people eagerly awaiting the first snowfall.

The Haven Brewery had a line out the door, and Max shouldered his way through, dragging her along in his wake.

They hung on the end of the bar, and Ava tapped the wrist of a waitress picking up a tray of drinks. "Is Dina here tonight?"

She pointed to a pretty blonde behind the bar, filling a pitcher of beer. "Dina! Customer over here wants to see you."

Ava thanked the waitress, and when Dina finished topping off the pitcher, she wiped her hands on a bar towel and approached them.

"Let's see, you want the Haven pale ale and you want the Haven IPA, right?" She winked.

Ava nodded, suppressing a smile. Cody couldn't resist going all secret agent on them.

When Dina slid the beers toward them, she slipped a key beneath Ava's mug.

Ava took a sip of beer through the foam, the malty taste filling her mouth. "This is good."

Max eyed her over the rim of his mug. "Do you really think you should be tipsy in the lab?"

"It's one beer."

"One very big beer, and I've already seen how you handle your booze, and it ain't pretty."

She punched his rock-hard biceps and took another tiny sip of beer. Her ears perked up when she heard the man next to them mention the ice-skating rink.

She glanced at Max, but she could tell by the hard lines of his face that he was already focused on the conversation.

"Yeah, it was weird. The guy went down like a sack of potatoes. I guess he tripped or something, but he wasn't getting up."

Max sidled closer to the man and said, "I was there watching my daughter skate. We left when he was still down. What happened to him? Did he die?"

The man took a gulp of his beer and wiped the foam from his upper lip. "No, no, that was the other guy in the bus station bathroom. That guy dropped dead from a heart attack, I heard. This guy was okay."

"Really?" Ava gripped the handle of her mug so hard, she half expected it to explode in her hand. "You mean he got up and skated away?"

"Nah, some guy, a family member I guess, came to his rescue and got him up."

Max traced a bead of moisture on the outside of his glass. "The attendant was going to call 911. Did the ambulance take him away?"

"Nope. His brother, or whatever, took him away before the ambulance got there." He elbowed his friend in the ribs. "Some brother. If it was me, I'd want to go to the hospital. That guy was out cold, from the looks of it."

"Yeah, me too." Max shoved his glass away from him. "We gotta go, honey. Olive will be happy to hear the man at the rink was okay."

Ava waved to Dina and pushed back from the bar.

Max paid for the drinks, leaving Dina a hundred-dollar tip.

When they hit the sidewalk, Max cursed and took her arm, hustling her toward the parking lot.

"What's wrong, Max? I know you think being in Tempest's clutches is the worst thing ever, but at least Adrian's alive."

"Being a Tempest drone is not being alive, Ava."

She puffed out a breath, happy for the hundredth time that Cody had secured the lab. Max would've never gone for her plan to return to Tempest only to be rescued by the antidote later, no matter how much whipped cream and hot fudge were involved.

He beeped the remote for their little car. "It's not just being under the spell of Tempest again. Tempest has Bessler and they'll be privy to any information he has—including info about Cody and maybe even the bug Bessler put in his place. Do you know if Cody was home when he called us?"

Max's words had instilled a cold fear throughout her body. "I think so. We need to warn him."

"I don't want you to call him. If Tempest does know about him, he'll be tracked."

She pressed a fist to her lips and then clapped her hands. "Dina! I'll give a message to him via Dina. She's already proven herself to be discreet."

"I'll drive you around the front of the bar and wait for you in the street."

He exited the parking lot and pulled the car in front of the bar, double-parking.

Ava ran into the bar, threading her way through the crowd. She gestured to Dina to join her at the end of the bar.

"Hey, thanks for the tip."

"Do you want another?"

The girl's heavily lined eyes widened. "Sure."

"I need to get a message to Cody but I can't call him on his phone. I don't want you to call him with this message either. Can you get him to come down here and talk to him in person?"

She smiled a slow, seductive smile. "I can get Cody to do anything I want."

"Too much information." Ava held up her hand. "When he gets here, tell him to leave town immediately and throw his phone away. Tell him it's life-and-death."

Dina's jaw dropped. "Seriously?"

"Seriously."

"I'll do it, of course."

"Thanks." Ava slipped her another hundred-dollar bill, courtesy of Max's stash. "Maybe you should join him."

She ran back to the car, still double-parked, and jumped in. "Done."

"We need to get out to that lab as soon as possible."

They left town just as a light snow began dusting the treetops. Max maneuvered the car down the mountain and they sped past Salt Lake City, heading south.

Ava clutched the piece of paper with the directions to the lab in her lap, crinkling the corners. "We're turning off in about four miles. What's the odometer reading?"

He poked a finger at the control panel. "I just reset it. I'll keep my eye on it, not that it looks like there are going to be a lot of options for turning off in the next five miles."

Darkness had descended and the snow had turned to slush.

Ava turned up the heat and folded her arms across her body. "Too warm for you?"

"It's fine." He flipped down the vent. "We don't have to

go through with this, Ava. We can drive on by and spend our last few days together someplace warm and safe."

"It's right within our reach." Her fingers danced along his forearm. "I'm not afraid."

"I know you're not. That's what scares me."

He took the turnoff and she continued to guide him by reading the directions from the notepaper. "I hope you have a flashlight in your bag of tricks because it's dark out here."

"What would you expect from a covert meth lab?" He scratched his chin. "Where did your brother get all those chemicals?"

"Don't ask." She turned in her seat. "You're not going to snitch him off, are you? I mean, about the meth lab and the drugs."

"I don't like the idea of someone out here making and selling illegal drugs, but I think under the circumstances I can let it pass." He shrugged. "Besides, the guy's out of business and his partner's in prison, right?"

"For now."

"That's all I have—right now."

He turned the car down what looked like an abandoned road, and a few buildings crouched together in a semicircle.

He cut the headlights. "Looks like there was a little light industry here at one point that never got off the ground."

She waved the paper. "It's the building on the left. It should have a keypad for the code he gave us and a padlock on the sliding door."

Max wheeled the car behind the building and parked. He dragged his bag out of the trunk and fished through it for a flashlight. He aimed the beam at the ground. "Stay close."

She hooked her finger in his belt loop and followed him around to the front of the building. As he shined the light on the keypad, she punched in the code with stiff fingers. Something clicked and she whispered, "That's a good sign."

Max inserted the key in the lock and sprang it open. He pocketed the lock. Then he yanked on the sliding door, and after a brief resistance, it slid open.

They stepped inside what felt like a cavernous space, and Max shut the door behind them.

Ava felt for the switch next to the door, and when she flipped it, white light bathed the room. She let out a long breath as she took in the gleaming stainless-steel surfaces and the neat placement of the lab equipment.

Max dropped his bag on the floor. "Wow, our meth cooker was a neat freak."

"It's perfect." She flexed her fingers. "I can do this, Max."

"Get to it." He gestured around the room. "I'm going to take care of security."

He watched Ava for a few minutes as she washed her hands, pulled on a pair of gloves and positioned a pair of safety goggles over her face. How the hell did he get so lucky to have this incredible, brave woman on his side?

He withdrew his weapon and loaded a second one. He placed it on the counter near Ava. "This one's for you. All you have to do is point and shoot."

She tapped a metal drum on the floor. "Can you crank this open for me?"

"Should I put on some gloves?"

"Yes, and some goggles. The fumes can sting your eyes."

"And you're going to be injecting me with this stuff?"

"It's better than the other stuff I'd been injecting you with for almost two years."

He opened the spigot on the drum for her. "Is this chemical flammable?"

She pointed across the room. "That stuff is. Why?"

He winked. "You do your thing, and I'll do mine."

While Ava continued to measure, pour, stir and heat, he secured the lab with a few booby traps using the equipment from his duffel. Tempest agents were always prepared.

If Tempest had their hands on Bessler, it was only a matter of time before they got information from him on Cody, including audio from the bug Bessler had set up in Cody's apartment. They should have some time on their side, since Bessler had been completely out of it.

Once Max outfitted the room, he slid open the front door. "I'm going to move the car away from the building. Be right back."

She said something unintelligible but didn't look up from her work, so he figured it wasn't important. Once outside, he surveyed the building and couldn't detect any light coming from it.

He moved the car another twenty feet from the structure, lining it up with a boarded window in the back—their escape hatch.

He returned to the lab and punched in the code to lock the door. He sat on a table facing the door. The building had no windows, so he couldn't see anyone coming but he could hear them.

"How are you doing over there?"

"It's coming along. Say what you will about Dr. Arnoff, but the man was a genius."

"Yeah, like a mad scientist."

"This formula is beautifully simple."

"I'll take your word for it. Let's just hope after all this hoopla, the damned stuff works."

"Count on it."

He let her work in peace, his muscles aching with the tension of the wait. Different noises came from the various equipment Ava was using, and then Max heard a low droning sound.

Tilting his head, he moved closer to Ava's work space. "What is that?"

She flipped the switch of some vibrating machine and the buzzing merged with the low drone.

He drew his finger across his throat, and she stopped the machine. "What?"

"Do you hear that noise? Is that something you're doing?"

She spread her gloved hands. "No."

Suddenly the drone turned into a roar, and the building shook.

Max clutched his weapon and tilted his head back to look at the ceiling, which seemed to be vibrating.

A voice boomed over a loudspeaker above them. "Give it up, Duvall. Come out with your hands up or we'll destroy that lab and everything...and everyone in it."

Chapter Eighteen

Ava dropped something on the floor and it shattered.

His heart jumped. "You okay?"

"Yeah. What do we do?"

"I'm not surrendering to Tempest, not now, not ever." He kept his weapon trained on the ceiling. "Get your stuff together. We're out of here."

"How are we going to escape? There's a helicopter up there, and I'm pretty sure they have weapons—lots of them. Besides, I…"

He held up his hand. "I know you're not ready yet, Ava, but I don't want to hear it. You have to abandon the antidote. Put down the test tube and pick up the gun I gave you."

The voice came through the bullhorn again. "We want to hear what you have to say, Duvall. Call the hotline. We'll pick up from the chopper."

Max reached for his phone, and Ava jerked her head up from pulling off her gloves. "What are you doing?"

"Buying time. I need to set our escape in motion, but I need you to pick up that gun and crouch down in the corner by the front door. Keep your goggles on."

He punched in the number for the Tempest hotline,

the line they used when they got into trouble. He'd never had to use it yet.

They must've patched the line through to the helicopter because someone picked up on the first ring and it was the same voice from the loudspeaker.

"That's better, Duvall."

"Who is this? Foster?"

"Does it matter? I'm Tempest. I'm authorized to speak for Caliban."

"What do you want from me?" Max put the phone on Speaker and then crept to the boarded-up window in the back of the building, past Ava's work area, where she'd been minutes away from saving his life.

The anonymous voice continued. "We don't want to kill you, Duvall. You're a valuable asset. Caliban thinks you're the most valuable agent we have. Give yourself up to us and we'll make sure Dr. Whitman gets out of here alive."

Liars. He checked the wires he'd set up earlier and glanced at Ava huddled in the corner, one hand shoved into the pocket of her jacket, the other clutching a gun.

"Is Dr. Whitman listening?"

"Yes."

"Dr. Whitman, you can take Dr. Arnoff's place. He neglected to tell us about that antidote. We'll allow you to mix up that antidote and more closely monitor our agents, including Max."

Max headed for the front of the building, with only one ear listening to the lies spewing from the phone. He checked his wiring there and lit a fuse hanging from the ceiling. There was no turning back now.

Max gave Ava a thumbs-up sign and muted the phone. He joined her in the corner and whispered, "Stay put but get ready to move through the back of the building once it blows."

Her eyes widened. "Blows?"

He put his finger to his lips and unmuted the phone.

Ava rose from her crouch and shouted into the phone in Max's hand. "Where's Agent Bessler?"

"He's safe and sound, Dr. Whitman. We treated him and he'll be fine."

"You mean he'll be a drone for Tempest."

"It's what our agents do, Dr. Whitman. Dr. Arnoff understood that and used the opportunity to conduct experiments that would've never been allowed in the medical community. You can do the same."

Max held up the phone and nodded.

Ava yelled, "No, thanks!"

Max punched in a three-digit number on his cell phone and the back of the building exploded outward, rocking the structure.

He grabbed Ava's hand. "Let's go!"

They ran toward the gaping hole in the wall in a crouch while machine gun fire sounded from above.

He pulled Ava close. "When we hit the opening, I'm going to lunge forward and I'm taking you with me. Get ready."

They stumbled through the gap, and Max launched himself forward just as the building behind them exploded. The force propelled them closer to the car, the heat intense on his back, the ends of his hair singeing.

The helicopter above them screamed and whined, and he twisted his head around to see it lurch onto its side, its spinning blades glancing the roof of the burning building.

Max dragged himself up from the ground and Ava popped up beside him.

She clambered into the driver's side and crawled across

the console to the passenger seat, dropping her weapon on the floor, and he gunned the engine before he was even sitting in the driver's seat.

Another explosion burst into the night sky as the chopper plowed through the roof of the building.

Max hit the accelerator as burning debris fell around them.

Ava turned around in her seat to watch the lab collapse. From his rearview mirror, Max witnessed a ball of fire rolling toward the sky.

Not until he reached the road that connected to the main highway did he let out a long, smoky breath.

He rubbed a patch of soot from Ava's white cheek. "Are you all right? Not hurt?"

She covered her face with her hands and said through parted fingers, "When you said you were securing the building, I didn't know that meant you were booby-trapping it."

"I figured the less you knew the better. You had other things to concentrate on. I didn't want to scare you or distract you."

"How'd you know they'd be coming by helicopter? How'd you know they'd be coming at all?"

"I didn't know about the helicopter, but car or helicopter, that explosion would stop either one. And once I heard they had Bessler, I figured it was only a matter of time before they found that lab. They'd debrief Bessler or shoot him up with truth serum or torture him, but one way or another they were going to find out everything he knew about us, including that bug he put in your brother's apartment."

She ran her hands through her hair, showering bits of debris into her lap. "I hope Dina got to Cody and he made it out of Snow Haven safely."

"Once you get to a secure location, you can call him. Tempest is not done with you, but once we part company

I'm sending you to Prospero. You can tell them our story. You can show them the formula for the antidote. They'll take care of you, whether they believe you or not."

"You still don't trust Prospero? You won't come with me?"

"Even if I had the time, which I don't, I wouldn't turn myself over to Prospero, but you should be okay."

"And who says you don't have the time?"

He grabbed her hand and circled his thumb in her palm. "We're not going to find another lab and get our hands on those chemicals in three days, Ava. It was a good try and we were close. I appreciate everything you did. I more than appreciate you. I love you. Always know that."

He steeled himself for more tears. It was a bittersweet victory that he was human enough now to be undone by Ava's tears.

She laughed.

He whipped his head around, but she continued to laugh, her eyes sparkling in the darkness of the car. Maybe the stress and tension had finally driven her off the deep end.

"I guess the idea of a doomed man falling in love could be funny and I'd rather see laughter than tears from you, but are you sure you're okay?"

"You're not a doomed man, Max."

"Three pills, three days."

She plunged her hand in the pocket of her jacket. She pulled it out and opened it wide, cupping a glass vial in her palm.

"Do you want to reconsider telling me you love me? This is the T-101 antidote, and you have a lifetime with me ahead of you."

Epilogue

Prospero's chief, Jack Coburn, cleared his throat over the phone. "We've been suspicious about Tempest's actions for a while, Duvall, so I'm inclined to believe your story."

Ava came up behind Max, sitting on the edge of the hotel bed, and draped her arms around his shoulders.

He captured her hand and pressed a kiss against her palm. "Do you know who Caliban is?"

"No, but we'd like to find out."

"I take it the CIA doesn't know either."

"Caliban reports to the director, just like I do, but Tempest has always been more secretive about its organization and actions."

"Now you know why."

"I repeat my offer for both you and Ms. Whitman. You can come in from the field and we'll protect you."

"It's not that I don't trust you, Coburn."

Jack Coburn interrupted him. "But you don't trust me. I understand, but to stop Tempest we need to know more about its operations. We want to debrief you."

"I get that, but we'll have to do it over a secure connection and from a safe distance. We will take you up on the offer of the new identities though, and Ava will turn over the formula for the T-101 antidote."

"That's a deal. Be careful out there and we'll keep you posted as we move forward with this investigation."

"What's next?"

"Nina Moore, Agent Skinner's fiancée. We have reason to believe she's being watched."

"Whatever you do, take care of her."

"We're on it, Duvall. You need to disappear now."

Max ended the call and reclined on the bed, pulling her down next to him. "We're done with Tempest—for now. We'll let Prospero handle them. You know, I think that's what Caliban wanted all along—some kind of face-off between Tempest and Prospero."

"Well, it looks like he's going to get his wish." She waved a hand around the hotel room. "Do we need to disappear any more than this?"

"Prospero will send us a couple of new identities. We can go even further underground."

She caressed his strong face, which had lost its hardness since he'd taken the antidote. "Can underground include a tropical paradise somewhere?"

"Absolutely." He kissed her mouth. "But we're not joining your brother and Dina in Hawaii, if that's what you're thinking."

"Hawaii?" She snapped her fingers. "We can go more exotic than Hawaii, can't we?"

"We can go wherever you want, Dr. Whitman."

She slipped her hand beneath his T-shirt and swirled her fingernails over his hard belly. "Now that you have your life back, are you sure you want to spend it with me?"

"If you can handle a cyborg for the rest of your life."

"Cyborg?" She snuggled next to his side and rested her head against his chest. "You're all man, Max Duvall, and you're all mine—forever."

* * * * *

The showdown between Prospero and
Tempest is just heating up!
Look for the continuation of Carol Ericson's
BROTHERS IN ARMS: RETRIBUTION
miniseries next month when
THE PREGNANCY PLOT goes on sale.

"You hurt me, Dylan. Because what you think you want and what you really want are two different things."

"I want you," he whispered, backing her up against the wall. "*You* are what I think I want and what I really want."

"But you might change your mind." Shelby began to look away again.

"I am not going to change my mind." Dylan brought his hands up on either side of her head, burrowing his fingers in her damp hair. "I hurt you, because I'm so used to pushing everyone away, and I'm sorry. You are what I want. I won't hurt you again."

Dylan could see the doubt in Shelby's eyes, and it killed him. He was afraid she would pull away. But she leaned toward him, putting her lips gently against his.

He kissed her back gently. But then the hunger— the *heat*—that had sparked between them since the first moment they'd met flared again. And all thought of soft and gentle was left behind.

LEVERAGE

BY
JANIE CROUCH

MILLS & BOON

Published in Great Britain 2015
by Mills & Boon, an imprint of Harlequin (UK) Limited,
Eton House, 18-24 Paradise Road, Richmond, Surrey, TW9 1SR

© 2015 Janie Crouch

ISBN: 978-0-263-25311-5

46-0715

Harlequin (UK) Limited's policy is to use papers that are natural, renewable and recyclable products and made from wood grown in sustainable forests. The logging and manufacturing processes conform to the legal environmental regulations of the country of origin.

Printed and bound in Spain
by CPI, Barcelona

Janie Crouch has loved to read romance her whole life. She cut her teeth on Mills & Boon® romance novels as a pre-teen, then moved on to a passion for romantic suspense as an adult. Janie lives with her husband and four children overseas. Janie enjoys traveling, long-distance running, movie-watching, knitting and adventure/obstacle racing. You can find out more about her at www.janiecrouch.com.

Chapter One

Sometimes a man just wanted to be left alone.

Dylan Branson didn't think that was too much to ask. He'd served his country for years, both on American soil and off, and had the scars—both physical and emotional—to show for it. But that was behind him now. Far behind him.

Not that you would know it from the voice talking at Dylan from the phone.

Dylan held the phone out at arm's length, staring at it as if it were a snake about to bite him. He'd rather be handling a snake. Seriously, give him a cottonmouth over what was at the other end of this phone line.

It was Dennis Burgamy, Dylan's boss when he worked at Omega Sector, a covert interagency task force. A crime-fighting, problem-solving, *get-stuff-done* unit, made up of the most elite agents the country had to offer. And Dylan had been one of the best of the best.

But not anymore.

Despite its arm's-length distance, Dylan could still hear Dennis Burgamy clearly on the other line. Dylan hadn't held the phone against his ear in at least two minutes, but evidently Burgamy hadn't missed Dylan's input into the conversation because the other man hadn't even noticed Dylan wasn't talking.

Which was pretty typical of Dylan's former boss. The difference now was that Dylan didn't have to listen to the other man. Burgamy wasn't his boss anymore.

Finally silence came from the other end of the phone. Dylan cautiously brought it back to his ear.

"Are you there, Branson?"

"Yeah, I'm here." Dylan sat on the porch of the house he'd mostly built himself and looked out over the pinkish light of early evening hitting the Blue Ridge Mountains surrounding him on three sides. Those mountains had been the only thing able to bring him a measure of peace over the past few years since his wife's death, and he tried to draw on that peace again now. To no avail. "You do remember that I don't work for you anymore, right, Burgamy?"

Dylan's statement was met with a dramatic sigh. There had never been any lost love between Burgamy and any of the Branson siblings. Dylan's sister and two brothers were all active Omega agents, and all had butted heads with Burgamy at some point.

"You are in the charter airline business now, Dylan," Burgamy reminded him. "I'm not asking you to do anything you wouldn't do for any other paying customer."

It was true. For the past four years Dylan had been flying customers and cargo wherever they needed to go all over the East Coast with his Cessna. But Dylan wasn't so desperate for business that he wanted to be at Burgamy's beck and call.

"I'm all booked. Sorry."

"Look, Dylan…" Dylan recognized the change in Burgamy's tone. Evidently Burgamy realized threatening Dylan wouldn't get him what he wanted, so he'd decided to try a different tactic. "How about if you do this for us, then I'll erase all record of Sawyer's little incident last year."

The *little incident* referred to Dylan's youngest brother, Sawyer, punching Burgamy in the jaw and knocking his boss unconscious during an operation that was going wrong. Sawyer managed to keep his job at Omega, but only barely. And although Sawyer was able to keep his job, the occurrence would still keep his brother from ever being able to move up in official ranks. Of course, until recently, Sawyer had no interest in ever moving higher than the rank of agent. Doing so would mean a desk job, which had frightened him no end. But now that Sawyer was married to sweet little Megan and expecting a baby, a desk job might be more appealing to him.

And damn it, this made saying no to Burgamy much more complicated.

Dylan looked out at the mountains. He didn't want to set foot back inside Omega. He'd done it a couple of times since he'd quit over six years ago, and each time had been fraught with disaster. Dylan still had residual discomfort from the beating he'd taken while trying to help his brother Cameron on an Omega mission a while ago.

In Dylan's experience, every trip to Omega led to some sort of pain. And he wasn't interested in experiencing that again if he had any other option.

"It's important, Branson," Burgamy continued. "We need these codes. And Shelby Keelan, the lady with the codes, is a friend of your sister-in-law. I'm sure Megan will take it as a personal insult if you don't help us with this matter."

Dylan closed his eyes. Burgamy didn't know it, but Dylan was already in. And if Dylan hadn't been, bringing up Megan would've done it. Dylan liked Sawyer's wife—the brilliant computer scientist—a great deal. She was good for his brother; had somehow managed to tame the playboy of the family without even trying.

And now Sawyer and Megan were having a baby.

Which was totally great for Dylan's parents, who had wanted grandkids for the longest time. They'd finally get their wish.

For just a second, that old ache crept into Dylan's chest. He pushed away the thought of the baby that hadn't made it when his wife had been killed. Nothing could be done about that now.

If Megan wanted him to pick up some codes or whatever from a friend of hers and bring the codes to Omega, Dylan would do it. He loved his brother, loved his sister-in-law and wanted to do anything he could to keep that baby growing happy and healthy inside her.

Of course, he didn't know why Megan's friend couldn't just email the codes. Why Dylan needed to hand deliver them to Washington, DC. Or why this lady couldn't just deliver them herself. But whatever. He knew better than to ask. With Omega, things were never simple.

Effective? Yes. Simple? No.

For example, things could've been much simpler if Megan or Sawyer had just called Dylan themselves and asked him to fly in the codes. He'd already be gassing up his Cessna right now. But Burgamy couldn't resist an opportunity to lord power over any member of the Branson family. It bugged Dylan to submit to Burgamy, but he might as well get it over with.

"Fine, Burgamy, I'll do it."

"Good. Because Shelby Keelan is on her way to you right now. She should be arriving in Falls Run in about thirty minutes. Meeting you at the only restaurant your blip on the map seems to have."

Dylan hung up the phone without saying anything else. Burgamy had obviously told the woman to come out here even before asking Dylan, sure he would get Dylan's cooperation. Dylan hated being a foregone conclusion.

He watched the pinkening sky for a few more moments,

allowing the phone to fall next to him in the swing on his porch rather than crush it against the wall the way he wanted to.

There were things Dylan regretted about his deliberate walk away from Omega six years ago. But having to listen to Dennis Burgamy wasn't one of them.

Dylan would get the codes from Megan's friend, fly them to Omega, say a quick hello to his siblings and get the hell out. There would be no traversing up the sides of yachts, emergency takeoffs with people shooting at him or being beaten to within an inch of his life.

Like his last visits.

Dylan grabbed his phone and stood up. He'd have to get going if he was going to make it into town by the time Shelby Keelan arrived. His phone buzzed again in his hand. Dylan grimaced, hoping it wasn't Burgamy.

It wasn't.

"You are not my current favorite sibling, Sawyer." Dylan's words were tough, but his greeting held no malice.

"Ha. Well, I'm still Mom's favorite, so that's all that matters," Sawyer responded. "I guess I'm too late to catch you before Burgamy does."

"Just got off the phone with him."

"Damn it. I'm sorry, Dylan. I told Burgamy I would handle it, but you know him."

Dylan rolled his eyes. Yes, he was quite familiar with Burgamy's tactics. "Looks like I'll be delivering some codes to you tonight." Dylan looked out the window; menacing clouds were rolling in behind the setting sun. "Actually, it might be much later tonight. It looks like a storm is rolling in."

"Thanks for doing this, man. The codes are—" Sawyer broke off midsentence and Dylan could hear his muffled words to someone else before they stopped entirely.

"Dylan?" A much softer female voice came on the line.

"Hey, Megan. How are you feeling?"

"Fine now that I'm not hurling my guts out multiple times a day." Dylan could hear the smile in his petite sister-in-law's voice. "I'm sorry about Burgamy, Dylan. Sawyer wanted us to leave him out of it totally, but I wouldn't let him."

"It's no problem, hon. I can handle Burgamy."

"Thanks for meeting Shelby. She and I knew each other in college. She's…special."

Dylan didn't know what to make of *special*. That could mean a lot of things. "Well, I hope you don't mean special as in special needs like your husband."

Megan laughed. "No, Shelby is definitely not special needs. The opposite, in fact. A brilliant computer-game programmer."

"Well, either way it's no problem. I'll see you guys soon. I've got to get going if I'm going to meet Shelby on time. Burgamy didn't leave much wiggle room."

"Thanks again, Dylan."

"Anything for you, sweetheart. You just keep my little niece or nephew safe, okay? Bye."

Dylan disconnected and went inside his house of the past four years. He had never brought a woman here; he'd preferred encounters to happen at their place instead. It made leaving much easier and awkward talks about why he couldn't stay much less necessary.

Dylan preferred his solitude and planned to keep it that way. He'd tried dating, but many women thought being a widower meant he needed to be smothered with attention. With love. They wanted to wrap their arms around him and help chase his demons away. Dylan knew they meant well, but he couldn't tolerate that kind of unrelenting attention.

Dylan would face his own demons. Always had.

So he kept things casual with women, and kept them

out of his personal space. Sometimes, much more rarely now, he got physically involved, but he was sure to let a woman know up front that his heart was off the table. A future with Dylan was not an option.

Dylan walked into his bedroom and changed out of the dirty work clothes he'd had on for normal plane maintenance. He decided to take a quick shower, cursing Burgamy again when he couldn't linger under the hot water to help loosen some of the residual soreness from old wounds. Thirty minutes wasn't a long time to get to Falls Run from his house.

And yes, Sally's was the only sit-down restaurant in the small town, more of a diner than anything else. There were also a couple of fast-food places, a gas station, a bar, hardware store and bank. Falls Run wasn't *that* small. And it was perfect for Dylan's purposes in a town: small enough that he didn't have to worry about too many strangers wandering around, and large enough that he was able to get what he needed regularly enough for both his business and personal needs.

He'd chosen Falls Run on purpose. At the borders of Virginia, Tennessee and North Carolina, it allowed him access, via his Cessna, to almost anywhere on the East and Gulf coasts. Plus, the town was surrounded by the Blue Ridge Mountains. In Dylan's opinion, you couldn't ask for better real estate than that.

And it was far enough from Washington, DC, and Omega for him to stay away from his past there.

Dylan rolled his eyes. At least he *thought* Falls Run was far enough away. Evidently not, given the past few years. Dylan got dressed in jeans and a button-down shirt, grabbed his keys and wallet from the dresser and headed out the door to his pickup truck.

What the hell. He'd enjoy a nice meal at Sally's—he was tired of his own cooking anyway—and meet Megan's

Chapter Two

For the first time she could remember, Shelby Keelan cursed her gifts when it came to math. Normally she was very appreciative of them: they allowed her to make a great living doing something she enjoyed—making games kids loved to play. But not this time. This time her abilities had brought her out of her nice comfortable home to a strange town to meet a strange person she had no real desire to meet.

Of course, Shelby rarely had the desire to meet anyone new.

She easily found a parking spot at the restaurant in Falls Run, although the lot was across the street from the diner due to the narrow shape of the town forced by mountains. Shelby had been told there was only one restaurant and she couldn't miss it, but she'd still been a little worried. What kind of town had only one restaurant?

Evidently the town of Falls Run.

Shelby didn't mind small towns. She didn't mind big cities either. It was the people in both that tended to cause her stress. Shelby just didn't do people very well.

Even now, pulling into a mostly empty parking lot, she was pretty stressed out. Shelby knew she would need to make small talk. With strangers. Multiple strangers maybe. She had many talents, but chatting with people wasn't one of them. She was an introvert through and through.

Her introversion had driven her flamboyant mother crazy when Shelby was a child. Her mom wanted to show her off—as if people really wanted to hear some four-year-old recite pi to the two-hundredth digit—but young Shelby had just wanted to be alone.

Adult Shelby just wanted to be alone, too. Back at her own house in Knoxville, where everything had its place and was comfortable and safe and familiar. Where she didn't have to think too hard about what she did or what she said or if she was coming off as rude or unfriendly or standoffish.

It wasn't that Shelby was afraid of people, she really wasn't. She wasn't agoraphobic, as her mother tried so often to suggest. Wasn't afraid something terrible would happen to her if she left her house. People just...*exhausted* Shelby. So she chose to be around them as little as possible. Fortunately, she had a job developing games and software that allowed her to spend most of her time away from people. Perfect.

Plus, she had plenty of friends in her life, just mostly of the four-legged and furry variety. And none of them were disappointed when Shelby wasn't up to making small talk. They kept one another company just fine. And Shelby had a couple of the two-legged-friend versions, too.

But it took pretty grave circumstances to get Shelby to willingly leave her house and be around people she didn't know for extended periods of time as she was doing now.

Like a terrorist-attack countdown in the coding of a children's computer game. One that Shelby happened to discover two days ago. One that anyone else in the world would've missed.

But Shelby hadn't missed it, the way she never missed anything having to do with numbers. She had known immediately the numbers she saw were not part of the game. They clearly had been planted, and once Shelby dug into them a bit, she realized they were, in part, a countdown. But she couldn't figure out any more than that on her own.

Sure that she had stumbled on to something potentially criminal at best, downright sinister at worst, Shelby had emailed her computer engineering friend from their college days at MIT, Dr. Megan Fuller.

Except Megan was Dr. Megan Fuller-*Branson* now, and expecting a little baby Dr. Fuller-Branson in a couple of months.

Shelby had explained the coding she'd found and what she suspected. Most others would've scoffed or accused Shelby of overdramatizing, but Megan and Shelby had developed a healthy respect for each other years ago at MIT. They may not be the type to chat with each other over coffee, but they took each other seriously.

And it ended up that Megan was now working with her new husband at some sort of clandestine law enforcement agency that specialized in saving-the-world type of stuff. Quite convenient for the matter at hand. Especially since the codes had been planted by some terrorist group known as DS-13, who was evidently really bad news.

Spotting the codes and realizing their nefarious purpose had been the easy part for Shelby. The hard part had come when Megan had asked Shelby to travel to Washington, DC.

Shelby understood why Megan needed her to come in. The string of coding Shelby saw in the game had only come up for a moment before deleting itself. Very few people would've been looking at the game in its raw-data form, and nobody would've been able to catch the countdown codes and the coordinates embedded in it in the split second it was available.

Unless you were Shelby, who was able to memorize thousands of numbers at once just by looking at them. A complete photographic memory when it came to numbers. And coding, whether it be as innocent as games, or as deadly as a potential terrorist attack, was essentially numbers.

Shelby now had the numbers she saw permanently stuck in her head. She couldn't get rid of them even if she wanted to. Megan had the decoding software that would help make sense of it all. They needed to put together Shelby's brain and Megan's computer. And fast. Because whatever the countdown was for was happening about sixty hours from now.

Megan knew about Shelby's dislike of being around people. Driving to DC from Knoxville was too far, so Megan had mentioned her brother-in-law's charter airplane service. The way Shelby saw it, one person in a small airplane was much better than airports and large planes *full* of people. And it was Megan's husband's older brother. That shouldn't be too bad.

So here she was, pulling up to a restaurant based on a text message she'd received from somebody named Chantelle DiMuzio, personal assistant of Dennis Burgamy. The assistant had requested that Shelby call Burgamy, but Shelby couldn't remember the last time she'd used her phone to *talk* into. Her outgoing voice-mail message pretty much summed up her opinion about phone conversations:

Sorry, I can't take your call. Please hang up and text me.

Shelby could text much faster than she could talk. She could type twice as fast as that. She was off the charts on a numpad.

Finally, the Chantelle lady had left a message that Mr. Burgamy had arranged for Dylan Branson, Megan's brother-in-law, to meet her at the town's only restaurant. Branson would fly her into DC tonight.

Shelby put the car in Park. Okay. She could do this.

She was already a little shaky from an incident about fifteen miles back when some moron had literally driven her off the road. That was the problem with driving in the mountains: if someone wasn't paying attention—or worse, doing something stupid like texting and driving—and nearly hit you, then it was pretty much game over. These mountain roads with their sheer drops were pretty scary.

It was only because of Shelby's hypervigilance behind the wheel that she'd managed to stay on the road and not drive off the side of the mountain altogether. Shelby wasn't 100 percent sure of her driving skills—she really didn't drive terribly often, and never on roads like these—so she'd wanted to make sure she was paying extra-careful attention.

And thank goodness, because that idiot hadn't even seen her. Didn't slow down, stop, give an "oops, I'm sorry" wave or anything. Shelby could've been flipped upside down at the bottom of the ravine right now and she doubted the other driver would've even noticed. He, or she, just sped on.

So, all in all, not a great start to this adventure. And *adventure* was very much Megan's word, not Shelby's. Shelby's idea of adventure was more along the lines of trying the new Thai place across town, or branching off in a new direction for a video game she was developing. This whole scenario was way beyond *adventure* in Shelby's opinion.

Shelby opened her car door and heard thunder cracking in the darkening sky. Great. More adventure to add to the adventure. Could small planes even take off in a thunderstorm?

Shelby walked to the door of the diner and entered. How would she know who Dylan Branson was? Inside she looked around. There were a couple of middle-aged guys and a woman at the counter, an older lady at the cash register and a teenage waitress carrying food to a couple at a table near the door. Some dark-haired Calvin Klein–looking model sat back in the corner booth—yeah, Shelby *wished* she could be that lucky—and a shorter, stockier man in khakis and a pretty bad polo shirt sat at a table near him.

Nobody was wearing a Trust Me, I'm the Pilot T-shirt or held a sign with her name. So evidently Shelby wasn't going to be able to slip in without having to talk to anyone except Megan's brother-in-law.

Shelby approached the lady at the cash register. "Hi, excuse me—"

"Oh, my goodness. Honey, you're not from around here. I would remember that hair anywhere." The woman's voice wasn't unkind, but it was loud, drawing the attention of pretty much everyone at the diner.

Shelby sighed. Remarks about her hair weren't uncommon. It was red. Not a sweet, gentle auburn, but full-on red: garnet, poppies, wisps-of-fire red—Shelby had heard all the analogies. If she'd been born a few centuries earlier, she would've been burned at the stake as a witch just for her coloring.

Shelby tended to forget how much it grabbed people's attention when they first met her. "Um, yeah. It's really red, I know. I was wondering—"

"You couldn't get that color out of a bottle, I imagine. Especially not with your skin coloring. Your hair must be natural."

See? This was case and point why Shelby tended not to want to talk to people. Because really, did she have to go into her natural coloring with someone she'd known for less than ten seconds? Shelby didn't want to be rude, but neither did she want to talk about which side of the family her coloring was from.

And Shelby was sure that question, or something very similar, would be the next inquiry from the cash register lady.

"Yeah." Shelby remained noncommittal about the hair. "I'm looking for somebody. A pilot. His name is Dylan Branson. He was supposed to meet me here."

"Oh, yeah, honey, he's right over there." The lady gestured toward the corner, and Shelby looked over. Great, it was the balding guy in the bad polo shirt. Shelby thanked her and headed that way before the woman could ask any more questions about her hair.

Dylan Branson was eating what looked like meat loaf at his table and had just put a huge forkful into his mouth when Shelby walked up to him.

"Hi, Dylan Branson, right? I'm Shelby Keelan."

The man looked over at Shelby and his eyes bulged. He held his hand up in front of his mouth, rapidly chewing, and began standing up.

"No, don't get up. I didn't mean to interrupt your meal."

Shelby sat down across from him. Of course, the polite thing for Branson to do would've been to wait until she got there and then eat together, rather than shoveling food in right when he was supposed to meet her. But whatever. Shelby just hoped Megan's husband was a little more considerate than his brother.

And for the sake of her friend, Shelby hoped he was a little more handsome, too. Not balding and portly, like Dylan here. But maybe follically challenged didn't run in the Branson family, just this one brother.

And he was still chewing. How big of a bite could he have taken, for goodness' sake? The look he was giving her over his moving jaw was clearly confused.

"Take your time." Shelby smiled. She didn't want him to choke or anything. That wouldn't get her to DC very quickly.

"Oh, honey, not Tucker," the lady called out from behind the cash register, pointing to the man eating. Then she looked past Shelby to the booth beyond her in the corner. "Dylan Branson, shame on you. You knew this young lady was looking for you. You should've said something."

"I would've, Sally. But I wanted to see if Tucker would actually choke on the meat loaf while trying to talk to her first."

The deep voice came from the booth behind Shelby. She didn't need to look up to see who it was. She knew. The dark-haired, sexy-as-sin Calvin Klein model.

Chapter Three

The attraction punched him in the gut. Dylan had been punched enough times to know clear and well what it felt like: it stole your breath, caused you to wonder which end was up, made your whole body tingle.

Of course, it was usually followed by agony. But in this case it might be worth it.

Striking was the only word for Shelby Keelan. Her red hair fell around her face and shoulders in long wisps and curls that had escaped from the loose braid she seemed to have attempted at some point. Her eyes —now looking at him rather than Tucker—were a clear emerald green with a hint of gold in them.

But, for the love of all things holy, it was her freckles that were killing him. Scattered across her nose, her cheeks, her forehead. They were quite possibly the most alluring thing he had ever seen.

Shelby Keelan wasn't a traditional beauty, but she was striking.

From his corner booth where he could see the main entrance, kitchen entrance and emergency exit—old habits died hard—Dylan had seen her come in. He'd been almost positive who she was from that moment, and then her brief conversation with Sally had confirmed it.

He should've said something when she sat down at the

table near his booth and started talking to Tucker, but he couldn't resist seeing how that played out. Poor Tucker still looked as if he was going to have a heart attack.

Shelby Keelan sat in her seat at Tucker's table, her green eyes zeroed in on Dylan. She did not look amused.

"Confused strangers are the top entertainment around here, I take it?"

Uh-oh. Dylan stood, giving Shelby his most charming smile. "Not usually, I promise. I just couldn't resist seeing how Tucker was going to react."

Tucker was still staring at Shelby. "I, uh, I mean, I'm not Dylan Branson." He finally got the words out, much too late to be helpful.

Dylan walked over and slapped Tucker on the back good-naturedly. "I think she caught that much, Tuck. Ms. Keelan is dropping off some items for me to deliver." Dylan looked over at Shelby and held out his hand for her to shake. "I'm Dylan Branson. A pleasure to meet you."

Shelby stood and grasped Dylan's hand. Dylan shook it, then kept it, glad when she didn't snatch it away, and led her over to his booth. "Let's leave Tucker to finish his meat loaf."

A huge crash of thunder shook the windows in Sally's diner. "I can't take off in this anyway. I'll need to let Megan and Sawyer know I'll be delayed for a few hours."

Shelby looked out the window at the rain now pouring down and nodded. "Yeah, that's probably a good idea."

"Maybe you'll let me buy you dinner to make up for my rude behavior. Since we have some extra time before I can fly in this."

Shelby didn't look convinced, but Dylan wasn't going to let it go. The way he saw it, this situation was the best of all worlds: a chance to spend some time with a gorgeous woman, but one who would only be around for a couple of hours. Once the weather cleared and she gave him the codes, they'd go their separate ways. No complications.

But for now he could just enjoy her; her company and her beauty.

"Unless you're in a hurry and just need to drop everything off and run." Dylan gave her another smile. "But I hope that's not the case and you'll have dinner with me."

She gave him a confused look, but then nodded. "Okay, dinner. A chance to redeem yourself." One of her eyebrows arched as she looked at him.

"Deal. Let me contact Megan and Sawyer to tell them about the storm." Afraid he might yell at Megan for not preparing him for how beautiful Shelby was, Dylan just sent a text to Sawyer.

Shelby in pocket, but storm will delay flight. Will contact with updated ETA soon.

Dylan received a reply just moments later from Sawyer.

Roger that. I'll inform Burgamy.

Good, let Sawyer handle Burgamy. Dylan wanted as little communication time with his ex-boss as possible. He caught the attention of the young waitress who brought them both menus. Shelby began looking through it, but Dylan didn't even need to.

"Already know what you want?" Shelby asked him.

"Yeah. Sally's chicken pot pie is my favorite. I usually get that."

"That sounds good. Perfect for a rainy night and to recover from my near-death experience a little while ago."

As far as Dylan knew, most people didn't have near-death experiences around Falls Run. He hoped she wasn't talking about poor Tucker. He wasn't *that* bad. "What happened?"

They both ordered pot pie and sweet tea then Shelby told him about the car that had driven her partially off the side of the road. It sounded as if the driver never even saw her.

"Wow, first almost being run off the road, then almost having to have dinner with Tucker. That's a double whammy."

She laughed and relaxed back against the booth. Her eyes sparkled with genuine amusement. Dylan assumed he was forgiven.

"Yeah, the roads around here can be dangerous even for someone who's driven them for years," he continued. "And somebody not paying attention? You're really lucky."

"I thought the same thing after my pulse settled down to something below two hundred beats a minute."

The waitress brought them their iced tea.

"So you and Megan went to college together? Were you close?"

"Well, sort of. Megan was so young when she was at MIT, child prodigy and all that, so she's younger than me. Plus, I'm not a real outgoing person, so I tend to keep to myself. But we banded together a little bit because we were both females in an overwhelmingly large group of men." Shelby took a sip of her tea. "So she married your brother?"

"One of the two, yes. Sawyer. The playboy of the family. It was amazing how fast he fell." Dylan chuckled at the thought.

"And now they have a new baby on the way. I'm happy for Megan. I know back in college she always felt concerned she'd never really fit in anywhere." By the way her face lit up, Dylan could tell Shelby authentically cared for Megan.

The waitress brought their food and they began to eat.

"So how many siblings do you have?" Shelby asked between bites.

"I'm thirty-five and the oldest of four kids. Sawyer is the youngest. Cameron is a couple of years younger than me and our sister, Juliet, is sandwiched between Sawyer and Cameron."

"Anybody else married?"

"My other brother, Cameron, to a woman he was involved with a few years ago. They reconnected recently." Dylan didn't mention that Cameron and Sophia had *reconnected* when Cam had taken Sophia hostage while working undercover. That would probably come across as a little weird. "Juliet just got engaged to our longtime family friend Evan. They work together."

Again, mentioning that Juliet and Evan had fallen in love after living through an attack by a crazed stalker probably would be an overshare. Love in the Branson family tended to be less than traditional.

And that was part of the reason Dylan tried to stay as far as possible from it.

"How about you?" Shelby peeked over her pot pie at him.

"Married once, a long time ago. But not in the cards for me any longer." Dylan definitely did not want to talk about that. "You?"

"Nah. Haven't found anyone yet I like more than my pets."

Dylan laughed. "I don't blame you. Are you a dog person? Please, not cats."

"Both, actually." Shelby smiled at him and began telling him a story about some trouble one of her dogs had gotten into. Dylan matched that story with one of a dog he once had. Soon they were both laughing so hard they could hardly eat.

They were still talking about all sorts of things—her

job as a programmer, his as a pilot, her cats that tended to act more like dogs—as they finished their meal, ordered some of Sally's pie and finished that.

Dylan couldn't remember feeling this comfortable and attracted, hell, this *invested*, in a woman in a long time.

He found himself wishing this was more than just a meeting to pick up some data from his sister-in-law's friend. That he and Shelby had more time to spend with each other. But glancing out the window, Sawyer realized the storm would be passing soon. He needed to get the codes to Omega.

The thought of Omega brought all the memories flooding back. All the reasons why Dylan couldn't— *wouldn't*—get involved with another woman.

Tension began to fill Dylan's relaxed body as he realized spending too much time with Shelby was not a good idea. Her smile made him think of things that just weren't in the cards for him. He didn't have it in his heart to love another woman. Burying Fiona and their unborn child, knowing their deaths were his fault, had killed something inside Dylan. He would be wasting time, both his and any woman in his company, by pretending he had anywhere to go in a relationship.

Not that Shelby Keelan had said anything about wanting a relationship with him, for heaven's sake. They were just enjoying a meal together, relaxed conversation. But attraction was fairly crackling between them. Their hands kept touching on the table as they each made some point in a story. He could even feel Shelby's smaller foot next to his leg under the table.

She wasn't being forward, they just had a connection. And Dylan hadn't tried to keep it in check, like he normally would've—not that he'd felt this way about a woman in a long time. Since he'd known he and Shelby would only be together for a couple of hours before she gave him the codes and left, Dylan had deliberately left their natural chemistry unchecked.

He wasn't sure he would've been able to stop it even if he wanted to.

But his plan was backfiring. The more he talked to Shelby, the more he wanted to *keep* talking to her. Her acid wit kept him laughing, her intelligence kept him intrigued, and those freckles…

Those freckles were going to be his undoing. Even right now it was all he could do not to reach across the table and begin kissing a line from one freckle to the next. Starting with the ones on her nose, over to her cheeks and down to the one big one he could see where her jaw met her neck.

He'd have to concentrate on that one especially.

Dylan realized he was inching closer to Shelby across the table and forced himself to lean away, shifting his weight all the way back in the booth, away from her. What the hell was he doing? This was more than mere attraction, it was almost as if Dylan was drawn to Shelby.

Well, that was unacceptable and Dylan needed to get himself under the control he was so well known for. He couldn't believe how close he was to asking Shelby out. To asking her to spend more time with him once he returned from Omega. Hell, to seeing if she wanted to wait *at his house* for the twelve hours it would take him to deliver the codes to Omega then get home, if he made the round trip as fast as possible.

And that scared the hell out of him.

Shelby wasn't the type of woman Dylan could get involved with. She wasn't a one-night-stand type of girl; that was already obvious. Plus, she was Megan's friend.

He'd let things step over the emotional line with Shelby because they only had a couple of hours. Well, a couple of hours were up. It was time to end this attraction right now. While he still could.

Get the codes. Deliver the codes. Get out.

Shelby was talking about pets. Finishing an entertaining story about how the mama cat had taken a puppy to raise as her own when the puppy's mother had died. Shelby's green eyes had softened while telling it and Dylan had been totally caught up in the story. But now he stopped her, almost abruptly.

"You know, it looks like this storm is making its way out of the area. It's been a pleasure chatting with you, Shelby. But if you'll just give me the codes, I'll be on my way for delivery."

It was rude and came out harsher than Dylan intended. He saw confusion wash over Shelby's face and then self-doubt. Damn it, she was trying to figure out what she had done to initiate Dylan's borderline rudeness. He hated how Shelby drew back and made herself smaller in the booth seat across from him. The smile that had lit her features for almost their entire conversation died.

Dylan hated it, but steeled himself against the apology he found on his lips. It was better this way. Cleaner. But the disappointment in Shelby's eyes actually hurt him. It had been a long time since anything involving a woman had had the power to hurt Dylan. Why should being a jerk to someone he'd only known a couple of hours be able to?

Even if she was the most engaging and fascinating person he'd met in a long time. And the first person who didn't make him want to excuse himself as soon as possible so he could get back to his house, alone.

All of which was just more proof he needed to get away from her as soon as possible.

Dylan could recognize the crookedness of his own logic though he didn't plan to do anything about it. He *couldn't* do anything about it. All he could do was just get away from Shelby before things went any further.

Shelby's brows were furrowed. "Um, I don't understand." Her tone was uncertain.

Dylan rubbed a hand down his face. Damn it, he was making a mess of this. "I think you should just go ahead and give me the codes. Then you can head on back home, or whatever, and I'll take off as soon as I have a chance. All I need is a break in the storms and I'll be fine."

Shelby frowned and shook her head. "But I can't."

"You can't leave Falls Run tonight? Well, there's a motel down the street. I'm sure it's not full." Dylan almost offered to walk her over there, but that was a terrible plan.

Get the codes. Get out.

"No, I mean I can't give you the codes."

"You don't understand, Shelby. It's okay. Megan knows I will deliver them straight to her at Omega. She should've told you I could be trusted, but we can call her so you can talk to her about it yourself. You'll just need to give me the drive, or disk or whatever the codes are on."

"No, *you* don't understand. I can't give you the codes because they're in my head. *I'm* what you're supposed to deliver to Omega Sector."

Chapter Four

You would think she'd just told him she had a nuclear device in her back pocket the way he was acting. Shelby watched from the booth as Dylan went over to pay Sally at the register for their meal.

Shelby tried to think through their conversation to figure out what had happened, where it had gone wrong. Shelby certainly wouldn't be surprised to figure out it was something she had said. It always tended to be something she'd said.

But things had been going so well with Dylan tonight. Laughing and talking with him had been easy. Not full of those awkward pauses that tended to populate Shelby's conversations. Especially ones with really hot guys.

Not that she tended to have too many of those.

Everything seemed to be going great, and then Shelby had watched as Dylan Branson just shut down right in front of her eyes. The light flirting, the laughing, the lack of awkward pauses they had enjoyed the whole evening— totally gone in a split second. The emotional temperature in the room had dropped twenty degrees in just a moment.

Generally, Shelby was always looking for a way to get out of conversations, to find a way to return to her natural solo state. But with Dylan she hadn't felt the need to withdraw. They both seemed to be enjoying the conversation.

Enjoying each other. So, yeah, his abrupt termination of *everything* hurt. More than Shelby expected.

Not that she'd been expecting Dylan to ask her to go steady or anything, but they'd been having a good time and then: *pow!* Right in the middle of a sentence he was suddenly finished with her.

See, this was why Shelby avoided people whenever possible.

And then when she told Dylan she had to go with him on the flight? She thought his eyes might bug out of his head.

She hadn't been sure how to respond. When it became clear Dylan wasn't going to elaborate, Shelby had tried to explain. "I have to go. The codes are in my head."

"Well, then write them down or something."

Write them down?

"Do you think Megan and I are idiots?" Shelby asked. "If I could just *write them down*, do you think I would be here with you right now?"

Dylan had shrugged. "I don't know. Maybe."

Shelby had struggled to keep her temper under control. How could this even be the same man she had been talking to so comfortably just ten minutes before? "Well, I wouldn't. If I was able, I would have already used that newfangled thing called the internet to send the codes to Omega. I have to go."

Dylan shook his head. "How big can the codes be if they're in your head?"

Shelby had just sat back and glared at him. "Big."

At that, he stood up, took the bill the waitress had brought a few minutes before and gone over to pay. The restaurant looked to be closing up soon.

Shelby didn't want to explain to him about her photographic memory of anything having to do with numbers. Fifteen minutes ago she wouldn't have minded talking about it, almost had mentioned it when they were discussing her job. But that was when she was talking to good Dylan rather than jerk-face Dylan, who had somehow taken his place. She really wasn't interested in telling him much of anything now.

Maybe Shelby should mention to Megan that schizophrenia might run in her husband's family.

When Dylan didn't immediately return, Shelby looked over at him. Through the window she could see he had stepped outside. He was on the phone now, obviously not happy with whomever he was talking to. Shelby hoped it wasn't Megan.

Shelby also wished she knew what she had done to turn Dylan so hard and cold. Besides just existing and needing a ride. Which was why she was even here. Although that obviously hadn't been explained to Dylan.

Shelby finished her tea as she watched Dylan talking on the phone outside. Another storm had come up and lightning played through the night sky. Shelby didn't think they could take off in all this anyway. Maybe she should drive or look into taking a commercial flight. She could live through being surrounded by all the people at an airport and on an airplane if she had to.

Plus, how much worse could it be than being in an airplane with someone who seemed annoyed by her very existence?

Shelby got up and headed toward the door. She would just go her separate way from Dylan Branson. And hope when she met Megan's husband, Sawyer, that he didn't have the same temperament as his brother.

Shelby opened the door. Dylan's back was to her as he spoke on the phone. "Yeah, I get it. She's needed, too. All I'm saying is that this should've been made more clear to me, Burgamy." Dylan turned around, looking at

Shelby while listening to the other person on the phone. "Yes, crystal."

Dylan disconnected the call without saying anything further. Good to know he was gruff with everybody, not just Shelby. They stood for a moment, not saying anything. Lightning flashed around them again.

"Look, I'm not sure what exactly happened here." Shelby gestured toward the inside of the restaurant. "But obviously there was some sort of misunderstanding. You weren't expecting me or whatever. And that's fine. I'm just going to make other travel arrangements."

Dylan rubbed his eyes wearily. "No, that's not going to work. DC is too far to drive."

"I can see about a commercial flight."

"By the time you got to an airport big enough, that would take nearly as long as driving. Listen, I'm sorry I was abrupt before. I just didn't have all the information." Dylan shrugged. "I can fly you to DC. But since this storm seems to have stalled out right on top of us, it's going to be a few hours. Probably three or four."

Four hours? Shelby looked at her watch. It was after 10:00 p.m. She didn't relish the idea of sitting in her car for that long, but surely Sally's diner was going to close soon. Shrugging, Shelby turned toward her car.

Dylan touched her arm. "Look, the airfield is out near my house. Why don't you just come stay at my place, get a few hours of sleep, then we'll be ready to go when this series of storms passes."

Shelby moved away from his touch. "Uh, no, thank you."

"Why?"

"Are you kidding me?" Shelby's voice was pretty loud. A couple leaving the closing diner looked over at Shelby and Dylan. Dylan waved, but Shelby ignored them.

"No, I'm not kidding you. It's a logical solution."

"Why would I stay with someone who out of the blue started treating me like I have the bubonic plague? No, thanks, I'll just stay here."

"You can't stay here. The restaurant is closing." Dylan's voice had raised to a yell, probably to compensate for the thunder overhead. Unfortunately, the teenage waitress came outside just in time to hear his shout, but not the thunder. She stared at Dylan and Shelby with wide eyes.

"Is everything okay, Mr. Dylan?"

"It's fine, Jennifer," Dylan told the girl. "Be careful driving home in this mess."

Jennifer kept watching them as she walked to her car. Looked as if Dylan's yell was the most excitement she had seen in a while.

But the fact that Dylan knew Jennifer's name reassured Shelby a bit, as did the fact that the girl was so shocked by how he was acting. Obviously, Dylan didn't normally stand around the parking lot yelling at women.

"Sally is closing up for the night. You can't go back in there."

"Fine. I'll just hang out in my car. Text me when you think it's safe to take off and I'll meet you at the airport."

Shelby heard Dylan's sigh. "It's not an airport, more like an airfield." A few drops of rain started to fall. It wouldn't be long until the thunderous clouds produced rainstorms again.

"Don't stay in your car," he continued. "There's a motel a couple of blocks down the road. Stay there at least. Not out in this storm."

He was right. Shelby didn't mind paying for a room she'd only spend a few hours in. Especially if it meant she wouldn't have to talk to any other people unnecessarily.

Or have to stay with a man who had made up his mind to dislike her for no apparent reason.

Shelby left the shelter of the overhang near the diner's

front entrance to cross to where her car was parked. "Okay, fine." She gave him her phone number. "Just text me or whatever when you're ready."

The rain was really starting to come down now. "I'll follow you in my truck. Just to make sure everything's okay."

That was the exact opposite of what Shelby expected. She said nothing, just pulled up the collar of her jacket for protection from the rain. She thought she heard Dylan say something else to her, but she just wanted to make it across the street to her car. She understood why they had built the restaurant on one side of the road and the parking lot on the other—the diner had amazing views of the Blue Ridge Mountains. They wouldn't want to use any of that prime real estate on parking.

But having to cross the street in the rain made Shelby wish they had put the parking closer.

She heard someone yell, but figured it was someone from the restaurant saying goodbye to Dylan. If he was trying to get her attention, he could just wait until they got to the motel. She wasn't having a conversation out in the cold rain.

Shelby heard the squealing of tires as she reached the other side of the road. She looked up to see a car barreling toward her so fast she couldn't even figure out what to do.

Her world tilted as a weight hit her from her right and she went flying sideways through the air. A split second later, the car sped through where Shelby had just been standing, not even slowing down. It sprayed water from puddles, soaking Shelby from head to foot.

From where she lay on the ground, Shelby sucked in deep breaths, trying to get her bearings. She'd been hit, right? But not by the car. She turned her head to the side and saw Dylan lying on the ground with her.

"Are you okay?" he asked.

"Yes. Are you? What in the world just happened?" Her limbs were tangled with Dylan's.

"That car almost hit you. I saw it speeding down the road and yelled, but you didn't hear me."

That wasn't totally true. Shelby had heard him, she just hadn't wanted to stop in the rain.

"Well, your reflexes are better than mine. Thank you."

"I had forward momentum going for me, otherwise I wouldn't have made it."

What he really meant was *Shelby* wouldn't have made it. Dylan could've stayed safely on the side of the road and would've been just fine.

They both began to sit up. Ouch. Shelby could already feel a rip in her coat at the elbow where she'd hit the hardest, although Dylan had taken the brunt of the fall.

"Are you okay?" she asked him. "You took your weight and some of mine."

"Yeah, I'll be fine." Dylan got to his feet then offered his hand to help Shelby up. She gratefully took it, grabbing her purse and working her way to a standing position. Now everything was starting to hurt. And this was what *not* getting hit by a car felt like.

"Did the person driving just not see me?" They walked the rest of the way to her car.

"It's possible."

"But?" Shelby could hear the but in his tone. She was trying to get her keys out of her purse, but found her hands were shaking pretty badly. Dylan reached over and held the purse for her so she could manage to fish them out.

"But it actually sped up. Definitely wasn't typical rainy-night-driving behavior."

"Drunk, I'll bet you. That's the second time I've been almost run off the road. People around here need to pay better attention." Shelby got her keys out and clicked open her car. She just wanted to get out of the rain.

Dylan was looking toward where the car had sped off. "Yeah. For sure."

They walked together around to her driver's side. He held the door open as she got into the car then shut it. Shelby cracked the window so she could hear what he had to say.

"The motel is just a couple blocks down on the right. Don't go anywhere else, okay? Just check in and rest until I let you know we can take off."

Shelby nodded. She wasn't planning on doing anything but taking a hot shower and changing into dry clothes.

"I won't. I don't think I'm up for much dancing."

A hint of a smile formed at Dylan's mouth. "You'd be hard pressed to find dancing around here anyway. Unless they've got the karaoke set up at the Blue Moon, Falls Run's bar."

The rain was pouring over Dylan. Shelby kind of felt bad for all the mean things she had thought about him since he'd saved her life and all. "Are you sure you're okay?" she asked him.

"Fine. Bye."

Evidently, gruff Dylan was back.

"Okay, let me know when it's time to go." Shelby rolled up her window and started driving slowly down the road, not even looking back at Dylan in the rearview mirror. She was irritated at him and her whole body ached.

This was why she tried to stay alone in her house as much as possible.

Chapter Five

Somebody was trying to kill Shelby Keelan.

Dylan hadn't wanted to say that to her in the parking lot of Sally's diner while they were both soaking wet and banged up by a hard fall to the asphalt. Although, there probably wasn't ever a good time to tell someone their life was in jeopardy.

And Shelby's was. By someone who was trying to make it look like an accident. The car that nearly ran Shelby down hadn't been a drunk driver. As a matter of fact, it had probably been the same vehicle that had nearly driven her off the road earlier today. Both attempts had failed, but just barely.

Dylan walked to his truck, opened it and hopped in, whistling through his teeth as he made it into the cab. Had he cracked a rib again? Damn it, he hoped not. Those hurt like hell. At the very least, his ribs were bruised. His shoulder, too. It had taken the brunt of the fall. But he was in one piece and so was Shelby.

He'd almost been too late. If he'd reacted two seconds later, or if he hadn't trusted his gut that told him that car was trouble, Shelby would be dead. No one could've survived being hit at that speed.

Dylan hadn't gotten any info about the car that would help them. Four-door, dark sedan wouldn't narrow down anything; it wasn't even worth calling in. And the car had been speeding by too fast for Dylan to catch helpful details.

Dylan watched as Shelby pulled out of the parking lot and began driving slowly down the street. He started his truck so he could follow her. He'd make sure she got safely inside, then would try to go get some sleep himself for a couple hours. Surely she would be safe at the motel.

But there had already been two attempts on her life. What would stop whoever was behind this from coming back to finish her in her motel room? That might actually be easier.

Dylan knew he needed to get her to come stay at his house. Dylan wasn't connected to her in any known way, so whoever was following her wouldn't be looking for her at his house. She could leave her car parked at the motel and Dylan could sneak her out the back door in case someone was watching.

Of course, he'd have to stop acting like a total jerk if he wanted to convince her to do that. How had Shelby phrased it? Treating her as if she had the plague.

Dylan ran a weary hand over his face as he parked his truck across the street from the motel and watched Shelby walk into the front office. Yeah, he definitely could've handled that whole situation at the restaurant better. But he'd thought Shelby would just give him the codes and they'd go their separate ways. She might think he was a little abrupt, but no real harm done.

How the heck was Dylan supposed to have known the codes were in her head and that she needed to be at Omega for all of this to work? How was that even possible? If the number sequence was too lengthy to be written up or easily transferred by an electronic medium, then how the hell could Shelby Keelan have them all inside her brain?

When his ex-boss had called, Burgamy should've made

it abundantly clear that Shelby would be coming with Dylan to Omega HQ. Dylan had mentioned that fact to Burgamy, who had just quipped back: What difference does it make? Your plane seats more than one, right? You can fit some codes and one woman.

Yeah, his Cessna sat more than one—up to eight, in fact—but that wasn't really the point. Dylan would've kept much more of a distance from Shelby if he had known they would be together for a few days.

Because Dylan wasn't sure he could keep his hands off Shelby Keelan for days. He hadn't felt this attracted to anyone in a long time. Not since Fiona. Hell, maybe not even *for* Fiona.

Which he couldn't even bring himself to think about.

There had been women since Fiona, of course. During the beginning downward spiral, there had been way too many women—just part of a series of bad choices Dylan made in the name of dealing with unbearable grief. But none of them had meant anything; none of them had touched him in any sort of meaningful way.

After just a few short hours in Shelby's company, Dylan wasn't sure he'd be able to say the same thing about her.

Dylan wasn't proud of how he'd handled the situation at the diner. A yelling match in front of Sally's was never a good plan. But the thought of spending more time with Shelby? It was both the most exciting and most frightening prospect Dylan had had in his personal life in years.

And now Dylan had to talk her into coming to his house. Her presence there, even for only a few short hours, was going to disrupt his peaceful, orderly life. Dylan just knew it. But what other choice did he have? He couldn't leave her in town alone. So even though she didn't seem too keen on the idea of staying with him, Dylan would have to change her mind.

And he would just have to keep the attraction he had for this woman, and her damn freckles, under control.

From across the street, Dylan watched as Shelby came back out of the motel's office, key in hand. She drove her car a little farther into the parking lot and parked in front of a room. After a moment, she got out of her car with a small suitcase and entered her room.

The Falls Run Motel wasn't fancy, but it was clean and family friendly. There was one building with two floors of rooms. The back of all the bottom-level rooms had sliding glass doors with small concrete patios; the upper-level rooms all had small decks, both providing views of the mountains.

Shelby's room was on the first floor, which made Dylan's plan much easier. He had to talk to her, but knew he didn't want to go through her room's front door. He needed to get her out in secret in case someone was watching. That left the back sliding glass door.

Dylan pulled his truck farther into the shadows of the bank parking lot that stood across the street from the motel. He turned off the engine and flipped a switch for the light in the cab so it wouldn't turn on when he opened the door. Just in case. He slid out of the cab, pushing all pain to the side. He felt a little ridiculous hugging the shadows as he made his way across the street in the rain, but he'd learned over the years that an ounce of prevention was worth three and a half tons of cure.

Dylan made his way around the back of the motel, keeping away from the lights. He silently walked along the line of trees until he was right behind Shelby's room. No lights were on in the rooms on either side of her, which was good. Shelby had pulled the curtain closed, so only a tiny bit of light cracked through the glass door. Dylan approached the door and tapped on it softly.

"Shelby." Dylan put his mouth almost up to the door.

He didn't want his voice to carry. He could see the shadow of movement in the room, but couldn't tell if Shelby could hear him. He tapped again, a little louder.

The curtain inched back and Shelby peeked out, but Dylan could tell she still couldn't see him from where he was in the shadows. He tapped again right where she was looking and brought his face close to the window.

Her short shriek made Dylan thankful there wasn't anyone in the rooms next to hers. The curtain flew back down, but Dylan heard the unlocking of the door a moment later.

"You scared the pants off me," Shelby hissed. She had a towel wrapped around her neck, drying rain out of her long red hair. It looked even more red against the white of the cloth.

"Sorry."

"What are you doing here? And why are you at the back door? Why didn't you use the front?"

Dylan put a finger up to his lips. He didn't want her to announce to everyone he was here. "I'm trying to talk with you without anyone knowing I'm here. Do you mind if I come in?"

At least she didn't hesitate as she opened the door farther and stepped back, which surprised Dylan a little bit. He wouldn't have been surprised if he had to plead his case from a cracked door after how he'd acted. He walked in and slid the door closed behind him, pulling the curtain to give them privacy from any possible prying eyes.

"Come back because you found just the right words to let me know how you don't like me?" Shelby stood, arms folded and eyebrow raised, by one of the beds in the room.

Dylan winced. He supposed he deserved that, at least a little.

"I'm sorry about before."

If anything, Shelby's eyebrow arched even higher. She didn't say anything.

"Listen, I was going to leave you alone here, let you get some rest, go home and do the same myself before we leave in a couple hours. But the fact is, someone tried to kill you tonight."

Shelby looked shocked then sat down on the bed and began smoothing her wet hair with the towel almost absently. "First of all, thanks for saving my life. But me almost dying and someone trying to kill me are two different things, Dylan."

"I know. I don't use the terms interchangeably." Dylan took a step closer, more to keep his shadow away from the curtain than anything else. But his action drew her attention. She stood and began walking farther away without a word, turning her back to him.

Dylan sighed. He guessed he deserved that, too.

But instead of taking the plastic chair at the farthest point away from him in the room, as Dylan thought she was going to do, Shelby walked into the bathroom and came back out with another towel a moment later. She tossed it to him and sat back down on the bed.

"You look as miserable as I feel. Maybe that will help dry you off enough so that you're at least not dripping."

Dylan began to towel off his face and hair. "Thanks."

"Don't look so surprised. I'm not a she devil, you know."

"I never thought you were."

Her eyebrow rose again.

Dylan changed the subject. "That guy tonight wasn't a drunk driver who got sloppy. That car was someone coming at you with the specific intention of running you down."

Shelby stopped drying her hair and clutched the towel

to her like a security blanket. Her green eyes were huge in her pale face. "Do you really think that's true?"

"Well, let me ask you this. Do you remember anything about the car that almost ran you off the road earlier today while you were driving up here?"

Shelby shrugged. "Not too much. I'm good with remembering numbers, but not much of anything else."

Dylan didn't want to just feed an image into her mind. He wanted to see if he could help her remember. "Was it a light or dark color, or maybe a specific color you remember, like red or yellow?"

"No, definitely not a bright color. It was dark, maybe black or gray. I can't really recall."

"That's okay." Dylan sat down on the bed across from hers. "Is there anything you can remember about the model of the vehicle? Maybe it was an SUV or a noticeable brand of car, like a VW or a Jeep?"

"No, I don't know anything about cars. But it wasn't anything like that. I just remember thinking it was an old person's car. That maybe it was some old person who shouldn't be driving at all if he or she was going to run people off the road."

"Okay, an old person's car." That was the info Dylan had been hoping for. "A sedan."

"Yeah, a sedan." Shelby nodded. "But I don't know what make or anything."

"That's okay, you don't have to. But I think you might find it interesting that the car that tried to run you down tonight was also a dark sedan. Someone has tried to kill you today. Twice. Both in ways that would seem like an accident."

Shelby bounded off the bed. The towel was still clutched in front of her. "What am I going to do?"

"I don't think it's safe for you to stay here tonight in

case that person tries to come back and finish what he started. It would be too easy to find you."

Shelby nodded almost blankly.

"I know you were pretty resistant to this idea before, but I think you should come back to my house. Nobody would know you're there and we'll leave in the plane as soon as possible. It's not safe for you to be alone anymore."

Chapter Six

Shelby could hear what Dylan was saying, but it was as if she was processing it too slowly to make sense. Someone was trying to kill her? On purpose?

The whole concept was pretty foreign. And Dylan was afraid someone would find her here at the motel?

"How would they find me here?" she asked.

"It's the only motel in all of Falls Run. If you assumed that what happened earlier was only an accident, you'd probably check in here, get some rest. If I was a killer, I'd look here first."

Shelby walked over by the curtains. She wanted to peek out, to open the door and see if the boogeyman was on the porch ready to attack them, but knew she couldn't.

Was Dylan right? Could someone actually be trying to kill her? They were dealing with DS-13, which Megan assured Shelby was definitely a group to take seriously. Shelby had the codes in her head and knew the numbers were some sort of countdown. But she had no idea what they were counting down to; that's where Megan's computer decryption program came in. Shelby and Megan's computer program had to be in the same room together so Shelby could feed in the data and eliminate what wasn't necessary. Only Shelby could do that. And once she did, they'd be able to figure out the what and the where the countdown referred to.

Were the numbers in her head worth someone killing her for? She didn't want to think so, but the aches and bruises from her close encounter with a speeding car—which did look a lot like the one she'd seen earlier today, now that Dylan mentioned it—told her otherwise. So, yeah, maybe someone was trying to kill her.

Yet another reason why she should have just stayed home.

At least Dylan didn't seem so irritated by her very existence anymore. He wasn't the sexy, flirty Dylan he'd been a few hours ago, but at least he wasn't yelling at her. She didn't necessarily want to go back to his house with him, but neither did she want to stay here with a possible attacker. Uncomfortable was definitely better than dead.

She nodded at Dylan. "Okay, I'll come with you."

Dylan tossed the towel down on the bed. "Good. That really is the safest thing."

"Should I bring my whole suitcase? Everything I brought?"

"If you need everything, I can carry the whole suitcase out. But it would be better if you had just a small bag with a few necessities. Makes us much more mobile getting to my truck."

"Okay."

"Plus, if someone does break in here, it makes it look like you're still around somewhere. It would cause the perp to think maybe he missed you somehow. Buy us more time while he waits for you to come back."

Shelby shuddered at the thought of someone coming in here, waiting for her. She looked quickly at the front door and the glass door. Two ways someone could get in. Shelby definitely didn't want to stay here.

"Let me pack a bag." Shelby grabbed a shirt, a pair

of jeans and some underwear, rolling them into a ball
with the delicates—did it have to be a red-and-black
thong?—on the inside. Shelby grabbed a toothbrush and
a comb, thankful she'd never been one for wearing much
makeup. The tennis shoes and socks on her feet would
be fine.

This should be all she needed. The rest she could buy
once she got to Washington, DC.

"I don't have anything to put this in," Shelby told
Dylan.

"That's okay. I've got a small duffel bag you can use
once we get to my house. Just put your comb and toothbrush in your back pocket and ball up your clothes."

Shelby did as he said. "Are we going to need to run?"

"We will at first, out to the tree line behind the motel.
There's no way around that. We've got to get away from
the building as quickly as possible. But otherwise, I hope
not. Two people sprinting across the street draws a lot
more attention than two people just walking fast to get
out of the rain." Dylan looked around the room. "You
don't have a baseball cap or hoodie, do you? Anything
with a hood?"

"No."

Dylan shrugged. "Your red hair is hard to hide without something covering it. Just stay as close to me as you
can as we're crossing the street. If I stop, you stop. Don't
ask questions, just do it."

Shelby wasn't planning on asking for justification for
everything he did while he was getting them out of here.
It would be nice if he would take her for a little bit less
of an idiot. "Fine."

If Dylan noticed Shelby's annoyance, he didn't mention it. He walked over to the front door and turned off
the lights in the room, plunging it into darkness.

"Let's give our eyes a chance to adjust. Then we'll head out."

Shelby nodded then realized he couldn't see her. "Okay."

After a few moments, Shelby's vision adjusted. Dylan had made his way over to the sliding glass door already and was peering around the curtain.

"Is somebody out there?" Shelby asked after what seemed like a long time.

"Probably not. Whoever wants to hurt you would probably come through the front door. Most motel rooms don't have doors at the back, just windows that don't open. Unless he's familiar with this motel specifically, then he'd think the front door was the best bet."

"Oh." Shelby couldn't think of anything more intelligent to say. How did Dylan, a pilot, know all that? Maybe he sat around and watched too many crime shows on television.

"Are you ready?"

Shelby took a deep breath. "Yes."

"Okay, Freckles. Remember, stay as close to me as possible and try not to talk."

Did he just call her Freckles? Shelby didn't even have time to get offended. Dylan was already out the door. She followed him quickly, clothes tucked under her arm, sliding the door shut on her way out.

Dylan made a dash for the tree line, a hundred feet or so from the hotel. Shelby made sure to keep up with him. Once they were in the cover of the trees, Dylan stopped for a minute.

"Okay?" he asked her.

"Yeah."

"We'll make our way along the trees to the side of the motel by the office, then we'll cut across the street. My truck is parked at the bank."

They made their way silently along the trees, keeping

to the shadows as much as possible. Dylan kept hold of the hand Shelby wasn't using to carry the clothes, keeping her close to his side. Every once in a while Dylan would stop and peer out. Shelby forced herself not to ask what he saw, if anything.

When they reached the side of the motel, the trees stopped. They'd have to walk out in the open now. Shelby peeked around Dylan's large shoulders. As far as she could tell, nobody was out. Why would they be? Anyone with any sense was inside, not outside in the wet cold. Shelby shivered.

"Are you ready?" Dylan asked, turning his head back toward her so she could hear him over the rain. "We'll walk side by side to my truck. I don't see anybody, but don't dawdle."

Shelby nodded and Dylan took her hand and they began to walk through the parking lot and across the street. Compared to the cover of the trees, Shelby felt exposed out in the open. She kept her head tucked down and walked as quickly as possible, but the steps across the street seemed to take forever.

When Dylan slowed down and curved Shelby into the crook of his arm, Shelby glanced up. She knew he wouldn't choose now to turn this into a lover's pose unless he had to.

"What?" she asked him.

"A car just turned onto the road up the block. A sedan."

"The same one?"

"I don't know, but I don't want to take any chances. I need to keep you out of sight and away from anything that might associate you with me." Dylan turned them away from where his truck was parked. "Detour."

Shelby kept up as Dylan now rushed across the street toward the bank building rather than his vehicle. He didn't stop until they were standing up against the wall of the bank, the opposite side from where the car was coming. Shelby clutched her balled-up change of clothes to her chest with one arm.

"Okay, we're going to work our way around to the back side of the building and see what that car is doing."

They stayed against the wall as they walked back. Dylan had yet to let go of Shelby's hand. When they got to the back where they could glance out to see the road, Shelby stayed behind Dylan while he took a look.

"I don't see anybody. Maybe that car wasn't even the same guy."

"That's good, right?"

Dylan nodded and let go of her hand. Everything seemed safe. Shelby wondered if this whole thing was just a case of overactive imaginations. Admittedly, it was unlikely that two cars similar in make and model would almost hit her twice in one day, but it wasn't impossible.

"Okay, I don't see anyone," Dylan told her again. "Let's head to the truck."

Shelby nodded and they began walking, neither of them quite as worried about secrecy.

Shelby felt Dylan stiffen a moment before she noticed the car again herself. It was pulling out of the parking lot directly adjacent to the bank, moving slowly, obviously looking for something or someone.

Okay, maybe not overactive imaginations.

Dylan grabbed Shelby's hand again and pulled her forward, then put his other hand on her head to get her to stay low. They ran to his truck, keeping as low as possible. Dylan opened the passenger-side door and jumped in, sliding across the seat and reaching to help Shelby at the same time.

"Hurry. Stay down." Dylan's voice was curt as he kept a watchful eye out the windshield while trying to stay out of sight himself. Shelby threw her clothes toward him, grabbed his hand and climbed. She pulled the door closed as quickly as she could, glad that no lights had come on in the cab. She ducked down low in the seat.

"Is he still coming toward us?"

"Yes, but I don't think he saw us. It looks more like a sweep-through than anything. He's past us now."

Shelby peeked up and saw the rear of the car as it drove slowly by. The person driving was looking for someplace. Or someone. But the car was moving on now.

Dylan straightened up in his seat. "I think it's safe now. But let's get out of here before he comes back. Once he's sure the street is clear, he'll try to find you at your room."

"Okay." Shelby sat up and reached to grab her clothes which had fallen all over the cab when she'd thrown them inside. She found her pants and shirt with no problem. But kept feeling around the darkened cab for her underwear.

"Um, I think this is what you're looking for."

Hanging from Dylan's finger was Shelby's black-and-red lace thong.

Chapter Seven

Dylan didn't allow himself to dwell on that tiny scrap of lace during the drive to his house. He needed to stay focused and make sure no one was following them. Although he knew following them on the windy road that led from town to his house with no headlights would be nearly impossible.

But that gave him too much time to think about red-and-black material, so he focused instead on being doubly sure no one followed.

No one did.

The storm still raged as they reached Dylan's house fifteen minutes later. Although he normally wouldn't park there, he pulled into the garage so they wouldn't have to get wet again. Shelby was just beginning to stop shivering. She hadn't said much of anything on the drive here. Once she'd snatched the thong off his finger, she'd kind of hunkered down over on the opposite side of the cab.

About as far from Dylan as she could get.

Dylan turned off the ignition and opened his door. He would've gone around to help Shelby, but she'd already made it out fine on her own. So he opened the door that led through a small mudroom before entering the main part of his house.

Dylan's house wasn't too large. Three decent-size bedrooms, a living room with a large fireplace and a kitchen with an eat-in nook. Dylan had designed and built most of it himself, based on his own needs and preferences. It definitely had not been built with entertaining in mind. Hell, except for family, Dylan never entertained anybody at his house. Any meetings concerning his charter business were conducted at his office by the airfield a half mile away.

Dylan wasn't a sloppy person—his mother hadn't allowed it growing up, neither had the army—but still he looked over his house with a critical eye. He'd never brought a woman here before, and for the first time had a moment's doubt. What did his house look like to Shelby? Too sparse, too masculine, too rough around the edges? There definitely weren't a tremendous amount of creature comforts here.

Dylan wondered if Shelby would start complaining right off the bat, or if she'd be too polite to do so. She hadn't seemed to hold back any of her opinions so far, so Dylan didn't expect her to do so now. But when he turned to look at Shelby as she walked farther into the living room, she didn't seem to be put off at all by his house.

"This is a great space," she told him, looking around. "Lots of windows. I'm sure that lets in great light during the day."

Dylan had to admit he was impressed. He didn't think Shelby would notice the windows, his favorite feature, first. He thought she might notice the kitchen was small and rather rustic—Dylan wasn't much of a cook—or that the television was pretty tiny in the living room and off to the side.

"I like the feeling of trees around me. The windows help almost bring them indoors." Dylan walked over and moved a book that lay open on the couch cushion and put it on the stack of books already on the end table. "Do you want to sit down? Or do you want to rest? As soon as this storm breaks we need to take off."

"How far is your airplane from here?"

"Less than a mile. There is a stretch of flat area and I built a runway, not a big one, but big enough for my Cessna. The hangar and my office are up there, too."

Shelby was still clutching her bundle of clothes. "I guess I'll rest. It's getting pretty late. Can we take off in the dark?"

"Yeah, dark is fine. Just not in the storm." It was almost midnight now. Dylan estimated they'd be able to take off in about three hours.

He led the way down the hall. "The guest room is right here." He opened the door and turned on the light, then winced. He'd forgotten that he had piled his book collection on the guest bed until he could get around to building the new bookshelf he wanted.

Shelby walked in and crossed to the bed. "Looks like my bed space is already taken up by Zane Grey and Louis L'Amour. Although I think I'm seeing a little C. S. Lewis in there, too. Pretty extensive collection."

"I'm sorry. Look, I can get this cleaned off in just a minute." Dylan grabbed a stack of books and began moving them across the room, but Shelby touched his arm.

"Dylan, it's fine. Just leave them. If you've got a blanket and a pillow, I'll just sleep out on that giant couch you have."

Dylan hesitated. Was that rude? He'd lived alone for too long. He didn't want to deliberately alienate Shelby; he'd done enough of that already this evening.

Shelby ended up answering the question for him. "Truly, it's okay. We've only got a couple of hours. No point using a chunk of that cleaning off a bed. Just hand me a towel so I can take a shower, and dump a pillow and blanket on the couch."

She was right, it would take him twenty minutes to clean off this bed enough that someone could sleep on it. Maybe he should offer her his bed.

No. Dylan had the feeling if he let Shelby sleep in his bed he'd never stop thinking about her there. "Okay, I'll get you a towel. Sorry about this."

Dylan got her what she needed and showed her to the guest bathroom. He went in there before her to check the status of the tub. It was pretty dusty—the whole room was pretty dusty; Dylan didn't get in there much—but it was relatively clean and usable.

"I'll leave a couple of blankets and pillows on the couch. Try to get a little rest. As soon as the storm breaks, we'll head out." Dylan closed the door behind him without looking at Shelby again.

Dylan took the items Shelby would need to sleep and placed them on the couch, then walked into his bedroom. He needed to try to catch a little sleep himself. But he could hear the shower running in the guest bathroom.

He definitely was not going to get any sleep thinking about Shelby, and her adorable freckles, in the shower. Or the never-to-be-mentioned black-and-red thong sliding onto her body afterward. Dylan needed a shower himself.

A cold one.

SHELBY LAY ON the couch looking up at the high ceiling of Dylan's house. Here, under blankets that weren't hers, on a couch that wasn't nearly as comfortable as her own bed, in a house she wasn't familiar with, Shelby knew she should be freaking out.

She did not do well out of her own house for very long. And although she had prepared herself to go to Washington, DC, Shelby had thought she would be staying with Megan. An old friend. A *safe* friend who understood Shelby's need to be alone after a time in other people's company.

Instead, she was at the house of a man who constantly made her either want to slap him or kiss him. He was definitely not safe, the opposite, in fact. And yet she was here in his house, quite comfortable.

Shelby wasn't freaking out at all.

As a matter of fact, she was a little freaked out that she wasn't freaking out. She kept preparing a speech in her mind that she would use on herself when the panic came.

But it didn't come.

Shelby wasn't just under the blankets, she was *snuggled* under the blankets. And looking up at the tall rafters of Dylan's ceiling, she found the space and the openness... calming.

Shelby had been called a lot of things in her life, but calm was not one of them. She liked things to be the way she wanted them. Her house was exactly the way she liked it, everything had its place and Shelby knew where that place was. She'd lived in her downtown Knoxville condo, right smack in the heart of the city, with views of World's Fair Park and the Sunsphere, for over eight years, and she loved it. In all that time, she'd never felt comfortable anywhere else. She liked the constant sound of traffic right outside her windows, and even the noise of neighbors in the building.

So Shelby couldn't quite figure out how she felt so comfortable lying here in the gentle peace of the mountains surrounding Dylan's cabin. But she wouldn't question it anymore. She'd just rest. She didn't think she would be able to sleep. Resting was one thing, but sleeping would be something totally different. She didn't sleep in strange houses. In fact, she hadn't been able to get a full night of sleep outside of her own bed in years. But she could rest.

The next thing Shelby knew, Dylan was gently shaking her shoulder to wake her up.

"Hey, there's a break in the storms. Time to head out."

Shelby opened her eyes to find Dylan crouched down beside her.

"Okay, I'm not asleep, just resting."

Dylan snickered at that.

"What?" Shelby demanded.

"Well, for somebody just resting, you had the most adorable little snores coming out of you." Dylan stood up and began walking into the kitchen.

"I do not snore." Wait, did she? It wasn't as if there had been anyone around to let her know about her sleep-breathing patterns in a long time. But Shelby was pretty sure she didn't snore. Plus, she hadn't been sleeping. Shelby sat up on the couch. Had she been sleeping?

No, because that would mean she had been comfortable enough to sleep at Dylan's house. So, no, she hadn't been sleeping.

Shelby looked over to where Dylan was fixing coffee and breakfast in the kitchen. "What time is it?"

"Almost four o'clock."

Over three hours since she'd lain down. She *had* been sleeping.

"I do not snore," Shelby muttered again under her breath as she got up and began folding the blankets she'd slept on. She didn't want to think about sleeping or not sleeping.

"Coffee?" Dylan asked from the kitchen. "And I have breakfast. Not much, though. Toast, cereal. And I have some yogurt."

"Coffee, please." Shelby shuffled into the kitchen. Although she felt better after her…*rest*, she could still use some caffeine. She sipped it gratefully after Dylan poured her a mug.

"As soon as you're ready, we'll head up to the airstrip. It looks like we have about a forty-five-minute window before the next storm set moves in."

"Okay." Shelby nodded, sipping her coffee faster. "I'll hurry."

"You can bring breakfast with you. I'll need to do a quick preflight check on the plane, and you can eat in the hangar."

Dylan was all business, but was at least being pretty friendly. As friendly as a person could be when it was four o'clock in the morning and your day was already starting. Shelby finished her coffee and grabbed what she wanted for breakfast to take with her. She ran into the bathroom to comb out and braid her hair and brush her teeth with the toothbrush and comb that had survived the trip from the hotel. Dylan had given her a small bag, so she put last night's clothes in there.

The drive to the airstrip didn't take long. It still drizzled outside, but there wasn't any thunder and lightning. Shelby waited in Dylan's truck, parked in the hangar behind his plane, as he ran through his preflight checklist.

This was a pretty nice setup he had here. The airstrip was on his land, and it was only his plane that took off or landed, so Air Traffic Control wasn't a problem. The only problem, Shelby was sure, had been getting an area flat enough and safe enough for a plane to take off around here, surrounded by the Blue Ridge Mountains. But Dylan had done it.

She watched him move around his plane with ease, obviously familiar with what he was doing. When his checklist was complete he made his way back over to Shelby and the truck.

"Ready?"

"Yeah."

Dylan helped Shelby out of the truck then grabbed a

backpack from the back. Shelby picked up her own small bag of items and walked with him over to the plane. She looked up at the sky. Even through the darkened night, she could still see the clouds, not as thick and threatening as they were before, but still there.

"We're okay with the weather?"

Dylan nodded. "I studied it through some weather sites and FAA reports. We don't have a whole lot of time, but we have enough."

Dylan helped Shelby up the stairs of the plane, entering behind her. She shifted to the side so he could pull up the stairs and close the door, securing then double checking it.

"Trust me," he told her, "I wouldn't be taking us up if it wasn't safe."

Dylan's plane was different than Shelby expected. Nicer. As he'd told her, it could fit up to eight people, with two sets of leather seats facing each other across tables and another single row of seats behind them. The setup was a great way to do business or just talk with someone while traveling to a destination.

Shelby turned to Dylan. "Somehow I thought you did more cargo trips than passengers. But you're certainly set up for people."

Dylan walked up to the cockpit. "It's about fifty/fifty right now. Passengers generally pay more, but I prefer cargo if I have the option."

"Oh, yeah? Why is that?"

Dylan gave her a half grin. "Cargo doesn't talk."

Shelby returned his smile. Not wanting groups of talking people? *That* she understood. "Should I stay back here or come up there with you?"

"Either way. The seats recline, so if you want to get some rest, I understand."

Did he want to be alone in the cockpit? Shelby would love to come up there, to see how a plane such as this one really worked, but she didn't want to make a nuisance of herself.

"I'm not going to sleep, but I can stay back here if you'd rather be alone."

Dylan tilted his head a little to the side as if he was weighing the pros and cons. Shelby didn't know whether she should be offended or not.

"Why don't you come up with me? I'm sure that will be more interesting." Dylan turned and walked into the cockpit.

Yeah, Shelby was sure that would be more interesting, too. She followed him.

Dylan handed Shelby a pair of headphones. "These make it easier to talk without having to yell."

Shelby nodded and sat down in the seat next to him. She pulled the headset over her head and adjusted the mic just slightly. Dylan showed her how to buckle in. A harness belt was much different than the ordinary lap belt on most airplanes.

Dylan finished his cockpit preflight checklist quickly, something he'd obviously done hundreds of times. But never did he seem to be rushing. Shelby couldn't help watching him. He was clearly sure of himself and what he was doing. He didn't hesitate, but moved efficiently through the list. Sure, confident.

It was downright sexy.

Shelby decided she better stop staring at him and looked around the cockpit instead. She'd never been in this part of an airplane before. It was exciting.

"Ready?" Dylan asked her. She could hear him without any problem in the headphones.

"Yep. Do I need to do anything?"

"Yes. When I give the signal, stick your arms out the window and flap them up and down really hard. It helps us to get airborne."

Shelby looked over at him with a grin on her face. Mr. Serious just made a joke. Shelby hadn't been sure he had it in him.

"You just be sure not to hit all the trees around here."

Dylan chuckled slightly. "Actually, the trees at the end of the runway are a concern. Not for us since we're so light today, but with a full load I do have to be aware of them."

Great. She hadn't been nervous, but she was a little now. Shelby hoped Dylan was as adept at flying as he had been prepping the airplane. She sat back and held on to the edges of the seat belts that covered both her shoulders.

The plane built up speed a few moments later and soon they were airborne.

Chapter Eight

Dylan saw Shelby finally release her death grip on the seat belt. He knew that the first time in a cockpit could be a little unnerving to a novice, but now that they were in the air, she seemed to be relaxing a bit.

Dylan still wasn't sure why he had invited her up here with him. Like his house, he considered his Cessna's cockpit to be his own personal space, not to be shared lightly. And yet he'd invited a quirky little redhead into both the places most sacred to him.

Through the lighting of the panels he could see her looking around with wonder in those big green eyes. The sun was just beginning to come up, giving them a little bit more natural visibility.

He wasn't likely to forget the picture she made sitting in the cockpit in the early morning light.

Which was the exact reason why he probably shouldn't have invited her up here.

Dylan looked down at the control panel and the weather printout he had. They'd have to go out of their way to avoid the storm, but that couldn't be helped. There was no way they were flying through it; that was a risk no good pilot was willing to take if he had any other option.

Dylan waited for questions from Shelby about flying and which buttons and controls did what. Curiosity was only natural from someone in the cockpit for the first time. But although Shelby looked around constantly, she didn't ask any questions. Maybe she just wasn't curious about what he did as a pilot.

For the life of him, Dylan could not figure out why that bothered him.

"No questions?" he asked, growing even more irritated when he found he couldn't keep his irritation out of his voice.

Shelby's look was a little wary. "Actually, lots. But you said 'cargo doesn't talk,' so I figured you preferred quiet. I totally understand."

And just like that, Dylan felt like a total jerk again. She was just doing what he had implied he wanted and he had proceeded to get irritated at her for it.

What the hell was wrong with him? Shelby Keelan twisted him in knots.

"Ask away," he told her. "I promise not to bite."

She smiled just a tiny bit at that. "Honestly, Dylan, you don't have to entertain me. I know what it's like to just want to sit quietly with your own thoughts."

"Well, I appreciate that, but I honestly don't mind your questions."

The sun was beginning to make its way a little bit more over the horizon. They were flying east and soon it would be bright in their eyes. Sawyer reached into his pocket and pulled out his sunglasses and put them on.

"Aviators?" Shelby asked with one eyebrow raised.

"They're called that for a reason. I'll need them a lot in just a minute. There's an extra pair in the Velcro pocket, a little bit behind you to your right."

"How long have you been a pilot?" Shelby asked as she maneuvered around to access the pouch with the glasses.

"I started my charter business almost four years ago. I actually started flying as a helicopter pilot in the army.

I got out of the army about ten years ago and went into law enforcement, and also got my private-pilot's license. So I've been flying a long time."

"Something you love?"

Dylan hadn't really ever thought of that question. Did he love flying? "I enjoy the challenge of it, the concentration and control it takes to fly a small jet like my Cessna. I like owning my own business and being able to take the jobs I want."

Shelby nodded. "Yeah, I like that about my job, too."

She developed computer games. She'd talked about that last night.

"How did you get into coding games?" he asked her.

"I'm good with numbers. And at the end of the day, that's what computer coding is—numbers."

"So you're good at your job?"

She shrugged. "I'm the best."

She said it so matter-of-factly you could hardly doubt her. "Is that so? Have you done any games I would've heard of?"

She looked around at the plane's gauges as she answered. Dylan was shocked to hear the names of a couple of the most popular games *in the world* come out of her mouth.

"You developed those games?"

"Yep." Shelby ran her fingers over the air-speed indicator and didn't say anything else.

"Those are really popular games." Dylan wasn't a gamer by any means, but even he had heard of those. They were popular because of the strong female leads, plus parents loved them because they proved games could be addictively challenging and fun without gruesome violence and gratuitous language. But teenagers adored them because of all the add-ons players could download after

buying the game. New ones every couple of weeks, unlike other games where you had to wait months or longer.

"Yep." Obviously Shelby wasn't one to brag.

"Did you do all the downloads, too?"

She nodded this time, not saying anything at all.

"You're like a celebrity then, aren't you?"

"Maybe if you're a seventeen-year-old boy with acne."

Shelby would be a celebrity for any seventeen-year-
old boy for reasons having nothing to do with gaming,
but Dylan kept that thought to himself. "Everybody loved
how fast those add-ons came out. Did you do them all?"

Shelby shrugged again. "Yeah."

"How? Not sleeping at all for two years?"

"No, I'm just really quick with numbers and therefore
coding. Most programmers have to write, then go back
through and see if what they did works on the screen. It's a
lot of back-and-forth." Shelby repositioned the sunglasses
on her nose as the sun made its way up even brighter. "I
have a photographic memory with numbers. So I only
have to code things once and know exactly what the re-
sults will be."

"And that makes you fast?"

"Really fast. And I don't make any mistakes, so I don't
have to recheck anything like normal programmers."

"You never make a mistake?"

"Not when it comes to numbers. I remember everything about them."

"You're a genius with numbers." It wasn't a question.
Dylan already knew it was true. "That's why you went
to MIT and that's how you met Megan."

"Megan's the true genius. I just happen to remember
digits. But she can figure out, build, tear apart or fix
just about anything having to do with computers. It's
pretty amazing."

"Yeah, she's helped Omega Sector out on more than one occasion."

"Omega Sector, that's where she works, right? And her husband, Sawyer, too."

"Yeah, actually, all three of my siblings work there."

Shelby nodded. "Is that where you worked when you were in law enforcement?"

Astute little thing, wasn't she? He'd only mentioned law enforcement in passing. "Yes, I worked for Omega for a few years."

"But you quit."

Dylan didn't want to get into this. He wanted to keep Fiona's ghost down on the ground where it belonged, not bring it up here in the cockpit.

"So, you want to fly the plane for a couple of minutes?" he asked her.

Dylan's diversion tactic worked perfectly. Shelby slid her sunglasses down on her nose and looked over at him with big eyes. "Really? Can I? Will we die?"

Dylan chuckled. "I'm pretty sure we won't die. I still have my control column right here in front of me in case I need to take over."

"What do I do?"

Really, at this altitude and since they were just flying straight and not changing direction or speed, she wouldn't be doing much, but Dylan didn't want to say anything that would cause the excitement to fade from her eyes. "You'll just take the yoke right in front of you and hold it steady, and I'll let go."

Shelby reached out for the control column, the plane's steering wheel, that was in front of her chair.

"Then, just try not to do anything to crash us," Dylan continued. Shelby's hands flew back away from the yoke without touching it.

"Wait, what would make us crash?" Dylan winced as she yelled it into the mouthpiece of her headphones.

"I'm just kidding, Shelby. You won't do anything to make us crash." He laughed. "Just keep it steady. Don't pull back or forward quickly and we'll be fine."

She reached over and slapped at his arm, difficult with the harness holding her in. But then she slowly reached out and took the control column.

"I'm going to let go now, okay?"

"Okay." Shelby nodded, but didn't look at him. She had a tight grip on the column.

"Just relax." Dylan let go of the control column, but kept his hands on his knees in case he needed to take back over quickly. "You're flying the plane, Shelby."

"I am?" Shelby glanced quickly over at his hands. "I am," she repeated, wonder clear in her voice this time.

Dylan let her enjoy the moment of realizing she was flying an airplane. She didn't seem in any danger of jerking the steering column.

"Why don't you ease the yoke back toward you just a little bit?"

"That will cause us to go up, right?"

"Yep."

"Don't you have to check with Air Traffic Control or whomever?" Shelby sounded pretty nervous.

"Not to go up just a hundred feet. They allow a little leeway. Plus, there aren't any planes around in the traffic pattern for miles."

"Okay, then. What do I do?"

"Just pull the yoke back toward you, gently and slowly."

The plane began to climb slightly as Shelby did as Dylan instructed. A surprised laugh fell out of her mouth. Dylan grinned.

"Now you're really flying."

Neither of them were expecting the roar and loud

popping noise that came from the engine to their right, before it stuttered to silence. Dylan immediately grabbed the control column.

"Oh, no, Dylan, what did I do?" Shelby's voice was frantic.

"That definitely wasn't you, Shelby. That was an engine flameout."

And there was absolutely no reason it should've happened at their rather benign speed and altitude.

"Are you sure?"

Dylan fought to keep the plane steady, more difficult now with only one good engine. They could still fly with just one engine, but they would need to get on the ground soon.

"I'm sure it wasn't you, Shelby. You didn't do anything wrong, I promise."

Dylan needed to call the situation in to Air Traffic Control. Immediately. They needed to get on the ground.

"ATC, this is Cherokee four four six one nine en route to private UNICOM airfield six two four seven. We've experienced an engine flameout in one engine. Over."

"Roger, Cherokee four four six one nine. You okay? Over."

Dylan looked over at the paper sectional chart then his electronic GPS system. The closest airfield was about sixty miles. They would be able to make it. "Affirmative. Request clearance for set down at unmanned airfield five miles east of Christiansburg. Over."

"Roger that, Cherokee four four six one nine. No traffic reported—"

The Air Traffic Control's words were drowned out by another roar, this time from the left engine. Dylan could see the glare of the flames out of the corner of his eye for a moment before it went out.

Now they were flying with no power in either engine.

Shelby's gasp was audible in the silence that now filled the aircraft. There was no way they would make it to that airfield.

"Mayday, mayday, mayday. ATC, this is Cherokee four four six one nine. We have lost the second engine. I repeat, neither engine is responding. Over."

"Roger, Cherokee four four six one nine." Dylan could tell he had the controller's full attention now. "What are your exact coordinates?

Dylan found it hard to look down for the coordinates from the GPS while trying to keep the Cessna under control. They were in essence a glider now. Dylan fought to keep the nose of the plane up.

Dylan glanced over gratefully as Shelby tilted the GPS toward her and read off the coordinates to the air traffic controller.

"Tower, we will be making an emergency landing, location yet undetermined."

"Roger that, Cherokee four four six one nine. We'll contact emergency services in that area."

Dylan looked around for anywhere they could possibly land. The mountains and trees made it difficult. And there was nothing ATC could do to help him now. Dylan didn't know where he would land, so the fire trucks wouldn't know where to go.

"What do we do?" Shelby asked. It was much easier to hear her now with no engine noise.

"We need to find a place to put her down. Fast. Any open area."

It was difficult to see anything around them except trees. He definitely could not land on trees. They were losing altitude quickly. They had only minutes left.

"What about over there?" Shelby pointed to a slight break in the trees maybe two miles away. It wasn't a field, and definitely wasn't a runway, but it was better than the beautiful, but deadly, trees around them everywhere.

Plus, it was the only option. Dylan began to maneuver the plane in that direction.

"C'mon, baby," he muttered as the plane shuddered slightly, resisting his ease toward the opening in the trees.

"Shelby, we're going to be coming down hard and fast. Make sure your harness is on as tightly as possible." Dylan did the same to his own.

The clearing wasn't as large as Dylan had hoped, but they were too low to do anything else now. He slowed the plane as much as possible and prayed they'd live through the next thirty seconds.

The Cessna hit roughly on the top edges of some trees then bounced hard against the ground, flying back up, then coming down roughly again. The impact was bone-jarring, but at least they weren't a ball of flames. Dylan slowed the plane as much as he could and then turned the yoke sharply so the plane began to slide to the side. Working against their own speed snapped them around hard, collapsing one side of the plane as the landing gear gave out, but it slowed them down.

He watched the trees speed toward them and braced himself, hoping he had slowed them down enough not to die in the impact.

He reached out his hand for Shelby, who took it right before they hit the tree line.

Then there was only blackness.

Chapter Nine

Shelby's eyes opened and it took her a minute to get her bearings. She was hanging in the seat sideways, the harness holding her in. The whole cockpit seemed to be tilted at some sort of canted angle.

But she could move all her fingers and toes without much pain and didn't seem to be bleeding. As far as she was concerned, that was the best possible outcome considering what had just happened.

Of course, the whole plane was filled with smoke, so they weren't out of danger yet. She wasn't sure if anything might ignite, but she didn't want to stay around and find out. And she hadn't heard anything at all from Dylan.

"Dylan? Hey, Dylan, are you okay?"

No response. Now Shelby was even more panicked.

"Dylan! Can you hear me?" She struggled to loosen herself from the seat-belt harness, difficult to do when it was supporting a lot of her weight. She finally managed to get the release clasp to function, and fell out of her seat onto the control panel.

She eased her way down to Dylan's seat, where he lay motionless against his belt. Shelby sucked in a panicked breath. Was he dead?

Shelby was reaching to take Dylan's pulse, when he groaned and moved slightly. Oh, thank God. Not dead.

"Dylan? Can you hear me? We're alive. But I think we need to get out of here because there's smoke everywhere."

Shelby braced her legs against the cockpit's small side window, which was now on the ground since the plane was mostly on its side, and used both her hands to ease Dylan's head back from where it hung from the harness. She brushed her fingers through his black hair. "Dylan. Can you wake up? We've got to get out of here."

Maybe she was going to need to get Dylan out on her own. Maybe his injuries were more severe than hers. Shelby began to attempt to unfasten his harness, a feat much more difficult since she couldn't brace his weight with anything. Plus, the fastener seemed to be stuck.

And the smoke was really becoming an issue now. Something was definitely on fire. Not surprising considering they'd just crashed.

Shelby stopped and looked around. *Think.* She needed to get Dylan out of that seat and out of the cockpit, which could turn into a ball of flames at any moment. She needed some sort of knife to cut through his seat belt since she couldn't get it unbuckled.

Hadn't Dylan had some sort of fancy pocketknife earlier? That would be perfect. Which pocket had he kept it in?

Shelby tried to get her hand into one of Dylan's front jean pockets, difficult with how his body was angled in the seat. Shelby tried to force his weight up so she could reach farther into the pocket.

"I think molesting someone while they're unconscious is a crime."

Dylan's deep voice in Shelby's ear caused her to stumble a step backward into the control panel. She felt herself blush. "I, um, was trying to get your pocketknife. I couldn't get your belt to unfasten."

Dylan smiled and pulled at the belt, grunting. "Yeah, I think the clasp is broken. My knife isn't in my pocket, it's in my backpack in the storage compartment behind my seat."

From her stance underneath him, Shelby felt something drip onto her shoulder. She touched the drop with her fingers and saw the red.

"You're bleeding."

Dylan's voice was tight. "Yeah, I think it's my arm. I can feel the burn."

Shelby realized she hadn't even checked to see if Dylan had any injuries. But that would have to wait. She needed to get him out of the harness belt and out of this cockpit.

"Okay, just hang in there. I'm going to get the knife."

The smoke was getting heavier and Shelby was beginning to cough. She maneuvered around until she was behind Dylan's seat, careful not to step on him.

"The storage container is to the left," Dylan told her, coughing between words.

From her vantage point, Shelby could see that the cabin on the plane, although intact, was definitely burning toward the rear. They had to get out of here fast or the fire would block the door.

Shelby found the container and opened it, quickly pulling out the backpack Dylan had stored there, as well as the first-aid kit. "Where's the knife in your backpack?"

"Side pocket." Dylan's voice was noticeably weaker.

Damn it. "Hang on, Dylan. I've got it."

Shelby threw the first-aid kit in the backpack and worked her way back down to Dylan's seat. She got underneath his large chest and pushed up with her arm and shoulder, trying to take some of Dylan's weight. Once she cut the straps, he was going to fall.

"Ready?" She didn't wait for his response, just opened

the knife and sliced through one of the canvas straps at his shoulder, then the other.

There was no way Shelby could hold Dylan once he was released from the belts. He was six foot one of sheer muscle, and probably at least seventy pounds heavier than her. But she did her best to keep him from crashing into the plane instruments below. Although all he really did was just crash into her instead.

She helped Dylan to his feet, a little unsteady herself.

"Okay, let's get out of here," Dylan wheezed, beginning the climb over the pilot seats. He grabbed some sort of map as he was on his way up.

"We have to hurry, there's definitely a fire in the back." Shelby noticed Dylan's arm was bleeding even more now and he didn't look very steady. But he managed to pull himself up and through the flimsy cockpit door that had broken away and into the main cabin, reaching back to help Shelby.

"I'm fine," she told him. "You get the outer door open. I'll get myself out of here."

The outer door was completely blocked because of how the plane lay on its side, but Dylan was able to get the emergency window open. Dylan climbed through, then reached back for Shelby. Both made their way outside, Shelby still carrying the backpack. Smoke poured out of the open window behind them.

They gulped fresh air and stumbled from the wreckage toward the trees. Shelby kept expecting an explosion behind them, but it never came. Finally they sat down against some trees, both of them breathing heavily between coughs. Shelby looked back at the plane. It may not have exploded, but the smoke and fire were now pouring out of it.

It was a miracle she and Dylan were alive at all.

They sat in silence for long moments, both of them

trying to catch their breath and process the fact that they had just survived that burning death trap a few hundred yards away.

"So…the landing was a bit bumpy. Sorry about that," Dylan said.

Shelby closed her eyes and began to laugh. "Yeah, maybe if you'd just had a few more flight hours under your belt, it wouldn't have been so rough. Be sure to work on that."

But Shelby knew the truth. If it had been a less capable pilot than Dylan flying the plane, they'd be dead right now. Shelby had no doubt about it.

"What happened up there, Dylan?"

"I don't know, exactly. One engine flaming out? That can happen. It's highly unlikely, but it can happen. But both engines flaming out? No."

Shelby wasn't sure what that meant. "But both did, right?"

"Yeah, but it wasn't a coincidence. It happened because it was helped along."

"You mean someone sabotaged the plane?"

Dylan nodded. "I thoroughly checked her out before we took off. I take preflight seriously. And there was nothing out of the ordinary to be seen."

"What would have caused the engines to cut off like that?"

"If I had to guess, probably some sort of fuel or oil contamination. It ate away at the integrity of the fuel, and then basically starved the engines. It would be a pretty easy way to deliberately sabotage a plane going on a route like ours through mountains and forest terrain, with no easy place to land. And a crash would burn away all the fuel, making the tampering virtually untraceable."

Shelby leaned her head back against the tree behind

her. What could she say to that? Had someone really tried to kill her *three* times in the past twenty-four hours?

"It just seems so far-fetched."

Dylan began to stand. "I know. Whatever those numbers are that are stuck in your head? Evidently they're more important than you or Megan or anybody at Omega thought. We need to get you there as soon as possible." Dylan had to grab the tree for support. Shelby scrambled to her feet to help him.

"Before we go anywhere, we need to bandage that arm. Are you hurt anywhere else?" she asked him.

"I don't think so," Dylan muttered. "It's hard to tell. Everything hurts." He looked up at her. "Are you okay? I didn't even ask."

"Well, it's like you said—everything hurts. But nothing hurts too much to move it. So that's good."

Shelby took the first-aid kit out of the backpack. She sat down next to Dylan and rolled his sleeve up. The cut on his arm was still bleeding, but not too bad. It didn't look like it would need stitches. Shelby ripped open a small package of antibiotic ointment and squeezed it over the wound to help keep any infection out. Dylan winced, but didn't complain. Shelby covered the wound, then wrapped his arm in gauze.

"Thank you," he said softly when she was finished.

"Thank you for getting us on the ground in one piece when almost any other pilot would've scattered us in little-bitty bits around the forest."

"Well, that's pretty gruesome imagery. But you're welcome."

DYLAN STOOD UP and watched his Cessna burning. He was glad he was able to get himself and Shelby on the ground relatively unharmed, and not in little-bitty bits as Shelby had pointed out so delicately.

There was an old pilot's joke that any landing you could walk away from was a landing not a crash. But watching his plane burn, Dylan knew that wasn't true. He felt a pang of sadness. Even though insurance would cover the cost of a similar new plane, it wouldn't be the same. He'd traveled a lot of miles in that little Cessna. His time in that plane had gotten him through some of the worst days of his life.

Shelby didn't say anything to him and he was grateful. There weren't any words that could be said. It was a pile of metal, for heaven's sake.

But it was also so much more than that.

Dylan appreciated it even more when Shelby slipped her hands into his. Whatever she was thinking, it was supportive and it didn't need words.

Dylan stood there a few more minutes. Nothing could be saved from the plane. It wasn't even safe to go back in to try the radio or to get their cell phones. Air Traffic Control knew their basic whereabouts, but there was no way to get any rescue vehicles up here.

According to the GPS Dylan had grabbed, they were only fifteen miles south of a small town. The town hadn't had a runway, but they would have a telephone.

Dylan couldn't ignore the fact that only Omega knew Dylan was the one transporting Shelby to Washington, DC. It was possible that the person who had run Shelby off the road both times last night had followed her from her house, but this deliberate tampering with Dylan's aircraft could really only mean one thing.

There was somebody within Omega working against them.

Dylan didn't even like to think it, but it was the only thing that made sense. Whoever had sabotaged his plane had done it last night during the storm. Dylan had flown the Cessna yesterday and there hadn't been anything wrong with it.

And over the past year, all his siblings had grumbled about the possibility of a mole in Omega. Problems here and there within operations, but never anything that could be proven. But standing here watching his plane burn, knowing neither he nor Shelby should've been alive after that crash, Dylan had all the proof he needed of a mole.

And while Dylan wouldn't directly accuse anyone without more proof, he had to admit that a lot of this was pointing right at Dennis Burgamy, his old boss. Burgamy had sent Shelby to him, had known they'd be using Dylan's plane.

That was pretty damning evidence.

"We're not going to have to walk all the way to Christiansburg, are we? That's sixty miles away, right? I heard you tell Air Traffic Control." Shelby looked up at him, brows furrowed.

Dylan put his hand against her cheek and smoothed his thumb over her brows to ease the worry lines before he even realized what he had done. He rubbed his thumb over her lip and stepped closer to her, but then stopped himself. He lowered his hand and stepped back. Touching Shelby was not a good idea.

Dylan cleared his throat. "Um, no. There's another town closer. About fifteen miles. With this terrain, it should take us five or six hours to walk. We should get started."

Dylan turned away from her, trying to remember all the reasons why he needed to keep his distance. Damned if he could think of a single one of them.

Chapter Ten

Dylan had insisted on carrying the backpack, although Shelby had offered because of his wounded arm. After touching her so gently, then completely backing away, Dylan had busied himself taking everything out of the backpack. She noticed he was quite careful not to touch her again.

The backpack was obviously his overnight bag. It contained mostly a change of clothes and some toiletry items. But he also had a can of soda, a few packs of trail mix, some bottles of water and even a couple of trash bags. Plus the lunch he had packed for himself.

"Lunch?"

"I packed it last night while you were sleeping. The airstrip we would've used for Omega only has vending machines. I thought I might be turning around to go home right away."

"Weren't you going to see your siblings while you were in town? Have lunch with them?"

Dylan shrugged, but didn't look her in the eye. "Maybe. I wasn't sure. I didn't want to be in the way of whatever you were doing."

In other words, he would've visited with his family if it meant he wouldn't have to spend extra time with Shelby. But just in case being in Shelby's presence was unavoidable, he had packed a lunch so he could make a quick getaway in his plane.

"Nice," Shelby muttered. She wasn't sure why she was so hurt. Dylan Branson had made it abundantly clear multiple times he wanted to spend as little time with her as possible.

"Look, it's nothing personal," he told her, taking the useless items like shaving cream and toothpaste out of the backpack.

"It feels pretty personal."

Dylan looked up from where he was crouched, his hazel eyes pinning her. "Yeah, I suppose it would." He rubbed his fingers over his eyes. "There are elements to this story that you're not aware of. And I'm sorry I keep hurting your feelings, but it's just better for both of us if I stay away from you."

Shelby had no idea what she was supposed to say to that.

Not that she was going to get a chance to anyway. Dylan left the pile of items he deemed useless for their hike, repacked the helpful things—the clothes, food, drinks, trash bags—into the backpack and stood up. "We need to get going."

He turned and began walking. Shelby was left with the choice of following or being left behind. They walked in silence for a while. The terrain wasn't easy; there weren't any roads or paths this far away from civilization.

As trees and bushes got thicker, Shelby found herself walking closer to Dylan. He had wrapped his extra shirt around his good arm so he could move limbs and bushes out of their way without getting scratched. After the first time of Dylan having to wait holding a branch for Shelby to catch up, she stayed right behind him.

As they marched on, the weather became less cooperative. The temperatures were already cold and the clouds were beginning to threaten storms again. Shelby found she could keep the core of her body warm by the constant moving, but her fingers were freezing. Her feet were wet from the soggy ground and she had lost feeling in her toes an hour ago.

When it started to drizzle, Shelby just ducked her head down and pushed her chilled hands into her pockets, although it didn't help much. The cold rain occasionally dripped down her neck, but Shelby plowed on. She reminded herself that just a couple short hours ago she had been sure they were about to die. Being a little wet and uncomfortable was bearable.

But she still shuddered when another cold drop of rain found its way through the trees and down the neck of her shirt.

She forced herself to trudge on step after step, trying to think about anything but her own misery. Mostly that included trying to think of the *elements* of Dylan's story that she wasn't aware of. Although she knew she shouldn't care.

Shelby didn't realize Dylan had stopped walking and slammed right into his broad back. His reflexes were quick. He reached his good arm around his back to steady her against him.

"You okay?" he asked.

"Yeah." Cold. Tired. Hungry. Stressed. Miserable. "I'm fine."

"This storm is moving in quickly. It's only drizzling now, but soon it will be pouring. We're going to need to find somewhere to hunker down. Hypothermia can become an issue even in these temps if we let ourselves get too wet."

Shelby gritted her teeth to keep them from chattering. It was probably in the upper fifties, but she felt much colder in her shirt and lightweight jacket. "Where?"

She forced the word out, sticking her numb hands under her armpits.

"We're going to build a wickiup. It won't be perfect, but it will be something." Shelby watched almost in a daze as Dylan began gathering thin branches about four to five feet in length.

"A wickiup?"

"It's also called a debris hut. It won't be fancy, but it will get us through the next few hours. We're going to build it up against that overturned tree. It'll provide us with a good deal of shelter from the rain all on its own."

Shelby looked over at the tree Dylan pointed at. She felt as if her brain was processing information too slowly. Dylan, on the other hand, was moving quickly, efficiently. Not unlike when she had watched him go through his pre-flight checklist. He had done this before.

He looked around for something, and then evidently found what he needed: a stick of a specific size, about six feet long, thicker than the others.

"This will be our ridgepole." He wedged one end of the stick into the overturned tree, about four feet up, and wedged the other end into a spot on the ground. "Now we add branches to make a lattice."

Slowly, Shelby's brain began to process. He was making them a shelter. It wouldn't be very big, but it would maybe keep them drier and warmer. She looked up at the clouds that were now ominous overhead.

She needed to start functioning and help. Shelby began gathering sticks similar to the size Dylan was using to frame his construction. He seemed surprised when she handed the first few she found to him, but then nodded.

"Thanks. We'll need to hurry if we're going to beat this storm."

"How many more do you need?" she asked him.

"At least a dozen."

Shelby began to scramble for them as Dylan took some items out of the backpack. Trash bags.

"One of the disadvantages of owning your own charter business? You're also the cleanup crew. But these will come in handy keeping out the rain." He took his pocketknife and began to slice them lengthwise. "We'll use them as tarps."

The thunder boomed from the clouds overhead, causing Shelby to drop her sticks. She bent down to pick them up again and brought them over to Dylan.

"Good," he said as he stretched the trash bag over the frame he had built and pinned it to the ground. "Try to find as much dry pine straw, grass, leaves, anything we can use to put on the ground and over the tarp."

Shelby brought anything she thought might be useful. Some he used, some he didn't, but the rain was picking up, making gathering more material impossible.

Thunder boomed again and rain began to fall in earnest.

"That's it. We'll do more damage than good if we bring anything in now. It'll be too wet. Let's get in. I'll go first since it will be easier for you to work your way around me."

He wasted no time, throwing the backpack into the shelter then sliding himself headfirst into the small enclosure. There was barely room for Dylan. How was Shelby supposed to fit?

"Okay, I'm in. It's pretty cramped."

A blast of thunder eliminated any further hesitation Shelby felt. She climbed in as rain began to really pour down around her. She slid as far as she could. Dylan's arm reached around her and slid her fully inside.

The shelter was cramped, no doubt, but it was also warm and dry. Shelby took a moment to enjoy being out of the wet and wind; the tension she'd been carrying eased some. Dylan was lying flat, his head resting against the backpack. There was no room to sit or shift around.

The warmth felt delightful and Shelby felt herself relaxing. Her head slowly drooped until it came to rest on the hard ground. Except it wasn't the hard ground. It was Dylan's muscular chest. Shelby realized how much of her body was lying on Dylan's body. There really wasn't any way around it. There was no room.

But unwilling to trigger one of Dylan's cooties attack where he didn't want to touch her, Shelby tried to pull herself back and away from him. But his large body seemed to completely fill up the shelter.

"You might as well relax. We're going to be stuck here for a while. At least it's warm and dry." Dylan shifted and pulled Shelby closer, but she still resisted.

"What?" he asked her, his voice deep and soft.

Shelby sighed and closed her eyes. She could not be thinking how deep and soft his voice was. Not trapped in this little shelter with a storm raging outside.

And especially not because at any moment he might decide he couldn't stand to be near her. Again.

"I just don't want to make you uncomfortable. You seem to do okay, but then something happens and you…"

"I what?"

"I don't know. Panic or something. Like you've got to get away from me as soon as possible."

That was met with silence. Shelby didn't even know why she had brought it up. She leaned up on her elbow so she could try to see him in the mostly dark enclosure. "Look, you're not into me. I get it. It's not a prob—"

His lips stopped the flow of her words and wrecked Shelby's train of thought. Her eyes closed as his hand reached up to wrap behind her neck and pull her down more firmly against him. He teased her lips apart slowly, nibbling at them.

All Shelby could hear was the rain and all she could feel was Dylan. And that was just fine. His other arm came up to wrap around her waist.

The kiss went on as Dylan pulled her closer, shifting her weight until she was almost fully lying on top of him. He traced her lips with his tongue and she opened her mouth, giving them both the access they wanted.

But another large crack of thunder, directly over them, startled them apart. Shelby opened her eyes to find Dylan looking at her. He stared at her for long moments.

"I'm into you. That is definitely not the problem."

But Shelby noticed he didn't pull her back in for another kiss. Not that they could do much more anyway in the middle of the wilderness in a lightning storm.

Instead, he slid her weight off him by rolling slightly to the side so she was tucked next to him. Then pulled her head down against his chest so she rested against him. Shelby gave up any thought of trying to keep distance between them. She just relaxed. His arm around her began playing with her hair.

Neither of them said anything for a long time as the storm continued to rage overhead. Shelby was amazed at how well the shelter held.

"I can't believe we're still dry. You must have made one of these shelters before." She remembered the deftness he had shown when putting it together.

"Yeah. It was part of my training in the army. We had to build field-expedient shelters—ones made out of only natural objects. You can stay relatively dry in those, but having the trash bags really helped."

"How long were you in the army?"

"Six years. Got my college degree and pilot experience while I was in, so a pretty good deal for me overall."

"And then you went to work for Omega Sector." Shelby could feel Dylan begin to tense at the mention of the law enforcement group he once worked for, but had no idea why.

"Yes. They recruited me, actually."

"Were you a pilot for them?"

"On some missions, but not necessarily. I was an undercover agent. So I used whatever I could to give me an in with certain criminals. Being a pilot helped in a lot of situations."

"Your siblings all work for Omega?" It was difficult to concentrate with Dylan making circles on her waist and hip with his hand. "They like it?"

"Yeah. Everyone has had their ups and downs, but none of them seem to want to leave."

"Why did you leave?"

Dylan's hand stopped moving then. It dropped away from her body altogether. He was silent for so long Shelby thought he was going to refuse to answer.

"An operation went wrong. And some people were hurt because I made stupid mistakes. I got out right after that."

Shelby was quiet for a moment. She could feel Dylan's heart beating in his chest that rested under her ear. She trailed her hand that rested at his waist up his torso. She sat up so she could look him in the eye. She cupped his cheek with her hand.

"I'm sure it wasn't your fault. Anybody working at Omega has to know there are risks involved."

"These were innocent people. Not agents."

Shelby knew she should just leave it alone, but somehow couldn't. "But still, you can't control everything. I'm sure it wasn't—"

"It was my wife and unborn child that died. I led a member of a crime syndicate group right to them. He shot her right in front of me before I could do anything about it."

Dylan flinched from Shelby's hand that still rested on

his cheek, so she moved it. She lay back down, unable to stand the agony in Dylan's eyes any longer.

This explained so much of his hot-and-cold reactions toward her. Dylan was obviously still in love with his dead wife. Shelby knew he wished he didn't have to touch her right now, but she was unable to do anything about it in the cramped enclosure. Her head now rested on his arm rather than his chest. She stared up at the ceiling of the shelter, listening to the rain.

Dylan didn't elaborate any further. Nor did the arm that had been around her touch Shelby again. Shelby was amazed at how close they could be together, yet so, so far apart.

Chapter Eleven

Dylan never liked to talk about Fiona. She had been so young, so beautiful, so full of life.

Okay, Dylan knew that wasn't totally accurate. Really, Fiona had been a little spoiled and their marriage had been a bit rocky. But you couldn't really say those things about someone who had been struck down in the prime of her life.

Dylan didn't know if his marriage to Fiona would've worked out if she had lived. But he damn well knew he would've loved that child—his son—she had been carrying. No matter what, Dylan would've loved that child.

"She was only four months pregnant," Dylan murmured. "The baby never had a chance. Sometimes I've wondered if Fiona had been further along, if the baby possibly could've made it, even if she hadn't."

Dylan had never said those words out loud to anyone. He wasn't sure why he was saying them to Shelby now. They probably made him sound like the most insensitive jerk in the history of the world.

Dylan braced himself for whatever Shelby would say, because no matter what it was, it wouldn't be right. Nothing could be said to make the situation right.

But Shelby didn't say anything. She just reached up

and grabbed the hand of his arm that was under her head. She intertwined their fingers.

And somehow that was enough. No words were needed.

Dylan thought about Shelby as the storm raged on around them. The way she had handled this whole situation had been pretty impressive. She hadn't fallen apart, not during the crash, not afterward.

She'd marched on through the wilderness at a pretty punishing speed, although Dylan knew she had to be cold. Not once complaining. For someone who spent the majority of time by herself behind a computer, the way she was holding it together in this real-life dangerous situation was impressive.

Hell, everything about her was impressive. But Dylan knew he had to leave her alone. He had nothing to offer. He didn't even have a job now, for goodness' sake, not since his Cessna lay burned a few miles away.

The storm seemed to be moving away from them. Good, they needed to get moving. As soon as they made it into the little town, Dylan would call for a pickup. But he wouldn't be calling Omega directly, not while there was a mole. Dylan would call the people he knew he could trust: his brothers and sister. One of them would come get them and bring them to Omega.

But maybe Dylan wouldn't leave immediately. Somebody needed to stick close to Shelby and make sure she was safe. His siblings had their hands full with their own cases and duties.

But Dylan still planned to keep his hands off the tiny redhead resting beside him. Definitely no more kisses. Because he knew he wouldn't be stopping next time, whether or not they were in the middle of a lightning storm in the wilderness.

"Sounds like it's passing through," Dylan told her. "We should be able to get going again in a few more minutes."

"How much farther do we have?"

"Probably eight or nine more miles. Maybe three more hours."

He heard Shelby's sigh, the first indication of stress about the situation he'd heard from her. "You're doing great. Couldn't ask for a better hiking partner."

Shelby gave the most unfeminine grunt Dylan had ever heard. He couldn't help laughing.

Dylan released Shelby's hand and shifted around behind him to get the backpack. "Let's eat the food. No point carrying it when we're hungry."

"Definitely."

They made short work of the sandwiches and soda from Dylan's lunch. It wasn't enough to fill them up given the number of calories they were expending, but at least it took the edge off. They decided to save the trail mix and water for later when they'd need it.

Eating lying down wasn't easy, but they managed. By the time they had finished the sandwiches, the worst of the storm had passed. The thunder and lightning were gone.

"Are you ready to get going?" he asked her. He knew neither of them were thrilled at the thought of hours of walking in the cold, but it was just going to get worse if they had to go after the sun went down. They definitely didn't want to be stranded out in the wilderness overnight if they had any other option.

"Yep." Shelby didn't sound enthused, but she certainly wasn't complaining either. A lot of other women wouldn't be so tough. Fiona sure wouldn't have been. Damn it, Dylan had to stop comparing Shelby to Fiona. Shelby seemed to win every time, which couldn't be fair, right? Fiona was dead and couldn't defend herself. Shelby was very much alive.

For some reason, a quote from the one literature class

Dylan had taken in college came to mind. From Shake-speare, if he remembered correctly.

Though she be but little, she is fierce.

Yeah, that was Shelby. Fierce.

Dylan turned to her. "The walk is going to be tough, but you've been doing really well."

Shelby rolled her eyes. "Thanks. I don't necessarily feel that way, but thanks."

Dylan nodded. "We're going to try to salvage the trash bags, in case we need to reuse them. As a matter of fact, you might want to wrap one around yourself if you're getting dripped on too much."

"It's my hands that get really cold. I wish I had some gloves."

It was only the beginning of November, but in the mountains with the rain, it was easy to get chilled. Especially someone with as little insulation as Shelby.

"I have extra socks in the backpack. They aren't gloves, but they'll at least give you a little covering."

"I'll take them. Thanks."

Dylan slid out of the shelter, wincing a little at the ache in his arm. It was painful, but not unmanageable, so he put it out of his mind. The rain had mostly stopped, but he could tell the difference in temperature immediately.

Shelby slid out behind him. "Wow, we would've been in trouble without the shelter."

Dylan set down the backpack and took out the socks, handing them to Shelby. "Here, put these on."

"Let me help you take down the shelter first."

Dylan shook his head. "No, it's all wet. You need to stay as dry and warm as possible, not get wet taking this apart."

"But what about you?"

"I've got quite a bit more body mass than you. It'll take a lot more than some wet sticks to get me cold." He pointed to the socks. She was already shifting back and forth to keep warm. "Go ahead and put those on."

As she did so, Dylan grabbed the trash bag they had used on the ground, getting off as much of the leaves and debris they'd piled on it for warmth as he could. When he had shaken off as much as possible, he folded it and put it next to the backpack. Then he walked around the frame of the structure to get the other trash bag.

And nearly stepped on a large snake that was coming out from under some bushes.

Dylan immediately froze, hoping his stillness would cause the snake to just slither off in the other direction. But the snake coiled and slid its head back, ready to strike. Dylan knew by the shape of its head and coloring it was poisonous.

"Uh, whatcha doing over there, playing freeze tag?" Shelby began walking in his direction.

"No, Shelby, stay back!" Dylan's voice was barely more than a whisper, but as forceful as he could make it. If she came over here, it might cause the snake to strike.

"What is it?"

"A copperhead. Right in front of me. Ready to strike."

And the snake was angry.

Dylan knew if he got bit by a poisonous snake this far away from town, it would probably be deadly. There was no way Shelby would be able to get him all those miles by herself. And by the time she could get people back to Dylan…

A tree branch near Dylan swayed in the wind and the snake struck. Dylan jerked back, barely making it out of the snake's reach. It immediately coiled and reared its head back once more.

Snake attacks were based on movement. Dylan tried to hold as still as possible, hoping the snake would soon just go its own way. But the tree branches moving around

Dylan were keeping the copperhead on high alert. And from this angle, there was no way Dylan could scoop the snake away with a stick without being bitten.

Out of the corner of his eye, Dylan saw Shelby making her way around the far side of where the deadly pit viper was coiled.

"Shelby, what are you doing? Stop."

She totally ignored him.

"I'm not kidding, Shelby," Dylan muttered without taking his gaze from the snake in case it struck again.

"You can't get it from where you are, I can," Shelby murmured. Dylan saw the long stick in her hand.

He was about to warn her not to move any closer, when she scooped her stick under the snake and flung it—stick and all—as hard as she could away from them.

It wasn't necessarily elegant, but it got the job done. The copperhead was gone.

Shelby all but leaped at Dylan.

"It's gone, right? Please tell me it's gone and not coming back because I definitely do not have it in me to do that again. I really don't like snakes." A shudder racked her body.

"No, I'm pretty sure its twenty-foot flight through the air scared it away from here." He grabbed her shoulders to hold her still from the get-the-snake-away-from-me dance she was doing. "You shouldn't have done that. You could've been bitten."

The thought of that viper ripping into Shelby's delicate skin was something close to horrifying to Dylan. It made him angry to even think about it.

"No offense, but you were in much more danger of that than me. Ugh." She shuddered again. "Did you see me, Dylan? I was like something out of one of my games. Maybe I should write a situation like that into one." She elbowed him in the stomach and actually laughed.

Damn it, she wasn't even taking her close call seriously. How could she be that flippant with her life? Dylan took her by the shoulders and set her abruptly away from him. "Don't do something that stupid again. Why don't you use your brain for something more than just prying into my personal business, so we can both get out of here alive?"

As soon as he said the words, Dylan wished he could take them back. Damn it, that wasn't how he felt. Shelby hadn't been prying earlier, she'd just been making conversation.

He saw her eyes widen in shock from the sucker punch he'd delivered. He had to apologize. "Shelby—"

Her eyes dropped from his, her red hair creating a veil around her face as she studied the ground with a great deal of attention. She turned and stepped away. "No, you're right. I do need to stop being so stupid."

Somehow Dylan didn't think she was referring to copperheads. "No, Shelby, please…"

Dylan trailed off as she continued to step back from him, still looking down at the ground. "Like you said, we need to get going. I'll be more careful."

Dylan couldn't let this stay between them. He moved to stand right in front of her and reached over with both hands to tuck her hair behind her ears so he could see her face, then tilted her head back. Her eyes met his for just a moment then looked away.

"I'm sorry. What I said was unfair and untrue. You haven't pried at all. You…" *Distract me. Have my attention all the time. Make me forget that I'm no good for a long-term relationship. You make me want to kiss you just by standing there breathing.* "You scared me with that snake and I was stupid. I'm sorry."

She still wasn't really looking at him. Dylan took a half step closer so their faces were only inches apart. Then Shelby didn't have any choice but to look at him.

"I'm a pretty solitary guy, Shelby. I'm not around people too often and around gorgeous women like you even less. But that's no excuse for what I said. I'm sorry."

Shelby nodded slightly. "Okay."

Dylan stepped back. Or, he meant to step back, planned to step back. But instead, he brought his lips down to Shelby's and kissed her. Softly. With reverence.

An apology.

Although she didn't pull away, Shelby's lips were closed and unmoving under his. Dylan knew he should stop, should just end the kiss and let it go, but somehow he couldn't. He couldn't let her stay distant from him. He continued his gentle onslaught of her lips. Eventually Shelby sighed and leaned in closer, returning his kiss. Her arms traveled up his arms and wound around his neck.

A few drops of cold water falling from the trees above them reminded Dylan that they needed to get moving. He pulled back from Shelby, resting his forehead against hers.

"I guess we should get going," she whispered, her voice husky.

"Yeah. We don't want to get caught out here once it's dark."

They worked together to take down the other tarp and fold it up. They took a few sips of water and were on their way.

And although Shelby didn't seem to be hurt or angry anymore, there seemed to be a definite distance between them, despite their kiss.

Dylan knew that should be what he wanted. He knew her emotional distance shouldn't bother him. But it did.

More than he was willing to admit.

Chapter Twelve

Five hours later they made it into the small town they'd been aiming for. Pulaski, Virginia. Dylan had to admit, he was relieved. Although he was pretty adept with a geospatial map and compass, both of which he'd had in the backpack, even the best navigator could have problems in the weather and circumstances he and Shelby had been through.

The town was even smaller than Falls Run, and when Dylan and Shelby stumbled into the first building they came to—a small hardware store—they found they were already celebrities.

They were barely inside the door when a teenager working there squealed, "Oh, my gosh, you guys are the ones from the plane crash, right? You're alive. Oh, my gosh."

Dylan looked at Shelby, confusion mirroring on both of their faces.

He turned back to the girl, who was now getting her smartphone out to take pictures. "I'm sorry, how do you know we crashed our plane?"

"Are you kidding? *Everybody* knows. County emergency services came through this morning making an announcement that they'd been notified about an emergency landing of a plane somewhere nearby. Nobody knew exactly where."

"Wow," Shelby murmured.

The teenager didn't stop talking. "A couple groups of locals went out looking for you in the general direction emergency services thought you'd be, but they weren't sure how far to go, so I think they came back—

"Mom!" the teenager yelled in the middle of her own sentence, startling both Dylan and Shelby. "Those people from the airplane crash are here. Here in the store." Her voice dipped down to a more reasonable level. "No offense, but you guys look a little rough. Actually, I guess you guys look pretty good for having survived a plane crash."

"We were lucky," Dylan said. But listening to the young girl talk nonstop, Dylan was beginning to rethink that sentiment. Thankfully, the mother, a much more calm lady, came out of the back room.

"Oh, my goodness. A lot of people have been looking for you two." The woman looked over at her daughter who was still taking pictures with her cell phone. "Angi, get them some water bottles from the back."

The mom brought folding chairs over for Dylan and Shelby, which they gratefully accepted.

"Are you seriously injured? Do we need to call for an ambulance? The nearest hospital is about forty miles away, but we have a doc-in-a-box closer."

"No." Dylan shook his head then took the water bottle Angi brought them from the back. "We're both pretty bruised and banged up, but nothing too serious. I just need to use a phone if that's okay."

The hardware store door chimed behind them and Dylan looked over. A number of people were coming through the door. Even more were standing outside.

The mom shrugged. "Evidently Angi has posted your miraculous survival on all her many social media sites.

We don't get a lot of action in a town this small. You're a pretty big deal."

Dylan sighed. He didn't suppose much damage would come from one teenager posting their picture all over her instant-photo account, but he would've preferred not to have any record of him and Shelby here at all.

Shelby was sitting over in her seat staring blankly to the side. She was exhausted, not that Dylan could blame her. Dylan needed to call Sawyer and Megan to get them updated on the situation, and Sawyer could get down here and pick them up. But Dylan also needed some food for Shelby and a place where she could get a little rest.

Dylan stood up and walked with the mom a few steps away. "Look, Shelby and I really appreciate how worried everyone has been about us, but we really need to get some food and lie down, not talk to a bunch of people right now. Does this town have a hotel? Somewhere we can stay until our family comes to get us?"

The mom shook her head. "No hotel, but we have a furnished studio room upstairs you can use. We rent it out to campers during the summer. It's not fancy, but it has a bed and a shower."

"That would be perfect. Thank you."

"You take care of your wife. I'll get rid of the crowd and then get you a phone to use."

Dylan didn't bother to correct her, just walked over to Shelby and crouched beside her. "You doing okay?"

Shelby nodded. "Just tired. And hungry."

"I'm going to call Sawyer and Megan, then we'll grab something to eat. While we're waiting for them to get us, the lady has offered us the room upstairs to rest, okay?"

Dylan wasn't sure exactly how much of what he was saying Shelby was processing. She'd been quiet most of the past few hours. Some of it was exhaustion, but some of it was her keeping her distance from him.

Mrs. Morgan, the mom, shooed all the people away, knowing most of them by name. Someone said they would inform the county emergency services that Dylan and Shelby were alive. Everyone was excited. Dylan heard the word *miracle* muttered more than once.

"I'm going to go get you two some food," Mrs. Morgan came back to tell them after she'd gotten all the towns-people out of her store. "If you try to go out there now, I'm afraid you'll be mobbed. A friendly mob, but mob nonetheless."

"Thank you, Mrs. Morgan. We appreciate that," Shelby told the older woman.

Interesting that Shelby seemed to have enough energy to talk to everyone but Dylan. He could feel his face tighten.

"Here's the phone you wanted, honey." Mrs. Morgan handed Dylan a smartphone bedazzled with all shades of turquoise. "It's Angi's. Why don't you go back in the storage room if you need some quiet to talk."

Dylan knew he wouldn't have to worry about not being able to see in the closet because of all the multiple jewels shining on the phone.

He dialed Sawyer's personal phone number.

"Yes? This is Sawyer Branson." Dylan knew his brother didn't recognize the number.

"Hey, bro."

Dylan could hear Sawyer's sigh of relief. "Thank God."

"Are you where you can talk?" Dylan asked him.

"I'm at work."

"It's looking like that's not a place where you can talk." Dylan didn't want to make any accusations or suggestions while someone at Omega might overhear their conversation.

"Can I call you back at this number in five minutes? It won't be from my regular number. I'll be using a burner phone." Sawyer had learned how a known cell phone could be used against him on a case not too long ago.

Dylan waited for Sawyer's return call, amazed by the number of push notifications Angi got on her phone. Evidently she was the town's superstar since she had posted pictures of Dylan and Shelby on every social media site available. She'd even selfied herself into one of them, getting Dylan and Shelby in the background. Dylan rolled his eyes.

Ten more notifications came in before Sawyer's call came in a minute later.

"Okay, I'm out of Omega," Sawyer told him. Dylan could vaguely hear the sound of downtown DC traffic around Sawyer. "I texted Megan to meet me out here. She's been worried sick."

"So you know about the plane crash?"

"When you didn't show up at the scheduled time, we started checking for problems with Air Traffic Control. Your Mayday was at the top of their list. What the hell happened?"

Dylan rubbed a tired hand over his eyes. "We were sabotaged, Sawyer. Someone was deliberately trying to take us down and make it look like an accident."

Sawyer's muttered curse was foul. "How?" he asked after a moment.

Dylan appreciated that his brother didn't question his assessment of the situation. "If I had to guess, some sort of fuel contaminant. Something I wouldn't notice during preflight, but was sure to cause huge problems while in the air. Both engines flamed out."

Another string of obscenities were cut off midstream. "Hang on, Megan just got here."

Dylan could hear Sawyer tell Megan that he and Shelby were okay. He could hear Megan's relieved cries. And then she was on the phone.

"Dylan, you guys are really okay? Shelby, too?"

"Yes, I promise, Megan. A few cuts, shaken up, yes. And some smoke inhalation. But overall, we're in good shape. Shelby's getting something to eat right now."

"Okay. I'll let you talk to Sawyer again. We need to get you guys here quickly. See you soon, Dyl."

"Shelby will be glad to see you, Megan," Dylan told her softly. That set Megan off on a new round of tears.

"My hormonal, pregnant wife is now sobbing," Sawyer said.

"I'm sorry, Sawyer." Dylan hadn't meant to cause Megan undue stress.

"Don't worry about it. She cried this hard a couple of days ago because she saw a double rainbow."

Dylan could hear Sawyer's "ouch" as Megan evidently did him some sort of bodily harm at his comment.

"We need a pickup." Dylan gave Sawyer the name and location of the town. "And, Sawyer, this needs to be kept on the DL. Sabotage of my plane meant that someone knew *I* was delivering Megan. That info could've only come from Omega."

"Yeah, that thought already occurred to me."

"Shelby had already had two attempts on her life before we even got into the plane."

"Are you serious? Was she involved in the motel fire last night?"

That was news to Dylan. "What motel fire?"

"The motel in Falls Run. A fire burned half the building to the ground. There were no reports of injuries, so I figured Shelby hadn't stayed there."

Dylan cursed. "She would've been there. I got her out because I knew it would be too easy to find her there."

And a good thing Dylan had. Whoever had almost hit Shelby in the sedan obviously had come back to finish the job. If she had stayed at the hotel, she would've been an easy target. The killer could've either broken into the room or flushed her out with the fire and taken her out then. Could've easily made it look like an accident.

"Damn, Dylan," Sawyer said.

"Somebody has a real jonesing for getting rid of Shelby, that's for sure. Whatever codes are in her head must be pretty important."

"Agreed. And if it's someone at Omega who wants her dead, that's even more of a problem." Sawyer's voice was tight. Dylan knew his brother understood the gravity of the situation.

"I'm afraid it's coming from pretty high up, Sawyer."

"How high?"

"I just find it very interesting that Burgamy called me himself to set up this whole transfer. He definitely knew where Shelby would be and that we'd be on that plane."

Sawyer whistled through his teeth. "That would explain a lot of mishaps we've had in the past on different operations."

"I know. We've got to keep our location out of Burgamy's reach."

"Agreed. I'll work on the best way to come and get you that's completely under the radar. That'll probably be by car. So plan to see us in about four hours."

"Sounds good, we could use a little downtime until then. I'm not sure if I'll have this phone with me. But the owner can get me the message. We're at the only hardware shop here in town."

"Got it. Get some rest, bro," Sawyer said.

"Yeah."

"And, Dylan, we're glad you're all right. When they told us about your Mayday, I knew if I had to be going down in a plane, you would be my best chance of surviving."

"Thanks, man."

They disconnected the call. Dylan let out a quiet exhale. Knowing his brother was on the way took some of the pressure off, especially since Sawyer was circumventing normal Omega channels.

Dylan exited the storage room and found Shelby eating with Mrs. Morgan and Angi at a little table in the main room. Shelby seemed to be doing better, and although she wasn't saying much, was smiling at whatever stories the other two women were telling.

She looked over in Dylan's direction. Her eyes met his for just a moment before dropping away. Her smile faded completely.

"Finished your call?" Mrs. Morgan asked him. "We've got food here for you."

Dylan joined them and ate, and although Mrs. Morgan and Angi had plenty to ask him and talk about, Shelby had withdrawn. She didn't talk to him, barely looked at him.

Dylan realized she was emotionally removing herself from him and the situation. He couldn't really blame her after the way he'd run so hot and cold with her.

But Dylan knew, as he sat eating his fried chicken, looking at the woman who was looking everywhere else but at him, that he wasn't going to let her withdraw.

He couldn't.

Chapter Thirteen

Dylan was looking at her.

Of course, obviously he was looking at her because they were the only two people in the studio apartment that the friendly Mrs. Morgan and her slightly bratty daughter, Angi, had shown them to above the hardware store.

But he was *looking* at her. The way a man looks at a woman when he has something planned. That involved a bed.

And it was interesting Dylan was looking at her now, because Shelby had pretty much decided she wasn't going to look at Dylan anymore.

Because she'd only known him twenty-four hours and he had already ripped her heart out more times than most anyone else she knew. Not that she tended to let anyone close enough to do that, but she had been unable to help it in this situation.

Shelby understood Dylan's hot-and-cold behavior, she really did. His wife and unborn child dying right in front of him? That had to mess somebody up pretty badly. He still loved his wife. Shelby could certainly understand that.

But she couldn't keep allowing herself to get blind-sided by Dylan each time he realized he was acting on his attraction to Shelby. And Shelby knew he was attracted to her. But she also knew he didn't like it.

So the best thing Shelby could do was just keep her distance from him.

But he had to stop *looking* at her. Or else there would be no way she could do that.

Thankfully, Dylan turned away so he could lock the door that opened to the outside stairway that led down to the hardware store. Immediately he pulled the drapes all the way closed. Then turned to scope out the room, so Shelby did the same.

A king-size bed dominated most of it. Shelby stood staring at it.

"Much better than outside in the cold, right?" Dylan asked her. "Maybe we can get a nap."

She nodded, avoiding his gaze. "For sure. How long before someone is here to pick us up?"

"Sawyer's coming, but he needs to drive, so probably about four hours."

"What do you mean he needs to drive?"

"Normally for this distance he'd take one of the helicopters available through Omega. That would save a few hours."

"But he's not taking a helicopter now." Shelby wasn't unhappy about staying on the ground, but she didn't understand why Sawyer would delay their arrival.

Dylan looked as if he was going to say something then stopped.

"What?" she asked him. "Don't start keeping things from me now."

Dylan sighed. "When someone tried to kill you yesterday, that could've come from multiple sources. Somebody following you from your house, or perhaps an intercepted transmission or call between you and Megan."

"Yeah, that would make sense."

"But once it became clear someone had sabotaged *my* airplane, I realized that only someone from Omega Sector could've known you'd be with me. We were definitely not followed back to my house from town yesterday evening."

All Shelby could remember about the drive back to Dylan's house was seeing her red-and-black thong hooked on his big finger. Everything after that was a mortified blur. But if he said nobody followed them, she believed him.

"So it's somebody in Omega who is trying to kill me." The very agency Megan worked for, the same agency that was supposed to be protecting her and stopping DS-13.

"It looks that way. I'm sorry, Shelby."

Shelby sat on the edge of the bed. "I wish we didn't have to go to Omega at all if there is someone there trying to kill me. Someone who obviously doesn't care if they take you down with me."

"We have to. The hardware Megan needs to use with the numbers in your head is at Omega, so Sawyer must have a plan to sneak you in. He's getting here without Omega knowing."

"Yeah, I know." Shelby heard the hesitancy in her own tone, but couldn't help it.

Dylan came to sit beside her. "Thank you for not giving up. Most people who had survived three and a half attempts on their lives, not to mention hiking a marathon through the woods, might be ready to throw in the towel."

"Three and a half attempts?"

Dylan winked at her. "Well, I figured that copperhead should at least get half credit."

And there was *the look* again. Coupled with the dimple from his smile? How in the world was Shelby supposed to resist that? She had to get out. Right now.

"Okay, well, I'm just going to take a shower." Shelby stood up abruptly and made her way into the bathroom.

She saw Dylan's eyes narrow momentarily, but she didn't stop. She couldn't stay there on the bed looking at his gorgeous face.

She wasn't trying to be rude, she just needed some distance.

DYLAN WATCHED SHELBY all but run into the bathroom. He shrugged off his jacket, easing his wounded arm through the sleeve. Shelby had done a good job wrapping it. He'd planned to let the Omega doctor look at it, but that was out of the question now. It wasn't too bad. A full first-aid kit would probably be enough in the hands of any of his siblings who were trained as field medics.

But more important, Dylan didn't like the way Shelby was avoiding him. Maybe not physically—it was impossible for two people in their situation to avoid each other physically, although she was trying her best—but she was definitely closing down on him emotionally.

He'd started the emotional pull away first, so he couldn't blame Shelby. It was his own fault. It had been his MO for the past six years to keep himself separated from people, especially women.

And double especially for women who had insinuated their way under his skin in twenty-four short hours with their bravery, intelligence and beauty.

Damn it.

But those kisses today.

His body began to react just thinking about it. Those kisses had set them both on fire and it had been all Dylan could do not to make love to her right there in the middle of the wilderness only a few miles from where they'd almost died.

Dylan was a man known for his control. He liked to have control in all aspects of his world, and worked very hard to make sure he had it.

But a kiss with one small redhead had blown his control all to hell. Dylan would've made love to her in that tiny shelter, on the hard cold ground, if the thunder hadn't boomed and reminded him that they were in a pretty dangerous situation.

But now here they were: safe, warm, dry. And Shelby wouldn't look him in the eye. For the past six hours—since his asinine statement about staying out of his business—she had hardly spoken to him at all. Yesterday, Dylan might have welcomed the relief from her acerbic wit. But now he could see her withdrawal, could feel it. And it made him mad. Mostly at himself.

But Dylan would be damned if he was going to let Shelby shy away from him. He wanted her more than he'd ever wanted any other woman. Watching her in the forest had sealed it for Dylan. She had shown strength and courage under demanding circumstances that could've rightfully caused her to crumble. Would've caused *most* people to crumble.

But she hadn't crumbled. The opposite, in fact. And if it hadn't been for her quick thinking, Dylan would probably be dying of a copperhead bite right now.

Everything about her was attractive to him. And he hadn't even begun thinking about her freckles yet.

So this can't-look-you-in-the-eyes stuff was not going to cut it. If he wasn't going to withdraw, he wasn't going to let her do it either.

A few minutes later the bathroom door opened and Shelby stepped out, steam swirling around her. She was dressed in only a towel. She moved to the side, holding the towel with one hand and gesturing to the bathroom door with the other.

"All yours. I washed out my clothes, so they're still wet, but I got them out of the way enough, I think." Her smile was forced, and she was obviously uncomfortable in her state of undress.

Dylan stood up from the bed and walked slowly over to Shelby, stopping just in front of her. She was looking toward him, but still not looking *at* him.

"Shelby."

"Yes?"

"Look at me." He took a step closer to her, but she didn't look. He tipped a finger under her chin. "Look at me."

There were those gorgeous green eyes. Finally. "You're avoiding me," he whispered.

"How can I avoid you?"

"You know what I mean."

Shelby finally nodded. "I can't keep getting hurt by you, Dylan. Terrible things happened, I know, so you do whatever you have to, to protect yourself. Your defenses."

She was right. It was amazing that someone who had known him such a short time could understand so much about him. "Yes, but—"

"It's okay to have defenses, Dylan," Shelby continued. "I usually have them, too, with almost everybody. But for some reason my normal defense mechanisms don't kick in around you."

Something in Dylan eased. He knew it was selfish, but he didn't want her defenses to work around him. He wanted her to be open to him. "Shelby—"

"But you hurt me, Dylan. You keep hurting me. Because what you think you want and what you really want are two different things."

"I want you," he whispered, backing her up against the wall. "*You* are what I think I want and what I really want."

"But you might change your mind." Shelby began to look away again.

"I am not going to change my mind." Dylan brought his

hands up on either side of her head, burrowing his fingers in her damp hair. "I hurt you because I'm so used to pushing everyone away, and I'm sorry. You are what I want."

He bent slightly so they were eye to eye. "I won't hurt you again."

Dylan could see the doubt in Shelby's eyes, and it killed him. He was afraid she would pull away. But she leaned toward him, putting her lips gently against his.

He was humbled by her trust in him, and kissed her back gently. But then the hunger—the *heat*—that had sparked between them since the first moment they'd met flared again. And all thought of soft and gentle was left behind.

Dylan kissed her. Kissed her in a way that left no doubt that, no matter what, they would be finishing what they started this time.

Her arms reached up to wrap around his shoulders, but Dylan grabbed her wrists and brought both arms up over her head, never stopping the kiss. He heard her soft sigh as his hands slid up from her wrists to link their fingers together.

Her mouth opened, giving him fuller access, and he took full advantage, using his tongue to duel with hers. His body, pressed up against hers, was the only thing holding her towel in place. Dylan nipped gently at her bottom lip then let go of her lips altogether, but not of her hands, which he still held over her head against the wall. He waited for her eyes to flutter open, then deliberately took a small step back.

Her towel slid down her body and pooled on the floor.

Their eyes met, then Dylan brought his lips back down to hers. He released her hands and slid his fingers into her hair and cupped the nape of her neck, drawing her even closer. Her fingers slid under his shirt, pushing it up.

Dylan released her lips to tear his shirt over his head, then found her mouth again. This time he was the one moaning.

He reached down and swung her up in his arms. He walked over to the bed and laid her on it almost reverently.

Yes, she was very definitely what he wanted and he proceeded to prove it to her.

Chapter Fourteen

Shelby felt as though she'd been almost run over, had survived a plane crash and had hiked through miles of wilderness over the past twenty-four hours.

Oh, wait, she had.

To say nothing of the most incredible sex ever. That had probably come the closest to killing her. In the best way possible.

She had been determined to hold herself aloof from Dylan, especially after what he had said in the forest. He'd apologized, and they'd even kissed again, but Shelby had already emotionally withdrawn. She had just wanted to get out of the woods, get to Megan and help however she was needed, and then get away from Dylan.

But there had been no reason to sit around talking about her hurt feelings with Dylan in the forest, so Shelby had just bucked up and started walking.

Because if there was one thing Shelby's mother had taught her, it was to buck up and move on. Shelby had never been able to please her mother. Had never been outgoing and pleasant enough; had always been too rough around the edges. Eventually Shelby had just stopped trying to please someone who couldn't accept her the way she was. It had been a long and painful lesson that had taken up most of her childhood.

But Shelby knew how to hold her head up and keep moving forward even when a little piece of her heart had cracked. And she'd done it today with Dylan.

He still loved his dead wife. Shelby understood that, couldn't even fault him for it. His coldness was understandable. But when they'd made it into town, Shelby found that she couldn't look him in the eye. That somehow, her ability to buck up and move on had failed her.

He didn't want her. And that hurt.

She'd fled to the shower where she'd been able to pull herself together. All she needed to do was make it through the next few hours until they got to Omega. Then she could say goodbye to Dylan, get the codes to Megan and her supercomputer and get back to her house in Knoxville. And maybe never leave it again.

But then she'd walked out of that shower.

She had no idea what had happened to Dylan while she was in there. Yeah, he'd been giving her *the look* before she went in. But by the time she came out of the shower, he'd been determined to get what he wanted.

And what he wanted was her.

She lay on his chest now, his fingers trailing up and down her spine.

"Your freckles drove me crazy from the first second I saw you, you know," he said against her forehead. "You're lucky you made it out of the diner without me throwing you down on the booth."

Shelby kissed his chest and laughed. "I'm pretty sure Sally would not have approved."

"And poor Tucker definitely would've had a heart attack."

Shelby felt so close to Dylan now, not just because of the incredible lovemaking, but because he was more relaxed, at ease. After everything that had happened over the past day, lying here, just enjoying Dylan's arms around her, was all Shelby wanted.

But the other part of her was waiting for Dylan to realize what he'd done, which was, in essence, to cheat on his dead wife. She was sure it wouldn't be long before the freak-out happened. Before he pushed Shelby away again, found a reason to put distance between them. That was just a matter of time, she was sure.

Their lovemaking was probably just a one-time thing. They were two people attracted to each other, but their attraction had been pushed along at breakneck speed by everything they'd been through.

Trauma-induced sex. Was that a real thing? Shelby would have to look it up. It felt as if it should be a real thing even if it wasn't currently.

Shelby wished she had her smartphone. Or was at home with her computer. Or was at home at all, where she could fall apart alone.

Oh, hell, was she about to start crying?

"You doing okay over there?" Dylan asked.

"Just feeling a little overwhelmed by everything that's happened." Shelby could feel her voice shaking. She definitely didn't want to mention that a huge part of the emotional roller coaster she was on was fear of what Dylan was going to do in the next few minutes.

But Dylan rolled to his side so he was facing her, then slid both arms around her so he could roll onto his back, bringing Shelby's entire body on top of him.

"It's okay to be overwhelmed. You've held it together for much longer than I thought you would, much longer than anyone could've expected."

Shelby nodded, feeling the bubble of panic inside her begin to lessen. "Thanks. I'm just tired." She laid her head down on his chest.

"We probably should've used our free time to rest. Not…other stuff."

Oh, no, here it came. Dylan's withdrawal. His regret about their lovemaking disguised as worry about exhaustion. Shelby tried—and failed—to keep tension from coursing through her body at Dylan's silence after his statement.

So she totally wasn't expecting him to roll himself quickly over on the bed and take her with him. She let out a small shriek before she could stop herself. Dylan reached down and hooked one of her legs up over his hips. He held most of his weight on his elbows, gazing down at her, his fingers brushing her hair away from her face on both sides.

"Of course, there was no way I was going to nap when having you naked in this bed was an option. I didn't care how exhausted I was."

Shelby felt the tension ease out of her. It was hard to be tense when someone as gorgeous as Dylan was lying naked on top of you and *obviously* wanted you.

Yeah, he might freak out, but she'd deal with that later.

Shelby wrapped the crook of her elbow around Dylan's head and pulled him down to her. She playfully grabbed his bottom lip with her teeth then let it go. "We can sleep later."

Dylan smiled, wickedness gleaming in his eyes. "Yes. Much, much later."

SHELBY WAS ASLEEP. Dylan could tell by the snores coming out of her tiny body, which were both hilarious and the most endearing thing in the history of the world. She wasn't touching Dylan at all now. Although he'd pulled her against him to hold her after their second round of absolutely fantastic sex, once she'd fallen asleep, she had immediately pulled away and rolled over to her side. Now she was curled up in a little ball.

She was used to sleeping alone. So was Dylan. It was a fitting metaphor for both of them.

Dylan didn't want to think too carefully about what had just happened. Or how unbelievably great it had been. Or how all he wanted to do was get back in bed with Shelby and wrap his body around her little, balled up body. And teach them both how to sleep with someone else.

Or maybe show her all the reasons again why they should not sleep at all.

Dylan pulled a blanket up over Shelby before he let those thoughts gain any more traction. She needed rest.

Dylan took a shower and, unlike Shelby, he at least had a fresh pair of clothes to put on. Shelby's were still wet, hanging on the sink. They wouldn't be very comfortable to put back on when Sawyer got here in a couple hours. Maybe Mrs. Morgan had or knew of a washer and dryer nearby where Dylan could at least get Shelby's clothes dried so she wouldn't have to ride for hours in a car in damp clothes.

Dylan wrote a short note for Shelby in case she woke up and laid it on his pillow. He didn't want her thinking he'd just skipped out on her.

With Shelby's wet clothes in hand, including, Lord have mercy, that red-and-black thong—he was going to get her to model that for him very soon—Dylan made his way out the door. He locked it behind him using the key Mrs. Morgan had given them and headed down the outdoor stairs.

Darkness was approaching and the small town had shut down for the day. Dylan peeked into the front of the hardware store, but didn't see either Mrs. Morgan or Angi. Perhaps they'd gone home for the day. Dylan was a little surprised neither had come to check on him and Shelby before heading out.

As Dylan turned away from the glass, something caught his attention from inside. Just a slight movement of shadow within the already dark store. Someone was in there.

Dylan moved away from the window and began walking away casually. Maybe it was Mrs. Morgan or Angi in there in the dark, although he doubted it was Angi because Dylan would've been able to see that bedazzled phone. But it just struck him as suspicious that neither of the outgoing females would not come open the front door for him.

Dylan realized he'd been through a lot over the past twenty-four hours, and maybe was overtired and hypersensitive, but his instincts were telling him something wasn't right here. His instincts had served him well over the years and he wasn't going to start ignoring them now.

Dylan continued to walk away casually, hoping whoever was in the store would think he was just some local who'd been a little nosy. But as soon as he was around the corner and out of sight, he sprinted toward the back of the building. There had to be some other door.

Dylan found the emergency-exit door completely unlocked. He wished he had a weapon besides his pocketknife as he opened the door slowly, trying to keep it from creaking. He didn't see or hear anything inside, but that didn't necessarily mean that the building was empty. Dylan kept to the shadows, allowing his eyes time to completely adjust. He edged his way along the back wall waiting for any glimpse of the shadow he'd seen moving earlier.

Nothing.

After a couple of minutes, Dylan had convinced himself he must have been mistaken. Or if there had been someone moving around in here, that person was gone now. The emergency-exit door being open was a little suspicious, but this was a small town. People were sometimes different in a small town than a big city. More trusting.

Dylan was turning to leave when he heard it. A sort of muffled thump from the storage room where Dylan had made his call to Sawyer earlier.

Dylan grabbed a hammer—any weapon was better than none at all—and rushed to the storage room. He opened it, ready to pounce.

But there on the ground were Mrs. Morgan and Angi, both bound and gagged.

Dylan rushed to Mrs. Morgan's side and slid the gag out of her mouth. She was bleeding from where someone had hit her in the face.

"I'm so sorry," she told Dylan. "He came in with a gun, demanding to know where you were. I didn't want to tell him, but he threatened Angi. He just left." Mrs. Morgan was sobbing.

Dylan didn't wait around to reassure Mrs. Morgan that she'd done the right thing. He whipped out his pocketknife and cut through the plastic zip ties the perp had used to tie her with and ran out the door.

Mrs. Morgan could now get Angi out. But the shadow Dylan had seen a few minutes before now knew where Shelby was.

Dylan went out the front door of the store that was closer to the outdoor staircase leading up to the studio apartment. He got to the corner and stopped, whipping his head around it to look and then back. No one was on the stairs. The man was already inside.

Dylan took the stairs two at a time, praying he wasn't too late.

Chapter Fifteen

Shelby woke up out of a sound sleep as a hand covered her mouth roughly. The room was dark and she couldn't tell who was looming over her, but she knew whoever it was, it wasn't someone friendly. She jerked away and began thrashing her body, not even caring that she was completely naked.

The man's other hand grabbed her by the hair and jerked her up to a sitting position.

"Where are the codes?" The voice was pure menace in her ear. Now that he was close, she could see he was wearing something over his face so she couldn't clearly identify his features. That made him even more frightening.

Shelby shook her head since he was covering her mouth and she couldn't talk. He yanked hard on her hair again. "Where are the codes? Are they in this room or were they destroyed in the plane?"

The man removed his hand just the slightest bit so Shelby could speak, but kept a grip on her hair. She didn't know what to say. Evidently he didn't know the codes were inside Shelby's head, not on some drive somewhere.

"I don't know wh—"

The man backhanded her. Shelby could taste blood in her mouth where her teeth cut into her cheek. Her whole face felt as if it was on fire.

"You will tell me right now or I will kill you."

Shelby knew he was going to kill her either way. Where was Dylan? He'd been beside her when she fell asleep. Dread flooded her. Was Dylan already dead?

The man yanked her hair again, this time dragging her to the floor. "Where are the codes?" he snarled. He reared back and kicked her with a booted foot in her thigh and Shelby let out a scream as pain ratcheted through her.

Shelby curled into herself as the man bent down and grabbed her hair again. "No screaming. Where are the codes?" He slammed her head against the floor. Shelby fought to hold on to consciousness.

"In the bathroom!" she choked out. It was all Shelby could think of to say through the pain. "On a hard drive on the sink."

Shelby had hoped the man would go check by himself and give her a few seconds to try to get out. She knew she'd have to run outside naked, but didn't care. Naked was better than dead.

But instead, the man grabbed her by the hair again and began dragging her with him toward the bathroom. Shelby could hardly get her hurt leg under her, so he was mostly dragging her along the ground. It wouldn't take him long to figure out she'd made up the stuff about a drive being in there.

And then he was going to kill her.

She was trying to think of any possible way out of this when the door leading from the outside of the room crashed open. From where Shelby laid mostly sprawled on the floor, she watched as Dylan ran inside. A second later, a hammer flew from Dylan's hand hitting Shelby's attacker in the shoulder. He howled in pain and let go of her.

Dylan wasted no time and leaped through the room, landing on her attacker with a flying tackle. Shelby scooted as far out of the way as she could. She knew the best way she could help Dylan was to just stay out of the way.

It took all of two seconds to realize how skilled Dylan was at fighting. He'd obviously been trained in hand-to-hand combat. He did some sort of spinning-kick thing that knocked the intruder to the floor.

But the intruder was also trained at fighting. He immediately jumped up and threw quick punches and kicks at Dylan's head and torso. Some Dylan was able to block, sheltering his injured arm as much as possible, but a couple of hits he took square on the jaw.

The blows didn't even seem to slow Dylan down. It wasn't long before it became obvious that Dylan would win this fight. The other man may have been bigger, but he wasn't as quick or as smart in his moves. Dylan gave one more good punch and the intruder flew through the air and landed in an unconscious heap on the floor near the bed.

Shelby watched it all from the corner she'd backed herself into. Everything in her entire body hurt. She couldn't imagine what Dylan felt like after that fight. And she hoped that bastard lying on the floor would be in agony once he regained consciousness.

Shelby heard the distinct sound of a shotgun being cocked from the doorway. It was Mrs. Morgan.

"You two okay?" she asked, obviously ready to take down the intruder if necessary.

Dylan quickly grabbed the sheet from the bed and handed it to Shelby. She gratefully wrapped it around herself. The teenager Angi was once again taking pictures, now of the unconscious intruder. Dylan ripped the mesh material off the man's face. Shelby didn't recognize him at all, Dylan didn't seem to either.

"Mrs. Morgan, we need some of those plastic ties that

this guy used to restrain you and Angi. I need them now before he wakes."

"Angi, go get them," Mrs. Morgan told her daughter.

"But, Mom…" Angi was obviously more interested in collecting photos to post online.

"Right this second, Angi. Or I will take that phone away until you graduate."

Angi muttered under her breath about having the worst life ever, but took off.

"What exactly is going on here, Dylan?" Mrs. Morgan asked.

"The less you know about it, the better. Just know that I'm trying to get Shelby to Washington, DC, so she can help law enforcement with something very important."

"And that guy wanted to stop that from happening?" She pointed at the man on the floor.

"Yes," Dylan explained, coming over to crouch down by Shelby. He tucked a strand of hair behind her ear. "Do you need a doctor?" he whispered.

"I don't think so." Shelby's voice was hoarse even to her own ears. "My leg is hurt, but I don't think it's broken."

Dylan nodded, then reached down and kissed her forehead. Angi showed back up with plastic zip ties and Dylan secured the man's hands behind his back.

"Mrs. Morgan, I have someone from the agency Shelby and I need to get to on his way right now to pick us up. He should be here within the hour. But can you please call your local sheriff to come arrest this guy. He's definitely going to need to be taken in."

DYLAN'S HEART BROKE every time he looked over at Shelby huddled in the corner. She was hurt, bleeding and although she had insisted she didn't need a doctor, Dylan just wanted to get everyone out of there so he could talk to her.

Actually, what he really wanted was to take her somewhere far away from here and all the people trying to kill her, and keep her safe.

And naked in bed with him. He could do both at the same time.

"Mrs. Morgan, can you please go get some ice for Shelby's face? Also, down in the storage room, I dropped her clothes. They were wet and I wanted to see if there was anywhere I could dry them."

Angi, who had miraculously stopped taking pictures with her smartphone, looked over at her mother. "She's about my size, Mom. I can find her something to wear."

Both women nodded and left to get the needed items.

The man on the floor was beginning to groan, regaining consciousness. Dylan didn't want to deal with him yet. He grabbed the man by the collar of his shirt, lifted him a few inches and then coldcocked him. The man slumped back to the ground, completely unconscious again.

Dylan looked over at Shelby's bruised, swollen face and had zero remorse about hitting a barely conscious man. He rushed over and sat down, putting his arms around her and scooping her, bedsheet and all, into his lap.

"I thought he was going to kill me, Dylan. The only reason he didn't was because he thought the codes were on a hard drive somewhere, not in my head. He wanted to know if they had been destroyed in the crash." Shelby's words were partially muffled against his chest.

"If you had told him they'd been destroyed in the crash, he probably would've killed you immediately."

"I told him they were in the bathroom."

The image of Shelby being dragged across the floor, obviously injured, would haunt Dylan forever. If he'd been just a couple minutes later, she would've been in much worse shape or possibly dead. He pulled her closer to him and kissed the top of her head.

"Are you sure you don't need a doctor?"

"He kicked my leg pretty hard. I thought it might be broken, but I don't think so."

"Let me see it."

Dylan helped her stand up then crouched back down so he could see the outer part of her thigh when she lifted the sheet. An ugly purple bruise was already beginning to form. Careful not to touch the bruised area, Dylan pressed on the other side of her leg, up and down along the bone. She didn't have any sharp pain, which probably meant no broken bone.

"I don't think it's broken, but it's probably going to hurt like hell for a while."

"Yeah, my head, too," Shelby said. "Dude thought banging it into the floor a few times would be fun."

Dylan grimaced. She might have a concussion. He brought her over to the light near the bathroom. Her pupils weren't dilated, so that was a good sign. But still, it was one more thing that was going to hurt her. He pulled her against his chest and wrapped his arms gently around her.

"Your body must be wondering if the Third World War has happened, with all the pounding it has taken over the past day and a half."

"Yeah, no kidding. But at least I'm still here."

And she wasn't even falling apart. Amazing.

Though she be but little…

The Shakespearean quote came to Dylan's mind again. Shelby was definitely fierce.

The man was beginning to groan again. Good, Dylan wanted him to wake up. He wanted to ask him a couple of questions before the sheriff came to take him.

"Stay over here," he told Shelby, helping her sit in a chair.

Dylan crossed to the man and grabbed him up off the

ground and pushed him back against the bed. "Who do you work for?"

The dark-haired man looked at Dylan and shook his head, his rough features giving away nothing.

"You know the local sheriff is going to take you into custody, but it won't be long before you're transferred to Omega."

"Being in any prison would be better than what my organization would do to me because I failed."

"If they're so bad, tell me who you work for or who you work with. We can protect you."

The man smirked. "You cannot protect me. It's all you can do to protect yourself and your woman."

"How did you find us?"

"It was only a matter of listening to the transmissions of emergency services for this area. It's all they've been talking about for hours."

Dylan was about to ask more questions—although he honestly didn't expect to get any other information out of the guy—when Mrs. Morgan came back up, Angi and the sheriff in tow.

"Mr. Branson, I'm Sheriff Fossen. I understand you had a tussle with this fellow, who also broke in downstairs and threatened and unlawfully restrained Mrs. Morgan and her daughter."

Dylan walked over to shake the sheriff's hand. Since the sheriff already had enough to arrest the man, Dylan didn't mention that the man had also assaulted Shelby. That would lead to having to stay around here for too long. They needed to be free to go when Sawyer arrived.

"Well, I'm going to put some proper cuffs on him and take him in."

"Yeah. I think there's going to be a lot of people who have questions for him," Dylan told the sheriff. He was looking over at Shelby to make sure she was all right, when he saw movement from the bed out of the corner of his eye.

Dylan immediately moved toward Shelby to protect her, but the attacker wasn't headed her way.

Instead, the man ran across the room in the other direction and hurled himself, headfirst, out the second-story window.

The sheriff already had his weapon in hand and he and Dylan rushed to the window. The man lay on the ground twenty feet below, unmoving. The unnatural angle of his neck attested to his demise.

The man had killed himself rather than be arrested and brought in for questioning. Damn it. He definitely worked for DS-13, and now they'd never know if he had been sent directly from the mole in Omega.

Dylan crossed back over to where Shelby still sat in the chair. Mrs. Morgan was yelling at Angi not to take pictures of the dead man out the window. Sheriff Fossen was calling in what had happened on his radio and making his way out the door and down the stairs.

Dylan grabbed the clothes Angi had brought for Shelby from on top of the dresser by the door. He was just helping her stand and make her way into the bathroom so she could change when he heard his brother Sawyer from the door.

"Looks like I missed quite a party."

Chapter Sixteen

Dylan had never felt so relieved to see someone in his entire life. He walked over to hug his brother. "I'm glad you're here, man."

"What the hell happened, Dylan? Some sheriff guy just flew down those stairs like he'd heard the donut shop was about to close or something."

"Somebody attacked Shelby, was going to kill her."

They both looked over at Shelby who was still standing outside the bathroom door, wrapped in her sheet, staring at them. Sawyer walked around Dylan and sauntered over to stand right in front of her. Dylan watched as his baby brother, the flirt of the family, wrapped his arms around Shelby, picked her all the way off her feet and kissed her smack on the mouth.

Sawyer had been kissing girls on the mouth since he was three years old. And as he'd gotten older, he'd continued to love them, and kiss them. Sawyer had kissed all his brothers' girlfriends in that friendly manner. Hell, Sawyer had even kissed Fiona on the lips the day Dylan and Fiona got married.

Sawyer's kisses had never bothered Dylan before. But the sight of his brother's lips on Shelby's triggered an ugly jealousy inside Dylan. He managed to tamp it down, but only barely. His jaw ached from gritting his teeth.

Sawyer lowered Shelby back to the ground. "Hi, I'm Sawyer. Meg has told me so much about you. I'm glad you're okay."

Shelby was just looking at Sawyer with that stunned look women always got when looking at Sawyer. "Hi," she finally whispered.

Dylan rolled his eyes and crossed over to stand right next to Shelby, putting his arm around her shoulders. "Why don't you stop molesting your wife's friend and let her get dressed."

Sawyer put a hand up to his chest in mock woundedness. "Shelby is Megan's friend, which makes her like a sister to me." He winked down at Shelby. "A very hot sister."

"I am *so* telling Megan on you," Dylan said.

"Megan's used to my crazy antics." Sawyer shrugged. "Plus, she knows I am a one-woman man now."

"A tragedy," Shelby said, grinning.

Dylan had had enough. "You—" he pointed at Shelby, spinning her around "—go get dressed. Call me if you need help."

"Or me." Sawyer raised his hand and wiggled his fingers in a flirty wave.

Shelby just smiled and went into the bathroom.

"You leave her alone," Dylan told Sawyer the moment the door was closed. The words poured out of his mouth almost of their own accord. "I'm not kidding about this, Sawyer. You stay away from Shelby."

Sawyer's face immediately changed from friendly to viciously serious. "You know what, Dyl? I'm going to let that slide because you've been through a lot in the past day and a half. And obviously you have some sort of head injury, because you just insinuated that I might be interested in cheating on my pregnant wife with one of her good friends."

Dylan rubbed his hand across his forehead. Sawyer was right. Dylan knew Sawyer loved Megan to distraction. He would never cheat on her or hurt her in any way.

"You're right. I'm sorry. It's been a long night and day and night again."

Sawyer was not one to hold a grudge. He slapped Dylan on the back. "No problem. So what the hell happened in here?"

Dylan told the whole story of Shelby's attack and the guy jumping out the window to kill himself.

"Do you think he traced our call?" Sawyer asked. "Is that why he was able to get here so quickly?"

"No. He was just following emergency services for this area. This is a small town and Shelby and I were a pretty big deal when we showed up alive."

"We're up against someone pretty serious if the guy was willing to off himself rather than be taken in," Sawyer murmured, looking around the room.

"My thoughts exactly. Definitely DS-13."

"I noticed our friend Shelby didn't seem to have any clothes on under that sheet. Please tell me the perp didn't rip them off her or something sick like that. Or worse."

Sawyer's voice was tight. Their family was intimately familiar with the trauma of aggravated assault and rape. Their sister, Juliet, had only just recently begun to fully recuperate from an attack while posing undercover a couple of years ago.

The Branson family took attacks on women very seriously.

Dylan cleared his throat. "No, um, Shelby's clothes were already off before he got in here."

Sawyer looked over at him, one eyebrow cocked. "I see. So your stupid comment before had nothing to do with protectiveness toward Megan and everything to do with why Miss Keelan was naked."

"Shut up, Sawyer." Dylan loved his brother, but Sawyer knew how to push his buttons.

Shelby came out of the bathroom now dressed in Angi's pale blue sweater and jeans. She'd pulled her long red hair into a loose braid that fell down her back. And while Dylan appreciated that Angi's junior-size jeans were fascinatingly tight on Shelby's grown-woman-with-grown-curves body, he could tell right away that she was in pain from her leg. She tried to hide her limp, but Dylan noticed it immediately.

"I'm not sure these jeans are exactly legal on me." Shelby's laugh held an embarrassed tinge.

Dylan crossed to her and helped her sit down on the bed.

"Trust me, you look better in those jeans than any teenager ever could," Dylan said just loudly enough for Shelby to hear. She actually flushed.

Dylan shouldn't be surprised, given her skin coloring, that she was easily able to blush. But he was surprised at the crimson, given what had occurred between them this evening. Shelby wasn't used to compliments. Dylan might have to become better at giving them.

He bent down next to her to help her get her shoes and socks on so she wouldn't have to put undue weight on her leg. After he was finished, he gently touched the outside of her thigh where he knew it hurt the most.

"Are you sure you're okay?" Dylan asked, standing and helping her to stand. "We can still go to a doctor if you think we need to have it x-rayed."

"No, it'll be fine. Maybe just some aspirin or something once we get on the road."

"I'm going to go clear us out with the sheriff," Sawyer called from the door. He tossed a set of keys to Dylan. "I'll meet you guys in the car."

Sawyer and Shelby were both right. They needed to get

going. DS-13 surely had more henchmen at their disposal to send once they figured out this one was dead. The next might already be on their way.

Dylan needed to get Shelby out of here.

They gathered the rest of their items, not that there was much. Just the contents of Dylan's backpack. Dylan helped Shelby down the outdoor stairs. He could tell she was in pain, although she didn't complain. He touched her bruised face gently once they reached the bottom, wincing.

"You have some bruises, too, you know, where that guy got in a few good punches," she told him.

Dylan could feel them. Between everything they'd been through over the past day and a half, Dylan's whole body felt bruised and sore. And he didn't even want to think about all the paperwork and mental energy he would have to spend dealing with the insurance issues surrounding his Cessna's crash. That would be dealt with later.

Right now he'd stay and make sure Shelby was safe. It wasn't as if he had any job to rush back to now anyway.

Dylan was helping Shelby into the car when Mrs. Morgan walked over to them. She had a bag in her hand.

"Here's Shelby's clothes, Dylan. I'm sorry you didn't get a chance to dry them."

"Thanks, Mrs. Morgan. Sorry our arrival has brought such chaos to your store. I'm sure Agent Branson will be giving Sheriff Fossen his card if you need anything further."

"Don't worry about that." Mrs. Morgan touched Dylan on his uninjured arm. "All this hoopla will bring in more people to the shop tomorrow than in decades. Angi is out taking pictures of the whole thing."

"You might want to consider getting her a real camera with her proclivity toward picture taking," Dylan said.

"I tried that. But part of the appeal for her is being able

to put the pictures up on all her websites as quickly as possible." Mrs. Morgan shrugged then drew in a ragged breath. "I was so scared when that man put his gun to Angi's head." Mrs. Morgan leaned down so she could see Shelby more clearly in the car. "I'm sorry I told him where you were, honey. I just didn't know what to do."

Shelby reached out a comforting hand toward the older woman. "You did the right thing. A mother should always protect her child, no matter what."

"But those bruises on your face! I wish I had thought to tell him you were somewhere else."

"Mrs. Morgan, not to be gruesome, but that man was a trained killer. You're very lucky to be alive."

Mrs. Morgan's eyes got wider.

"He left you alive in that storage room for a reason— to check and see if you were telling the truth about where Shelby and I were," Dylan continued. "If you hadn't been, he probably would've come back and done a lot more damage."

Dylan decided it was probably best not to mention that the man would've almost definitely been coming back to finish off both Angi and Mrs. Morgan once he had taken care of business upstairs. One of DS-13's hired professionals would not have left loose ends.

"But thank you for coming up there with your shotgun, Mrs. Morgan," Shelby told her. "That was very brave."

Mrs. Morgan nodded. "You two be careful. Whatever's going on with you seems pretty dangerous."

"Yes, ma'am." Dylan nodded. "We'll be getting to a safer place soon."

"I better go make sure Angi is staying out of trouble."

They watched as the older woman walked back toward her shop, now surrounded by a number of flashing police cars and multiple bystanders, despite the late hour.

It wasn't long before Sawyer joined them back at the

car. "Evidently this county doesn't have a lot of suicidal would-be killers. Go figure. Some of those deputies are just about giddy dealing with the crime scene."

"Do they need us?" Dylan really didn't want to stick around here to answer questions.

"No, since the guy jumped while being taken into custody and because the sheriff was right there to witness the whole thing, it's pretty straightforward. I told Sheriff Fossen I was taking you guys and how to get in touch."

"Were you able to get a good look at Shelby's attacker? He wasn't familiar to me at all."

Sawyer shook his head. "I saw him, but he wasn't familiar to me either. Didn't seem to have any identifying marks or tattoos on him. How long did you guys fight?"

"Over five minutes."

Sawyer's eyebrows shot up. "Any particular reason for that?"

"Well, I had been in a plane crash a few hours earlier. And I'm no longer active, Sawyer."

"So?"

Dylan knew what his brother meant. Dylan was particularly skilled at hand-to-hand combat. He'd been well known during his time at Omega for finishing skirmishes in under a minute.

"I was a little distracted by Shelby, but yeah, the guy was highly skilled. Definitely not a thug hired off the street."

Dylan and Sawyer both knew that was particularly bad news. Smart, skilled, hired muscle tended to speak of much smarter, more skilled people working behind them. In this case, someone very high up in DS-13, and perhaps even the mole in Omega.

They had no proof who was behind all this, they just knew it was someone connected and dangerous.

A lethal combination.

Chapter Seventeen

Shelby awoke in a bed, not sure exactly where she was. Definitely not at her own house. Light was coming through the window, so it was daytime, midmorning by the looks of it. Maybe she was in Sawyer and Megan's home. That would make sense. She moved quickly to get up, but a sharp pain in her outer thigh caused her to slow.

The last thing Shelby remembered was getting in the car with Dylan and Sawyer. They'd both sat in the front seat so Shelby could stretch out her hurt leg in the backseat. She'd been about to fall asleep when they had stopped at a drugstore for supplies for Dylan's wounded arm and painkillers for Shelby. And a couple of prepaid disposable cell phones to replace the ones they'd lost.

Evidently a respite from the pain had been all Shelby needed to fall asleep, because she didn't remember anything else about the drive into DC. She didn't remember the car stopping or getting into this bed or sleeping all night. But evidently all those things had taken place.

She was still dressed in Angi's jeans and sweater. She needed to go to the restroom and she was starving. Shelby took care of the first need then headed down the hallway to where she heard voices. Dylan and a woman. And the woman definitely wasn't Megan.

"Yeah, well, at least you don't look as bad as the time it was the two of us in the airplane hangar."

Dylan groaned and laughed at the same time. "Woman, that night just about killed me. Don't bring it up."

The woman chuckled in a knowing, intimate past-history way. Had Dylan brought Shelby to an ex-girlfriend's house?

Not a current girlfriend. Shelby didn't believe Dylan was the kind of man who would cheat on a lover. And especially wouldn't be stupid enough to bring the woman he was cheating with to his girlfriend's house.

But they were obviously close to each other. The familiarity between them was immediately apparent as Shelby entered the living room in which they sat.

Sat together, on a cozy love seat, in front of the fireplace.

It was the woman—a gorgeous brunette with blond highlights—who saw Shelby first, to Shelby's continued chagrin.

"You're awake, good! Although I'm sure sleep was the best thing for your poor body." The woman stood and walked over to Shelby. She seemed unsure of whether to hug Shelby or offer her a hand to shake.

Evidently Shelby's facial expression wasn't real friendly-like because the woman ended up doing neither.

"Um, I'm Sophia Branson. This is my house. Well, mine and my husband's. I'm married to Dylan's brother Cameron."

This gorgeous woman was married to Dylan's brother. Thank goodness. But that didn't mean she and Dylan didn't have a history.

"Cameron? But you spent the night with Dylan in an airplane hangar?" Shelby could easily imagine just how well Dylan could get around in an airplane hangar with a woman. And he'd laughed and said it had almost killed him. The thought made Shelby a little sick. Dylan would know exactly what equipment could hold the weight of two peop—

The woman laughed, cutting off Shelby's thoughts of airplane-hangar antics. "Well, yeah. When a group of terrorists had me in their clutches. They used poor Dylan here as a human punching bag."

Both Dylan and Sophia winced.

Well, that wasn't what Shelby had thought at all. She shouldn't even have brought it up. Shelby stuck her hand out for Sophia to shake. "It's very nice to meet you. I'm Shelby Keelan. Thanks for letting us crash here."

Dylan came over to stand by his sister-in-law. "Sophia is the only member of our family who doesn't work at Omega. We thought it would be better for everyone else to go to work as usual. That will make it look like you and I aren't around this area at all, hopefully. After all, if we were here, we'd go straight to family, right?"

Shelby nodded. That definitely made sense.

"Plus, they're working on all the details for their grand plan to sneak you into Omega," Dylan continued.

"Do you really think the mole is someone inside Omega?" Sophia asked Dylan while she took Shelby's arm and began leading her into the kitchen.

"I don't know how it could be anyone else. It's either someone pretty high up inside Omega or someone with access to info he or she shouldn't have. That might be even worse."

Shelby agreed with Dylan's assessment, knowing how electronic leaks could be deadly to both companies and law enforcement. "Yeah, one mole would be better than having an unknown information leak. Something like that could be coming from hundreds of different electronic areas and would be nearly impossible to find."

"You have to be hungry," Sophia told Shelby as they entered the kitchen. "It's after eleven o'clock."

Shelby turned to Dylan. "How long have I been asleep?"

"Including your sleeping in the car? Almost fourteen hours."

No wonder she felt so groggy. And hungry. "Wow. Wait, what about the countdown I spotted in the coding?" Shelby instantly did the math in her head. "We have less than twenty hours left before whatever is counting down gets to zero."

Dylan slipped an arm around her shoulder. "I know. But you needed the time to rest. Plus, there wasn't anything you could do until we figured out how to get you into Omega."

Shelby was still feeling pretty anxious. As if there was something more she should be doing. But it didn't seem as though there was, so what could she do?

"Coffee?" Sophia walked over from the cabinet, carafe and mug in hand.

Shelby couldn't do anything else, but she could drink coffee. "Oh, please, yes. Thank you, please, yes."

Sophia laughed at Shelby's coffee enthusiasm. "I'm the same way about coffee." She poured Shelby a cup, offered cream and sugar and went back to the kitchen counter and began making sandwiches.

"You should have seen the Branson siblings in here scheming away on the best plan to get you inside Omega with minimal detection. Megan and Evan were here, too."

"Evan is my sister Juliet's fiancé. They both are active agents like Cameron and Sawyer."

"You've got a pretty kick-ass family there, Branson," Shelby told Dylan after taking another blessed sip of her coffee.

"Well, the eldest sibling obviously got the biggest slice

of the awesome, but the others do all right." Dylan winked at her.

Shelby completely ignored the little flip her heart did at Dylan's playful expression. Didn't pay it even one little iota of attention. Because that would be way too dangerous.

"I'm sorry I missed Megan." Shelby would have loved to see her friend right now.

Sophia turned from the sandwiches. "If I'm not mistaken, I think Megan is going to start having some 'pregnancy' issues and take a half day off work. She should be here not too long from now."

That sounded great. Because although Shelby liked Sophia, she needed a little time not around someone new. Not taking the mental energy to make sure she was being friendly and socially appropriate.

Megan didn't care at all if Shelby was socially appropriate. And actually, Dylan didn't seem to care too much about Shelby's quirky habits either. Neither of them were like her mother who seemed constantly flabbergasted by most of the words that came out of Shelby's mouth.

It wasn't as if she wandered around yelling profanity or racial slurs, Shelby just wasn't good at chitchatting and the social niceties that were so important to her mother and her mother's friends. Shelby just got straight to the point. And as far as Shelby could tell, her mother and friends never got to a point. Ever.

Sophia brought the sandwiches over and they all sat down at the kitchen table.

"So, did you all come up with a plan to get me in?" Shelby asked, then took a bite of her sandwich. Her eyes closed as she savored the bite. This had to be the best sandwich ever.

"Yeah, a good one." Dylan told her. "It's pretty complicated. They're building one ID for you to get you past front-desk security. Then a separate one to get you into the computer system. It won't fool the mole forever, but it should buy you and Megan a few hours to do whatever your wonder-twin powers can do."

Shelby stuffed another bite in her mouth. "Okay," she said, then cringed. *Never ever talk with your mouth full. Not even one small word.* Shelby had gotten plenty of smacks for that as a child.

But Dylan and Sophia didn't seem to notice. "We'll have to bring you in during the middle of the night when the least number of employees are around. Whoever the mole is knows we're alive, but doesn't know where we are," Dylan told her. "We'll use that to our advantage." He took a bite of his own sandwich.

"Do you really have all the numbers inside your head?" Sophia asked.

Shelby shrugged and nodded. She didn't like to make any sort of big deal about how she could remember numbers because it wasn't as if she did anything special. She just saw them and it was as though her brain took a picture. It didn't take any effort on Shelby's part, so she didn't like to take too much credit for it.

"Yes, she does have all those numbers inside her head. Plus every other number she's ever seen in her entire life." The words came from the hallway. Megan.

Shelby rushed over to embrace her quite pregnant friend. "Oh, my gosh, look at you, Megan. You're going to be a mom!"

"Yeah, tell me about it. I feel like a beached whale. And I'm still mad at you for not coming to my wedding."

Megan turned her cheek up as Dylan came by, kissed it and helped her take off her coat. Then she hugged Sophia.

Shelby was glad to see her friend had found the big extended family she'd always said she wanted back at MIT. But Shelby did feel bad for missing her friend's wedding almost a year ago.

"I'm sorry, Megan. You know me and crowds of people. Plus, I was under a huge deadline then." The excuse sounded thin even to Shelby's own ears.

But Megan was not one to hold a grudge. "Well, you're here now and that's what matters."

Megan linked arms with Shelby and brought her back to the table. Sophia slid a sandwich in front of Megan, and Megan gave her a huge smile. "How'd you know?"

"Whether it's a boy or a girl, that kid already has the Branson appetite. You need all the food you can get."

Megan didn't disagree, just started eating. "Interesting little rule came into play at Omega today," Megan said in between bites.

"Oh, yeah, what's that?" Dylan asked.

"All persons entering the building must be checked for any electronic devices that could store significant data. No electronic drives of any kind are allowed through the front doors. Only items one hundred percent vetted and approved by a temporary cyberdivision task force will be allowed on the premises. Effective immediately."

"Have they ever done anything like that at Omega before?" Shelby asked.

"Nope." Megan wiped her mouth with a napkin. "And I don't know why they started today. It's pretty odd. Plus, I'm not on the cyberdivision task force, what's that all about?" Megan's irritation was plain.

"That is kind of weird. Do you think it has anything to do with us and the mole?" Dylan stood and walked his and Shelby's empty plates over to the sink.

Shelby jumped in while Megan was still chewing. "Did

you tell anybody that I have the countdown codes in my head, Megan?"

"No, I don't think I explained your numeric photographic memory to anyone but Sawyer. It was just easier to tell the higher-ups that you had obtained the codes in a game. Why?"

"If I'm not mistaken, whoever is trying to kill me thinks the codes are on a drive. They have no idea they're in my head."

Dylan came back to stand beside Shelby. He put a hand on her shoulder. "That's right. When the guy attacked Shelby, he was asking her where the codes were. He thought they were on a drive, not inside Shelby's head."

Megan lowered her sandwich slowly back to her plate. "That explains so much. Whoever put out the directive for halting all hard drives and hardware from coming into the building is trying to keep us from bringing in the codes Shelby has."

"Do we know who sent out the directive, Megan?" Dylan asked.

"No, it was collaborative. Whoever the mole is did a good job convincing everyone at Dennis Burgamy's level and above that this was a necessary safety protocol, at least for the time being." Megan brought her sandwich halfway up to her mouth. "To be honest, as someone who works in tech, I can tell you it's not a terrible idea. We get all sorts of viruses and problems from corrupted drives and hardware that are brought in."

"But the timing is pretty suspicious," Dylan stated.

"Knowing that they think Shelby's data is on a drive, I would say the two can't be coincidences. There's just no way of knowing exactly where the directive came from without asking a lot of people a lot of questions."

Megan finished off her sandwich. "The good thing is, we don't have to get a drive inside the building. The mole is on high alert for technology. We've got something much better."

Megan reached across the table and grabbed Shelby's hand. "We've got Shelby."

Chapter Eighteen

What happened when you put five highly trained and industrious spies and a computer genius together and told them to figure out a way to sneak someone into the inner computer labs of a highly guarded top-secret facility?

This hugely complicated plan happened. That's what. Nothing with Omega was ever simple.

It was ten o'clock in the evening and they were sitting around Cameron and Sophia's living room after having had dinner together. The entire Branson clan—Dylan, Cameron, Juliet and Sawyer—were present, laughing, joking and figuring out a way to save the world.

Just like old times.

The plan was elaborate. Dylan's sister had created two separate false IDs and itineraries for Shelby. First, she would be Dr. Shelia Wonder, an American scientist who had been working in Australia, back to consult with Megan on some cyberterrorism research. Juliet knew the Omega computer and calendar system backward and forward from her time as an analyst. She'd already made it look as though Dr. Sheila Wonder had been scheduled to arrive tonight for months. Juliet's changes to the system wouldn't stand up to close scrutiny, but they would at least get Shelby through the door and past the guards.

"Seriously, Jules, Dr. Wonder from Australia? So that

would be Dr. Wonder from Down Under?" Cameron teased his sister as his wife leaned up against him on the couch. He leaned over and kissed the top of Sophia's head.

"Hey, I wanted to make it something easy for Shelby to remember." Juliet winked at Shelby. "You've got enough to worry about. Plus, coming in from Australia gives Shelby a legitimate reason to be getting in and working in the middle of the night."

"Wonder from Down Under. I shouldn't have any problem remembering that," Shelby said.

"Dylan will be going in as your assistant. That might be a little more tricky since he used to work at Omega, but the guards on night shift shouldn't know him. You both just need to look exhausted and a little bit lost when you talk to the guards at the door. Megan will do most of the talking. Everybody loves her."

"That's true." Megan beamed.

Sawyer lifted his head from where it lay in her lap near her belly so he could kiss her. "She's got that sexy-librarian thing going on."

"It's now just pregnant librarian." Megan rolled her eyes.

"You're damn sexy to me." Sawyer kissed her again.

Dylan saw Shelby smile. "Exhausted and lost won't be difficult for me."

"Once you're inside, you'll take on an entirely different ID. One that doesn't have anything to do with Megan. Whoever the mole is knows you're friends with Megan and might be looking for the two of you to go into the main lab together."

Dylan had to give it to his sister, she was a master planner. And she was just getting started.

"According to all electronic records, Dr. Wonder and Dr. Fuller—"

"Ahem, Dr. Fuller-Branson," Sawyer interjected.

"Pardon me," Juliet continued. "Dr. Wonder and Dr. *Fuller-Branson,* plus the assistant Dylan, will seem to be in the cybercrime unit, working on identity theft, a section completely removed from the main computer terminals."

"Your other ID will be a local police detective. No one of particular computer savvy or intelligence. You'll be going into the computer lab with Cameron. If anybody notices an electronic trace of that, it may seem a little odd, but won't draw attention like you and Megan coming into the lab together would."

"Megan will also be entering the room under a different ID, so you two can do whatever configurations you need to do," Juliet's fiancé, Evan, continued as Juliet linked her hand with his.

"It's all basically a bait and switch," Evan continued. "We're hoping the mole doesn't even know you're in the area and will focus his attention on trying to keep all electronic drives out of the building."

"But if the mole does think you're in the building, we're hoping they'll follow the Dr. Wonder path to cybercrimes. That will buy us more time," Juliet said.

Shelby looked over at Dylan, clutching at her arms, brows furrowed.

This was a lot for her, Dylan realized. Not just the plan—which, heaven knew, was complex enough to give anyone hives—but the being around all the people the way she had been all evening. Shelby didn't have any brothers and sisters, no real family except her mom. She wasn't used to the general craziness that came along with big families.

Dylan needed to get Shelby out of here. She needed protection right now just as much as she had against the attacker last night. His family was a different kind of threat. An unintentional and friendly one, but still a threat. At least to Shelby's mind right now.

Dylan moved closer to where Shelby sat propped against the couch. He didn't put his arm around her, but he did touch the back of her hand with his fingers. "Everyone else will be running interference as soon as Dennis Burgamy, their boss, arrives in the morning. If I had to guess, I'd finger him as the mole."

Dylan stood up and turned to his family. "All right, playtime's over." He reached down his hand and helped Shelby stand up. "Shelby needs some quiet away from you maniacs for a few hours. A chance to rest and focus on her role as Dr. Wonder from Down Under."

Dylan looked over at Shelby hoping she'd at least crack a smile at the corny joke, but if anything, her features were even tighter than before.

She'd stared down a poisonous copperhead snake yesterday and hadn't looked as frightened as she did now. He could tell his siblings and their significant others were all concerned for Shelby, but Dylan knew them voicing their concerns, or attempting to get Shelby to talk, would do more damage than good.

"We'll see you all at the scheduled rendezvous time in a few hours."

Dylan slipped an arm around Shelby's waist and led her all the way down the hall and into the bedroom where they'd slept last night. He deposited Shelby on the bed then turned to lock the door behind them.

Dylan sat down beside her on the bed, took her small hands that were closed into tight fists and rubbed them gently in his to get them to loosen.

"I don't think I can do this, Dylan." Her voice was barely a sound, even in the quiet room.

Dylan didn't know exactly what she meant by *this*. Pretend to be someone else? Break into a building? Figure out what the code was counting down to?

She turned away to look out the window. "I have an

overstuffed chair in my condo, I've had it for years. It's old, and not very attractive, and my mother hates it with a passion. I jokingly call it my time-out chair. I go there whenever talking and people and life are too much for me. I just sit there and listen to the traffic outside, and that somehow reassures me that everything is going to be all right." Her voice got even softer. "I wish I had my chair here now."

Dylan wished she did, too. Anything that would help her feel less overwhelmed. He touched her hand again. "Let's try to break down what's making you feel uncomfortable, okay?"

Shelby nodded the tiniest bit.

"Anything with the codes and the computer stuff?" Dylan didn't know exactly what she and Megan would be doing.

"No, that part I'm most secure about. I'm never wrong about numbers."

Dylan smiled slightly. He didn't doubt that.

"Is it pretending to be Dr. Wonder?"

Shelby shook her head. "No, I'm not going to win any awards for my acting, but I think I'll be okay."

"Then what?" he asked as gently as he could.

"I don't know if I can be around all the people, Dylan. Okay? It's been years since I've been in a building the size of Omega, full of people." Shelby's outburst took Dylan a little by surprise. And she wasn't finished. "I'm a very successful game developer, Dylan. I'm a millionaire because I'm good at what I do."

Dylan had figured out Shelby was a millionaire the first time she'd mentioned the game series she'd developed. "I know that, sweetheart."

"So I hire people, assistants, to do the stuff I don't like to do. That includes going anywhere there are a lot of people who would need to interact with me." She paused, then finally continued. "I can't hire anybody to do this for me."

"Shelby—"

"Dylan, I could barely be around your family, who are all very kind and nice and, holy cow, so darn in love with their respective others, for even a couple hours. How am I going to be able to be around an *entire building full of people*?"

She was shouting now, but Dylan didn't stop her. She stood up and turned to face him. Tears were streaming down her face.

"I can't do it." She brought her hands up to her face and began to cry in earnest. Dylan put both his hands on her hips from where he sat, but she took a step backward, shaking off his touch.

Dylan stood up and looked down at the tiny redhead so upset at the thought of having to *talk* to people. Dylan had to admit that he could not help smiling a tiny bit at the situation, but Shelby was obviously authentically upset and Dylan did not take her concerns lightly. He went and stood right in front of Shelby, gently running his hands up and down her arms.

"Shelby, you got run off the road, nearly run over by a car and were in a plane crash and you totally kept it together as if you'd done that every day of your life."

Shelby stopped crying a little, but didn't move her hands from her face. "But—"

"You got me out of a burning plane, saved us both from a poisonous snake, walked fifteen miles through the wilderness *in the rain* and then survived a pretty vicious attack. And kept focused and strong through all of it."

Shelby shrugged her shoulders, but at least she took her hands down from her face. Dylan reached over to the bedside table and grabbed a box of tissues and barely restrained a chuckle when she gave the loudest, most unladylike blow he'd ever heard.

Dylan couldn't help it. He reached over and pulled Shelby up against his chest.

"I know you don't like people. It's okay not to like people." Dylan put his finger under Shelby's chin and tilted her head up to look at him. "And you know most of the people in the Omega building are not going to want to talk to you."

"I know." A flush crept across Shelby's cheeks with the adorable freckles. "I know my discomfort is stupid and ridiculous. But I can't help it."

"Hey, everybody's got their own demons. Yours aren't any less real than mine just because I don't fight the same ones." Dylan couldn't help himself, he dipped his lips down and kissed her. "We've come this far. Don't give up now."

A tiny little sigh escaped Shelby. "I won't give up. I'll do it. I know how important this is."

"*You* are what's important," Dylan murmured against her lips. "And I will be with you the entire time. We'll all be there to help you and run interference where needed. Especially in the chitchat department. That's dangerous stuff."

"I'm sorry I threw a fit." Shelby's crooked smile was perhaps the most adorable thing Dylan had ever seen. "My mom never knew what to do with me growing up when I would get so hysterical about being around new groups of people. She was a social butterfly and loved interacting with everyone and trying to show me, and my ability to remember numbers, off."

"I can't imagine that went over well."

"Yeah, I could never be the socially adept daughter she wanted. Our relationship is pretty strained even to this day, although she doesn't like to admit that."

Her mother's pressure that Shelby be gregarious around crowds probably had only complicated and multiplied the discomfort she had about being around people. Dylan had such a loving, supportive relationship with his family, it hurt him to think of Shelby never having something like that.

"I know you haven't had a great experience with family, but you can trust, unequivocally, that my family has your back. Okay? If you get into a situation at Omega and you're panicking, you let one of us know and we'll help you get through it."

Shelby reached her arms up around his neck and pulled his lips down to hers. "Thank you," she murmured.

"For what?"

"For not calling me crazy. For not writing me off. For having faith in me."

There were things Dylan wanted to tell her, but they got lost as Shelby walked forward, forcing Dylan to step back until his legs were against the edge of the bed.

Dylan wrapped his arms around her hips and brought them both down to the bed. Their hands became more frantic, removing clothes as quickly as possible. Their lips only separated from each other when they had to in order to remove clothes. Dylan peeled Shelby's jeans down her legs, careful of the one that was still tender.

Oh, holy hell, she was wearing that black-and-red thong. And a very wicked grin.

All thoughts of the dangers and risks they would take later that night disappeared. All Dylan could think about was Shelby and this moment.

And that thong.

Chapter Nineteen

Dylan walked into Cameron and Sophia's kitchen to make a pot of coffee. It was just two o'clock in the morning, but they were all going to need the caffeine to get through the next few hours. Evidently most of his family had headed back to their own homes for a few hours of rest, since the living room was empty.

But his sister was sitting at the kitchen table.

"Got any more of that?" Dylan asked Juliet, pointing to the mug of coffee in her hands.

"I think the pot is just about empty."

Dylan nodded and began to make more. "Everybody head out?"

"Yeah. Megan needs as much rest as she can get, so Sawyer took her home. Evan wanted to be at Omega already, to make sure everything looked clear."

Evan and Juliet had both been known for keeping highly irregular office hours at Omega, even before they'd become a couple. Security wouldn't bat an eye at seeing either of them there in the middle of the night. After all, bad guys didn't work just nine to five, so good guys couldn't either.

"This is a pretty good plan you've come up with, sis."

Juliet handed Dylan two cell phones. "Here's a couple of phones for you and Shelby in case you need them." She took another sip of coffee. "Let's hope my plan is enough. It's hard to hide when you don't know exactly who you're hiding from."

"My money is on Dennis Burgamy as the mole."

Juliet shrugged. "Burgamy is a general pain in the ass and perhaps the greatest kiss up who's ever been involved in law enforcement. But a traitor? I just don't know, Dylan."

Dylan shrugged. "Well, whoever it is, we're going to need to be ready. Once they figure out we've got Shelby and her numbers into the system, it's going to cause them to move into action quickly."

"Where is Shelby, by the way?" Juliet asked.

Dylan didn't quite meet his sister's eyes. "She's in the shower. She'll be out in a minute."

"She seemed a little overwhelmed earlier. She going to be okay?"

"Shelby doesn't do well around a lot of people. Tries to avoid it as much as possible. So the thought of going into an entire office building full of people is a little traumatic for her."

"Because she's afraid they'll attack her or arrest her or something?"

"Um, no. Actually, I think her greatest fear is that they'll all want to talk to her."

"Talk?"

"Yeah, like chitchat." Dylan smiled and poured himself a cup of coffee. "Honestly, I think she'd prefer it if they were chasing her or shooting at her."

"Okay, then, we'll be sure to protect her from all the dangerous talking."

"She's not crazy, Jules."

"I'm not mocking, I promise. You're talking to the woman who slept on a closet floor for a year and a half because of the terrors I had built up in my mind. Fears are fears whether they seem legitimate to other people or not."

Dylan knew Juliet understood fears all too well.

"Shelby will be all right. Once we get her in with the computer system, it'll be like a playdate for her and Megan."

Dylan smiled just thinking about Shelby with access to the technology Megan had created at Omega. Dylan hoped he was around to see the pure geek joy. He smiled into his coffee.

Dylan looked up to find his sister staring at him. "Oh, my gosh, Dylan, you're falling for her."

The statement totally caught Dylan off guard.

"No." Dylan used his best this-discussion-is-over tone, but Juliet just ignored it the way she always had.

"I would warn you off, but the way she was looking at you this evening—like you were her lifeboat and she had no idea how she would survive without you—I think she's falling for you, too."

Had Shelby really been looking at him like that? No. Juliet had to be mistaking Shelby's panic for something more romantic. "Look, Shelby and I have had a traumatic couple of days. Yeah, it's led to a little sex, but that doesn't make it something serious." And if it did, Dylan definitely did not want to talk about it with his little sister.

Juliet laughed, obviously enjoying Dylan's discomfort. "Are you kidding? You guys were all over each other with the little touches here and there all evening long. You even carried her dishes over to the sink for her."

"She has a hurt leg, Juliet. I was trying to be a gentleman like Mom raised me to be. Besides, you guys were touching each other all night, too. You're like the poster children of PDA."

Dylan saw the trap he'd set for himself as soon as the words were out of his mouth.

"Because we're all *in love*, Dylan. It's just natural. And

notice how you and Shelby just fit right in with the rest of us."

Dylan shook his head. Hoping his silence would clue his sister in. It didn't.

"Is this about Fiona and the baby?" she asked.

Dylan groaned. "No. It has nothing to do with her."

"Dylan, I'm going to say this because it's time. I know Fiona was your wife and I know what happened to her was a tragedy and that we're not supposed to speak ill of the dead…"

Dylan raised his eyebrow when Juliet hesitated. He couldn't remember Juliet ever talking about Fiona before. "Yes?"

"Well, Fiona was kind of a shrew."

Dylan barely avoided spewing the sip of coffee he'd just taken.

"I know what happened was sad, especially because of the baby, but you can't stay frozen in that place any longer, Dylan. You don't want to do law enforcement anymore because of what happened, that's fine. We all support you and none of us blame you. But you've got to stop closing yourself off from the rest of the world."

"You're one to talk, Jules."

"Look, don't throw how I handled the rape back in my face. Yeah, it took some time, but I had to come to the same place you're going to eventually have to come to—I could choose to let one moment control the rest of my life, or I could decide my own destiny. I chose Evan. I chose love."

Dylan was so proud of the corner Juliet had turned lately in her personal life. She'd struggled for so long and Dylan was glad she'd found happiness. But… "It's not the same, Juliet. This is just a casual thing between Shelby and me. We'll both be going our separate ways in a couple of days when this is all over."

"You keep telling yourself it's a fling, big brother. And when you wake up a few months or a year or whenever from now and you realize you let the perfect woman slip through your fingers because you were too blind to do anything about it, well, then you remember this little cup of coffee we had tonight."

Something in Dylan's heart clenched at Juliet's words. Because yes, Dylan could very clearly picture himself waking up in the middle of the night and reaching for Shelby and her not being around. And that frightened him more than anything else had for a long time.

But Dylan didn't have time to think about this right now. There were other much more important things that needed to be done tonight. Sorting out his feelings for one tiny, gorgeous, quirky, freckled female was not one of them.

So Dylan didn't care if both his tone and his words were a little harsh. He just needed to shut his sister up— damn her for always being able to see too much anyway— so he could focus on the mission at hand. Dylan set his coffee cup down with a resounding thump on the table and told his sister the exact opposite of what he was feeling.

"Whatever, Jules. I have no plans to ever see Shelby Keelan again when this is over. There's nothing real between us. Nothing special. She's just another woman." There, that should shut Juliet up for a while.

He'd expected an angry or annoyed look from her, but when Dylan glanced up he saw his sister look over his shoulder into the doorway of the kitchen and cringe. Dylan didn't have to turn around to know.

Shelby was there and had just heard his statement.

IT WAS ALWAYS good to have things spelled out for you with utter clarity just to make sure you didn't have any delusions of romantic grandeur for the man you'd just had sex with. Shelby would've said *made love*, but that evidently was too strong a phrase for what she and Dylan had shared.

And whatever real connection she'd felt with Dylan, whatever passion and tenderness she thought she had seen in his eyes earlier? Those were evidently figments of Shelby's overactive imagination.

Shelby would've eased back out of the kitchen, but Juliet had already seen her. Had already given her that oh-I-am-so-sorry-men-are-such-jerks look. Which Shelby would've appreciated more if said jerk wasn't two feet away from her.

"Shelby—" Dylan turned toward Shelby with an arm outstretched.

Shelby left a large distance between his hand and her body. If he touched her now—if anybody touched her now—she would shatter into a million pieces.

"Is that coffee? Thank goodness. There was no way I was going to make it through this night without coffee." Her voice sounded tight even to her own ears.

But she wasn't sobbing on the floor as she really wanted to do, so she'd just call that a win.

Not that she had any reason to be sobbing. Dylan hadn't promised her anything. The opposite, in fact. He had told her that he didn't do serious relationships. Had basically announced he was still in love with his dead wife.

Everything that had happened between them had been based on adrenaline and their hazardous circumstances. Fate had thrown them together, they'd been attracted and they'd acted on that attraction.

No harm, no foul.

It wasn't until Shelby actually heard Dylan say that what they had was nothing real or special that she realized she'd been hoping for something different when this crisis was all over. Maybe not a ring and promises of forever, but definitely not "no plans to ever see each other again."

Ouch. But it was better to know, right? To know that Dylan thought so little of her, of what was between them?

Shelby realized she'd been staring at the coffeepot without moving for an unreasonable amount of time. The silence at the table behind her was deafening. She picked up the pot and poured some into her mug. Damn it, now she was going to have to turn around.

And look at Dylan. And not cry.

Shelby would give ten years off her life for some sort of witty, socially acceptable thing to say right now. Why hadn't she listened and learned from her mother?

"Good, everybody's up. I'm leaving to go to Omega in a minute. Everybody good?"

Shelby closed her eyes briefly in relief and turned around. It was Cameron, with no knowledge of the awkward situation floating around the kitchen. He came over to get a cup of coffee, giving her shoulder a friendly squeeze.

"You ready for this, Shelby?"

"More ready than I was five minutes ago, that's for sure. Time to get this done so you all can stop some bad guys and we can all move on with our lives."

"Shelby—" Dylan stood and began walking toward her.

"I've got to get my Dr. Wonder outfit on that Juliet provided for me. It won't take long." Shelby grabbed her coffee mug and began to leave, giving Dylan a wide berth.

"I'll come with you," Juliet said.

"No, that's not necessary." Shelby did not want to talk about what Dylan had just said.

"Just in case you have any questions about tonight, Dr. Wonder, that's all." Juliet linked her arm with Shelby's, brooking no refusal.

In the bedroom, Shelby turned and locked the door. She didn't think Dylan would come in, but wanted to make sure.

"I mean this strictly professionally, although in undercover work personal matters definitely come into play. Are you okay?"

Shelby looked over at the bed where she and Dylan had just been an hour before. No, she wasn't really okay. She deliberately turned her back to the bed.

"I'm going to get the job done. That's what really matters, right?" Shelby got the trousers and blouse out of the closet.

"It does matter. But it's not the only thing that matters, Shelby."

"Look, your brother never promised me anything, Juliet. We've only known each other for forty-eight hours, for goodness' sake, so what he said in there—"

"He didn't mean." Juliet was quick to cut Shelby off. "He was irritated with me and was trying to shut me up, so he said something obnoxious."

Shelby snuffed out the tiny piece of her heart that wanted to grab hold of Juliet's words. It didn't matter *why* Dylan had said the words, he'd still said them.

"You don't have to defend him, Juliet. Like I said, how involved can two people be after just two days?"

It sure felt a lot longer than that to Shelby, but she wouldn't mention that.

"Getting these numbers in my head into Megan's computer, figuring out what the countdown is leading to and where it will happen, that's the most important thing now. Hurt feelings between Dylan and I are pretty insignificant in comparison."

Juliet grinned at her. "Are you sure you've never worked undercover before? You sound like a seasoned pro."

Shelby slipped on the outfit to make her into Dr. Wonder. The blouse was a pale tan and the pants were a darker tan. They were as nondescript as you could get. "You probably won't still think that the first time I actually have to talk to people."

"You're going to do fine. Just let Megan or whoever you're with do most of the talking whenever possible," Juliet told her.

Shelby ran an exhausted hand through her hair before pinning it up in a bun to look like the professional PhD she was supposed to be.

Somehow she was afraid saving the world from a terrorist attack was going to be the easy part of the next few hours.

Chapter Twenty

"I see it's on the schedule, but I don't know why you're working this late at night, Dr. Fuller-Branson. You should be home getting your rest."

Shelby had been both completely ignoring Dylan and watching sweet, pregnant Megan charm the four guards at the front entrance of the Omega building for the past five minutes. Except she wasn't really charming them, she was just being herself. She knew each guard by name, asked each about their families and any ailments they may have ever mentioned.

Shelby was in awe of her friend. Having gone to MIT with Megan, she knew the woman was a genius, but Megan was able to interact and talk with people—put them at ease and make them feel important—in a way that was totally foreign to Shelby.

And it wasn't an act. Megan genuinely cared about others. Shelby cared about others, too, but was always so awkward and stiff that interchanges rarely went the way she intended.

"Michael, I went home and rested all afternoon," Megan assured the guard. "You know there's no way Sawyer would stand for it otherwise. I wouldn't be surprised if he showed up in a little while anyway."

All the guards nodded, smiling, in approval of Sawyer's

good husbanding. Shelby barely refrained from rolling her eyes. It was a good thing Megan wasn't one of the bad guys, because she probably could've gotten away with just about anything without ever even raising a weapon.

"Besides, Dr. Wonder and her assistant have flown all the way from Australia to work in the cybercrimes lab. It's the middle of the afternoon for them."

If Shelby didn't know it was Dylan standing next to her—sexy, virile Dylan—she might never have given him a second look. He had somehow contorted his posture until he looked unassuming and nonthreatening in any way. He definitely didn't look like the confident, strong man Shelby had seen wrestle an unwieldy plane safely to the ground or defeat her attacker. The ill-fitting suit, glasses and horrible slicked-back hair helped the ruse, but it was Dylan's demeanor that sold it.

For the first time, Shelby could understand just how good Dylan had been at undercover work.

The guards glanced at Shelby and Dylan and nodded politely; one of them handed her a visitor's badge with her name and info on it, but their concern was for Megan. Shelby was a little disappointed that not a single one of them made the Wonder from Down Under joke.

"I know you guys have extra security we need to go through. No drives, right?" Megan asked them, handing them her purse to go through the X-ray machine. Shelby and Dylan in turn handed over their purse and briefcase as well.

"Yes, ma'am." The guards all looked a bit sheepish. "Plus, we now have this new body scanner everyone has to walk through. They brought it in yesterday afternoon."

Whoever was trying to keep out a drive with all the numbers on it was doing a pretty thorough job. No one would be able to get any computer equipment or drives past that scanner.

"Um," the first guard spoke up again. "We already asked to make sure it was safe for a pregnant woman."

Megan's smile was obviously sincere. "Thank you, guys. I really appreciate it."

They walked through the scanner, one similar to the new fancy security scanners at large airports, individually. Everyone was deemed clear to pass.

"See you later, guys. Have a good night," Megan said.

Shelby and Megan moved quickly toward the elevators, Dylan one step behind.

"That's quite a fan club you have there," Shelby told Megan while they waited for the elevator doors to open.

"Elevators have cameras," Megan whispered as the door opened. "But yeah, they're all wonderful guys. Most hoping to be full agents one day."

They rode up in silence. Dylan kept his head down and pretended to be shuffling through some files he held in his hands.

"There are cameras in the elevators, but not the offices or hallways," Megan told her once they got out. "Sorry, should've mentioned that before." Megan shot a worried look at Dylan.

He nodded. "Yeah, we just have to be as alert as we can. We couldn't prepare her for everything."

Something as simple as making a joke in the elevator could bring down this entire operation. Shelby suddenly became very aware of how precarious everything really was.

"My plan is just not to talk to someone I don't know unless I need to."

Megan wrapped her arm around Shelby as they walked down the hall. "Aw, honey, that's always your plan." She kissed Shelby on the cheek. "And I love you for it."

Megan knew what it felt like not to fit in. That's why Shelby had bonded with her so completely.

Shelby was very aware of Dylan on the other side of her and the huge distance between them. She hadn't talked to him directly since what she heard from him in the kitchen. As far as Shelby was concerned, there really wasn't anything left to be said.

Dylan had said it all.

They made it to the cybercrimes office, which was empty at this early hour.

"Okay, as soon as we scan our IDs into this door, the clock is on. The Omega system will think we are all in there. That will only fool the mole for as long as there are no human eyes checking on us. If the mole is as high up as we're afraid he is, that will only take a phone call once people start reporting in."

Shelby nodded. That gave them a few hours, hopefully.

"I know I'm being monitored because you're my friend and I'm the computer guru. What helps us is the mole probably thinks we're spending all our effort trying to get you into the building with some sort of hard drive."

The elevator pinged down the hallway and Shelby startled in the quiet. Dylan slipped his arm around her to offer support, but Shelby shrugged it off.

It was Juliet's fiancé. That's right, Evan was providing them the second set of IDs.

This cloak-and-dagger stuff was already wearing on Shelby and she'd only been doing it for five minutes. She had no idea how people worked undercover for weeks at a time.

"Here's your local police IDs." Evan handed another set of scanner cards to Shelby, Dylan and Megan.

"Won't they realize these IDs didn't come through the front door?" Shelby asked.

Megan nodded. "Yes, that's possible, but it's two different systems. Someone would have to cross-reference the two."

They all looked at each other. That was a danger and they all knew it.

"Juliet's plan is good, but the best it does is open us pockets of time. You and I are going to have to work fast, Shelby," Megan said. It was three o'clock in the morning. At best they only had three or four hours. It wasn't going to be easy.

Shelby nodded. She was ready. Especially if it meant she didn't have to talk to Dylan.

Megan scanned the IDs for Dr. Wonder, Dylan and herself into the cybercrimes lab door. "Okay, that's it. We're officially on the clock. The mole is most definitely going to be watching for me. Hopefully he'll think I'm here in the cybercrimes office as long as possible, since my ID won't check in anywhere else."

"Let's get you two to the real computer lab," Evan said. "Cameron should be waiting for us there."

They walked through a series of hallways and used the back stairs instead of the elevators to avoid cameras. The whole building seemed dangerous in its partial darkness. To Shelby, it felt as if eyes followed them everywhere, that at any time someone would jump out. She didn't want to be attacked out of the blue the way she had been while lying unawares at Mrs. Morgan's house. She shuddered at the thought, the pain in her leg becoming more pronounced.

"You okay?" Dylan asked.

Shelby desperately wished she could lean into his strength. To just take a second and breathe in Dylan's calm and feel his arms fold around her.

But that had also been stolen from her while she was lying unawares. Shelby just didn't want to be attacked anymore.

"I'm fine," she told him.

But Dylan wasn't willing to let it go. He grabbed her arm as they walked. "Shelby, what you heard—"

"I don't want to talk about it, Dylan." She tried to snatch her arm away, but that was laughable when Dylan didn't want to let her go. Although she noticed nothing about his grip hurt.

Evan and Megan glanced back at them from their place in front, then sped up to offer Shelby and Dylan a bit of privacy. Privacy Shelby didn't want.

Dylan slowed them down so Evan and Megan pulled away even farther.

"What I said to Juliet in the kitchen was just to get her to shut up, Shelby. She was pushing my buttons and I said the most obnoxious things I could think of."

"We don't have any promises between us, Dylan. I know that. We're just a fling, noth—"

Shelby didn't even get the words out before Dylan stopped them both and backed her up against the wall. Hard.

And kissed her until she was breathless and clinging to Dylan.

He pulled back from her and cupped her face in his hands. "Damn it, Shelby, I know this isn't the time. I know there are bigger things at stake here than you and me. But I couldn't let you go one more second without you knowing how sorry I am for what I said. None of those words were true."

Dylan grabbed her arm and they began walking again at a quicker pace to catch up with Megan and Evan. Shelby now had no idea what to think. She wasn't sure if she should still be mad at Dylan or if what he said was the truth.

She wasn't even going to think about it right now. She didn't know if she would ever think about it again. And then it didn't even matter because they were at the door of the main computer lab. Cameron was waiting for them.

"Should both Cameron and Evan be here? Will that be suspicious?" Shelby asked.

"No, there would always be at least two Omega employees here with anyone from the outside. The only thing that is really suspicious is that it's three o'clock in the morning. But we didn't have much choice about that," Cameron explained.

"You ready?" Megan asked her. "Everything okay?" She looked pointedly between Shelby and Dylan.

"Yes." Shelby nodded. "It'll take me a little while to enter the numbers in, Megan."

"That's fine. The system will begin analyzing them as soon as you're done." Megan collected the second set of IDs from Shelby and Dylan to scan them at the door. "Let's hope this works."

"Many Bothans died to bring us this information." The words were out of Shelby's mouth before she even realized it. Megan gave her an odd look, but Shelby didn't take offense. Megan didn't get most pop culture references.

"It's go time," Cameron said to Evan. They actually bumped fists.

Megan and Shelby both rolled their eyes. "*It's go time?* Seriously?"

"Hey, you just quoted *Jedi*. Don't give us a hard time," Evan said, laughing. He scanned his ID at the door.

"All right, here we go. We're on clock number two now," Megan said, scanning the other IDs. Cameron followed up with his.

All joking stopped. If Shelby didn't get these codes out of her head and into Megan's system before the mole figured out they were here, then everything would be for naught.

Shelby turned to Megan. "You know what it will be

like for me while I'm entering in the data. Don't stop me, even when it's ugly. If I don't get it all the first time, I won't have the time to recoup and do it again."

Megan nodded and squeezed Shelby's hand.

Shelby was glad Megan understood. Shelby had to do this no matter what personal price she paid. Because if she didn't, they'd be too late to stop whatever the DS-13 countdown was for.

Chapter Twenty-One

Shelby, behind a keyboard, was amazing.

Dylan had never seen anything like it. Her fingers flew on the numeric keypad as she stared blankly ahead typing numbers from inside her mind that only she could see. She'd been doing that for over an hour.

"That's pretty freaky, man," Evan said from where they both stood at the back of the room. They spoke in hushed voices, but Dylan didn't think Shelby would notice them even if they were yelling.

Dylan had known Shelby was good with a keyboard because of her success as a video game coder, but this was almost like a superpower. She never stopped, never made a mistake, just typed in numbers at the fastest pace any of them had ever seen.

"I don't think I could type numbers that fast even if I was randomly pressing buttons," Dylan said.

And that she was remembering all of these in her head? That was beyond amazing.

Megan came over and sat down in one of the conference chairs near where they were standing. "She's pretty amazing, isn't she?"

Dylan nodded. Yes, she was amazing, but he'd known that before she started typing. He just hoped he hadn't screwed up any chance with her whatsoever.

What a stupid mess he had made in the kitchen. The look on Shelby's face. Dylan hoped to go the rest of his life without ever seeing that look on her face again.

Because what they had was special and she definitely wasn't just another woman. Dylan looked at Shelby now, and the things he felt were both terrifying and thrilling.

And even though he had no idea what to do or what sort of future they might have, he hoped to God he hadn't ended the entire thing by something said so carelessly.

"You know, DS-13 embedding their information in a children's internet game is pretty impressive. Brilliant, actually," Megan said.

"With an organization as widespread as theirs, it's a pretty effective way to communicate. They can get different levels of information to different people. No phone calls to be recorded or emails that can be traced," Evan continued.

This game was popular amongst grade-school children. A help-the-detective-type mystery. The game was unique in that it was only available once a week on Saturdays for only one hour.

Now that they knew what DS-13 was hiding in the coding of the game, they understood why it wasn't constantly available.

It was much more possible that someone would've found the pattern if the game had been continuously available. Not likely, but possible. So they'd only made the game—and thus its coding—available one hour per week.

"Shelby started following the game to get ideas for her own games. She likes to watch games in their code form because coding is in numbers and that's how her mind works." They all watched Shelby while Megan talked. Yeah, it was obvious her mind worked differently—more brilliantly—than theirs when it came to numbers.

"The game can't be recorded or played back, the coding

deletes itself after just a moment, so I'm sure they were feeling secure in what messages they were sending out in the games," Megan continued. "Because who would've ever believed that there was someone who could not only recognize that there was some sort of message going on inside the game, but also someone able to memorize the entire sequence after only seeing it once."

"The good guys caught quite a big break with Shelby," Cameron muttered.

"And we better use that to our fullest advantage. This could really be what we need to begin to bring DS-13 down completely," Evan agreed.

Dylan left them to talk and walked closer to Shelby. What she was doing was obviously taking a toll on her. She continued her constant data entry, but her lips were now tightly pursed and her face was paler than before.

"Shelby needs a break," he said to Megan as she came to stand beside him. "It's hurting her to do this. Why?"

"Have you ever given one hundred percent of your focus to one thing for an extended period of time? It's like using the same muscle over and over. At first it's fine, then it's tiring, then it's agonizing. That's probably the point she's getting to."

"Then she needs to stop. Stop her, Megan."

Megan laid a hand gently on his arm. "She wants to finish, Dylan. She knows we have a limited amount of time."

But in just the couple of minutes that they'd been talking, Dylan could tell Shelby was feeling worse. Her breathing was becoming labored. Dylan was horrified to see her nose begin to bleed on one side.

"We have to stop this," Dylan said.

"Give her a few more minutes. She's got to be close to finished. If we stop her now, she may not be able to get herself functional enough to restart and finish in time."

Evan and Cameron joined them. "Is it just me or is Shelby not looking so good? Is that blood?"

Evan's words were enough. Dylan was putting an end to this. He began walking toward Shelby, determined to stop her.

Megan—moving pretty darn fast for a little pregnant lady—got in front of Dylan before he could reach Shelby.

"Megan, look at her." Shelby was now trembling. Color had washed out of her face. But her fingers kept moving.

Megan put a hand on his chest. "It hurts me, too, Dylan. She's my friend. But she asked me to make sure she was allowed to finish."

"Have you ever seen her like this? At school?"

"Not this bad, no," Megan admitted.

Dylan looked at Shelby again where she sat at the computer terminal. He closed his eyes. "I have to stop her."

"Her body will stop her if it gets too bad—she'll pass out. It's the mind's way of protecting itself from unmanageable pain."

She shouldn't have to go that far. Dylan had no idea it would be this way. "Did Shelby know this would happen?"

"She knew she wouldn't be comfortable."

Wouldn't be *comfortable*? This was so far past that.

"She knows what's at stake, Dylan. It's DS-13. They're known for incurring as many casualties as possible in their attacks. It's a countdown and information that went out to every DS-13 operative. Whatever that countdown is to, it's *big*."

"I know that, Megan, but look at her!" Both nostrils were bleeding now and her shoulders were stooping. Dylan gently, but firmly, moved Megan out of his way. He couldn't watch this anymore.

But Megan grabbed his arm. "If the roles were reversed and you had the chance to stop DS-13 even though it meant pain to yourself, wouldn't you want the chance to do it? Don't let her suffering be in vain. Respect her enough for that."

Dylan stopped. Megan was right.

And he did respect Shelby's strength.

Though she be but little, she is fierce.

But Dylan would give anything if he could take some of the pain racking her small body into his own right now.

Shelby began to slump forward, tears rolling down her cheeks from eyes that were still closed. Dylan rushed over to her to hold her up, to lend his strength in any way possible. Her fingers kept plucking away at the numeric keypad.

"You can do it, sweetheart. Hang on." Dylan whispered the words in her ear. He felt her lean against him, so he wrapped both arms around her. He could feel her weakening.

Her fingers abruptly stopped their movement. Shelby's eyes opened. Her breathing was labored as she looked over at Megan, then Dylan.

"Done." Her voice was nothing more than the hoarsest whisper.

Dylan caught her as she fell to the side, completely unconscious. As gently as he could, he swung her up in his arms. Megan quickly sat down in the seat Shelby had vacated at the main computer terminal.

"She got it all in. Amazing." The wonder was clear in Megan's voice. "Is she okay, Dylan?"

Dylan sat in one of the other chairs, keeping Shelby clutched against his chest. There was no way in hell he was letting her go. "Her breathing is less labored, a little bit of color coming back into her cheeks." Evan handed Dylan a tissue and he used it to wipe the blood from Shelby's nose.

"Now I just need to allow the software to run the configurations of the data Shelby entered. It won't take long and we'll know what the countdown was leading to and where."

Shelby's eyes began to blink and then opened. "Did I finish?" Her voice was still a whisper.

"Yes. You were amazing." Dylan kissed her forehead, thankful that she wasn't trying to get out of his arms. Because he didn't think he could let her go. "Megan is running the configurations now."

Shelby nodded wearily. "Good, because there's more."

"More what?"

"It doesn't matter, they're later. We've got to worry about the imminent countdown right now."

Dylan wasn't sure what Shelby was talking about. He wasn't sure she knew what she was talking about. So he didn't push it, just held her.

Shelby brought the hand she'd used on the number pad up and cradled it to her chest. Her fingers were extended at odd angles.

"My fingers are cramping."

Dylan took her fingers between both of his and began rubbing gently. He wasn't surprised they were cramping at the rate she had been using them. She whimpered a tiny bit at his ministrations, but didn't pull away.

Megan was busy at the keyboard providing further instruction to the software she had created, feeding info back in when it was needed. Dylan just held Shelby while all this went on and watched as strength began to creep slowly back to her body.

Dylan could feel the exact moment when that strength tipped the scales and caused Shelby to remember that she shouldn't be sitting in his lap. He watched as her green eyes went from soft to shuttered right in front of him.

For the first time in a very long time, Dylan remembered what it was like to feel his heart crack. He hadn't let anyone close enough to do that sort of damage in years.

Shelby stiffened and began to sit up and move away. Dylan let go of the fingers he was rubbing and didn't try to stop her, although he stayed close by in case her sudden strength deserted her.

Shelby walked over to the terminal where Megan sat. Numbers were scrolling across the screen like something out of *The Matrix*. Dylan had no idea what any of it meant. He could tell Evan and Cameron didn't either.

Shelby put her hand on Megan's shoulder and Megan touched her hand gently in acknowledgment, but neither woman took their eyes from the screen.

"There."

Both women said it in unison. Shelby pointed to a group of numbers on the screen and Megan nodded. Megan began typing something else.

Across the room a phone rang. Cameron went to answer it, but Dylan knew it was bad news. Nobody would be calling this room at this hour except a member of his family with information they didn't want to hear.

"We're running out of time, ladies," Dylan told them.

"We're almost there." Megan kept typing as she spoke.

And then, as suddenly as Shelby's had, Megan's fingers stopped moving. Both stared at the screen, then looked at each other, horror clear on their faces.

"What?" Evan barked. "What is it?"

"The countdown is for a bombing here in Washington, DC." Shelby's voice was once again hoarse as she turned to look at Dylan. "Set to go off at eight thirty this morning."

That was a little less than two and a half hours from now.

"Where in DC? Do you know?" Dylan crossed to Shelby and put his hands on her upper arms. She looked as if she might collapse again.

"On the Mall, right in front of the Lincoln Memorial, in a maintenance tunnel."

A monument, even the Lincoln Memorial monument, wasn't too bad. An artifact, even one as important as this, could be rebuilt. Lives couldn't.

"Okay," Evan said. "That's not as bad as it could be."

Now Megan spoke up. "No, it's much worse. There are children's groups, elementary schools from all over the country performing at the Mall this morning. It's been all over the news. It's called Celebrating America's Future."

Dylan's jaw clenched. It was the most perverse and perfect target a group like DS-13 could think of. Attacking a celebration of *America's future*. DS-13 had probably been waiting a long time for something with such a degree of poetic justice.

"We'll stop the kids from coming in, keep them all out of the Mall area," Evan said.

Shelby shook her head, looking at Dylan. "The kids are already there, most of them have been there since three or four o'clock this morning. Part of the program begins at sunrise." Shelby grasped onto Dylan's arms. "They're planning to attack our children."

Chapter Twenty-Two

"Okay, things just got more complicated." Cameron hung up the phone he was on and ran over. "Burgamy just arrived at Omega. Juliet's calling in the bomb squad and FBI. We'll meet them at the site."

"What the hell is Burgamy doing here so early?" Dylan asked. It was highly suspicious. Especially when taking into consideration the DS-13 plans they'd just discovered. Did he want to be here so he could have a front-row seat to the destruction and death his organization was attempting to cause?

"There's more, in the codes, more information," Shelby said. "Did you see it?" she asked Megan.

"No, it was going by too fast."

"Was it stuff about today, Shelby?" Cameron asked. "We can't waste any more time. Unless there is more information about today, we've got to get to that bomb."

"Yes, I think. Maybe a way to disarm the bomb. I'll keep checking." Shelby's face was pinched.

Dylan walked to Evan and Cameron by the door. Evan was already back on the phone with Juliet providing her with all the info Shelby and Megan had given them.

"You guys need to be careful about any mass evacuation of those kids," Dylan told Cameron. "DS-13 could be watching and might trigger the bomb early if you try something like that."

Cameron nodded. "You need to stay here with Shelby and Megan, Dylan. Buy them the time they need to access whatever they can from those codes. Them finding a disarm code may be our only chance."

Dylan nodded. He knew he could do more good here than at the bomb site. There would be other people, much more qualified people, who would take care of that situation. And if the mole knew Megan and Shelby were pulling info about DS-13 from this computer location, he would be coming to eliminate them.

Dylan had no intention of letting that happen.

But Dylan also knew he was sending all his siblings, and one of his best friends, Evan, into potentially the deadliest situation they'd ever faced.

Dylan hugged Cameron. "You be careful and get everyone out of there alive."

"You do the same, big brother."

Evan slapped Dylan on the shoulder and followed Cameron out of the room.

Dylan turned back to the women. It was just a matter of time before they were found in this room. Who they were found by would determine the next course of action.

Megan was staring at the door Cameron and Evan had just run out of. Her face was ashen. "They're all going, aren't they? To the bomb site."

Megan meant Sawyer. She didn't say his name, but Dylan knew who she meant.

"I didn't even get to say good-morning to him," Megan said softly. "We always find each other whenever the later one gets to the building. To say good-morning. Always. We've never missed even once."

Dylan met Shelby's eyes just for a moment. Shelby was concerned about her friend's distress. Dylan was, too. Since Megan had a genius IQ, Dylan would try to appeal to her reason.

"Megan, it's an emergency. I'm sure if Sawyer could've—"

Dylan's words were cut off by the door flying open. It was Sawyer. He rushed over to his wife and put his hands on both her cheeks.

"Good morning." He kissed her tenderly, briefly, then put his hands on her pregnant belly for just a moment. "I'll see you later tonight at home. I promise."

Sawyer said nothing else, just turned and ran out of the room, slapping Dylan's back on the way out.

Dylan saw Shelby wipe away tears at the tender scene between his brother and Megan. Megan, who a moment ago seemed distraught, now was focused and secure.

"Let's get back to work," she told Shelby, pulling up another chair at the terminal. They immediately began sorting through numbers and information on the screen. Dylan didn't even pretend to understand what they were doing, just let them work.

Dylan knew what his job was. Protecting them from whoever walked through that door next, although he wasn't sure how he would do that with no weapon, no credentials and no authority. But the person who came through the door a few minutes later was not who Dylan was expecting.

Chantelle DiMuzio, Dennis Burgamy's personal assistant, walked in. Her head, as it almost always tended to be, was stuck in her electronic organizer.

"Oh, sorry, am I in the right room?"

Chantelle had started working at Omega after Dylan had left, so he didn't know her well. But he had met her a couple of times, most recently last year when helping out on a mission involving Juliet and Evan.

"Hi, Chantelle, I'm in here." Megan threw up her arm

and waved, but didn't get up from her seat at the computer terminal.

"I'm Dylan Branson, we've met before," Dylan said to the woman.

She seemed a little harried. Although she worked day in and day out with Dennis Burgamy, Dylan was a little surprised she wasn't constantly pulling all her hair out. Not only did Dylan think the man was the mole, Burgamy was also just a jerk in general. Nobody got along with him.

"Yes, I remember," Chantelle told him. "And you look just like your brothers."

She flushed a little at that. Evidently Burgamy's secretary had a little crush on one or both of Dylan's brothers. She wasn't the first, Dylan was sure. He decided to up the flirt factor, keep Chantelle talking about nothing for as long as possible.

"You're here early. I hope they pay you overtime for hours like this."

Chantelle rolled her eyes. "I wish. I'm salary, so no overtime no matter what."

"And you have to work with Burgamy all the time? That's a little cruel and unusual."

Chantelle looked down again. "I thought you had been in a plane crash."

Damn. "Yes, I was, but fortunately made it out alive."

"Oh, well, that's good. I didn't know that, but here you are." She gave him a smile, but didn't look him all the way in the eyes. "Mr. Burgamy said you had a woman with you, too, that she was bringing in some sort of numbers on a hard drive or something. Is she okay?"

"She was fine, too. Unfortunately, the hard drive was destroyed." Dylan hoped that information would be passed along to Burgamy. Give him a false sense of security about Dylan's being here.

"It was destroyed? I don't think that was reported to Mr. Burgamy's office yet."

"Sorry. One of my siblings was supposed to have done it yesterday, I think. They're such slackers." Dylan gave her his most engaging smile.

Poor Chantelle didn't seem to know what to do with Dylan's charm. She looked back down at her computer tablet. "Um, the computer log showed this room as being used by Cameron and Evan with guests. But then the front-door log showed that they just left the building. So I was just trying to figure out what was going on."

Now Megan stood up and walked over. Dylan didn't know how they would explain any of this. They didn't want to tell Chantelle anything about the bomb because that information would go straight to Burgamy.

"Evan and Cameron were here, but they had to leave. So I came in here," Megan told the other woman.

Chantelle really looked confused now. "Oh. Because the system says you're logged in to the cybercrimes offices with a Dr. Wonder. It doesn't have any record of you in here."

Megan caught Dylan's eye. Neither of them were sure what to say. "Yeah, the system must be glitching or something. I can look into that. I'm multitasking right now. Back and forth everywhere."

Something beeped on Chantelle's computer. "Okay, that's Mr. Burgamy. He's already here and on a rampage about something." She typed furiously. Then looked over at Shelby at the computer. "You guys didn't bring any hard drives in here, right?"

For just a second, Chantelle wasn't a frazzled, worn-down employee. She was taking in and weighing everything in this room.

"Are you kidding, Chantelle?" Megan laughed and linked arms with the other woman. "Nobody can get in here with any drive of any sort. Have you seen the new crazy security machine they have at the front doors? I felt violated just walking through it."

At Megan's words, whatever Dylan had thought he saw in Chantelle was gone. She was back to frazzled, over-worked employee with a terrible boss, barely able to take her eyes off her computer tablet.

"All right, if you guys are okay in here I'll just leave you to it. But I'll have to call a couple more agents to come in, Megan, because of the rules about visitors."

"No problem, Chantelle. Thanks. Sorry for your early morning."

Chantelle nodded and was already walking out the door, answering her phone and typing at the same time.

"Well?" Dylan asked.

"I think it's only a matter of time before Burgamy knows we're here. I didn't want to ask Chantelle to lie to him. It didn't seem right and would look suspicious since we don't have solid proof about Burgamy."

"I agree." Dylan looked over at Shelby, who was still frantically working on the computer. She was slowed down by having to use her left hand to type and enter data. Her right hand was still clutched against her chest.

"There's a lot more information in there than we thought," Megan said. "Shelby's looking for stuff concerning the bombing specifically right now, but there's other info, too. Important intel on DS-13. It's a huge break-through, Dylan."

Dylan nodded. "But right now, we've got to focus on the bomb. Anything that you can find to help them."

"Believe me, I know." Megan nodded and made her way back to where Shelby worked.

A few minutes later, four Omega employees entered the room. All size large. None of them looking personable.

The muscle had arrived. If Burgamy decided to put an end to the work Shelby and Megan were doing, Dylan wouldn't be able to stop all four men before they stopped the women.

Dylan gave a half grin at no one in particular. He may not be able to stop them, but he'd damn well try. Dylan slipped off his suit jacket so it wouldn't hinder his movements if quick action became necessary.

"I'm sorry, but I need to ask all of you to allow us to do a scan of your clothing and possessions," Big Guy Number One said.

Shelby looked over at Dylan for the first time. He nodded. She stood up so the man could use the scanner to eliminate any doubt that she had any electronics on her person. The same was done to Megan and Dylan.

One of the other guys reported in the finds—that all of them were clean—but Dylan didn't know to whom. Burgamy? Chantelle? Did it mean anything? The men then scattered around the room, casually but strategically.

Dylan doubted he'd be allowed to leave the room now even if he wanted to.

A few minutes later, a smaller man, obviously not muscle, entered the room. Where Megan had pretty much ignored the big guys except to submit to their scans, this person she paid attention to.

"Hello, Dr. Fuller-Branson. You're working early this morning," the man said in a singsongy voice, ignoring Dylan and the other men and crossing directly to the computer terminal. Everything about him screamed computer geek. Dylan was surprised he didn't have a pocket protector.

"You, too, Dr. Miller. I'm surprised to see you here." Megan's response was clipped. It was the first time Dylan had ever heard Megan be less than overtly friendly with someone.

There was no lost love here.

"I've been asked to come in and check that there are no contraband hard drives being used in the system."

"Asked by whom?" Megan demanded.

"Burgamy's office. If you must know." Miller's voice was just as rigid as Megan's.

Megan glanced over at Dylan, one eyebrow raised. Dylan gave her a small nod. He was becoming more and more convinced that Burgamy was the mole. They just needed to figure out a way to prove it.

"Fine, Dr. Miller. Check away. We have no external drives."

Miller thoroughly vetted the computer. Looked in places Dylan had no idea you could even attach an external drive. The man seemed genuinely shocked not to find one.

"You really don't have one?"

"No." Megan shrugged. "I told you that."

"Megan, where is this data from if not a drive?" The man's curiosity had obviously outweighed any ill feelings he had toward Megan.

"Jim, I know you and I have had our differences, but this is important. We're the good guys here. But—" Megan looked around casually at the men sitting in the room and lowered her volume "—perhaps not everyone in this building is."

Miller looked at Dylan, then back at Megan and Shelby. He nodded. "I'll let them know that there's no hard drive. But I'm supposed to stay here and report on what you're doing."

Shelby and Megan were already back at work, both of them frantically scanning data. They were running out of time with the bomb.

And with Dr. Jim Miller here to report on every move they made, things had gotten just about as bad as they could get.

Or so Dylan thought.

Because then Dennis Burgamy walked through the door.

Chapter Twenty-Three

Shelby heard somebody else enter the room behind her and cringed, gritting her teeth. It was getting really crowded in here.

She knew things were falling apart around them. That the mole—Burgamy or whatever his name was—was closing in. Maybe the computer would be taken away at any moment. Heck, for all Shelby knew, maybe they were all about to be thrown into some dark cell or killed.

She could hear talking going on all around her, could feel all the people, but tried to stay focused. She had finally found the thread she was looking for, the one that would lead to the code needed to disarm the bomb.

What time was it? How much time did they have left before the bomb went off?

All the voices in the room were driving Shelby crazy. She wished she could poke her fingers in her ears. But her right hand wasn't working anyway, still cramping every time she tried to move it, so that couldn't happen. She was already feeling sick from the effort to get the data in earlier. She needed quiet. She needed to be alone.

Damn it, she needed to know what time it was.

"Dylan." Shelby knew he was talking to someone, could hear their voices louder than the rest. But Megan was too busy talking to the other computer guy who came in to ask her.

Dylan was by her side in just a moment. "Hey." He brushed a strand of her hair out of her eyes. "You okay?"

She was so tired.

"I've almost got what I'm looking for—the code to shut off the..." Shelby trailed off. She wasn't sure if she was supposed to say anything in front of these people. She had no idea who was good and who was bad anymore. "What time is it?"

"Almost eight o'clock. Keep working, okay?" He kissed the top of her head and Shelby almost believed that he cared. "Everyone is waiting for our call."

"I've found the right string. I just need a few more minutes to follow it."

"Okay."

"It's getting crowded in here, Dylan. That's hard for me." Shelby desperately wanted Dylan to understand. She wouldn't be able to function for much longer.

Somebody said something from across the room, but Dylan held out an arm to silence the person. He crouched down next to Shelby, giving her all his attention. "Shelby, I know how hard this is for you." His words were whispered so no one else could hear. "You've already been so strong, baby. Keep it up just a little bit longer, okay? Get that code for my family to dismantle the bomb and I promise I will get you away from people for as long as you want."

Dylan did understand. He didn't think she was making stuff up just to get attention, as Shelby's mom had always felt.

Shelby nodded and turned back to the monitor. Using the last of her strength and focus, she pushed all the voices and presence of others to the background.

She saw the trail she was looking for in the massive

amount of code. She began to follow it, reading the numbers the way most people read books.

She only needed one small group of numbers. She knew they were there. But it was like finding one particular sentence in the middle of a large legal document. Even though you knew what to look for, it was hard to find.

But people, *children*, were going to die if Shelby didn't find that code.

So she shut everything out and focused.

There. There it was.

"I've got it," Shelby announced.

"She's got what? What has she got?" Shelby heard the angry words from behind her, but didn't know who said them.

"Go, Shelby, I'm ready," Dylan said, also ignoring the man who was yelling.

Shelby read off the eight-digit code. She looked over to find Megan with her cell phone also. Both she and Dylan were sending the code to the bomb site.

"Anything else they need to know?" Megan asked.

"No, that's it, according to this data."

Shelby sat back and spun the chair away from the computer terminal for the first time since she'd sat down in it. There really were a lot of people in here. No wonder she had been going a little crazy.

One guy in particular, Shelby had to guess he was Burgamy, based on what she had heard, was pretty livid.

"Why the hell didn't you notify me that you were here, Branson?" Burgamy asked Dylan. "And are you okay from your crash?"

"My plane did go down, but we somehow managed to survive. We somehow managed to survive a lot of things over the past few days."

Burgamy's eyes narrowed at that. "I'm not sure what's going on here, Branson, but we have protocols and rules that have to be followed. Perhaps you've forgotten that in the years since you've last worked here."

Burgamy didn't show any signs of stopping his tirade anytime soon. Shelby wasn't sure how long she could listen to him before she did or said something really inappropriate.

She just needed to get out of here for a while. As far as Shelby could tell, neither Megan nor Dylan had heard anything back from the bomb site. That was a good thing, right? Shelby hoped so, because she didn't think she could get back on that computer with all this human nonsense going on around her.

Chantelle DiMuzio, the lady who had been here earlier, came back in the room.

"Chantelle, why wasn't I notified that Dylan Branson was in the building? I thought he and Ms. Keelan had critical information that we needed."

"I did update the status report when I found them here earlier, sir. But Mr. Branson informed me that the hard drive with the data they were meant to deliver had been destroyed in transit, so I lowered their rank of importance in the system." Chantelle's voice was tight but level. Obviously she was used to this sort of conversation with her boss.

"At least you sent in some other Omega employees, as per protocol." Dennis Burgamy straightened his tie. Obviously protocol was the most important thing to him.

Shelby *really* didn't like that man.

She could feel something inappropriate building inside her. If she punched Burgamy, would she be arrested for attacking an officer of the law? Did that law still apply if the guy was obviously a total jerk? Shelby actually took a step toward the man.

It was Chantelle who stepped in and saved the day. She set her tablet down on the table and turned to Burgamy.

"Sir, these ladies have been in here all morning working. It looks like they need a break. If it's okay, I will escort them to get some coffee and will stay with them the entire time."

Burgamy hesitated and then nodded. "Fine. I want to talk to Branson anyway. About, for example, why none of his siblings seem to be here today."

Shelby looked over at Dylan and he nodded. Shelby sure hoped Burgamy was the mole and that Dylan would find a way to prove it or else it looked as if all the Branson siblings were going to be looking for new jobs.

Megan and Shelby followed Chantelle out the door.

"Thanks for getting us out of there, Chantelle," Megan said as they walked down the hall. "I think Shelby had had all she could stand and might have been about to do your boss bodily harm."

"Dennis can be a little much sometimes," Chantelle said.

"A little much?" A gross understatement, if Shelby had ever heard one.

"Okay, a complete pain in the ass most of the time," Chantelle snickered.

All three women laughed.

"How well do you know Burgamy, Chantelle?" Megan asked.

"We've worked with each other every day for four years and I constantly ask myself why I don't quit." Chantelle laughed again, shaking her head. "Hey, do you gals want to get coffee at the place next door instead of the break room? I could use a little fresh air."

Shelby could, too, and they readily agreed. It didn't take them long to work their way out of the building.

Shelby barely refrained from throwing her arms out and spinning around once they made it outside. She finally felt as if she could breathe. There was nobody around her and all she could hear was the sound of traffic and construction.

It was like music to her ears.

Shelby knew she had done a good job. She had gotten all the data in the system and she and Megan had found what they needed to stop the bombing.

She'd been an important part of saving a lot of lives today.

She and Megan would figure out what the other parts of the code meant and hopefully put a stop to even more of DS-13's plans.

But Shelby also knew this meant that she and Dylan would be going their separate ways soon.

She'd accepted that he hadn't really meant what he said in the kitchen. Dylan wasn't cruel; he wouldn't say something unkind to hurt her purposefully, even if he didn't want to continue whatever was between them. But the fact was, they hadn't made any promises to each other, and it didn't seem likely that Dylan was going to be ready to make any promises anytime soon.

If there was one thing Shelby knew from programming, it was this: timing was everything. She and Dylan had the chemistry for sure, and cared about each other. But the timing wasn't right.

Shelby was brought back into the present by Megan linking arms with her. "Did you hear Chantelle's suggestion?"

"No, I'm so sorry, I was in a different world."

"There's a new coffee place that opened the next block over that has fabulous chai tea. Chantelle thought we could try it out."

"Sounds great to me."

Actually, nothing sounded great to Shelby, but she knew she was just going to have to move on. The wind picked up. She wished she had a jacket.

"Let's cut through this alley," Chantelle said. "It'll get us out of the cold quicker."

"Good. I'm freezing," Megan said, grabbing Shelby's arm more securely.

"So what were you guys working on so hard in there? Shelby looks like she's been through ten rounds," Chantelle asked. "It's such a shame that hard drive was destroyed. There weren't any other copies?"

"Not to speak of," Shelby said.

"So I came to realize when I checked you out a little further, Shelby…" Chantelle said.

Megan and Shelby both stopped walking. Shelby realized the wind wasn't whipping around them any longer.

Because Chantelle had led them down an alley that had no opening on the other side. It was a dead end. And there wasn't another soul around.

Chantelle didn't even look like the same woman who had been up with them in the computer lab. This woman wasn't browbeaten by an overbearing boss. She was someone very much in control.

And she was someone pulling out a gun and putting a silencer on the end of it.

"You're the mole, not Burgamy," Megan said.

Chantelle rolled her eyes. "Burgamy is a sycophant and a moron. He doesn't have enough intelligence to play both sides. Especially not to work for DS-13."

Chantelle pointed her gun at Shelby. "You. I can't believe someone like you, who can hardly have a coherent conversation with more than one other person, is the one causing DS-13 so many problems."

She twisted the silencer the rest of the way onto the muzzle of the gun. "I spent too much time trying to keep any sort of hard drive out of the building. I thought that would be enough. Shame on me for assuming. But honestly, who even knew that someone like you existed? Someone with all the codes *in her head*. Freak."

Shelby and Megan looked at each other, but said nothing.

"I want you to take out your phone and call Dylan," Chantelle continued. "Tell him you made a mistake with the bomb-disarming code and that you just figured out it was wrong. Give him a new number to relay to his siblings."

"No," Shelby told her. "I don't care if you shoot me. I won't do it."

"Oh, but, Shelby," Chantelle said with a half smile that almost looked friendly. "I won't shoot you. I'll shoot Megan here. Right in the belly."

Chapter Twenty-Four

Dylan watched Burgamy dismiss three of the four guards that had been posted in the room. Dr. Miller had ducked out as soon as possible after the women left. That left one other Omega employee, Burgamy and Dylan.

Dylan had no plan to leave Burgamy alone in this lab with the computer if he had any other option.

"What's going on, Dylan?" Burgamy asked. "Where are your siblings?"

Dylan knew he couldn't tell Burgamy anything. Hopefully, Burgamy had no idea that they knew about the scheduled bombing. Dylan didn't want to give him the opportunity to tip off DS-13 before the bomb unit and his family had a chance to disarm the bomb.

"I don't know where they are." Dylan shrugged. "I don't work in law enforcement, so they're not at liberty to tell me all of their whereabouts."

Burgamy rolled his eyes. "Fine. I'll deal with them later. Tell me what was going on in here. Why would you sneak in here? You've walked through the doors like you own the place enough times."

Maybe it was time to start putting a little pressure on Burgamy. "I just thought it was pretty interesting that the first time I pick someone up for Omega, *both* engines on my plane suddenly fail."

"It was sabotage?"

Dylan nodded. "Somebody trying to kill Shelby Keelan and make it look like an accident. But you know what's even more interesting? There were only a few people who knew *I* would be the one flying her in."

"What are you trying to say, Branson?"

"I'm not trying to say anything. I'm just pointing out some facts the way they happened."

"What? Are you kidding? When Chantelle and I heard that you had made it out of the crash alive, I was thrilled. You can ask her. I wasn't sure why you hadn't reported in."

Something wasn't right, Dylan realized. When he first talked to Chantelle this morning, she had said she thought he had crashed. Then asked about the hard drive. Why would she do that, unless…

Dylan's phone began to vibrate. He took it out of his pocket.

Shelby. Calling him. On the burner phone they had bought. He distinctly remembered her aversion to talking on the phone. She'd even let him listen to her voice-mail message while they had joked at Sally's that first night: *Sorry, I can't take your call. Please hang up and text me.*

Shelby Keelan did not talk on the phone if she had any other option.

"Hey, Shelby. Everything okay?"

"Hi, Dylan."

Dylan could tell immediately that Shelby was on speaker and outside. "Are you outside? Where are you?"

"Um, yeah, Dylan. We're just going to get coffee at that new place around the corner. Look, this is important. Do you mind reading back to me that number I gave you earlier to pass along to your brothers and sister and the bomb squad."

Puzzled, Dylan grabbed the notepad and read them back to Shelby.

"Yeah, that second-to-last number isn't right. I'm so sorry, Dylan. I just made a mistake. It should be a three not an eight. I feel so terrible making a mistake on something so critical. It's really important that you call them and let them know I made a mistake."

"I will, Shelby. You don't worry about it, okay. Just go enjoy your coffee. I'll see you soon."

The phone instantly cut off.

"Will you please tell me what the hell is going on?" Burgamy roared.

Dylan had been wrong about Burgamy. He wasn't the one who worked for DS-13.

Chantelle DiMuzio was. And she had Shelby and Megan.

"Your assistant is a double agent for DS-13. And there's a bomb in DC about to kill a bunch of people if Omega doesn't stop it."

Burgamy's curse was vile. "I knew we had a leak, but I didn't know who." Burgamy cursed again. He walked over to the other Omega employee still in the room. "I assume you're carrying?"

"Yes, sir."

"I need your weapon right now."

The man handed it to Burgamy. Burgamy turned and handed it to Dylan.

"Let's go get Shelby and Megan. And take that bitch Chantelle down," Burgamy told him.

Dylan was already running out the door. He went straight past the elevators to the stairs and began taking them two at a time.

"I assume your siblings are already at the bomb site? Don't you need to call them?" Burgamy asked between breaths. The older man hadn't seen active duty in a lot of years, but he was managing to keep up.

That was good, because Dylan wasn't going to wait for him.

"No."

"I thought Shelby told you to call them. What were those numbers you were writing down?"

"They were nothing. Shelby was buying time and Chantelle was trying to make sure the bomb goes off."

"Are you sure?" Burgamy questioned.

"Absolutely." Dylan had no doubt, especially after what he'd seen her do today. "Shelby never makes mistakes with numbers."

Dylan made it out of the staircase and sprinted through the main lobby. He could tell the guards were going to stop him. He slowed, not wanting them to shoot him by mistake.

"I am Director Dennis Burgamy. Clear the path for this man!" Burgamy yelled it while swiping his badge for Dylan to get out the front door of Omega.

Dylan took back every bad thing he had ever said about Burgamy.

Outside, Dylan was unsure which way to go and stopped. Burgamy came up behind him.

"She said they were going to the new coffeehouse. But Chantelle wouldn't take them to a populated place."

"The new coffee place is around the block, actually behind the building. If you could get there from the alley next door, it would be great. But I don't think that leads anywhere."

Which would make the alley a perfect place to take two people if you were trying not to be seen or heard. Dylan took off running toward the alley, praying he wasn't too late. Burgamy was right behind him.

"We need to take her alive if we can, Branson."

Dylan nodded, but he wasn't willing to make any promises. He forced himself to slow down and be more calculating with his movements. Rushing up on Chantelle guns blazing would do nothing but get Shelby and Megan killed.

Dylan turned back to Burgamy. "Let's split up. I'll go down this side of the alley, you work your way down the other side. Stay a few paces behind me."

Burgamy nodded. "Alive, Dylan."

"If she's hurt Shelby or Megan then I promise nothing."

"Fair enough," Burgamy muttered then crossed to the other side of the wide alley.

Dylan dashed from blockade to blockade, trying to move as quickly as possible, but not do anything to tip off Chantelle that he was there. He was thankful for the Glock Burgamy had provided for him.

Although he couldn't see them from this angle, Dylan finally got close enough to hear someone speaking. Chantelle. Still talking with Shelby and Megan.

For the first time since Dylan realized a murderous operative who had fooled trained agents for years had Shelby in her clutches, he felt as if he could breathe. Shelby was still alive. Dylan would make sure she stayed that way.

"I see that it's after the scheduled time for the bombing and it still hasn't detonated. You may have stopped this attack, but I'm going to make sure you don't stop any more," Chantelle was telling them.

"There's going to be a lot of suspicious people when we were last seen with you and our bodies are found in an alley." Shelby didn't sound scared. She sounded mad.

"That's so naive of you. But you don't have to worry about anybody finding your bodies here. Someone from DS-13 will be along to clean that up five minutes after I let them know you're dead."

"It won't work, Chantelle." Megan sounded decidedly more frightened.

"Of course it will work. I've been working undercover for DS-13 for years with Omega. You know what the key to my success was? Not trying to do too much. I wasn't trying to bring down Omega. This wasn't personal. I didn't help every bad guy and criminal organization that came along. I just did a little slip of information here and a tiny drop of false information there. I've gone undetected for years, and I'll continue to do so."

Dylan peeked for a brief second around the corner of the garage container that hid him. He instantly broke out in a cold sweat. It was like something out of the nightmares of his past. An assassin, a gun and a silencer.

Pointed straight at the woman he loved.

No. Dylan could not lose Shelby this way. Dylan knew he'd promised Burgamy he'd try to take Chantelle alive, but that just wasn't going to happen.

"So I'll just finish you two off and go in and wipe all the data Shelby entered. You may have stopped today's attack—and after all the planning that went into that, I'll be a hero with DS-13 for killing you—but you won't be around to stop anything else."

Dylan steadied the Glock in his hand and got ready to jump out. He didn't have a great shot at Chantelle from this angle, but he wasn't going to sit here and do nothing. Not again.

One, tw—

"Drop it, Chantelle!"

Dylan heard Burgamy's words and dived out, firing as soon as he could see Chantelle. She was startled and fired her weapon right at the women, while turning to fire at Burgamy. Shelby screamed and leaped at Megan, trying to pull her out of harm's way.

Dylan's first bullet hit Chantelle in the shoulder. He

squeezed off two more rounds that hit her in the heart. Chantelle fell dead to the ground. Both Shelby and Megan were crying, which reassured Dylan.

"Burgamy, are you hit?"

"Yes." The older man bit out the word from where he lay on the ground. "But I'll live. I'm calling it in. Check on the women."

Dylan ran over to Shelby, who was crying hysterically now, sitting on the ground near Megan. Blood was all over their clothes.

"The baby, Dylan. Megan's been shot. The baby. Just like your baby. Oh, no!" Shelby was inconsolable.

Dylan's heart stopped. He looked over at Megan, who was obviously still alive, but covered in blood. Megan couldn't lose the baby. Please God, no.

"Megan." Dylan rushed to her side where she sat on the ground. Her face was as ashen as Shelby's. "Where are you hit?"

"Dylan, nothing hurts except my butt where I hit the ground when Shelby grabbed me." Megan's voice was shaky. She took a couple of deep breaths as Dylan started pressing along Megan's body to try to figure out where she was hurt.

"Dylan!" Megan said loudly. "I just felt the baby kick. The baby's fine."

Then where was all this blood coming from? Dylan and Megan both looked over at Shelby, who had her hands over her head and was rocking back and forth.

Dylan put his arms around Shelby. "Shelby, listen to me. Megan is fine. The baby is fine."

Shelby refused to be consoled. "No. I saw the blood."

Dylan looked down at Shelby's beige blouse. The blood was definitely coming from Shelby. "You got shot, Shelby. Not Megan. You did."

"What?" Shelby finally stopped sobbing.

Dylan put his forehead directly against hers and began trying to find her wound. "Megan is fine. *You* are hurt."

"The baby's okay?"

Dylan nodded.

"Megan's okay?"

Dylan nodded again.

"You're okay?"

Dylan rolled his eyes. "Yes, we're all okay. You're the one who's hurt." And at the rate blood was beginning to drip from her blouse, Dylan was seriously becoming concerned. He laid Shelby down against the pavement. Her face was waxen, her skin was clammy. Her breathing more and more labored.

Dylan ripped open her blouse to see the wound. It had gone in the fleshy part of her side, but might have nicked her kidney at the rate blood was rushing. Dylan tore off his shirt and began pressing it against the wound.

"Burgamy, we need a medic back here, stat. I mean, like five minutes ago," Dylan yelled out. He heard the man relay the info.

"Dylan, I don't feel so good," Shelby muttered.

"Hang in there, baby. If you don't, I'm going to call you and make you talk on the telephone every day for the rest of your life."

Now Megan was crying. "She pushed me out of the way, Dylan. If she hadn't…"

Dylan didn't say anything. He didn't have to. Both he and Megan knew if that bullet had hit Megan in the same area it had hit Shelby, the baby would be dead. Megan probably, too.

Dylan could hear reinforcements running down the alley. He kept his hand firmly pressed on Shelby's wound. "Help is almost here. You stay with me, okay?" Dylan put his head right next to Shelby's.

Shelby's green eyes looked up at Dylan, but he didn't think she really saw him.

"Dylan?" Shelby whispered.

"Yes, Freckles?"

"I promise I won't die."

Dylan leaned down and kissed her tenderly. "I'm going to hold you to that promise."

Chapter Twenty-Five

Shelby kept her word and didn't die, but it was touch-and-go for a couple of days. Days of agony and soul-searching for Dylan. He refused to be moved from the waiting room while the doctors operated on Shelby to repair the damage the bullet had done to her kidney, stop the bleeding and save her life.

His family joined him one by one in the waiting room as they came back from the scene of the would-be bombing at the Lincoln Memorial. The bomb had been shut down, dismantled and removed from the location without any fanfare. Omega Sector didn't need glory or accolades from the press. They just did their job and got out. The public didn't need to know how close they had flirted with disaster.

Dylan's family sat with him in the waiting room, as the one small woman who had done the biggest part to save thousands of lives, fought for her own.

When the doctors came out to give a report and asked if they were family, everyone gave a resounding *yes*. Shelby was theirs now, regardless of whether Dylan decided to pursue her or not.

The doctors weren't hesitant to let the Bransons know how close a call it had been. Just an inch farther… Just a minute or two more… The picture that *could have been* was bleak. And they all were thankful it wasn't what it could have been.

Burgamy was also in the hospital, a bullet to the shoulder. Nothing life threatening. The man had already sent down his regards and well wishes for Shelby. Dylan was glad he had been wrong about Burgamy. The man may have been a pain in the ass, but at least he was one of the good guys.

Once Shelby stabilized and began waking up, Dylan's family left. It had been a long, exhausting couple of days for everyone. Juliet was the last one to leave.

"Do you want to come home and get a little rest? Take a shower?" she asked Dylan.

"I will. After I've talked with her. Made sure she's okay."

"You sure you don't want to tell me she's not important again? Just another woman?" Juliet's eyebrow was raised.

Dylan couldn't even joke about it. "I will never say anything so stupid again for the rest of my entire life."

Juliet hugged him. "I'm glad to hear you're getting smarter with age." She walked toward the door, but then turned and took a few steps back toward him. "Dylan, Fiona wasn't the one for you. Her life was cut short and that's so sad, and a baby was killed and that's tragic."

"Juliet—"

"Dylan, I don't want to see you lose Shelby."

Dylan walked over and put his hands on his sister's shoulders. He could remember not so long ago when she would've flinched if he had done that and was pleased to see she didn't now.

"Jules, if you're going to say that I've used Fiona's death as an excuse to keep everyone at arm's length, you're right. And that it's not only her death that's haunted me, but the fact that I knew I had gotten married to the wrong woman. And that's why I haven't let myself get close to anyone. I've already figured that out."

Juliet laughed and reached up to kiss Dylan on the cheek. "Actually, I was just going to say don't screw this up with Shelby."

She winked and left, leaving Dylan alone in the waiting room.

Yeah, Dylan had been afraid of letting Shelby get too close. But seeing her bleeding out right in front of him, watching her slip away from him in a way he couldn't stop?

That was when Dylan had learned true fear.

A nurse came out. "Ms. Keelan is awake. Would you like to see your fiancée?"

Dylan hoped Shelby wouldn't be upset by that little piece of news. It was the best way for him to be allowed to see her, since he wasn't her relative. And the fact that he had his entire family there backing him up had helped.

Shelby's mother was on her way. She should be here soon. Dylan wasn't very sure how she would take the fiancée news either. But he'd burn that bridge when he got to it.

Dylan followed the nurse into the intensive care unit. "You can only stay for ten minutes. But I'll be surprised if she's awake that long."

Shelby looked so tiny and frail in the bed. Little, and not at all fierce. He slid a lock of her hair back away from her face and her eyes opened. They still seemed a little unfocused, but at least they weren't clouded with pain this time.

"Megan and the baby are okay?" Shelby whispered.

"Yes, they weren't hurt at all."

"And we stopped the bomb at the memorial?"

"Yep, nobody hurt there, either." Dylan ran a finger down her cheek. "Nobody got hurt at all, but you, Freckles."

"And Chantelle DiMuzio is a—"

Dylan half coughed and half laughed as a filthy set of words about Chantelle DiMuzio flew out of Shelby's mouth. Even a nurse looked over, eyebrow raised, from the station in the center of the room.

But seeing the state Shelby was in, knowing how much she had fought just to be alive now? Dylan didn't mind Shelby saying that and could add a few choice words of his own, although he didn't.

"Um, yes. Chantelle was not a nice person. And was the traitor. And is no longer among the living, so we probably don't need to call her any more names."

"But I want to. I don't like her." Shelby's voice was beginning to slur. Dylan could tell she was fading.

"Sleep now. You can say as many terrible things as you want when you wake up," he promised.

THREE DAYS LATER Shelby was beginning to wish she had died in that alley. Okay, maybe not really, but a little bit.

This hospital was her description of hell.

There were people around her all the time. She was never alone, someone was always talking to her, asking questions. And Shelby had to answer them politely. Because they were her caregivers and were only doing their job. And what kind of terrible person would Shelby be if she was mean to the people who had taken such good care of her?

She wondered if she could sneak out. Maybe go out the window.

Probably not, since she couldn't even walk five feet to the bathroom without assistance.

And to make all of these matters worse, Shelby's mother,

Belinda, was here. She'd already asked Shelby, oh, so sub-
tly, if Shelby would like her to put on a little makeup—*you
know, sweetie, to cover up some of those freckles*—and do
Shelby's hair. It was important to look good, even in the
hospital—*you know, sweetie, because there's just so many
attractive nurses around*—for one's fiancé.

Fiancé.

Dylan had explained that it had been the easiest way for
him to have access to her when she'd first been brought
into the hospital. Shelby didn't blame him, as a matter of
fact, thought it was kind of sweet.

But then a nurse had told her mother about Shelby's
fiancé. And that had been it. After meeting Dylan, her
mother had actually cried tears of joy. Belinda had thought
Shelby would never find someone who would put up with
her and all her awkwardness.

That was a direct quote. That Belinda had said to pretty
much everyone.

Shelby had tried to explain. Even Dylan had tried to explain. But every time they did, Belinda just started crying
and thanking heaven her little girl was alive and had found
someone to love. And then promptly changed the subject.

Shelby closed her eyes and shook her head. She knew
when she opened them, the huge stack of bridal and wedding magazines her mom had brought in and set by her
bed would be the first thing she saw.

So, yeah, a little bit Shelby wished she had just moved
on to a better place in that alley.

The sole peace she got was when she worked with
Megan to decipher more of the DS-13 code. Now that all
the data from Shelby's head was in the Omega system,
Megan could bring it in to the hospital in smaller chunks
on a laptop. Although Shelby was only able to work short
spurts at a time before exhaustion set in, they'd cracked
away at it multiple times each day.

They'd found four more potential bomb sites and dates as well as information about the key people responsible for each likely attack. Megan, as well as all the other Bransons who stopped by, assured Shelby that the information from the codes would put an end to DS-13 for good. Arrests were already being made.

So although the mental exertion tired Shelby, she was glad to help. Plus, Megan always shooed Belinda out of Shelby's hospital room while they worked, making deciphering the code Shelby's favorite activity ever.

They were releasing her from the hospital tomorrow, but Shelby would need someone to help her around the clock for at least the next week. She was glad to be going, to be getting away from all these people, most especially her mother, before she went absolutely crazy.

Her mom came bouncing through the door, no doubt having just been flirting with some doctor significantly younger than her. Shelby knew she couldn't wait any longer. She needed to tell her mother her plans for once Shelby was released from the hospital.

"Mother, I've decided to go home tomorrow after they release me."

"Home where, darling? With Dylan?"

"No. To my home. To my condo in Knoxville. I'm just going to hire a temporary nurse to take care of me."

Belinda immediately went over and began pressing the nurse call button next to Shelby's bed.

"Mother, what are you doing? That button is supposed to be for emergencies."

"It is an emergency. Listen to the crazy way you are talking!" Belinda's volume never rose, but her intensity did.

And, of course, Dylan picked that moment to walk in.

"Evening, ladies. Everything okay?"

"Oh, thank goodness you're here, Dylan. Something is wrong with Shelby."

Dylan looked over at Shelby with concern, but Shelby just rolled her eyes.

"There's nothing wrong with me, Mother."

Just then, the nurse walked in, so Shelby repeated her assertion that she was fine and apologized for accidentally hitting the call button.

"Dylan, Shelby plans to go all the way back to Knoxville and have some stranger care for her. You simply cannot allow her to do that. Tell her."

"The doctors estimate I'll need care for one week, Mother. I am pretty wealthy. Hiring someone for a week shouldn't be a problem," she told them both. "I've already got my assistant looking into it."

Dylan leaned over and whispered something in Belinda's ear. Belinda nodded and patted his hand, then walked out of the room.

"I don't even want to know what you just said to her."

Dylan chuckled. "Yeah, you really don't."

Dylan came over and sat on her bed. "I know this fiancé thing has gotten a little bit out of control with your mom, and I'm so sorry."

"Yeah, my mother is one of a kind." Shelby rolled her eyes.

"I want to ask you for one thing. Let me handle the details of your next week's care. I think I can safely say that I've learned a few things about your needs and your quirks, as you call them."

"Dylan—"

"Shelby, give us a chance to get to know each other with no plane crashes, or snakes, or bombs, or guns. If after a week we're ready to get rid of each other, then that's okay. But let me do this for you."

Shelby didn't want him to feel as if he was responsible for her. "Are you sure you want to?"

"I've never been more sure of anything."

Shelby hesitated, torn. Was she just prolonging the inevitable? If Dylan was still in love with his wife, what would a week change?

"Please, Freckles."

Shelby nodded. "Just promise, whoever's house we're staying at, tell them not to give their address to my mother."

Chapter Twenty-Six

Borrowing a plane from Omega hadn't been a problem for Dylan. After all Shelby and Dylan had done, and because now Dennis Burgamy was their friend rather than adversary, Dylan had been given access to whatever he needed.

"Whose house are we going to?" Shelby had asked as they left the hospital. "Back to Cameron and Sophia's?"

Dylan didn't want to share Shelby with anyone. He was taking her back to his house in Falls Run.

He'd already been home yesterday, before Shelby had even agreed to let Dylan take care of her. There were some changes he'd had to make around his house before she got there. Some were medically necessary to help her out over the next week.

Some he hoped would be enough to help erase the hurt he'd caused her with his careless words at the table a few mornings ago. And some he hoped would convince her to stay longer than a week.

She'd been surprised when after leaving the hospital they'd pulled up at a small airstrip outside town rather than at the house of one of his siblings. "Where are we going?"

"Back to Falls Run. To my house."

Because of her injury and surgery, Shelby couldn't fly in the cockpit with Dylan. He helped her get situated in the cabin, lying across two reclining seats. He kissed her on the forehead and told her to get some rest. Soon they were in the air.

It was probably good that they couldn't talk during the flight. Both of them had heavy things on their minds.

Shelby made her concerns known immediately after they landed, before she would even get out of the plane.

"I didn't know we were going to your house when I agreed to do this," she told him.

"I know." That's why he hadn't told her. He was afraid she'd say no.

"You're still in love with your wife." Shelby believed in getting to the point. It was one of the things Dylan enjoyed most about her.

But about this, she was wrong.

"No. Shelby, I grieve for the loss of her young life, and definitely the baby's, but I wasn't even in love with her when she died. I realized that's the biggest part of what kept me trapped with her ghost for so long. Not so much the fear of losing, but the fear of *choosing* wrong like I had with her."

Shelby seemed to ponder that.

"Are we still okay? Will you still give me the week?"

Shelby nodded and Dylan scooped her up in his arms and carried her off the plane and down to his truck. He went back and got the little luggage they had, then closed the hangar door behind him. He drove slowly over the rough road leading to his house and parked as close to the front steps as possible.

He got out and walked around to her side of the truck and opened the door. This was it.

Dylan had never felt more unsure of himself in his entire life. It wasn't a feeling he was used to or enjoyed.

He trailed a finger down Shelby's cheek and helped her out of the truck. "I know that Sawyer and Megan's good-mornings that meant so much to them touched you. Sawyer has always been great with romantic stuff like that. But I'm not, Shelby. I'm sorry."

Dylan felt completely inadequate. What he'd done wasn't romantic. She was just going to think he was nuts. He helped her walk up the porch stairs slowly.

"I know you only promised me a week, Shelby, but I hope you'll give me—give us—much longer. And you trusted me to make you as comfortable as possible—" Dylan opened his front door "—so I hope you don't mind that I did this."

He helped Shelby through the front door and into the living room. Where he had moved her favorite overstuffed chair from her condo, the time-out chair she had told him about, that helped her know everything would be all right. He'd put it in between the front window and the fireplace, thinking she could enjoy the view and be warm.

"How?" she whispered.

"I contacted your assistant and she let me into your apartment yesterday. After thoroughly vetting that I was who I said I was and that I wasn't just robbing you, of course."

Shelby was just standing there, saying nothing, staring at the chair.

Dylan laughed and it sounded awkward even to his own ears. "I was trying to be romantic, but I'm obviously not as good at it as Sawyer."

Dylan walked over to the MP3 player on the end table by her chair. He turned it on. "And I recorded about six hours' worth of traffic from right outside your window. I know how you love that traffic sound."

Shelby still hadn't said anything. Dylan turned off the MP3 and looked at her. She had both hands covering her face and was crying.

"Shelby, are you okay? Are you hurting?" Dylan rushed to her side.

Shelby immediately put both hands on his cheeks. "This is the most special and romantic thing anyone has ever done for me. It's good-mornings enough to last a lifetime."

"Then promise me you'll stay a lifetime here with me and know that every time you turn on the sound of that traffic that I love you."

"You can bet on it because I love you, too."

He tenderly picked her up in his arms and sat them both in her time-out chair. He'd take time-out with her there every chance he got. The two of them together were a perfect fit.

* * * * *

MILLS & BOON®

The Rising Stars Collection!

1 BOOK FREE!

This fabulous four-book collection features 3-in-1 stories from some of our talented writers who are the stars of the future! Feel the temperature rise this summer with our ultra-sexy and powerful heroes. Don't miss this great offer—buy the collection today to get one book free!

Order yours at www.millsandboon.co.uk/risingstars

**Don't miss Sarah Morgan's
next Puffin Island story**

Some Kind of Wonderful

Brittany Forrest has stayed away from Puffin Island
since her relationship with Zach Flynn went bad.
They were married for ten days and only just
managed not to kill each other by the
end of the honeymoon.

But, when a broken arm means she must return,
Brittany moves back to her Puffin Island home.
Only to discover that Zac is there as well.

Will a summer together help two lovers reunite or
will their stormy relationship crash on to the
rocks of Puffin Island?

Some Kind of Wonderful
COMING JULY 2015
Pre-order your copy today

0315/MB507